DANCE WITH THE DAWN

CITY OF VIRTUE AND VICE: BOOK 3

SUSANNAH WELCH

CONTENTS

Cover Concept and Design by Art Muse (Patricia E. Badalo)
Editing by Red Loop Editing (Victoria Basnuevo)

eISBN: 978-1-7365770-4-2
Paperback ISBN: 978-1-7365770-5-9

www.susannahwelch.com

ALSO BY SUSANNAH WELCH

City of Virtue and Vice Series

Dance with the Wind

Dance with the Night

Dance with the Dawn

The City

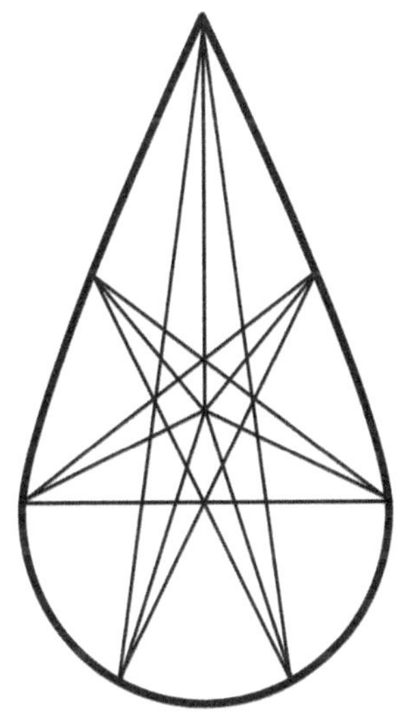

1

———

Ylena woke in the Heart of the Grottos, wrapped in velvet curtains. After Caed left, she had pulled the curtains from the stage and made herself a bed near the staircase she had created. No one had walked down the stairs in the last three days. She was still alone.

Alone, except for occasional visits from the strange child who said he was the City. He seemed comforted by her presence, but his appearances made her anxious. She wasn't sure what it meant that the City had been born by her tears. Was she responsible for the child? Was she responsible for the City?

She sighed and pulled herself out of the warm curtains, then walked over to the stage, where she had gathered her supplies. The people had run away from the Spectacle in a hurry, so they'd left items behind for Ylena to scavenge. She had divided everything into piles of food, alcohol, weapons, and some things she still couldn't identify.

Anything that looked like tea, she had poured into the crystalline pool.

She took a long drink of a clear liquid that burned like fire. Apparently, no one had brought water to the Spectacle.

Her food pile was the smallest and only contained questionable food sources. She was chewing a bite of jerky, wondering what kind of meat it was, when the City appeared at her side.

"What are you doing?" His soft, black hair hung in loose curls around his small face, and his dark eyes were wide with curiosity.

"I'm eating."

"You eat every day?" He cocked his head thoughtfully and studied her mouth.

"Yes. Every day. And if I'm very lucky, multiple times a day." She remembered eating so many times a day during Pageant rehearsals that she actually grew tired of eating. Food was not as abundant in the Underneath, and since the Wardens had locked the doors again, food was going to become hard to find.

"Do I need to eat?"

She turned to study him. He appeared to be about six years old, but if he was born when her tears hit the basin during the Pageant, he was only a few weeks old.

"I don't know. Do you feel hungry?" she asked.

"Hungry?" His forehead creased as he considered the word.

"Does your stomach hurt? Is it making a rumbling sound?" She held out the last bit of the dried meat. "Does this look good to you?"

He was still confused, so she handed him the food. "Try it. I guess we will find out what happens."

He smelled the meat, then took a tentative bite. "Interesting ... This is what food tastes like?"

She snorted. "Not all food, thank the Goddess." Ylena winced at the name. She didn't want that name on her lips right now. She wasn't sure if the Goddess was completely to blame for the situation in the City, but she was definitely complicit.

Ylena left the boy eating the meat and went back to sit on the velvet curtains in front of the staircase. She had done nothing else for the last three days.

She imagined what it would be like if Caed walked back down the stairs. There were so many things she wanted to say to him about that night. All of their plans had gone awry, but he had come to her with hope that the two of them would solve it together. But instead, she'd hurt him with a kiss that revealed her betrayal. His stunned expression was burned into her mind.

His face had looked like Wilder's. Ylena hadn't been honest about her feelings, and as a result, she'd hurt them both. She rehearsed her apologies in an endless loop, even though she realized she might never get the chance to apologize to either one. She took another drink of the burning liquor and curled back up on the curtains to watch the stairs.

"Is this the only thing you enjoy doing?" The boy sat on a curtain at her side.

"I don't enjoy this," she mumbled.

"But why do you do this every day if you don't enjoy it?"

She sighed. "There's nothing else to do. Everything is broken, and I can't fix it. I'm waiting to see if he can forgive me so I can move again."

"You are waiting for someone? Is that the thing you enjoy?"

She snorted. "No. Not at all."

The boy looked at her with a puzzled expression. "You want to fix something?"

"Yes. More than anything."

"Maybe we can fix something together."

She studied the child's earnest face. "I appreciate you trying to comfort me, but it's unnecessary. I'm fine."

He studied her rumpled clothes, messy hair, and the hand that clung to the almost empty bottle. "I don't think you are fine."

She raked her hand through her hair. "I admit, I've been better. But you're a kid. You shouldn't have to solve my problems."

"I'm a kid?" he asked.

"Well, that's a valid question. I have no idea what you are."

He shrugged. "Okay. So, what can we fix?"

"Nothing." She sighed.

"Nothing? I'm sure there is something we can fix. Before you came to my Heart, I felt you walking around. Were you fixing things when you were out there?"

She considered all the times in various Grottos when she heard the baby, this boy, crying. Did she fix anything? She'd thought she was fixing something, but it all fell apart. "I don't know. It's debatable."

"What is out there that needs fixing?"

"A lot. I don't even know how bad it is right now." It had been days since the Wardens had defeated the High Priests and taken their place as rulers of the City and the Underneath.

"You could go out there and see how bad it is. Then you would see what needs to be fixed."

She almost laughed at the boy's simplistic thinking, but he had a point. She couldn't do anything until she discovered what was happening out there. But there was a deeper problem.

"I'm scared," she whispered.

He tilted his head. "Why?"

"What if it's worse than I imagine? What if I find out

more of my friends have died? What if I see the anger in their eyes and realize they won't ever forgive me?"

"Oh, I understand! If you stay down here forever, they will stay alive and forgive you." He nodded sagely.

She looked at him through narrowed eyes. "You definitely don't talk like a kid."

"If you get scared when you are out there, you can always find me." He grinned.

"How do I do that?"

"I'm not exactly sure. But you found me when I was a baby." He shrugged.

"I never found you. You came to me in my dreams. Sometimes, I heard you crying even when I was awake."

He looked at her like she was the child. "How could I find you? I was just a baby!"

She opened her mouth to reply but then closed it.

"Go look around and then come right back!" he said cheerfully. "If it is as bad as you imagine, you can tell me about it. Then, we can figure out how to fix it."

She chuckled at his optimistic tone. "Sure. Why not?" She stood and stared at the staircase without actually stepping onto it.

The boy cleared his throat. "You might want to change into something else first."

She looked down and realized she was still in the Goddess costume, the inappropriate version that the Underneath preferred. "You are probably right. I guess I have a few other costumes around here to choose from."

She matched together a few different pieces from the costumes of the Little Wardens and grabbed her cloak from her dressing room. It was the cloak Caed had found backstage and given her when she escaped after the Pageant. Wearing the cloak felt like a bittersweet way to remember him, but she needed something to cover the white streaks in her hair given to her by the Little Warden of Peculiarity.

"Now you are ready to explore!" The boy handed her a bag filled with the dried meat Ylena had collected. "Here is some food. I know how you enjoy food!" He took her arm and led her to the staircase. "Go up there and see what is happening. Then, come back and tell me all about it!"

She looked down at his hopeful face and nodded, then took a deep breath and began her way up the staircase.

DISCIPLINE

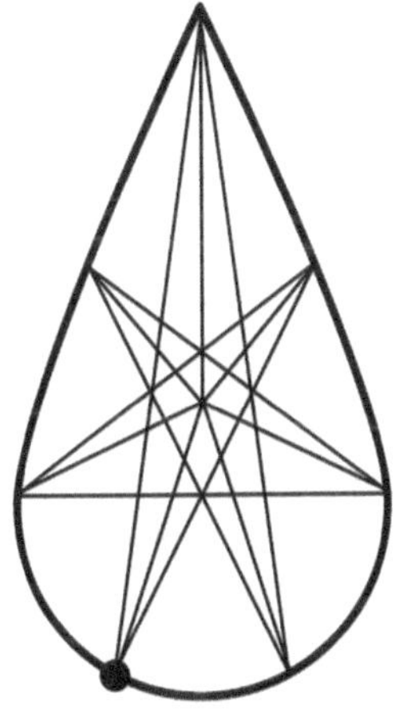

INDULGENCE

2

—————

Ylena walked up the last steps and slowly slid a wooden plank off of the opening to the Underneath. Caed must have covered the staircase to keep it hidden. She slid the plank back into place and stood up inside the cramped area beneath the stage. The last time she had been in the amphitheater, she had been with Caed. And the stage above her head was where she had found Pim and the others dead.

She considered escaping back into the Heart but took a few steadying breaths and kept moving ahead, mainly because she didn't want to see a judgmental look on the face of the boy when she returned so quickly.

She peeked out the door underneath the stage. The amphitheater was empty. And the sun was so bright.

She stepped out into the orchestra pit and turned her face up to the sky. The sun warmed her cheeks, and light blazed through her closed eyelids. She opened her eyes and looked around. Every color seemed brighter. She had grown accustomed to the crystal spires casting a purple light on everything in the Grotto.

She avoided looking at the stage. She could still imagine

the lifeless bodies of Pim and the others when she closed her eyes. Instead, she focused on the crystal basin that glowed purple.

Now that she had been to the Underneath, she knew that this was only the top of an eighth spire in the City. The crystal stretched below this basin, through the Underneath, and into a pool of crystalline. She walked closer and tentatively stretched out her hand to the crystal.

The last time she had touched it, her tears had been what relit the dark crystals. That seemed to be the moment that the boy, the City, was born. She wasn't sure it was a good idea, but she laid her hand flat on the crystal.

There was no flicker, just a steady glow. The crystal pulsed warmly underneath her hand. She thought she sensed what the boy was thinking, but perhaps she was only remembering his last words. *See what's happening up there, then we can fix it.*

She began the long walk out of the amphitheater and into the City.

Since the amphitheater was at the center of the City, she was more or less the same distance from each of the temples. But she never considered starting anywhere other than Discipline.

She crossed the empty place in front of the amphitheater and headed into the first few rows of houses in Discipline Diocese. She expected to see people roaming around, but it was completely silent. Maybe everyone was hiding inside the houses, or maybe they had fled.

Or maybe worse ...

Caed had said that he was hiding near the amphitheater with some others who'd escaped the attack by the Wardens. She had hoped that she might find him somewhere as she walked through the City, but now, she realized that would be ridiculous. If he was in one of these houses, he was hiding so the Warden's soldiers wouldn't discover them. She would never find him.

She kept walking.

It was a lot harder to sneak around in broad daylight. The shadowy light of the Underneath was much better for sneaking. She moved quietly from building to building, keeping her eyes open for anyone who looked like a soldier.

She finally heard voices around the corner.

"Yes, I know it's boring, but that's the best kind of job you can have as a soldier. I'd much rather be out here than closer to the temple."

"But there is no one here! It's stupid to just keep marching around!"

"You're young. You'll learn. Marching around is most of the job. Besides, they've got to be hiding somewhere. We haven't rounded up nearly enough people in the City. We are obviously missing some."

The younger soldier grunted. Ylena missed the rest of their conversation as they moved away.

It seemed like a good sign that they hadn't found all the people. She continued further into the City, walking past a lot of shops and homes that looked abandoned. The City always had plenty of room available, thanks to the frequency of the High Priests' executions, but now, it seemed empty. As she drew closer to the temple, she found a group of people being supervised by soldiers.

The men and women wore fashionable clothes completely unsuitable to the manual labor they were doing. They carried wood planks and hurried to avoid the eyes of the soldiers, who would occasionally shove or kick someone not moving fast enough. Ylena had always found the people in the City beautiful, but now, their faces were lined with exhaustion, and their once perfectly healed skin was covered in cuts and bruises.

The soldiers' attention was focused on the people they were supervising, so they didn't notice Ylena creeping past them. She slid into an alley as a guard moved away, then quickly climbed up the building and onto the roof. From above, she could see the people were building a wall. She only saw parts of the wall through the buildings, but it looked like it circled the inner portion of the Diocese.

The Wardens had ruled over Grottos separated by long tunnels, so they had well-defined boundaries of who ruled what. Upstairs, each Diocese had no external markers, even though all the people she'd met knew clearly where the dividing lines were. Judging by the soldiers' watch of the workers, Ylena guessed this wall would not just be a way to keep others out, but to keep people in.

She couldn't believe the people wouldn't try to fight back. The soldiers were outnumbered, yet the people blindly did as they were told. How could they tolerate being so closely watched and only working because they were afraid of punishment? She thought back to the High Priests' reign, when the Sentinels marched through the streets and executed anyone who made a mistake. Life under the Wardens must feel exactly the same.

3

———————

The sun was setting by the time Ylena made it to the temple. In the Underneath, time seemed a lot more fluid, and she rarely kept track. But the setting sun was a clear warning for the people of the City. They scattered into their houses at the commands of the soldiers, crowding into the homes closest to the temple. Ylena wasn't sure if that was because it made the people feel more secure to be in a group or because the Wardens wanted everyone close to keep track of them.

Even though people dispersed into their houses, the temple was still active. She wasn't close enough to see their hair from her hiding spot, but she assumed the workers were Priests. She hadn't seen Priests in the rest of the City, at least none with a recognizable white streak in their hair.

She waited until the courtyard emptied, then ran up the circular steps, hiding in a shadow against the building. The courtyard still had its clever equipment to exercise and train; however, it was all empty. Several doors and arches led into the center of the building, but she was hesitant to walk through one.

The only time she had snuck into a temple was with

Lady Erenne. At the time, Ylena thought Lady Erenne knew of a secret door, but now, she wondered if she had used her Gift with stone instead. Ylena moved to the same stone wall where Lady Erenne had "opened" the door, cried--an easy thing to do lately--and touched her tear to the wall. The stone flowed away until she faced a narrow corridor that was completely empty.

She stepped into the hallway and melted the stone to close behind her. As she continued down the hallway, she traced a mental map in her mind. When she thought she had walked far enough, she placed her hand on the wall. The stone flowed around her fingers until she made a hole large enough for her to look inside.

No one was in the room. The stone around her fingers flowed to the sides in a rush, and she stepped inside. Rows of cribs stood empty.

She couldn't decide if this was good or bad. If baby Priests still filled the room, that would be bad. She didn't want those children to be raised under the harsh care of the Wardens like the children from the Underneath had been. But what did it mean that they were all gone? She didn't want to think about it. She stepped back into the hallway and closed the stone.

She continued down the narrow hallway as it looped in a circle through the building and peeked into another room and found children and teens practicing their combat skills. These were obviously the children with Gifts the Wardens had kept hidden.

The children practiced the fighting style she saw demonstrated by the Discipline Priests, the same type of fighting performed by two small girls in the arena in Grotto Rivalry. The style was violent and quick, but Ylena still found it beautiful. These young people had the Gift and leaped higher than should be possible. They flew through the air in a straight line to sweep a leg out and tumble a larger opponent. They could spin and yet come to a stop with grace. The fighting was like a dance, and she always found it fascinating.

Ylena gasped. The children were being taught by some Priests with white streaks in their hair. The Priests didn't appear to be using their Gifts, but they were giving the kids instruction on how to better command the wind. She couldn't imagine why they would choose to help the people that had taken over the temple until she saw soldiers watching them from the corner. Other than training, they said nothing of interest, so Ylena continued on to her destination.

She opened another peephole and found the room empty. She melted the stone away gently but realized she needn't have bothered. The vines of white roses covering the walls and ceiling of the dance studio were dying.

Dried, brown leaves drifted down from the ceiling like snow. The room smelled musty, and as she walked inside, she stepped on leaves, making the scent stronger. Some vines were coming unattached from the wall and hung in skeletal pieces.

She remembered the night she first saw Caed dance true. Her tears from watching him dance had created the beautiful indoor garden. She couldn't believe what had become of it.

The flowers were dead. Caed was gone. There was nothing left.

She escaped into the courtyard through the archways and slammed into a soldier. She wasn't sure which of them was more surprised.

"What are you doing out here?" he asked.

"I'm sorry. I didn't know—I was—" She backed away slowly as the soldier stared at her with narrowed eyes.

"There you are!" A red-haired, young woman with freckles grabbed her by the arm. "The other soldier told us to clean the inner courtyard, not the outer one. We'd better go."

The guard looked confused. "Wait! What other soldier?"

"I don't know his name … Short hair, several scars, very cranky."

The guard chuckled. "Yup. That's him. Better get going."

The girl pulled Ylena along and whispered, "Thank the Goddess. The short hair was a complete guess, but the other two are always true."

"Who are you?"

"Rose. No more questions for a bit. We've got some more guards to get past."

A pair of guards approached them, and Rose gave more half answers with a smile until she got them into a room Ylena didn't want to enter: the space she rehearsed in for the Pageant. She worried it would bring back too many memories, but the room was so different she soon forgot about her fear. Rows of beds lined the walls, and people sat at long tables, eating a meal. Not just people, Priests. Ylena saw the white streaks in their hair.

She studied Rose's red hair more closely. "You have a white streak. You are a Priest."

Rose raised an eyebrow that seemed to imply Ylena's stupidity. "Yes. You have a couple white streaks yourself. You really are an observant one."

Rose walked to a long table with benches and sat down. She gestured for Ylena to join her.

"Did you sneak in here on purpose?" asked Rose.

"Um … I guess I did?"

Rose shook her head in disbelief. "If you hadn't been captured yet, why in the world would you get this close to a temple?"

"I wanted to see what was happening." Ylena wasn't sure if she could trust this Priest or not, but sometimes, telling the truth was strange and vague enough to get by.

"Now you know. What are you planning to do about it?"

"I have no idea."

Rose chuckled darkly. "Well, join the club."

4

———

Rose convinced her to eat dinner. Even though the room was the same, the food was nothing like what they ate during the Pageant rehearsals. Bland soup and a dry biscuit replaced the fresh fruit and vegetables and fish and bread. Ylena examined the biscuit with critical eyes.

"It helps if you dip it in the soup," said Rose. "It's less dry that way but takes on the terrible flavor of the soup, so ..." She shrugged. "I'm honestly surprised they feed us at all, so I guess we shouldn't complain."

Ylena had eaten worse food when she and her grandfather had waited for the spring to bring the traders back to their mountain. She choked down every bite of soup-soaked biscuit.

"So, which temple are you from?" asked Rose. "And why did you venture over here to Discipline?"

"Um ... Perfection. I guess I just wanted to know how this temple was doing."

"Well, from what I've heard, our temple had the most Priests escape before the Wardens arrived. It obviously didn't help me, but it would have been a lot worse if we didn't get warning right before the attack."

"Oh ... Someone gave a warning?" Caed.

"Yeah. That's how we got our babies away before the Wardens could take them."

"Mims," she whispered.

Rose narrowed her brown eyes. "You know Mims?"

"Um ... yeah, I met her once. It's a long story. But you say she got the babies out?"

"Yes. A few of us stayed behind to distract the Wardens enough to give them time to get out." She ran her fingers absently through her red hair. "They are the only Priests in the City who can freely use their Gifts. We have to protect them. Plus, who knows what the Wardens do with them when they are that young. I don't like the way they treat their own Champions."

"Champions?"

"That's what they call their kids with Gifts. They can't exactly call them Priests."

"That makes sense. The Wardens don't seem very fond of the Goddess."

"You know all the Wardens personally?" Rose looked at her like she was crazy.

"No, I just—I assume they don't believe in her." She tried to avoid Rose's eyes by scraping the last bit of soup out of her completely empty bowl.

"Well, the point is, we have relatively few Priests here. I know it has caused the Warden to be extremely jealous of the other temples."

Ylena tried to remember the Warden of Indulgence, who had formerly ruled below this temple. She remembered him wearing a fedora and pouring her shots in the Central Tavern, but that was all.

Rose stood up. "We better get to work. Otherwise, someone will assign us to something worse."

Ylena followed her into the inner courtyard that circled the glowing crystal. She hadn't visited the inner courtyard when she'd lived in the temples during rehearsals. The Priests' rooms surrounded the interior, so the acolytes avoided it. She had done plenty of sneaking through shadows, but the inner courtyard was the brightest place in the whole temple. The one time she'd glanced inside, there were beautiful stone statues and comfortable places to rest. Now, rows of smoking contraptions made of metal and glass filled the courtyard.

"The Warden is moving his distillery into the temple." Rose frowned at the stills as she handed Ylena a mop. "It is blatant sacrilege."

Rose and Ylena both ducked their heads and began mopping as two guards walked out of what was formerly a Priest's room. The guards passed them like they didn't exist.

"They aren't worried that you will try to hurt them?" As Ylena mopped, she noticed there were people checking on the stills who were equally disinterested in the two of them.

"What would we do to them?" Rose looked at her like she was crazy. "They are trained fighters."

"I've seen some Discipline Priests who can fight."

"Only a portion of our Priests are fighters. The rest of the Discipline Priests are dancers and gymnasts and runners. The soldiers cut through this temple with very little resistance." Her brown eyes filled with tears, but she blinked them back before they became dangerous.

Ylena dropped her voice. "But if we join together, we can use our Gifts to overpower them before ..." She touched her white streak.

Rose raised an eyebrow. "What are you going to do?

You're a Perfection Priest. Will you heal the soldiers so they are healthy when they crush us?"

"Well ... maybe I'm not helpful, but the rest of you can use the wind to attack—"

"Use our Gift to harm? Does your temple appreciate your heresy? Or is that why you left?"

Ylena's breath left her in a rush. She wanted to deny it, but she had intentionally used the Goddess's Gifts to hurt people. And several times, it was someone she loved.

"I'm sorry." She bowed her head. "Honestly, I'm not a Priest."

Rose snorted. "You can't get out of being a Priest that easily. The moment your tears hit the basin, you became her Priest. You can't escape your duty to the Goddess by being an idiot."

Ylena stared at her in disbelief. No one added Ylena's tears to the basin when she was a baby, but that didn't remove the fact that her tears had eventually made it in. Rose continued mopping around another still, and Ylena scrambled to follow.

"So, if we can't fight, what are we going to do?"

"I know what I'm going to do." Rose lowered her mop and looked Ylena in the eyes. "The question is, what are *you* going to do?"

"I have no idea!" Ylena tried to keep her whisper from rising in panic. "That's why I came up here—over here ... to see if there was anyone who knew what was happening. To see if I could fix what I ..." She harshly wiped the tears from her eyes. "It's all just broken, isn't it? There is no fixing this."

Rose narrowed her eyes and considered Ylena's words. She looked around at the people monitoring the stills and pulled Ylena closer to the center of the temple.

"This is a dark moment for us all. You must ask yourself the same question we all have to ask: am I going to lie down in the middle of the road like a lazy dog, or am I going to get up and live to fight another day? I can't answer that question for you. So again, I ask, what are you going to do?"

Ylena turned away from Rose's penetrating eyes. She focused on the bright purple light of the crystal. What was she going to do? She thought of all seven crystal spires soaring into the sky and plunging deep into the earth. She was so small in relation to the whole City. Wardens set on evil now filled each temple, and she was barely more than a girl. She couldn't fight them all.

She placed her hand on the crystal.

A deep note resonated through it. She felt it vibrate the stone of the temple and tremble through her bones. The crystal around her hand rippled like water and then smoothed back to stillness.

Ylena pulled her hand back with a gasp. Rose was staring at her with wide eyes.

"We have to go." Rose grabbed her by the hand, and they dropped their mops.

The people monitoring the stills hadn't seen Ylena's hand on the crystal, but they'd felt the vibration through the floor. They ran into the hallway.

"Are we being attacked?" one of the Warden's people questioned a soldier.

"Unknown. We dispatched extra guards to the perimeter and the entrance to the Underneath, but we don't have a report yet."

Rose backed down a hallway and pulled Ylena along with her. Once they were far enough away from the guards, Rose ran.

"Hurry!" she whispered.

Rose was fast, and Ylena struggled to keep up. Rose slid to a stop in front of a curving staircase and waved at Ylena to make her run faster.

Ylena followed as fast as possible without tripping down the stairs. At the bottom, Rose looked around carefully before opening a door into a storage room. Ylena closed the door behind her as Rose lifted a rug and slid a piece of stone tile out of the way.

A hole led down into darkness.

"Get in." Rose's voice was demanding, but Ylena couldn't move. Rose stood and pulled Ylena closer to the opening into the earth. "Get out of here. Do you hear me?"

The voices of guards echoed through the building as the last note from the crystal faded away. Ylena looked into the darkness.

"You're not coming?" she whispered.

"I have a few more things to handle before I leave. You'll be fine. This tunnel leads straight out. Don't worry about getting lost. Just keep going until you see the light."

Rose helped Ylena lower into the tunnel. It was narrow enough she could brush the top and sides with her fingertips. Her breath sped up as she thought about the darkness ahead. She looked up as Rose grabbed the tile cover.

"I'm not sure what I think about you yet, Ylena. You are interesting, but you are also kind of a disaster." She shrugged and slid the tile into position.

Ylena was in the dark.

5

Ylena walked in complete darkness. There was no sound other than her shuffling footsteps and her gasping breath. There were people walking in the City above and in the Underneath below her, but she felt so separate and alone. She occasionally slowed her steps and considered lying down in despair, only to speed up with a need to escape at all costs.

She was a disaster. Rose had called that one accurately, although it seemed like a mean thing to say. Other than Caed, Ylena had little experience with Priests, so maybe they were all that rude. They obviously weren't all as terrible as the High Priests, but it still surprised Ylena to be called names by a Priest. Especially one who called her out for heresy.

Replaying their conversation helped distract her from the seemingly endless tunnel. She thought back to when Rose discovered her outside the room with the flowers. That really had been convenient.

And Rose had called Ylena by name.

Ylena stopped walking. She relived every moment and realized she had never told her name. In fact, if Rose had asked, Ylena would have given a fake name. So, how did Rose know her?

Did Caed tell her? Ylena's heartbeat sped up even more. What if Caed told Rose to watch in case Ylena came to the temple? Her heart lifted at the thought.

Except ... Caed helped the babies escape, and they left Rose behind. After that, Caed came to the Underneath, where he'd planned to stay with Ylena. Until he discovered she'd betrayed him. She couldn't figure out when he would have mentioned Ylena to Rose if she was already trapped inside the temple.

It made no sense, but she could add that to everything else she didn't understand. She couldn't explain the crystal's reaction to her touch. It had to be related to the boy who called himself the City. Would that happen every time she touched a crystal spire?

She saw a faint light up ahead, but in the complete darkness, it shone like a beacon. Ylena ran the last few steps, trying not to trip but desperate to get out.

Moonlight shone through a hole in the stone. Stone stairs led inside the cliffs that surrounded the amphitheater. A ledge of stone hid her from view as she stepped out. Instead of walking around the outside of the amphitheater, she used some of her dried tears to open a hole in the stone inside.

The amphitheater was as empty as when she arrived. Now that she'd learned the Wardens were building walls around their stolen temples, she realized the center of the City was deserted.

She found the entrance to the Heart and slid the plank over the opening. She barely made it to the bottom of the stairs when the boy accosted her.

"What did you discover? Did you find out what needs to be fixed? How are we going to fix it? What can I do?

Can I come with you next time? Do you think I can leave?"

"Hey! Slow down. That's a lot of questions at once, and I have zero answers to anything." She walked over to her crumpled bed curtains and flopped down. "I hoped I might learn some things, but I just have more questions."

The boy's eyes lit up. "Oh! More questions! Like what?"

"Like what happened when I touched the crystal? Did you ... feel that?"

"You mean when you called my name?"

"I didn't call your name. I don't know what it is. Wait ... Do you remember your name?"

He cocked his head and considered. "I remember you calling it, but I don't remember what it was."

"Of course." Ylena massaged the bridge of her nose. "Because that would be an actual answer, and we don't have that."

"What other questions did you find? I'm great with answers!"

"No offense, kid, but I'm not sure you are. Maybe you'll know more when you grow up. If you grow up ... I'm not sure how you work yet."

He shrugged. "Me neither. But I still want to help! You can talk to me about it, and we can figure it out. Did you find that boy?"

"Which boy?"

"The one you've been waiting on to come back."

Caed.

She sighed. "He's not a boy. He's older than you."

"He is?"

"I don't know, okay?" She rubbed her forehead. "Listen, kid. I'm not in a great mood right now. Can you just give me a minute to lie here on my curtains and think in peace?"

"Sure! Go ahead!" He smiled and stared at her.

And kept staring.

She groaned. "Can you just go back into your crystal or whatever it is you do?"

"What's that mean?"

She couldn't handle any more questions when she had no answers to give. She stood and walked backstage to grab a handful of coins. "Sorry, I've got to get out for a bit. I will be back. Are you okay here alone?"

"Of course!" He was cheerful, although she was about to lose her mind.

She searched through the costumes until she found a blond wig to hide her white-streaked hair.

"Don't get into trouble while I'm gone." She wasn't sure what trouble he could cause, but the words felt right.

He smiled up at her in adoration. She patted him awkwardly on the shoulder before escaping into the quiet tunnels.

6

The opening above the stairs was covered with only a wooden plank, but the tunnels leading to the Grottos were impenetrable without the Gifts required to disable her gates. She melted the stone that covered the entrance and touched her hand to the water that was poised to crash down on her. The stone flowed back into place behind her as she stepped into the small hurricane that held back the water. Beyond the storm, she moved vines from her path. She stepped into the empty tunnel and smoothed all the gates back into place.

If the Little Wardens wanted to get in, they had the Gifts to do it. But only if they all worked together. She hoped they weren't foolish enough to attempt it. Especially considering that the last time they had seen her, she had not only defeated them with their own Gifts, but she had done it spectacularly for the whole Underneath to see.

Guilt prickled at the thought of using the Goddess's Gifts to harm. Mostly, she had just captured them and not injured them, but she definitely hadn't used those Gifts for their intended function. Was that truly heretical, like Rose said? Should she have let them capture her and Wilder? She never learned what they planned to do with the two of them after the Spectacle, but it wouldn't have been good.

She finally saw the end of the tunnel leading to Indulgence. The first time she walked through the tunnel on the way to the Heart, she'd found it disturbing, but compared to the completely dark tunnel Rose sent her through, the crystalline in this tunnel shone bright. As she neared the opening, she heard people talking. She didn't know who they were, but if she stepped out, they would carry word to the Warden. If by some chance they attacked, she wasn't ready to deal with the theological implications of fighting back.

She touched the stone at her side and melted a new tunnel. When she was far enough away, she opened a peephole to look out. She could barely make out the figures of the people guarding the entrance. She opened up a full door and stepped out, marking the stone behind her so she could find the tunnel easily when she returned.

Ylena wandered alone through Indulgence. She was grateful that her cloak and blond wig made her less conspicuous. Her white-streaked hair was too recognizable, considering that she was the only Gifted person in the Underneath. Even though everyone in the Underneath had seen her on stage during the Spectacle, most people were far away from the stage and drinking copious amounts of alcohol. She hoped the wig was enough of a distraction to keep her safe.

The Underneath had undergone some changes since she had last been out. Before the Spectacle, the people were getting desperate because of the lack of food. She knew the food was being delivered again, because her stomach rumbled as she smelled the bright curry she loved. However, she noticed more people begging on the streets or eyeing her to see if she was an easy target. They hadn't recovered from the food shortages, and obviously, the

Wardens didn't care about distributing the food deliveries fairly.

She wandered to the Central Tavern without thinking. It was the largest structure in Indulgence, so it wasn't surprising that she found it again, but it was surprising she would get close considering how it went the last time. Before that night, she didn't know about alcohol and had ended up drunk and injured Caed using her Gift. But she couldn't blame her actions on the alcohol. She was angry with him and had lashed out. Her anger always floated just below the surface, and the alcohol only amplified it.

She took the steps up to the Central Tavern. Multiple bars ringed the enormous, circular building, and she chose a different one than last time. She ordered one of her favorite sour drinks with a sugar rim and smiled as she remembered drinking with Wilder, Rev, Quinn, and Tayeh. Sure, the night ended poorly, but she also remembered laughing with them. If she could go back in time, she would do so many things differently.

She savored the peace of not being bombarded with questions from the boy. He meant well, but Ylena had no idea what to do with him. Was she responsible for him now? Did she need to take care of him for his entire life?

Was she his mother?

The idea sent her into a panic, and she flagged the server for another drink. She wasn't old enough to have a six-year-old child. How does someone even raise a child?

She never knew her mother.

Her grandfather had been kind to her. He'd taught her how to climb and fish and swim. He had found someone to answer her questions about becoming a woman.

He had also lied about her parents, about her Gifts, about his connection to the Wardens. The secrets he kept completely shattered her world. He should have prepared her for this instead of letting her get thrown into something she wasn't ready to handle.

Would her mother have done the same thing? Did her grandfather raise her the way all parents do? Pim talked about her own mother in a way that sent a sharp longing through Ylena's chest. Surely that's the relationship Ylena would have experienced with her mother. But the only stories of her mother came from her grandfather, and she wasn't sure which of his stories to believe.

She got another drink.

If the City was now her responsibility, how was she going to raise him? She would start by telling him everything he wanted to know. She would not be like her grandfather, avoiding questions, dodging the truth. She would tell him everything, no matter how many annoying questions he asked.

She was also going to care about him, no matter what he turned out to be. Grandfather suppressed her Gifts for her entire life because he didn't believe in them. Why should he have any say over her Gifts? The Goddess gave her those Gifts, and her grandfather could jump in the Abyss for all she cared.

She ordered another drink.

The sugar on the rim was always so good! Maybe she would bring a drink home for the boy? Wait, were kids supposed to have drinks like this? What if the kid in question was some sort of mystical City? Was that okay?

She would figure out what the boy should eat and drink, and she was going to care for him like a real mother should. Yes, she was young herself, but she had lived through a lot recently and felt older than her eighteen years. She was going to be a great City mother. She would show her grandfather how it should have been done.

After several more drinks, she stood to walk back to the

Heart, but her feet slid out of her control. She grasped hold of her stool unsteadily and looked at the floor with blurry eyes. The floor slanted strangely, and she couldn't stand up correctly. She vaguely remembered that happening the last time she was in the Central Tavern and wondered when they would fix that.

She hugged the wall for help with the sloped floor and eventually made it out onto the street. It seemed to curve a bit more than she remembered, but she used the crystal as a guide to make sure she headed in the right direction.

A lot of friendly people along the way offered her a variety of services. She wasn't sure what all the offers entailed, but she was glad the Underneath was so generous.

She stood in front of the crystal. The Warden's Den was close, and Ylena realized she should probably be worried about that for some reason. She actually didn't need to be here. She needed to head toward the tunnel, back to the Heart. But the purple light of the crystal was so bright, and it drew her in.

The crystal spires really were so beautiful. The light had always been a lovely amber color until Ylena's tear had extinguished them. Then, she'd somehow lit them back up in purple.

She reached out her hand and touched the crystal.

7

Ylena was not herself.

She stood in a large, open field with small houses in the distance. Much further beyond, mountains rose into the clear sky.

"We need to play up each of the Virtues in this first act."

Ylena turned at the man's voice. He was standing beside her on the grass in front of a wooden stage. Several actors on stage listened to him speak. "When you sing about Order, that's when they will drop the vines from above. You will each have to help move the vines into place." The actors nodded and practiced with the stagehands hidden in the rafters above the stage.

"What do you think about those vines? Do they look too fake?" He rubbed his dark beard as he looked at the stage. It took Ylena a moment to realize he was speaking to her.

"Um ... no, they're fine." She shifted awkwardly and smoothed down her full skirt. Her full skirt? What was she wearing? And her hands ... they weren't hers.

"Fine? That's all? Just fine?" He grabbed his chest like she wounded him. "You are vicious, as usual."

"Vicious? No, I'm ... They look terrific. Really terrific."

The man shook his head. "You're in a mood today. But no matter. This show is happening, and it will be fabulous."

The actors looped the vines through the set pieces, and then they sang. Their song caused a shiver to run through her chest. It was a song from the Pageant, but slightly *off*.

She understood the music from the Pageant better than anything she had ever learned in her life. She recalled each perfect note sung by a team of skilled performers. These actors were skilled, but there was something a little more relaxed about their performance. They didn't appear to be surrounded by deadly Sentinels, so perhaps that helped them be more carefree than her fellow performers had been.

She walked closer to the stage. It was a lot smaller than their stage at the amphitheater had been, but someone had crafted it well. She stood at the front of the stage and ran her hand across the smooth, wooden boards. She turned from their performance to face the mountains.

The grass was bright green with life, despite the cool breeze blowing down from the mountains in the distance. The chilly wind flowed around the scattered houses in the wide valley, across the open field, and swept her hair back from her face. A wave of disorientation hit her.

This was the City.

Before the City.

Ylena woke to someone digging in her pockets. She kicked out and heard a yelp. By the time she pried her eyes open, the thief had run away.

She found herself slumped over on the ground in front of the crystal. How long had she been asleep? She remembered leaving the Central Tavern, walking up to the crystal and ...

The memory came back to her in a flash. What was that? Was that something that'd actually happened? How could she remember something from that long ago? The City had always been here. At least, that's what she imagined. She wondered how she could find out if the memory was true. She couldn't ask any of the Priests about it. The memory itself was heresy.

She moved to stand but had to sit back down because of the nausea. Only then did she finally realize how much she'd had to drink. She reached out to lean against the crystal but pulled her hand away quickly. She didn't feel well enough for anything else unexpected. After staggering to her feet, she stepped a safe distance away so she wouldn't fall over onto the crystal and hit her head.

Is that what happened? Was the memory a result of alcohol mixed with hitting her head? Priest Rose accused her of heresy. Maybe she was still so upset about the accusation that this was her mind's way of dealing with it.

She began the walk back to the Heart. This time, she would be the one asking the boy all the questions.

"I don't know what you are talking about, Ylena." The boy's usually cheerful face was worried.

"I touched the crystal and was suddenly in someone's memory. Did you see it?"

"See it? How? I've been here the whole time." He waved his arm around the empty Heart of the Grottos.

"I know, but when I touched the crystal in the temple, you said you heard me call your name. Did that happen again?"

The boy bit his lips and looked scared to answer.

"What? What is it? Why can't you tell me?" Ylena grabbed the boy by the arms and studied his face. A tear started rolling down his cheek.

She let go of his arms quickly and stepped back.

"I don't know what you are talking about." The boy's voice was little more than a whisper. "I'm sorry. I thought I could fix it, but I don't know what you are talking about."

His little body curled in on itself. Sometimes, he talked like an adult, but right now, he seemed no older than his apparent six years of age.

She sank down to her knees until she was his height.

"I'm sorry. I didn't mean to scare you. You don't need to have all the answers."

The boy looked into her eyes and ran straight into her chest. She hugged him back for a moment before he toppled them both over. He cried silently on her arm for a while and then curled up next to her on the bed of curtains and fell asleep.

Ylena watched him sleep. His dark curls framed his face, so peaceful while he slept. She was angry with herself for harassing him for knowledge he didn't possess, but she still wanted answers.

It seemed like there was something important in the crystal spires. The spires didn't exist in the memory she saw, but they had to hold more clues. She wasn't sure she should head back to the same spire so soon, but there were plenty left to choose from.

PURITY

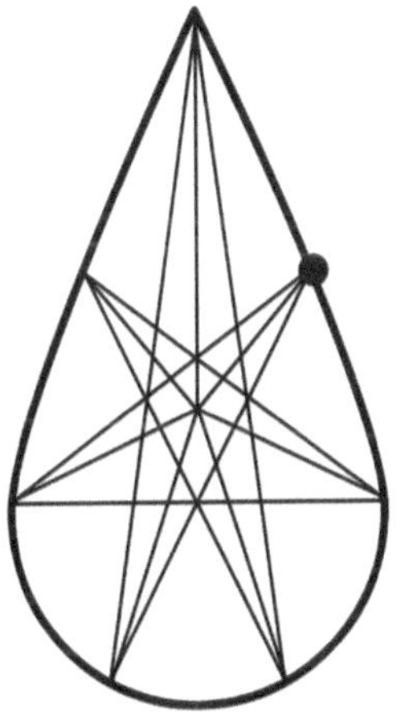

DESIRE

8

When Ylena woke the next morning, she had more energy than the last several days. She picked out some dark red pants and a sleeveless, gray blouse from the costumes. It was simple enough that she hoped it would blend in whether she was Upstairs or down. She grabbed the short, blond wig again and tucked her hair inside.

The boy was still curled up, asleep. His arm was flung out to his side, and she pulled the curtains up to tuck him in. She wasn't exactly sure how much sleep a City needed but didn't want to wake him if it wasn't necessary.

She emptied her pockets except for a few coins tucked down her blouse. If she passed out again after touching another crystal spire, she didn't want to get robbed. Or worse. She wished she had someone she trusted to keep her safe, but the boy was all she had. She couldn't talk through what was happening with him, because he was just a child, if a strange child at that. The only thing she had was a plan to figure out some of her questions.

She decided to not waste any time. She opened all of her gates and found her way through the tunnel, with another offshoot tunnel to avoid any spies. Then, she walked straight toward the crystal in Desire.

She received a lot of propositions along the way but didn't have time to blush at any of them. She was sad to see more than a few children scavenging for food behind restaurants. When she noticed a little girl eyeing a brothel with a hungry look, she used some of her coins to buy her a meal. But unfortunately, she knew there weren't many other places to work in Desire.

Her steps were angry and purposeful by the time she arrived at the crystal. The people in most Grottos avoided the area, and she wasn't sure if that was because the light was so bright or because it was too close to the Wardens' Dens. She could see the Den from where she stood. It was one of the few places in the Grottos carved by seemingly conventional means. She knew from experience that the Den went further into the cave wall than it appeared on the surface. The Wardens had held armies of child soldiers behind those walls. But now, she hoped the Den was as empty as it looked.

It was possible she would pass out again, so to keep from injuring herself, she sat down at the foot of the crystal, where it plunged further into the stone ground, and scooted to the far side of the crystal, away from the Den. She took a deep breath and touched the crystal.

Nothing happened.

She frowned. Maybe the strange experiences with the crystal were just one-time occurrences? But there had to be more to the vision she had seen. Then, she realized she had not cried since she woke up and washed her face. That seemed like an achievement! However, she needed to make some tears quickly.

There was an endless supply of sad things to think about, but this time, she thought about the last time she had been in Desire, remembering kissing Caed underneath a water droplet sky. She had never felt so happy. And she'd ruined it all.

The tears flowed easily. She wiped her eyes and settled back into a comfortable position, then touched the crystal spire.

A low note resonated throughout the Grotto. She heard exclamations of surprise from the men and women hanging out of the brothels. A few people walking along the street ran into buildings.

Her hand sank into the crystal with a ripple.

Dozens of guards streamed out of the Den. She pulled her hand away and scrambled to her feet but realized the guards were running toward the stairs that lead up to the temple.

Once again, they thought they were being attacked, that it must be an outside threat. They couldn't imagine that the sound was from a girl sitting next to the crystal.

She was disappointed that she didn't get the memory immediately but realized she should have expected the same vibration as last time. She flexed her fingers and touched the crystal again.

Nothing.

She frowned and gathered more tears, but still nothing happened. Her head tipped back as she studied the spire thrusting through the stone overhead, where it continued on through the center of Temple Purity.

She sighed.

Before venturing Upstairs again, she stopped for some coffee to help with her pounding headache.

The same stripper from last time served her. She blamed her hangover for forgetting what kind of coffee shops they had in Desire.

"Oh dear! You are a sad one. Let me try to cheer you up!"

The woman put on an enthusiastic show, but Ylena's heart wasn't in it. She couldn't even bring herself to blush out of courtesy.

"Hmm ... I must be off my game today. I apologize." The woman buttoned her shirt with a disappointed expression.

"It's not you. That was just as lovely as last time. I'm sorry. I have a lot on my mind."

The woman looked at her again, and her eyes widened in surprise. "It's you!"

Ylena spilled her coffee in her rush to stand.

"Relax, dear." The woman put a comforting hand on Ylena's arm. "I won't say anything. Sit down. No need to make a scene and draw attention to yourself."

Ylena slowly lowered back down in her seat. The woman grabbed another cup of coffee for Ylena and one for herself before joining Ylena at the table.

"I'm glad to see you again after ..." She didn't need to say "the Spectacle" for Ylena to understand. She should have remembered that the woman was the stripper Wilder had recruited to contribute to the show. "I wasn't sure if you would be okay after the way it ended."

"I'm not exactly okay, but I'm alive."

"I'm glad." The woman leaned forward and whispered, "I can't tell you how exited I was to see you give those Little Wardens a good lashing. The Wardens set them up as rulers down here in their absence, but those brats are just as bad as the originals."

Ylena looked around to see if anyone was looking at them. She wanted to escape as fast as she could.

"I don't know exactly who you are, but we thank the Goddess for you every day."

Ylena's head snapped to the woman. "We?"

"Those of us in the Underneath who follow the Goddess. My group of followers bless your name every day."

"They know my name?"

"Of course. News like that spreads fast down here. Even the smallest spark of hope spreads through here like fire."

"Hope in what? Everything is a wreck!" Ylena spoke the words louder than she intended, but the woman's calm expression never changed.

"Of course it is a wreck. That's why we have hope. If you had fixed everything already, that wouldn't be hope, would it? That would be proof." She winked at Ylena as she stood. "Enjoy your coffee. Goddess bless you, Ylena."

9

After she finished her coffee, she walked back to the Heart, grabbed a few extra costumes, told the boy goodbye again, and started on her long walk toward Temple Purity. Using the Heart as her home meant she did a lot of walking to get anywhere. It would be so much more convenient if she could walk straight up the stairs into the temple, but that stairway was the most guarded place in the entire City.

She made it through the silent center of the City, which the guards had ensured was empty. The soldiers in Purity Diocese forced the people to build the same type of wall as the one in Discipline. She couldn't believe how different the Wardens could be, and yet also so similar.

She climbed over buildings, causing well-timed distractions to get past the perimeter of soldiers. Once she arrived at the temple, she stopped to consider her options.

At the last temple, she had just run up the front steps when the guards had walked past. The temple was a huge, circular building surrounded by an open courtyard. It was not the most easily defended structure, but the Wardens had to occupy the temples as a symbol of their authority and to protect the doorways to the Underneath. However, since Ylena needed to get to the crystal at the center of the temple, she considered a more direct route.

The Priests of Temple Purity could manipulate water, and as a result, they covered the temple in fountains, pools, and waterfalls. She made a wide circle around the surrounding buildings until she found the stream she was looking for. Most of the water in the City flowed through underground pipes, but Purity Diocese had a clear stream that meandered through the shops and homes. She took a deep breath and waded into the cold water.

She swam through the slow-moving water, keeping her head just barely above the surface while watching for soldiers. The stream eventually flowed into a tunnel that led under the temple steps. She gathered a pocket of air around her and swam into the pipe.

She let the water push her along as she kept track of where this pipe would take her. When it branched, she aimed closer to the center. The stream emptied her out into a large pool with great, splashing fountains running along the center. She reached out with her Gift to feel the edges of the water. When she realized how many people were in the pool, she cursed, then immediately bit her lip. She wasn't sure if they could hear her from inside her pocket of air at the far end of the pool, but she needed a change of plans. Luckily, she had prepared her wardrobe in case she got in a bind.

Ylena adjusted her bubble of air until she was at the bottom of the pool, and then she sat down and stripped off her clothes. She pulled off everything until she was only in a flowy, little dress from the Spectacle. The dress looked like what the Warden's followers wore when she had seen them in his Den, and she hoped it was close enough to what they wore here, too. She tied her discarded clothes to the bottom of the pool with a press of water and slowly floated to the surface.

She hid behind the farthest fountain and found what she expected. The Warden lounged at the steps leading into the pool, surrounded by a group of beautiful, barely clad followers. Most of them laughed and splashed playfully with one another, but Ylena noticed that five of them seemed strangely still. The Warden had his arms around one woman, and his leg was resting on a man. The other three hunched over awkwardly, uncomfortable and afraid.

All five had white-streaked hair.

Fury rose inside Ylena, and she struggled to not drown the Warden on the spot. The only thought that held her back was the admonition by Rose that using her Gift to harm was heresy.

The Warden reached out a hand and lazily trailed it down another woman's freckled arm. She flinched, and Ylena saw her face.

Rose.

How did she end up in this temple after she was just in Temple Discipline? Did she get captured while trying to escape? Ylena didn't know what happened, but she knew what she had to do. Rose had helped her escape from the last temple, and there was no way she was leaving her—or any of those Priests—here with the Warden.

She needed a new plan.

The whole temple flowed with water, and it would be so easy to flood the entire place. She imagined pulling an entire river down from the mountain and drowning the Warden ... But no. Besides the heresy, that would place the blame on the Purity Priests who remained in other parts of the temple. She knew she wasn't leaving without taking these Priests out of the Warden's hands, but she wasn't strong enough to get them all. She needed to save these five

Priests without using water. And she needed them to be prepared.

She ducked under the water and swam to the fountain closest to the steps. She raised her head and saw the Warden twirl Rose's red and white hair around his fingers. When the angry tears came, she whispered to herself, wrapped her whisper in a gentle breeze, and flew it directly into each Priests' ear.

"When the chaos begins, swim to the far end of the pool. There is a way out."

She saw each of their heads snap up to look directly at her. Rose saw her and frowned.

Ylena touched her hand to the stone fountain and sent a ripple through it. Her mind reached out through the stone lining the bottom of the pool and traced every curve of the building. She felt the stone arches in the studio where she had danced with Caed. She crumbled each arch into dust.

She could have melted it into liquid, but instead, she separated the stone into individual chunks and then ground them together in the loudest, most jarring sound imaginable. The Warden's followers all turned to him in panic, except for the five Priests, their eyes still glued on Ylena.

The Warden called out to the soldiers at the door. "What is that?"

"We don't know, Warden."

"Find out!" he screamed at the them and jumped out of the pool, streaming water behind him as he stalked out of the room. His followers scrambled to follow him, but the Priests dipped quietly into the water and swam to Ylena.

When the Priests popped their heads up near her, she whispered, "The water is being held back from this pipe. Once you swim down there, you will crawl through the tunnel and out of the temple. Hurry!"

The Priests all obeyed without a word, except for Rose.

"What are you doing here?"

"You helped me escape before. Please help them get away, too." Ylena swam for the edge of the pool, but Rose grabbed her arm.

"Where are you going?"

"I have something to do. There's not much time. Please help them."

Rose bit her lip but nodded and swam down to the pipe. Ylena swam to the edge of the pool and lifted herself out, pulling the water from her short dress as she ran toward the center of the temple.

No one was in the inner courtyard. Soldiers yelled at each other in the outer courtyard, but to buy herself more time in the confusion, she crumbled an arch on the opposite side of the temple as well.

She looked at the crystal and took a deep breath. She hoped she would wake up before anyone found her passed out here.

Maybe she wouldn't pass out?

She touched the crystal and fell to the ground.

10

Ylena stood in the wings. She could see the performers on stage and the Director standing out on the grass as he had before. When the man on stage started singing, her head whipped around to find him. His voice reminded her of Wilder.

My Lady,

My heartbeat pulses with the rhythm of a fiery lute, and I will strum your spirit to life.

My fingers pluck the strings of a delicate harp, and I am gentle enough to awaken your soul.

My lips curve around tender notes of love, and I will breathe a new fire into your heart.

She remembered the first time she heard Wilder sing those words. She, along with every girl in the room, had stopped breathing. He was an excellent singer and understood exactly how to sing such bold words. The Director wasn't convinced this performer did.

"Come on now! This is a love song!" The Director slapped his hand against the wooden stage. "You need to show enough passion to woo her. Amuse her with your cleverness.

Stir up a desire deep within her that heats her pulsing blood until she can't control the blush on her cheeks." He looked at Ylena offstage. "Yes, thank you for that lovely example." She groaned at being caught blushing once again. He winked and turned back to the singer. "This is the most important story of our lifetime. I won't be satisfied with your performance until at least half the audience swoons. Understood?"

The singer chuckled. "Understood."

"Then please begin again. Prove to me you have the audacity to play the role of the Companion."

The singer began his song again, and the Director's words must have made an impression on him, because he sang with a passion he didn't have before. He sang for the woman playing the role of Goddess, and Ylena could see an honest blush crawling up her cheeks. The more reaction he got, the more courageous his song became, until the Goddess looked like she would melt into a puddle on the stage.

At the end of the song, the Director clapped his hands and cheered. "That's exactly what I was talking about! I can't wait to see the audience's reaction!"

Ylena's thoughts drifted away from the memory, but she struggled to wake.

"What was she doing there?" asked Rose.

"Who knows?"

Caed.

His voice was gentle. "Ylena always surprises me."

Rose cleared her throat.

He growled. "I know. I'm an idiot. Believe me, I know."

"Yes, you are."

Ylena's thoughts focused, and she blinked her eyes open. She looked around the room, but Caed wasn't there.

"Good morning, sunshine." Rose sat up in the chair she had been lounging in.

"Were you just talking to ...?" Ylena's head felt fuzzy from her vision of the past, and she wasn't sure if she had imagined his voice.

"It's just me and you. It's been pretty boring around here." She leaned back and stretched. Rose was no longer in the skimpy clothing the Warden preferred. She was wearing black pants and a short jacket, with her red hair pulled up in a ponytail. She appeared confident and healthy.

"Are you okay?" asked Ylena.

"You're asking me? You're the one who just woke up from being passed out."

"True. But the Warden of Desire captured you. He forces ... um ... Are you okay?"

Rose sighed. "Why do you have to be so sweet? I'm trying to be upset with you, and you're making it difficult."

"Upset with me? Why? I got you out of there!"

"Do you realize how hard it was for me to get into his harem? And you had to ruin it on my first day in!"

Ylena's mouth dropped open. "You were there intentionally?"

"Yes. And now I need to come up with a whole new plan. Thanks a lot." Rose rolled her eyes.

"Oh. I thought the Warden would force you to ..." She swallowed. "The five of you looked miserable. I didn't know. I'm sorry."

Rose raised an eyebrow. "Apologizing to me? That's interesting ... Well, to be honest with you, the other four really were miserable. They were not there by choice and had been receiving his ... attention... for days. If they were here, they'd be crying at your feet, and all those tears are too dangerous for them right now."

"They got away? They're safe?"

"Yes. Well, as safe as anyone can be right now."

Ylena looked around the small room she was in. There were heavy curtains over the windows, and the room was almost completely empty except for Ylena's bed and Rose's chair.

"Where are we? How did I get here? I don't remember anything after ... I touched the crystal."

"I made sure the others made it through the pipes and into the arms of one of my colleagues. I guessed where you went, and when I made it to the inner courtyard, I found you passed out on the ground. It was a real pain pulling you out of there. You are heavier than you look."

Ylena scowled internally at the jab but kept her words polite. "Thanks for pulling me out. I wasn't sure if I would wake up soon enough to make it out without being discovered. I appreciate you coming back for me."

"So, you suspected you might pass out? You didn't pass out the first time."

"Um ...."

Rose rolled her eyes. "Did you at least accomplish what you set out to do?"

"Yes, although I still have a few more to go."

Rose leaned forward to glare at her. "Are you telling me you plan on breaking into every temple like you did today?"

"Not *exactly* like that, but ..." She shrugged.

Rose rubbed her forehead. "I can see now why it is so difficult for some people to disentangle themselves from your schemes."

"My schemes? So far, I've found you in both temples I've broken into. It seems like you are doing plenty of scheming yourself."

Rose chuckled. "You are a feisty one, at least. And yes, I am doing plenty of scheming. However, unlike you, I'm not doing it myself."

Ylena focused on smoothing out her sheets. "Yes, well, I don't have any options except to do this alone right now."

Rose leaned back in her chair. "Don't you have any friends you can ask for help?"

"It's a long story, but let's just say I made several exceptionally terrible decisions and ended up ruining every good relationship I had in my life. So, all of my schemes from now on need to be a one-woman show."

"That's very limiting. And it doesn't sound like a good long-term plan."

"I don't have any long-term plans. I have no idea what my life will be like in the next seven days."

"That's the truth for all of us right now." Rose tapped her fingers on the arm of her wooden chair and studied Ylena's face. "I might regret this decision, but I have a proposition for you. I need to get into another temple and look around. Maybe the two of us could team up."

"Really? You trust me enough to partner up?"

"I don't trust you at all." Rose stared at her with hard eyes. "You are too unpredictable, but if we team up, at least I'll know where you are at. You won't accidentally stumble into my plans and wreck everything."

"Well, it's not the most enthusiastic alliance, but considering my lack of friends right now, I guess it's the best I can get. Sure. Let's combine our efforts."

Rose nodded. "Tomorrow night. I'll meet you outside Temple Perfection. I assume you can plan a suitable distraction for us to get inside?"

Her lips curved up in a smirk. "I'll come up with something."

"Good. If you get us in, I can help get you out. Will you pass out again?"

Ylena shrugged noncommittally.

"Well, my plan didn't get me into the temple for several more days, so I'm willing to take my chances with you. I hope I'm not making a huge mistake."

11

When Ylena got out of bed, she realized she was still wearing the short, white, draped dress she took from the costumes. She thought about the four other Priests dressed in even less, and a fiery rage rushed through her again. The rest of her clothes and her blond wig were at the bottom of the Warden's pool, but she would walk back to the Heart with pride, knowing she at least got those four Priests out of the Warden's hands.

She peeked outside and looked around to get her bearings. The safe house was in Purity Diocese but in the center area close to the amphitheater. She adjusted her tiny dress and headed to the center of the City.

She had only walked past a few houses when she found Lady Erenne sitting on the steps of a porch, drinking tea. She didn't appear to notice Ylena until she stood right in front of her.

"Ylena. It's good to see you." Lady Erenne had circles under her eyes, and her dark hair was disheveled.

"What are you doing here?" Ylena studied the house that was as cozy and perfect as every other house in the row. "Do you live here?"

She chuckled. "I don't live anywhere. I'm just resting for a moment."

"Are you actually resting? You look tired."

Lady Erenne raised an eyebrow. "You could have kept that opinion to yourself. Honesty is not one of the Seven Virtues."

"It's just surprising. I've never seen you tired before." Ylena had never seen her appear less than perfect, and it made her even more anxious than sneaking into the temple.

"I've been doing work that is far beyond my usual skills. Babysitting."

"The babies! They are with you? You have them?" Ylena looked into the windows of the house to catch a glimpse.

"They aren't here. I wandered away to take a moment to myself." She sipped her tea and leaned her head against the porch railing. "I heard you put on quite a show with the Little Wardens."

"It didn't turn out the way I expected."

"It rarely does. But I am sad I missed it. My soul needs a good show where the Goddess triumphs over the bad guys. That's not the way it's working out up here. There are more captured Priests than those of us in hiding. It looks pretty bleak."

Ylena wasn't sure how to respond. Lady Erenne had been confident of her plans from the first moment they met. Now, she looked fragile and sad.

"But you got the babies out! That's something to be proud of."

"We got them out of one temple. The other six Wardens still have a full nursery of our children, along with all the Priests who didn't escape. And now, the Wardens are walling up each Diocese. They won't be satisfied until the entire City is just as broken as the Underneath."

"Well, it was already pretty broken to begin with."

Lady Erenne gave her a sharp glance which reminded Ylena that she had previously been a High Priest.

"Um ... no offense. It was always beautiful up here. It's just ... there were a lot of executions, you know?"

"Yes, I know!" Lady Erenne snapped. She took a deep breath and a sip of tea. "Yes, I know," she said more calmly. "Why do you think I became a High Priest? I was trying to fix it from the inside."

"You could kill one of the Wardens and try to take their place?" Ylena said it as a joke, but Lady Erenne stared at her with hard eyes.

"Despite what you believe about me, Ylena, I do not murder people to achieve my goals. I did not murder the High Priest of Purpose to take his place. I confronted him about what he was doing to those children and forced him to come to grips with what the Goddess thought of his behavior. He was unable to stand up under the weight of his sin. He didn't die by my hand, but I accept the blame. I would never have caused his death intentionally, but for the sake of those he hurt and those he would have continued to hurt, I honestly can't bring myself to feel regret."

"The Wardens kept children locked up for almost two decades to use them as their own army. Maybe they need to be confronted in the same way."

"As you should remember from your role in the Spectacle, the Wardens have little respect for the Goddess or her Virtues. I can guess that much from seeing your costume. I don't think the Goddess blushed often, but that outfit might do it."

Ylena didn't allow her to get off topic. "But we have to stop them. They will be even worse than the High Priests. There has to be a way to fight them."

Lady Erenne shrugged. "I don't know. Perhaps this is the best we can expect from this City."

"It can't have always been this way ... What do you know about how the City began?"

"You mean the Scriptures? I assumed they drilled theology into you during your preparation for the Pageant."

"No, I mean before that."

Lady Erenne's voice was sharp. "There was no 'before that,' Ylena. The Scripture says, 'First, chaos reigned. There was no pattern. No form. No purpose.' It was chaos and nothing and then the City."

"But what if—?"

"No. I don't want to hear about it. That's all there was. This City is where it all began."

Rose had already accused Ylena of being a heretic, so she didn't press any further. "I'm sorry for offending you. I only wondered if, in the beginning, everything was different. When the Goddess created the City, was it the way she wanted it to be?"

She sighed. "I don't think this City has ever lived up to her expectations. Based on Scripture, she was never happy here."

"Why do you say that?"

"You sang all the songs, Ylena. Don't you see it? Sure, there is a love story, but the Goddess's Companion dies in the end. Tears awaken her Gifts. Her Priests dress in black. All of our beliefs come from tragedy. Why should we expect more for ourselves than the Goddess herself received?"

Ylena couldn't form an answer. Every song of the Pageant replayed in her mind, and she realized that what Lady Erenne said was true. Sadness and loss ran through the Scripture. Maybe that was the best they could expect.

"I must get back. Not that Mims needs me to take care of the babies, but I will cook us a meal. That's one thing I can actually accomplish." Lady Erenne stood and brushed off her rumpled dress. "It was nice to see you, Ylena. I hope to see you again someday."

She picked up her teacup and walked away. Ylena watched until she turned a corner, and then she headed back to the amphitheater.

❧

Ylena lay down on the curtains at the bottom of the stairs. She couldn't shake the melancholy feelings that Lady Erenne had stirred up. Ylena had been sad for days but hoped she would get over it at some point. After her conversation with Lady Erenne, she wondered if she should even hope for that.

"Hi!"

Ylena jumped at the voice of the boy. She sat up and found him sitting right next to her.

He appeared to have aged several years since she last saw him.

"Hi, kid. You look ... older. Do you feel any different?"

"Different? No. I still feel like myself." He studied her face with a frown. "You look older, too."

She suddenly understood what Lady Erenne meant about keeping the honest comments to herself.

"Thanks, kid. Unfortunately, I do feel different."

The kid nodded slowly like he understood.

PERFECTION

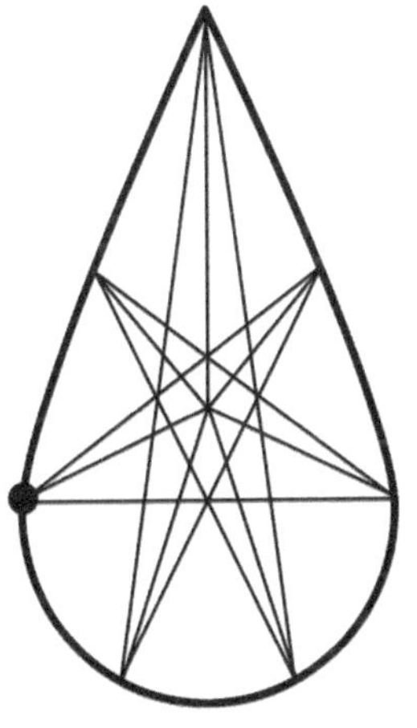

PECULIARITY

12

Ylena woke late the next morning and headed toward the crystal spire in Peculiarity. Upstairs in Perfection and in Peculiarity in the Underneath, the people wore similarly bizarre outfits, so she picked out a bright purple dress and a red wig that formerly belonged to a stripper from the Spectacle.

She told the boy goodbye and wondered how big he might be when she returned home that night. She made it through all of her gates and headed straight to the crystal.

This time, she knew what to expect. There were a lot more people near the Den in Peculiarity than in some of the other Grottos. She looked at the items for sale by the vendors who gathered around the crystal and casually touched her hand to the crystal as she crossed to another vendor.

Once again, a low note vibrated through the crystal and throughout the Grotto. Soldiers streamed out of the Den, and all the vendors ducked behind their carts. Ylena froze in place like everyone else. The soldiers ran toward the stairs, trying to determine where the low note was coming from. She pulled her hand away and backed through the crowd.

She headed away from the running soldiers, further into Peculiarity. The first time she visited this Grotto was soon after she discovered the Underneath. She had been numb with grief at Pim's death and angry at Wilder for abandoning them all. It was only a few weeks ago, but it felt like a lifetime.

As she walked, she tried not to get her hopes up, but when she arrived at Rev's house, her heart sank anyway. Someone had repaired the door of Rev's house, but judging by the strange people going in and out, the house no longer belonged to Rev. The last time Ylena saw the house, Sentinels had wrecked it and left Rev's possessions scattered like trash. Rev had gathered a few critical items, then headed out with Wilder and Ylena without a backward glance.

Rev had followed Ylena and Wilder, even though the High Priests were hunting them. She followed them, even though the Wardens had trapped them in an unknown game. Through everything, she remained at their side.

And Ylena had betrayed her as surely as she betrayed Wilder.

Rev had warned Ylena that Wilder had feelings for her. And deep inside, Ylena knew she was right. She should have been honest and told Wilder the way she felt about Caed. But she had been too afraid to lose how Wilder made her feel. From the first day she met him, Wilder looked at her like she was the only woman in the room. After a lonely childhood spent with only her grandfather for company, Wilder's attention was intoxicating.

She understood how it spiraled out of control, but that fixed nothing. She ruined her relationship with Wilder, which bled over into her relationship with the rest of the crew. They were gone, and she wouldn't get them back.

She watched a few more people go in and out to reassure

herself it wasn't Rev's home. Rev could have escaped to any Grotto in the Underneath along with the rest of the crew. Ylena hoped the four of them were together somewhere.

Just because she was alone didn't mean they had to be.

~

Ylena returned to the Heart. After discarding her wig, she went up the stairs and headed toward Perfection Diocese. She wasn't planning on meeting Rose until later that night, but she wanted a chance to see if it was the same as the other Dioceses.

She walked through abandoned neighborhoods similar to the others at the center of the City. Everything was quiet, except for the far-off sound of a wall being built. She walked through a stand of trees and found herself in front of the healing center she visited during the Pageant.

The healing center where Wilder had killed the Priest.

Her first reaction was to walk swiftly the other way, but she stopped once she remembered the people inside. If the Wardens had rounded up all the Priests, what did they do to all the people they had been caring for? She couldn't imagine the Wardens worrying about those people at all, and she realized they might have left the people locked in their rooms.

She burst through the front door, but inside, it was silent. If there were guards stationed anywhere within, they definitely heard her enter. She walked down the hallway where she had seen the patients.

The people in these rooms lived with illnesses of the mind that the Priests couldn't heal. The Priests took care of them ... Priests like Alys. She was caring for Walter when she healed Ylena and discovered her secret.

Ylena looked into each room, but they were all empty.

She wasn't sure if that was good or bad. She hoped that, like the empty nursery, it meant that someone got the patients out. As she turned to leave, she heard someone humming.

She crept down the hallway until she arrived at the humming sound right outside Walter's door. She looked through the window and saw Walter seated at his table. He saw Ylena and waved her inside.

"Hello, young Ylena! How have you been?"

She froze in the doorway. "You remember my name?"

"Of course! I'm not so old that I forget everything." He looked at her like she was a simple child. The first time they met, he seemed to go in and out of the conversation, so she thought he would have forgotten the entire day.

"Are you here all alone?" She had seen no sign of life anywhere else in the healing center, but his room appeared clean, and the remnants of a salad were on a plate in front of him.

"Yes. When the loud ones arrived, I hid. I didn't want to go with them. I prefer it here." He picked up one of his notebooks and began writing.

"Who brought you that salad?"

"I made it. Salads are pretty easy to make. I'm not helpless."

"Of course you aren't. But I doubt you have much food here. Maybe I can find you another place to go."

He looked up at her and smiled. "No, thanks." He returned to writing in his notebook.

She didn't know what to do. She didn't think she could force him to leave. When she got too close to him before, he lashed out at her almost by reflex. She didn't want to restrain or frighten him, but he couldn't remain in his room all alone.

"I really wish you would consider coming with me. I can find somewhere much safer than this."

He chuckled. "You remind me a lot of your father. Very stubborn."

Ylena gripped the doorframe for support. "My father? You knew him?"

Walter seemed transfixed by his notebook. He scribbled strange letters and drawings, then would stare off into the distance for several moments, only to return to adding more strange letters. He started laughing to himself and looked up to find Ylena staring at him.

"Sorry! I was just thinking of this silly pun a cat whispered in my ear a couple of decades ago. It finally made sense!" He started laughing again, and Ylena frowned.

He tilted his head as he studied her face. "Ah! When you frown, you look like him, too. Ylain frowned a lot."

That was his name. Lady Erenne had taken her to see his grave and said he was a Priest in Perfection.

"Did he work here? Was that what he did? He worked with the people here?"

"I haven't seen Ylain for a while. I wonder where he has been."

Her father killed himself before she was born. She assumed that the other Priests wouldn't tell their patients that, though. It would probably be too upsetting.

"Will you tell me about him?" She didn't want to disturb Walter, but she knew nothing about her father other than his name. She had to know more.

"Ylain frowned a lot, but when he smiled, he lit up the room. He had a dry sense of humor, and not everyone understood it, but those of us who did lived to hear him tell his stories. He was also a brilliant artist. That's the way he wooed his lady love. His art was stunning." He stared off into the distance again, then turned back to his notebook.

"Do you remember anything else? Please," she begged.

"Hmm? I remembered another of the cat's puns. I need to write it down." He continued to scribble.

She sighed. "Okay. Thank you for sharing what you remember. I have to meet someone, and I can send her to check on you later. Just to make sure you have plenty of food, okay?"

He nodded absently and dug into the stack of his notebooks and flipped through the pages.

"It was nice talking to you, Walter." She headed out the door.

"Don't forget to take that with you." He set a notebook on the edge of the table and reopened the notebook in front of him.

"Oh. Okay. Thanks, Walter. You are very kind." She moved slowly to pick up the notebook without startling him. She took the notebook and closed the door gently behind her.

She flipped through the pages as she walked down the hallway. She expected to see the same strange symbols that he had been writing, but beautiful drawings covered every page.

There were pictures of flowers and birds and butterflies. Faces of people smiling, people crying, people at their ease. Halfway through the notebook, the pages were suddenly all the same woman, and written under the portraits, her name.

Mae. Her mother.

She sat down in the hallway and flipped through each page slowly. Her mother sniffing a flower. Her mother sleeping on a blanket in the grass. Her mother reading a book. She was doing common things, but her father found her beautiful in every way.

She cried carefully to keep her tears from falling onto

the pages. Each portrait was a piece of their story, and she wanted to read every word.

She never thought about them being in love before. For most of her life, her grandfather only told her they'd died. She knew nothing about their life until she came to the City and found out that they had both been Priests. How did they meet? When did they realize they were in love? Did they ever fight? What if she hadn't been born? Would her mother and father still be alive and in love?

She wanted to study every line of each picture to see what it would reveal, but the sun was setting, and it was time to meet Rose. She tucked the small notebook into her shirt. It was the most precious possession she had ever owned.

13

Ylena arrived at the meeting place later than she'd planned. She didn't see Rose and wondered if she was too late. She could see the temple from her hiding place, and she timed the guards as they passed.

"Nice of you to show up." Rose's voice startled her, and she was angry at herself for flinching.

"Sorry. I was checking on someone."

Rose snorted.

"So, what's our plan?" asked Ylena.

"First, you come up with one of your stunning distractions so we can get inside. Next, we go find something in one of the storage rooms on the lower level. Then, you go to the crystal and do … whatever you do. After that, I drag you out. Simple."

"Yes. Sounds very simple." She stared at the guard, who walked past again. "I've got an idea for a distraction to get in. But we haven't ever really discussed *how* I come up with some of these distractions …"

Rose rolled her eyes. "It's old news, Ylena. Besides the fact that you demonstrated all the Gifts in the Spectacle, you have also performed quite a few in front of me, remember?"

"Oh. Yes, I guess that's true. And you are okay with that? It's not something heretical?"

"If you have all the Gifts, it's because the Goddess gave them to you. Sometimes, the Goddess gives Gifts to people that don't deserve them. I mean, why would she give Gifts to the High Priests? It makes no sense, but it's not heresy."

Ylena frowned. "I'm not sure I like the comparison, but I guess that's better than I expected." She sighed. "Time for a distraction."

She clicked her tongue, and a dog with golden fur scampered up. He bounced around until Ylena scratched behind his ears. "Yes, buddy. You are such a good boy. I need you to do what you do best, okay?" The dog huffed quietly. She patted him on the back, and he ran toward the temple.

The guard passed in front of the arch closest to them as the dog ran up to him. The guard bent down and reached out to pet the dog. He scampered back playfully, and the guard laughed. The dog ran into one of the inner rooms, and the guard ran after him.

Rose stared incredulously. "That was it?"

Ylena shrugged and ran up the steps.

She found the secret door on the outer wall and melted the stone away. She ushered Rose inside and closed the door up behind them.

"Wow," said Rose. "That's not what I was expecting, but okay. This works for me."

Ylena led her down the small inner hallway until they arrived at the spiral staircase. They headed down.

"I don't know where this staircase ends. I haven't taken it to the lower levels before."

"If you can get us to the lower level, I should be able to tell where we are fairly quickly."

They reached the bottom step, and Ylena touched the stone wall. She was glad Walter had given her the notebook, because it meant she had plenty of tears to use. She melted a small piece of the wall and let Rose look out.

"This is good. Yes, open the door here. We will head down a corridor on the left and then take the second door on the right. We've got to be quiet, because I don't know if there will be guards or not. And since we are out of dogs, I don't know how we'd get past them."

Ylena rolled her eyes and opened a door in the wall, following Rose down the corridor. Rose pressed her ear up against the second door; then, after a moment, she let them both in.

Inside, she found the High Priest of Perfection sitting in the middle of a cage.

Rose closed the door quietly while Ylena stared. The last time she had seen him, he sat in the front row at the Pageant. He had been wearing his tall crown and long, flowing robes. Now, his dark skin was mottled with bruises, and his clothes were stained with blood. He had a scraggly beard, and one of his eyes had swollen shut.

"Wow, Idra. You look terrible." Rose strode up to the cage and studied the lock on the door. "You really got yourself into a mess, didn't you?"

"Who are you? By your white streak, I'm guessing you are a Priest, but if so, you are a terribly insubordinate one."

"Nope. Not insubordinate. You aren't a High Priest anymore, so you and I are on equal terms." She tapped the bars of his cage. "Well, maybe not quite *equal* terms."

He glared at her but didn't respond.

"So, here's the deal. You tell me your secret, and we will try to get you out of here."

He attempted to cross his arms defiantly, but Ylena sensed his left arm was broken. He held the arm carefully in place without flinching. Despite the pain, his face looked remarkably calm.

"Do you understand what the Warden has done to me, girl? Every day, she takes me out of here and tortures me. She's come close to killing me multiple times, but she uses her healers to bring me back to barely enough health to survive. She has done that day after day after day, and still, I have not broken. So, I can guarantee that there is no way I will reveal anything to you."

"What a shame. I assumed as much, but I thought you'd be more angry at the Warden than the rest of us. No? Then I guess we're headed out. Good luck with the Warden!" Rose headed to the door.

"Rose!" Ylena stopped her in her tracks. "Are we seriously going to leave him down here?"

"Yes, *Rose*," said the former High Priest. "Are you seriously going to leave me?"

Rose scowled at Ylena when he said her name. "You aren't very skilled at this, are you?"

"No. I am not skilled at leaving someone to continue to be tortured. Are you?"

Rose's brown eyes turned cold. "I didn't think that I would need to remind you of this, but he is one of the High Priests that had all of your friends in the Pageant executed."

The High Priest whipped his head around to stare at Ylena. "You! You are the one who started this! If we could have killed you that night, the Goddess might have forgiven us and not let the Wardens take over."

"Wow. That is some messed up theology, Idra." Rose turned to Ylena. "This is who you think we should save?"

Ylena couldn't stop staring at him. There was a part of her that was literally ill with the physical sense of his injuries. And yet, there was a part of her that wanted to do worse to him.

"It just feels wrong," she whispered.

"You are once again nicer than I imagined, so I'll make

this easier for you. Check out his cage. How would you propose we get him out?"

Ylena studied the cage and lock. Her lock picks were back at the Heart, and there was nothing else in the room she could use. The cage was metal on every side, so she couldn't melt stone to get him out. There weren't any plants or water in the room, and she wasn't sure how she could use that against a metal cage. She thought through every other Gift and came up short.

"I don't know. How can we?"

"We can't."

"But you said if he told you—"

"I was bluffing, and he knew it. They built this cage to prevent him from being rescued by anyone using the Goddess's Gifts. Although, why anyone would risk their life to use their Gift to free him is beyond me."

His glare was haughty, but he didn't respond.

"So, if it makes it any easier to walk away, we can't get him out, even if we were stupid enough to try."

Ylena stared at the cage helplessly. She didn't really want to help him, but she didn't want to be the type of person who could allow someone to suffer, no matter how awful they were.

"Would you allow me to heal you?" she asked.

He widened his eyes in shock.

"They will probably hurt you again tomorrow, but I can heal you for today."

He didn't speak, but he stretched his non-broken arm through the bars. Ylena touched his hand, and he gasped. He pulled his arm back in and shook his body like all the pieces were falling back into place.

He took a deep breath and said, "Thank you."

Rose stared at him in shock. "Well, toss me into the Abyss. I did not expect you to thank her. Because of that, I feel like offering you a gift myself." She reached into her pocket and handed him a little box. "I assume you know what to do with poison dust."

He gave her a flat expression. "I'm familiar." He clutched the box to his chest. "Thank you."

Rose nodded once and headed for the door.

"Wait!" Rose looked irritated at Ylena for interrupting her dramatic exit once again. "The Wardens have a cure for the dust. You won't be able to kill them with that."

He chuckled darkly and looked at Rose. "You brought a child down here with you?" Rose shrugged. The High Priest turned back to Ylena. "This isn't for the guards. It's for me."

Ylena turned to Rose with wide eyes.

"Let's go." Rose opened the door and then closed it behind them.

14

They walked in silence back to the secret hallway and up the stairs. Before Ylena opened up a new doorway, she turned to Rose.

"I'm not a child."

Rose studied her. "No. You aren't. But for someone like him, your mercy seems naïve. Even for someone like me, it's … surprising."

"I know that everything I do is strange and that I don't belong here. You aren't the first one to point that out." Rose opened her mouth to answer, but Ylena melted a door in the stone, and they had to be silent.

They stood in a bedroom off the inner courtyard. Rose cracked open the door and peeked out. She rubbed her forehead and sighed.

The inner courtyard was a circus.

Gymnasts practiced their flips as clowns ran around in circles. A woman stood on the back of a horse as it galloped around the crystal. A man adjusted the leash attached to a sleepy lion.

It was a bit more crowded than Ylena expected, but she planned to use the commotion to their advantage. She looked around the bedroom to see what she had available. The room had formerly belonged to a Priest, but one of the circus performers had obviously seized it. Sparkly costumes littered the room, draped on every surface.

"Can you do the splits?" whispered Ylena.

"What?" Rose snapped.

"Never mind. Just pick something quickly. We're joining the circus."

Rose rubbed her forehead again but grabbed an outfit out of the closet.

Ylena squeezed into a sparkly leotard. She carefully tucked the book inside and found a short, sequined jacket to wear on top that hid the rectangular outline.

"Do they not own any pants?" asked Rose. She was tugging the glittery leotard, trying to get it to cover more.

Ylena took pity on her and dug through the costumes until she found a sheer skirt. "That's the best you are going to find. We need to do this now." She gathered up their discarded clothing and closed the pile behind the stone. Rose stared longingly at the hole as it closed.

"I have to get to the crystal. I don't have to touch it for long, but I'm pretty sure I will pass out. Are you sure you can get me out? Maybe I should leave this exit open?"

"I wouldn't be able to close it without you. I will have to take you out the front door. Any ideas?"

"Um ... can you ride a horse?"

Rose sighed and ushered Ylena out the door.

Ylena made eye contact with the lion. He cocked his head, then roared and broke his leash.

The lion chased the horse, and the rider jumped off and ran away. Gymnasts screamed and ran toward the door. The lion chased them as the clowns tried to catch it again.

Rose and Ylena ran to the crystal in the confusion. The horse walked calmly to their side, and Rose patted it with a hesitant hand. Ylena gave Rose one final look, then touched the crystal.

~

The fire was warm on her face, but her back was cold from the night wind blowing off the mountain.

She was part of a circle of people gathered around a fire in front of the stage. It was where the crystal basin would eventually be, but for now, it glowed with a normal fire and not crystal.

She hadn't seen many flames since she came to the City. Most of the light came from the spires or crystalline, so the fire immediately reminded her of the fire pit she had in the cave with her grandfather. She remembered sitting next to him and watching the flames in silence. The silence had felt comfortable, but now, she wondered why he couldn't have broken it at least once to tell her the truth.

A woman across the fire sang. The group hushed and turned to listen. Ylena recognized her as the woman who was playing the role of the Goddess in the Pageant, and she sang her love song to the Companion. Her voice was strong but didn't travel beyond the confines of their intimate circle. She sang it as a gift for them alone. The group all sighed and smiled in contentment. Ylena knew they must have practiced these songs so many times together, yet the simplicity of the woman's voice in the still night caused the group to bow their heads in reverence.

The Pageant had ended so terribly that she avoided considering it as the City's form of worship. She enjoyed learning the music and the dances, but that joy was inextricably tied to her fear. Even now, she found it difficult to separate the two. The group around the fire enjoyed the

75

song as if witnessing a holy prayer, and she wept with the desire to be a part of the moment.

She looked at the tears she wiped from her eyes and wondered if she had any Gifts in a vision.

The woman finished the song, and the group murmured thanks to her for sharing something so beautiful. Next to her, the Director stood and began his own song. It started out with a simple melody about a shepherdess tending a field, but soon, the group started giggling. Ylena listened closer to the lyrics and realized that every time the shepherdess bent down to tend her sheep, she seemed to fall out of her clothes.

The Director walked around the fire as he sang, and he knew the right lines to sing to the right people to cause the most giggles and blushes. She couldn't believe that this was how he followed up one of the Goddess's holiest songs. However, when he sang the line about the shepherdess purposefully loosening the ribbons so she could keep the sheep entertained, she remembered the stripper she had seen in Desire. She clapped her hand over her mouth so she wouldn't laugh out loud at the image.

The Director took her laugh as a victory, and he sang the last verse even louder. He grabbed her hand and pulled her to her feet, spinning her around until she couldn't stop laughing. The crowd laughed and clapped along. His voice was powerful, and his hands on her waist reminded her of dancing with Caed.

She imagined Caed seeing her dance with this strange man and immediately felt guilty. She pulled herself to a stop and woke up.

15

———

Ylena woke in Caed's arms. She believed she was dreaming again, so she snuggled in closer to his chest as he carried her.

"I was doing fine, Caed," said Rose.

"You were riding a horse through the City in a leotard with an unconscious girl slung across your lap. You were slightly conspicuous."

Ylena realized she was actually awake. She took a deep breath and politely cleared her throat.

Caed froze.

"It looks like she woke up quicker this time," said Rose. "See? We would have been fine on our own."

Ylena blinked her eyes open as Caed slowly lowered her feet to the ground.

"Caed." She breathed his name and tried to say everything she could in the word.

"Ylena." His voice was hard, and in the one word, he said just as much.

"This is really fun. Really fun." Rose looked around the empty street. "Sorry to speed this along, but we can't have this conversation here."

Caed nodded and started walking ahead. Rose rolled her eyes.

"Come on, Ylena. Don't worry about him right now. We need to keep moving."

Ylena walked beside her but couldn't stop herself from worrying about him. Everything about him seemed different. Or more truthfully, the way he looked at her was different.

"So, were you successful?" asked Rose.

"Huh?"

"Um ... the whole reason we caused anarchy at the circus. Were you successful with that?"

"Oh. Yes. Maybe." She remembered dancing with the strange man. She looked ahead at Caed walking with stiff shoulders and felt guilty again.

"Maybe? That's fantastic. I'm so glad we did all that for a 'maybe.' I'm so glad I'm walking through this City in a leotard for a 'maybe.'"

Ylena looked down and realized she was also in a leotard. Her hand shot to her chest. When she felt the hard edges of the notebook, she relaxed.

"Although, we were a glorious sight." Rose actually smiled a little. "When you dropped to the floor, I picked you up and threw you over the back of the horse. The horse leaped down the stairs with no prompting from me. We rode out of there like we were in a magnificent circus of our own." She gave a dreamy sigh.

Ylena turned to stare at her. "I'm glad at least one of us is enjoying this."

"Don't be so sarcastic," Rose snapped. "That's my job. You need to go back to being sweet but strange."

"That's harder to do when I remember how awful I've been." She watched Caed stalking and sighed.

"Really? You've been awful?" Rose was obviously

searching for gossip, and Ylena felt so guilty that she confessed.

"I hurt Caed because I wasn't willing to have an honest conversation with someone else. Then, of course, everything spiraled into the Abyss in the worst possible way. I was stupid and ruined everything."

"Well, at least now you are being honest about how stupid you've been."

Ylena stopped in the middle of the road. "What is your problem? I don't even know you, and you have been consistently rude to me. Are you this terrible to everyone or just me?"

Rose crossed her arms and gave her a hard stare. "I'm only this terrible to people who break my little brother's heart."

Ylena blinked stupidly while her thoughts caught up, and then she groaned. "This is just great. The first person I run into up here is Caed's sister? How do I have such terrible luck?"

"Luck had nothing to do with it. Caed asked me to watch the temple because he had a feeling you would show up. I don't like to admit when he is right, because he can be irritatingly smug about it. But instead of being smug, your presence is making him even moodier than usual. I didn't even think that was possible."

They started walking again. Ylena stared at Caed and didn't hide her longing. "He asked you to watch for me? Why?"

Rose rolled her eyes. "Why do you think? Because he's a glutton for punishment. He wants to see if he has any little pieces of his heart left for you to crush."

"I don't want to hurt him again. But I don't know how to fix it."

"Well, you better figure it out quick. There is too much

going on in this City for him to waste time moping around. You need to get him back to his cheerful, bubbly self now."

"I should go. I'm just going to make it worse."

"That's interesting ... You're willing to take on a stage full of Little Wardens, but you want to run away from a heart-sick boy?"

"I ... You think I should stay?"

"I think you need to do what you should have done a long time ago. Decide what you want and fight for it."

"Oh. Yes ... that was the problem, wasn't it?"

Rose grunted. "Normally, I'd say take your time. Remain a silly girl for as long as you want. But there's a lot going on right now, so you need to decide real quick if he is someone you will fight for. If not, then it's probably best we go about our business separately."

Caed stopped walking at the edge of the clearing surrounding the amphitheater. Rose and Ylena continued through the stand of cherry trees until they caught up to him. He didn't speak, but his body said he would continue on with Rose, and Ylena was dismissed.

"Can I speak with you, Caed?" Ylena looked at Rose, who stood with her arms crossed. "Alone, please? Just for a moment."

Rose raised an eyebrow and silently walked away.

"Caed ..."

"Ylena, I don't want to talk about it. It's been several days. I've moved on. I'm fine."

He didn't appear to be fine, but it wouldn't help her case if she fought with him about that. "We don't have to talk about it, if you don't want to."

He nodded and started to walk away.

"Wait!" He froze in place at her word. "Please, Caed. I need to talk to you. Not about that ... But I need you—I need answers, and no one else will even listen."

He crossed his arms. "One of your major complaints about me was that I kept information from you. Why do you assume I will answer now?"

"Because my questions are heretical, and you might be the only one who will risk answering them."

He raised his eyebrow, and his expression reminded her of Rose, even though they weren't blood related.

"Okay, I'm listening."

She sighed with relief. "What can you tell me about the time before the Goddess created the City?"

"They say it was chaos and that nothing had any form."

"I know that's what the Scripture says, but what do *you* say? What was here before the City?"

"I don't really know. I have seen the ancient books in the Library from the time before the City, but no one has been able to translate them. At some point, the people put those books away and switched to our current language. There was clearly enough civilization during that time to not only create books, but to create a new language and ask everyone to adopt it as a society."

"That definitely doesn't sound like chaos, so I see where the claims of heresy come from."

"Exactly. I believe those people had the technology to build this City using knowledge that was contained in the old languages. Over time, they explained the things they didn't understand as the work of the Goddess. And eventually, they attributed everything in this City to her."

Ylena shook her head. "They believed in the Goddess before they built the City. They performed the Pageant before there were crystal spires."

He narrowed his eyes at her. "That idea is heretical in its own way, so I'm not sure where you came up with it."

"Oh ... This is the part you might have a hard time believing ..."

"Ylena, my lack of belief is why you came to me for answers."

"That's true." She brought her hand near her eye. "Can I show you?"

He narrowed his eyes. "The last time you showed me something that way, it didn't end well."

That easily brought the tears to her eyes.

He sighed and casually held his hand out. She wiped her tears and took his hand.

She showed him the City from before. A simple stage in an open field. The clear view of the mountains before the crystals and the surrounding wall. Cold wind. Music around a fire. The dancing—

She let go of his hand before he could see too much of her dancing with the strange man. She didn't want to betray him with any more images.

Caed slowly opened his eyes. He whipped his head around to stare at the glowing crystals where the vision had shown open fields between mountains. His face lit up with wonder. Ylena could almost hear the thoughts spinning in his mind. She had just shown him something that contradicted what he believed to be true, but instead of breaking him, it fascinated him.

He continued to stare into the distance as he spoke. "They must have already believed in the Goddess before they arrived. I didn't see any signs of the advanced technology required to build this City ... Did they bring that knowledge with them? Or is the City much older than we thought?"

She studied him in the crystal's glow. The warm air blew his white-streaked hair softly around his face. He was no longer wearing his Priest circlet, but he still dressed in all black. He tapped his lips absently, and the memory of his lips on hers stole her breath.

He flipped his head back around. "This is fascinating! I
—" He noticed the look on her face and stilled.

She stared into his eyes and knew what she wanted. She
knew what she had wanted since the first moment they
danced together. It was going to take work for him to forgive
her, but this was the mountain she was prepared to climb.

"Caed." She didn't whisper this time. She spoke with
power, and the breath of his name floated from her lips and
rested in the palm of his hand.

He opened his mouth to speak when a bird chirped. His
head turned. "It's Rose. There must be a soldier close by. I
have to go." He turned back toward her. "I'll meet you at the
next temple. I ... want to know more." She nodded, and he
headed to find Rose.

As he walked away, she saw his hand close, her breath
held in his palm. Her lips curved in a smile, and she walked
back to the Heart.

Knowledge

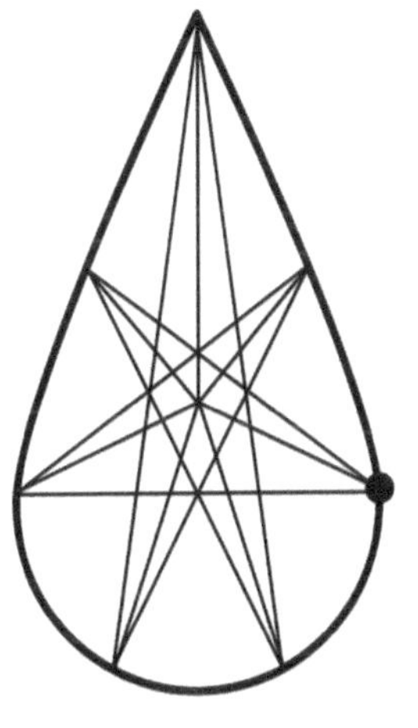

Instinct

16

———

Ylena sensed someone staring at her while she slept. Her eyes popped open, and she gasped. The boy was lying on his stomach on the floor in front of her bed of curtains.

"You were smiling." His face was so close to hers that his breath warmed her cheek.

She rubbed the sleep out of her eyes and sat up. "Please don't watch me sleep. It's disturbing."

"You usually don't smile in your sleep."

She remembered the dream she just had about Caed.

"Yes! That's the smile! Are you happy now? Did you fix everything?"

She stood and walked into the dressing rooms to find some clothes and a new wig. "I guess I'm happier than I was. I haven't fixed anything yet, though."

"I'm sure you will fix it soon." She heard the boy as he waited for her on the edge of the stage. She was adjusting her red wig when he said, "Where did you get this pretty book?" Her hands stilled. She ran out of the dressing room.

"Don't touch that!"

The boy froze in place with the open notebook in his

hands. His eyes were wide with fear, and she felt guilty for scaring him again.

"I'm sorry for yelling. It's okay. But … be careful. That is the most important thing I own."

The boy looked down at the book with reverence. "Did you make these drawings?"

"No. My father did." She sat down next to him on the stage. "I never knew him. He died before I was born."

"That's sad." He flipped carefully through the pages. "Who is this woman?"

"It's my mother. I never knew her either. She died shortly after giving birth to me."

"She's beautiful." He traced the drawn lines of her cheek. "She looks like you."

"Do you think so?" She studied the drawing. "I always wondered, but my grandfather never mentioned it."

He flipped through more pages. "He drew her a lot."

"I think they must have been in love, but this book is all I have as proof."

He traced another drawing with his finger. "You were born. That's also proof."

She studied him. "What do you know about all that? We haven't discussed where babies come from. Are you a kid or not?"

He frowned. "I'm not sure … But I know they were in love and that they loved you."

"It's possible my mother loved me, but not my father. The knowledge of me was enough for him to take his own life."

The boy looked confused, and Ylena felt bad for telling him such a tragic story. It wasn't fair for her to put that burden on a child. She wondered if that's why her grandfather never told her the truth, but she pushed the thought away.

The boy flipped through until he was at the last drawing. "But this ... See? You're right here."

She took the book from him and stared at the drawing. Her mother was standing with her open hands cupped in front of her stomach. A small flower bud had formed in her hands, and the roots curled lovingly around her fingers. She had a soft smile and a knowing glint in her eye.

"He obviously loved you, too."

Ylena gasped and tried to catch her tears before they hit the page. "Are you sure? I was told that ..." It was her grandfather that told her about her father taking his life because of her. Maybe that was another thing he'd lied about.

"It's definitely you. Isn't it obvious?" The boy looked at her like she was the child.

Her doubts said that her father had just drawn her mother using her Gift. But there was something about her mother's smile, and Ylena *knew*.

"Yes. It's obvious. Thanks for showing me."

"Glad I could help." He patted her on the shoulder. "You're a good kid, Ylena. I'm glad to see you smile."

As the boy wandered off, she realized she still had no idea what he actually was.

17

Ylena had a bounce in her step as she walked through Grotto Instinct. She had tucked the notebook safely away in the Heart before she left. She didn't like leaving it behind, but she was too afraid to keep it with her as she broke into the next temple.

Her cheerful steps slowed as she approached her destination. She wasn't looking forward to this conversation, but she couldn't solve this on her own. She needed help. He might not be here, but she had to take the risk.

She walked through the casino and headed straight to the Fifths table. She found Quinn winning, as usual.

She stood at a distance and watched him study his cards. His eyes moved around the table, doing complex calculations that were totally beyond her. Considering the pile of coins in front of him, the rest of the table should be glaring at him. But Quinn was so friendly that everyone still appeared to be enjoying themselves.

"I'm surprised you showed up."

Ylena froze at the sound of Tayeh's voice beside her. She swallowed down her fear. "Hello, Tayeh. I appreciate you not punching me on first sight."

Tayeh grunted. "I saw what you did on that stage. I'm not an idiot."

"No, you aren't. But I've definitely acted like one." She turned to face Tayeh's penetrating eyes. "I'm sorry for keeping secrets from you and for the way I hurt Wilder ... for everything. I'm so sorry."

"You don't owe me an apology. You might owe one to Wilder, but he's a grown man. He'll live. And your other secret that you revealed at the Spectacle? Honestly, that was probably a good idea to keep to yourself. The way you demonstrated it to the Little Wardens was very satisfying." An evil grin spread over her face.

"Oh, I didn't expect that apology to go so well ... How do you think Quinn will—"

"Hi Ylena! I like your hair!" Quinn ran up to her side. "Did you see me playing? I just made a lot of money."

Tayeh hushed him. "Quinn! Don't say that out loud! Why do you have to make my job so much harder?"

He dropped his voice to a whisper. "Sorry. Want to celebrate at the bar? I know how you like fancy drinks, Ylena!"

Tayeh shook her head, but Ylena chuckled. "Sure. I'd love to have a drink with you."

After they took seats around a small table near the bar, Ylena spoke. "I'm not just here to apologize and share a drink with you. I need your help, Quinn."

"Sure! What's up?" He grinned and leaned forward with interest.

"What do you know about the City before it was the City? Beyond the chaos that Scripture mentions, what else was there?"

"Oh!" His eyes lit up. "That's such a good question. There are a lot of books from the time before the City, but I've only seen a couple of them. The writing comes from several complex societies, but not much else is clear. We don't know how long ago that was or how the people arrived here or why they gave up that knowledge to start over."

She frowned. "That's almost exactly what Caed said."

"Caed? Is that the Priest we found sneaking around down here?" asked Tayeh.

"Um … yeah. I may have downplayed the relationship I have with him. Well, the relationship I used to have with him."

"Why does this even matter?" asked Tayeh. "There is plenty going on down here right now. Why are you worrying about ancient history?"

"The City is trying to help me discover something important." They both looked at her with confused expressions, and she sighed. "It's complicated. But I think there might be an answer in the past to help us solve our current situation."

"That sounds a little too religious for me," said Tayeh.

"I think it's an interesting idea!" said Quinn. "Maybe there's a weapon in our past that could help us destroy the Wardens." He got a far-off expression on his face.

"Oh … I hadn't considered that …" said Ylena.

"Yes, and maybe the Wardens will also discover that weapon." Tayeh gave her a hard stare. "There might be a reason they chose to forget."

Quinn shrugged. "That is a possibility. Sorry I couldn't be more helpful."

"There is one more thing you could do … How do you feel about helping me break into the Library?"

Quinn's mouth fell open.

"Look what you've done, Ylena. Quinn has stopped breathing." Tayeh slapped him on the back.

"I'm fine. I've just never heard such beautiful words before." He pulled out a notebook and started scribbling in it.

"What are you doing?" asked Ylena.

"I'm writing a list of all the things I need to buy to do this correctly."

Tayeh rolled her eyes.

They left the casino to go shopping. Besides everything Quinn decided he needed, Ylena bought some more food to keep in the Heart. She wondered again if the boy needed to eat. She wasn't doing a great job as his mother.

When they finished shopping, Ylena led them to the crystal near the Warden's Den.

"I don't normally come here unless absolutely necessary," said Tayeh. "Even though the Wardens took most of the soldiers Upstairs, the Little Wardens still have plenty in their Dens."

"I don't like it either," said Ylena. "But I have to do something real quick. Stand back here, just in case."

"Just in case what?" asked Tayeh.

Ylena shrugged and walked toward the crystal. She touched her hand to her eye, then to the crystal.

The cavern hummed with a low note. As her hand melted into the crystal, she looked toward the Den and found soldiers swarming out on cue. She tried to mimic the confused looks of the people around her as she hurried back to Quinn and Tayeh.

"That was interesting," said Tayeh.

"Yes, it was!" said Quinn. "What was that? How did you know that would happen?"

"Not now," said Ylena. "We should probably go, just in case."

"Yes," said Tayeh. "Just in case."

As they neared her secret entrance to the Heart of the Grottos, she slowed down. "Um ... I don't know if I should warn you about this or not ..."

Tayeh immediately went on alert.

"No, nothing dangerous. It's ... do you remember before the Spectacle that I kept hearing a baby crying?"

"Sure!" said Quinn. "You thought it was a child being held by the Wardens."

"Yeah ... It wasn't that. I guess I'll just let you meet him and see what you think."

Ylena opened up all the gates into the Heart and closed them behind them. They walked toward the stage.

"I love what you've done with the place." Tayeh looked at the pile of curtains by the staircase. "This is where you've been living since the Spectacle?"

"I didn't really have anywhere else to go ..."

"It's nice," said Quinn. "Considering that almost every person in the Underneath could fit in this cavern, it's probably a bit more room than one person needs."

"Speaking of that ..." Ylena looked around the Heart. "I want you to meet the boy."

"Is he here right now? Can you see him?" Tayeh asked. She and Quinn were both looking at Ylena strangely.

"No, he must have wandered off somewhere. Why would you ask if he's here if you ...? You think I'm crazy."

"No! Of course not!" said Tayeh.

"I didn't say that!" said Quinn.

Ylena sighed. "It's okay. It makes sense. In fact, some days, I feel crazy. I don't blame you for doubting me."

Quinn patted her on the arm. "He might show up before we leave. Let's get ready for our trip to the Library. Can I put this food ..." He looked around the giant cavern. "In your kitchen?"

"You can put it on the edge of the stage. That's where the boy and I usually eat."

Tayeh and Quinn exchanged a worried glance, and Ylena continued to search the cavern for the boy.

18

Ylena led Quinn and Tayeh up the staircase. "I have to meet up with some other people later tonight, so I'd like to break into the Library pretty quickly." She slid back the cover on the staircase, and they entered the area under the stage. "I'm not sure how heavily guarded the Library will be. Maybe the Wardens will completely disregard it. Hopefully, we can walk right in ..."

She headed to the stage door and realized Quinn and Tayeh were no longer following her. She turned around and saw them both by the edge of the stage, staring up at the sun with tears running down their faces.

"Oh! I forgot ... You've never seen ..." She stopped talking and let them both take a moment to compose themselves.

Tayeh turned around to wipe her tears away and said in a rough voice, "What were you saying? We can just walk right in? Where's the fun in that?"

Ylena smiled and turned her face up to the warm sun. "I can't imagine what it's like for you seeing this for the first time, but even in my short time in the Underneath, coming up here was a shock."

Quinn turned in a circle, staring out across the City.

From inside the amphitheater, the rest of the buildings weren't visible, but they could see the tall crystal spires and the mountains in the distance. Quinn whispered, "I've read books about it, but I didn't know. The sky is so blue!"

Ylena smiled and gave them both some more time to admire the sky.

After a few more moments of wonder, Quinn said, "I'm ready to break into the Library."

Ylena led them out of the amphitheater. They took a few more moments to stare at the open field and the trees that circled them.

"Everything is so ... alive." Tayeh hesitated at the edge of the field. "Do people really walk on this?"

Ylena chuckled. "I wondered the same thing when I arrived! Growing up on the mountain, I would never have stepped on any plant. In the City, the Priests grow whatever food they need, and they even grow plants to walk on." She leaned down to touch the soft grass. "Although, now that the Priests can't use their Gifts, I wonder if that will change."

They began their slow walk through the center of the City. They had some time before they arrived at the part of the City the soldiers were occupying, so they could explore. Quinn stopped at every plant he walked by.

"Quinn!" said Tayeh. "We have most of these plants in the Underneath. You've eaten a lot of them!"

"Yes, but I've never seen them growing like this. It's amazing."

Tayeh rolled her eyes but also stared at everything she passed. Ylena remembered her first time in the City and realized how obvious it must have been that she didn't belong.

She gasped. "Pim thought I was from the Underneath." The idea hit her suddenly, and she stopped walking.

"What did you say?" asked Tayeh.

"My friend, Pim. She hinted a few times about the reasons I might not know things I should have obviously known. I just realized that she thought I might be from the Underneath." She hadn't cried for Pim for several days, but fresh tears sprang to her eyes.

Quinn put his arm around her. "She didn't force you to tell your secret. She was a good friend."

Ylena nodded, because she couldn't speak.

Tayeh didn't touch her, but she moved close and kept watch as Ylena cried.

After Ylena carefully wiped her tears, they set off again toward the Library, slowing their steps when they heard the sounds of construction. They looked carefully around the corner of each building until they finally came upon the wall.

Soldiers were prodding the people as they carried boards. The people who weren't fast enough got kicked until they either sped up or fell down. When Ylena first saw the people of the City, they were all beautiful and dressed so flamboyantly. Now, their clothes were dirty and ragged, and they had scratches and bruises all over. She wondered if any of them had ever lived with a bruise for more than a day before getting it healed.

"This is shocking," said Tayeh. "Why are they allowing this?"

"What do you mean? Those soldiers will hurt them if they don't obey."

"Count the soldiers, Ylena, then count the people. The people could overwhelm the soldiers in a heartbeat."

"The people here never learned how to fight like you do in the Underneath. They are used to obeying everything the

High Priests and Sentinels told them. I guess they don't know how to fight back."

"It's pathetic." Tayeh shook her head in disgust.

Ylena felt defensive of the people she had lived among. "How is this any different from the Underneath? You let the Wardens rule you in the same way."

Tayeh looked at her like she was an idiot. "The Wardens controlled the only door to the food. Without that doorway, all of us would starve. The staircases up to the temples are so narrow you can't stage a battle there, even though many have tried. Even if we made it up the staircase single file and defeated the Sentinels, the Wardens would be at our backs, killing us from behind. That's why the Wardens cleared everyone out of the Grottos and sent them inside the Heart for the Spectacle when they staged their battle. They were only fighting on one front. Since they had the remedy to the poison dust, along with their own Gifted children, it meant that they swept through the temple before the Priests could seal the doors. I hate the Wardens for it, but it really was a brilliant strategy."

"Wow ... I guess I hadn't considered their strategy at all. And if I hadn't considered it, then I guarantee these people never have. Their lives have been very different."

Tayeh rolled her eyes. "Obviously."

"I wonder why they don't just have their Gifted children build the wall," said Quinn.

Tayeh looked at the dejected people as they shuffled along. "Probably because this is busywork to keep the people occupied. This wall isn't to keep intruders out. It's to keep those people locked inside. They are having them build their own prison."

Ylena shivered. "I can't let this continue. I need an answer."

"And you think the answer is inside a book?" Tayeh clearly did not believe that was possible.

"I don't know. But if not, at least Quinn will get to be inside the Library."

He grinned.

19

Sneaking through the City with three people was both easier and more challenging. It was helpful to have someone else provide a distraction when necessary. However, getting the three of them past the wall took longer than it had before. It was also harder to sneak around in broad daylight, but luckily, Quinn and Tayeh had honed their skills in the Underneath, so they made it to the Library without being seen.

They approached the seven-story building and Quinn whispered, "Are you telling me they filled this entire building with books?"

"Calm down, buddy." Tayeh chuckled. "We can't have you falling in love with a building."

"Too late." He winked and ran up the steps.

They listened at the door and then slipped inside. Sunlight streamed in from the windows at the back of the room. Everything looked exactly the same, except that the Library was completely empty of people. The last time she had been here, people walked on each of the seven levels that were open to the foyer, but now, the entire building was silent.

Quinn had a reverent look on his face, but Tayeh broke the silence. "Where do we start?" Her whisper echoed through the room, so Ylena led the way without speaking.

She remembered her first trip to the Library and the Priest she met that day. The young, red-haired woman was kind and had used her Gift of Knowledge to ease Ylena's mind. She had also been the one to mention that the Library held books from the time before the City was created.

Ylena led them to what the Priest had called the South Annex, following a few signs that pointed them in the right direction. They walked through several dark rows of shelves but didn't want to turn on any lamps that were visible from outside. They had to walk down one short staircase, turn a corner, and then walk up another staircase. When they finally opened the door into the South Annex, it was remarkably anticlimactic.

The room wasn't that impressive. Narrow windows at the top of the wall lit the room, casting shadows at odd angles. The bookshelves crowded together in narrow rows, as if the builders hadn't planned how many shelves they would need before they started. There was a worn, wooden table in the corner of the room with a crystalline lamp nearby on the wall.

"It's beautiful!" Quinn breathed. "I never knew there were so many books from before! And they are just sitting here. They didn't even lock the door. Weren't they concerned about someone discovering this?"

"When I came here before, the Priest mentioned this room, so I don't think it is a secret. She said the writing proved that there was chaos before the City and didn't seem concerned about that."

"Fascinating." Quinn lightly ran his fingers over the spines of the books as he walked along the row. "I wonder if they made any progress with interpretation. Maybe they have some notes around here to give me a head start? It would help me decide which books to take with me—"

"No one is taking any books." A dark-haired woman with a white streak stepped out from the far end of the bookshelf and held a knife up to Quinn's throat. Ylena felt a presence at her back and cool metal near her throat.

"I'm not sure what you ladies are planning here, but I think you need to relax." Tayeh held her hands up in front of her and looked between Ylena and Quinn.

"Look at our faces. We are perfectly calm. And you need to listen to us carefully if you would like to walk out of here on your own. You, girl." She focused on Tayeh. "You will walk out of here without looking back. If you make it out the door without turning around, we will send these two out after you."

A cold fire burned behind Tayeh's eyes. "Not happening." Her weight shifted slightly forward.

"Tayeh, please!" said Quinn. "Don't try it! If she cuts me, I might get blood on the books!"

Tayeh sighed and rubbed her forehead.

The Priest turned her head to study Quinn's face. "You're concerned you might bleed on the books? Not that you would be too dead to steal them?"

"These books have existed through generations and will hopefully survive generations after I'm gone. I don't want this single moment to ruin that. Also, I didn't say I wanted to steal them. Just borrow a couple for a little while."

"Who are you people?" The woman behind Ylena spoke in a familiar voice.

"Are you the red-haired Priest who works here?" Ylena asked. "I met you the last time I was here."

Tayeh looked at the Priest behind Ylena and raised her eyebrow. Ylena guessed correctly.

"Okay ... so you know who I am. But you haven't said who you are yet."

Ylena slowly held her hand out to her side. "Take my hand, and I will show you." The woman sucked in a breath but didn't move. "It's not a threat. You shared your Gift with me, so let me show you."

The Priest holding Quinn was shaking her head, but Ylena felt the red-haired Priest take her hand.

Ylena stood on the stage of the Pageant as the crystals blinked off.

Ylena bent over Pim's cold hand on the stage as tears poured down her face.

Ylena looked up at the crystal spire as it drove through the high ceiling of the Underneath.

Ylena wrapped the Little Wardens up in vines and ropes of air and sent twin white wolves to protect her friends.

The Priest released Ylena with a gasp. The dark-haired Priest tightened her grip on Quinn.

"Let him go, Adah. These aren't simple book thieves." She walked to Ylena's side and stared at her. "I don't think our blades would be that successful. At least, not on this one."

Priest Adah released Quinn, and he hurried to Tayeh's side. The red-haired Priest addressed Ylena. "My name is Nya. I remember you coming in here before the Pageant. That feels like a lifetime ago."

"I could not agree more," said Ylena.

"What are you doing here? There are a lot of terrible things happening in the City. You showed me what you can do. Don't you think you'd be more beneficial somewhere else?"

"I didn't show you the whole story, because there is too much, but let's just say I believe there might be an answer to our current problems somewhere in our past. What happened before the City was formed? I need more than the simple answer '*chaos.*' I need to understand why."

Nya studied her face. "You're still asking the same question."

"Excuse me?"

"That day, you asked me if this City turned out the way the Goddess planned. You're still asking the same thing."

"I guess I am."

"Child, there have been Priests studying these books for generations. We've had to be clever about it. Too much focus on these books might draw the wrong attention, but that didn't stop those of us who hold Knowledge above all. And even with all that, we still haven't found the answers you seek."

"But I have to try! And things are different now. Isn't the fact that I exist at all proof that something new is happening?"

Nya nodded slowly. "You may be right. Your Gifts, the crystals shifting colors, the balance of the High Priests being destroyed... All of those things are unprecedented. But you can't read any of these books either. I don't think you can spend your time in here reading."

"No, but I can!" Quinn spoke up from his place by Tayeh. "I've studied three books from this time period. Two were in the same language, and one looked based on that language but separated by time or location. I feel like if I had more samples to study, I could make some connections."

The dark-haired Priest Adah stared at him. "We have found no connections between the languages. I'm curious to learn what causes you to connect the two."

Quinn opened his mouth to answer, but Nya stopped him. "I can't let you take these books out of here. This is the treasure of our ancestors, and I must keep it safe. In fact, it is disturbing that you have three books that might not exist in this collection."

"I don't have to take the books out. I'll stay here."

Both Priests shook their heads. "It's not safe," said Adah. "Both of us are prepared to fight to keep this Library intact. Our worst fear is that the Wardens will try to burn down the Library and destroy our history. I believe in Knowledge, but I'm actually a Priest from Purity. There is a stream close by that I plan to use if there is any threat of fire."

"But you can't ..." Ylena touched her own white streak of hair.

"Yes. But I will." Adah's voice was hard as ice.

"We will not let this Library fall." Nya's voice was just as strong.

Tayeh nodded in appreciation. Quinn had returned to staring longingly at the books.

Ylena had to convince them. "I believe you both will do what it takes. But wouldn't it be helpful if you had a few more hands?"

"Yes! Tayeh and I both know how to fight if we need to!"

Tayeh rolled her eyes. "Quinn, don't lie to these nice ladies. You are not allowed to fight."

Ylena raised her eyebrow. The women who just a few moments ago had knives to their throats, Tayeh now called "nice ladies."

"Okay, fine. I'm the brains, not the brawn. But I promise, I will be useful. It's also possible that I have those three books in my bag right now."

Nya and Adah stared hungrily at his backpack. A look passed between them, and Nya nodded. "Okay, you can stay. And so can you, if you want?" She looked at Tayeh.

"I can't leave him, or he will get into trouble. Plus, I can be pretty handy in a fight."

Ylena snorted at the understatement.

"Then that's settled. And what are you going to do?" Nya studied Ylena's hand that had touched hers. "I assume you have more things to discover out there."

Ylena looked at the sun setting through the narrow windows. "Yes, I do. I might not be back for a few days, but if you need me, you know where I live."

Quinn was already pulling books off the shelves, but Tayeh looked at Ylena and shrugged. Ylena made her way out of the Library and headed toward the temple.

20

Ylena hid inside a dress shop and waited for the sun to set. She planned to meet Rose at full dark and wondered if Caed would show up with her. She paced inside the empty shop and waited for the time to pass.

Lady Erenne walked past the window.

Ylena opened the door a crack and whispered her name. Lady Erenne flinched, then looked around for anyone watching before she slipped inside the dress shop.

"What are you doing here?" asked Ylena.

"I might ask you the same thing." Lady Erenne narrowed her eyes. "In fact, I am asking. What are you doing here?"

"I just wanted to check out this temple and see how they are doing."

"There are dozens of Priests trapped inside, and they have no idea how to overthrow the Warden or how to escape, so they are all just sitting there waiting for their Gifts to drain their life away." Ylena widened her eyes at Lady Erenne's matter-of-fact description. "So, now you can avoid the trip inside."

"Well ... thanks for the information."

Lady Erenne sighed. "I don't know why I thought telling you that would keep you from going. No matter what I say, no one changes their mind." She sank to the floor with her back against the door. "I'm just going to rest here a moment, if that's okay with you?"

"Sure." Ylena sat down next to her. "Are you all right? You don't seem like yourself."

"I've been better. But I've been a lot worse, so I guess I should be thankful."

"Maybe ... Although, there is a lot going on right now to be upset about. I have only been in the City a short time, and I find it difficult to watch the few people I've met suffer. I can't imagine what it must be like after living here your whole life. You must know so many of the people in the City. I'm sure seeing them suffer is painful."

Lady Erenne closed her eyes. "Yes." The word was almost a sob.

Ylena wasn't sure how to respond, so she just squeezed Lady Erenne's hand and sat with her in silence for a moment.

Lady Erenne turned to face Ylena. Her sad face curved into a little smile. "You are kind, Ylena. I didn't know that about you when I threw you into the Pageant, but you have been a blessing to me."

"Being in the Pageant changed my entire life, and you've never said why you picked me."

Lady Erenne considered her words. "I knew your parents. The miracle of your birth was enough reason for me to keep an eye on you. I thought the City might need you some day."

Ylena's voice was a whisper. "Can you tell me about them?"

"I'm afraid I didn't know them well—"

"Were they in love? Were they happy?"

"Were they in love? Yes, that much was obvious. Were they happy? That question is more complicated than you might think."

"But if they were in love—"

"I was in love once." Lady Erenne closed her eyes again. "He was a charming and infuriating man. Was I happy? Yes. Was I anxious? Yes. Was I sad? Oh yes." She sighed. "All of it was a manageable ebb and flow. Until he died. When I lost him, the ebb and flow became a flood, and I drowned in it. I was underwater for a long time ... I was hopelessly alone, even when surrounded by people. But occasionally, a person would speak, and I could hear their voice. One of those voices belonged to Mae."

"My mother ..."

"She wasn't singing for me. She sang for your father, and I was close enough to hear. Her voice was as beautiful as yours. I always loved music, and there was something about her songs that brought me up from the depths. She didn't realize that she saved my life. I barely got to know her before she was gone."

Ylena's breathing slowed, and she focused on her words. "The Priests can't heal illnesses of the mind ... You were sick ... You were in the healing center ..."

Lady Erenne held her gaze.

"My father didn't work there, did he?"

Lady Erenne shook her head slowly. "No. The same flood of sadness that threatened to drown me flowed around him in a continual stream. He fought it. He fought it every day. But one day, it was too much. He didn't make it out."

Tears streamed down Ylena's face. "He died, but it wasn't because of me."

"It was not because of you, Ylena."

They sat in silence and an abundance of tears until the sun finally set. Lady Erenne kissed Ylena on the forehead and said goodnight.

~

Ylena stepped into the alley, and Caed and Rose stopped their conversation. There was no doubt they had been talking about her.

She offered them the courtesy of a lie. "Were you making plans for how we are doing this?"

"Yes, of course," said Rose smoothly. "You send a little doggie to distract the guard. We run in and see if we can find a captured High Priest. You touch the crystal and take a nap while we figure out how to get you out. Sound about right?"

Ylena shrugged. "More or less." She peeked around the corner of the building to see the guard patrolling around the temple courtyard. She turned back to Caed. "Can you say, 'What are you doing?' in your toughest, most manly voice?"

He raised an eyebrow, and Rose snorted.

"Please?" she asked again.

He sighed and said the words. Before the question had fully left his lips, Ylena gathered the sound in a breeze and spun it to the far end of the courtyard before she let it go.

"What are you doing?" Caed's voice caused the guard to turn and run toward the sound.

Ylena grinned, and they all ran inside. Once they were in the temple, Ylena let Caed and Rose lead the way. They had years of experience sneaking through the temple, whereas she only had a few months. Rose led them down a staircase until they arrived in some storage rooms. Ylena wasn't sure where they got their information, but Rose headed straight to the High Priest.

The door was unlocked. There was a similar metal cage, except this time, the High Priest was slumped over on the floor. Caed approached the cage with cautious steps, and when he got close, he dropped to his knees and sighed. He reached his hand into the cage and pulled out a small package from the hand of the High Priest.

"Someone got here before us," he said.

"Goddess-damn it," said Rose. "I'm fine with the result, but I wish we could have questioned him first."

"It's unlikely he would have told us anything," said Caed. "Look at him. They were torturing him for days. He chose the poison dust instead of going through that anymore."

"There are countless people who would choose to murder this one themselves, but who else would have offered him the mercy of dying on his own terms?"

Ylena remembered the sad look on Lady Erenne's face as she had walked past. She had come from the direction of the temple. Ylena shook her head, because she could not fathom it.

"We have to go," said Caed. "I think we might be the first to discover he is dead. I want to be far away before they find him."

He led them up toward the inner courtyard. The sounds of gambling came from inside. It was a significantly smaller space, but it sounded even rowdier than the casino. She placed her hand on the outer wall of one of the Priest's former bedrooms and peeked through the stone. When she saw it was empty, she led the three of them inside.

Outside the bedroom door, people played cards at tables filling the inner courtyard. There were dozens of people, and they didn't appear ready to leave soon. She cupped her fingers in front of her lips and took a deep breath. The words left her mouth with no sound, but her hands were full. She opened the bedroom door a little further and threw.

"Help! They are attacking at the door to the Underneath!" The voice came from the staircase.

"They are trying to take the children!" The voice came from the hallway on the right.

The people at the tables froze, then ran in various directions. She wondered which call would be most effective. A few stragglers still sat at the tables, surveying the coins laid out in front of them. Ylena sighed and tossed more words right into the middle of the courtyard.

"The Warden is coming!" came the panicked cry.

That got everyone moving. Ylena had met the Warden of Instinct. His smile was cheerful, but his eyes were deadly.

The three of them ran out into the empty courtyard and directly toward the crystal.

"You should throw out a few more shouts before you touch that," said Caed. "It would help us get you out if they were even more distracted."

Ylena smiled. "I've got something else in mind." She held up a rose petal. "I've scattered these throughout the temple as we walked. I'm going to give them a show." She touched the petal to her eye, where she still had tears from crying about her father. It sprang to life into a vine that curled around her hands and dropped to spread across the floor.

"You can't just drop petals and expect them to all bloom. That's not how the Gift of Order works—" said Rose. She cut off as the petals around her feet sprouted and spread across the room. They heard more shouts from the hallway as every other petal branched into vines covering every floor and climbing up the walls.

She turned to look at Caed. He was staring at the vines

as they curled along the crystal and wrapped their way up. He touched a flower, and tears sprang to his eyes.

She floated her whisper to him only. "You showed me what I could do. Each time I use my Gifts, I can't help but think of you."

"Ylena …"

"Catch me." She touched the crystal.

21

Ylena stood at the bottom of a ladder. Her foot was on the bottom rung, and she was holding it with both hands.

"Does the vine look more natural now?" The Director was at the top of the ladder. He adjusted a vine that hung from a series of pipes that stretched across the top of the stage.

"More natural? Sure ..." she said.

"Come on, tell me seriously! I want it to be symmetrical but not *too* symmetrical, you know?"

"Yes, of course. Not too symmetrical." She had no idea what he was talking about.

"You're patronizing me like you always do!" He laughed and started down the ladder. She backed out of the way, and he jumped off, running out into the center of the grassy area where the audience would sit. He rubbed his beard while he considered.

"It's perfect!" he declared as he walked back to where Ylena stood by the ladder. "Now I just have to hope the actors don't get it all twisted up in the first act."

"Aren't the Priests going to help?" She looked at all the

vines strung across the stage. It seemed similar to the way they had it for the Pageant, except the Priests used live plants and caused them to grow on cue.

"Priests?" he asked. "Well, aren't you fancy today?" He chuckled. "The stagehands will be ready to assist in the reset before Act Two. I'll let them know you think we should call them Priests. They will get a kick out of that!"

No Priests? This was definitely the Pageant with the same songs mentioning the Seven Virtues. How would they have all that but no Priests?

The Director touched her arm and murmured. "Are you all right? You seem far away."

"Um ... yeah, I'm fine. Just distracted by all the excitement." She put on a fake smile.

He seemed to recognize its fakeness and frowned. "Okay. I'll be here if you want to talk." He squeezed her hand before he began folding up the ladder.

Ylena walked to the center of the empty stage. She looked out over the grassy area and tried to imagine it filled with the people. She wondered how many people currently lived in the City. Only a few houses lined the open field and trees that circled the simple amphitheater.

The stage was in the same place that it was when she had performed, though much smaller and made entirely of wood instead of stone. And the seating here was just grass. Her amphitheater had giant cliffs that had stone benches cut into them to fit all the people of the City. She tried to imagine these people building the cliffs, building the entire City, and had no idea where it came from.

A familiar hand rested on her back. She spun out to the side, then back into his arms. She looked into his face and realized it wasn't Caed.

"Want to rehearse the scene with me? Will you be my

Goddess?" The Director smiled at her. She took a deep breath and woke up.

～

Ylena's sense of smell was the first to wake. She smelled crushed flower petals and the cold mountain stream scent of Caed. She kept her eyes shut for a few moments longer, savoring the sensation of her cheek pressed against his muscular chest as he carried her. His heartbeat rang in her ear, and she smiled.

"I can tell your breathing changed, Ylena." Caed's laugh rumbled against her ear. "But you can fake sleep a little longer, if you really don't want to walk."

Her eyes sprang open, and a guilty blush bloomed on her cheeks. "I'm sorry. I can walk."

He chuckled again and set her down. Rose stopped a few feet ahead and turned back.

"Good morning, sleepyhead. Glad to see you joined us again."

Ylena smoothed her hair back and rubbed her face to wake up. Despite Rose's greeting, it was still early evening.

"I wasn't out as long as the last time, was I?"

"No, you weren't," said Caed. "We just made it past the wall a few moments ago. We've still got a walk ahead of us."

Ylena walked close to Caed's side. "This time, I found out that they didn't have Priests yet. They had a Pageant, Virtues, the Goddess and Companion, but no Priests and no Gifts."

"Interesting ..." said Caed. "I assumed the Gifts came first and they eventually attributed them to the Goddess. Maybe the Gifts are more tied to the City itself than they are to the idea of the Goddess."

Ylena stopped in her tracks. "The City ... The Gifts come from the City?"

Caed shrugged. "Since there are no Gifts or giant crystal spires in your visions, I wonder if they show up at the same time? Hopefully, you can have more visions to find out."

Rose whistled a bird chirp. She noticed they had stopped walking and gestured for them to keep going.

"I wish there was something more I could do right now. Trying to figure this out is taking so long. I want to do something helpful."

"I had an idea about that, but I'm not sure what you will say." Caed ran nervous fingers through his white-streaked hair.

"Please tell me!" Knowing that he thought about her enough to make a plan involving her caused her heart to leap. She would do whatever he asked.

"It's the babies we rescued from Temple Discipline. We keep moving them from house to house in the center of the City. It would be safer if they could stay somewhere more secure."

"You think we could bring them to the Heart?"

"It's a lot of babies to make room for ..."

"And the Heart is such a small place?" She laughed. "I'm not sure why you think this would be a big deal!"

"It would also be Mims."

"Oh. Your mom ..."

He nodded.

"I'm just curious... Considering your sister's reaction to me ... how angry is Mims at me right now?"

He didn't answer.

She sighed. "That's fair. If she's willing to bring the babies, I will stay out of her way."

"We have to make a plan to get them all to the amphitheater safely. It will take a lot of people."

"I don't have many friends right now, but I'll see who I can find to help."

Ylena was thoughtful as they continued their walk. "Thanks for carrying me out of there, Caed."

"It was no big deal."

Ylena raised an eyebrow. "Your sister said I was a lot heavier than I look, so apparently, it is a big deal." He chuckled. "But I knew you would get me out. And it was nice to be on a mission with you. Before, I was always several steps behind you. Today, we worked side by side."

"It never felt like you were that far behind. With everything you can do, I always felt like you were one step from leaping away."

"You thought I would leave?" She never considered it.

"You have more Gifts than any of the other Priests in this City. I'm not sure this is where you belong."

"You remind me of my grandfather." Her voice hardened. "I guess I should just keep drinking tea for my whole life so I can fit in here."

"No, Ylena!" He walked in front of her and stopped. "That's not what I meant. You are something unique. Something I don't understand. I like to understand all the rules, but you came into my life and proved that I know nothing. What you did with those flower petals ... the drops of rain ... the music at the Spectacle ... None of that should be possible. I don't think you even realize how remarkable you are."

"All of that is as natural as breathing. But this ..." She placed a hand on his chest over his heart. "This is what feels remarkable. I didn't even know enough to dream about this. I don't want to leap away and miss it."

Caed took her face in his hands and pulled her closer. She leaned into him, longing for his kiss. Before his lips met hers, he blinked and focused on his hands, touching the tears on her cheek. His hands slid away.

"I can't do this, Ylena."

"I promise I won't use my Gift like that again. That was an accident, and it wasn't—"

A bird chirped far ahead. Rose.

Caed looked around. "I'm not sure if she is trying to speed us up or if she actually sees something. We should keep walking."

Ylena sighed and watched the moment slip away.

Purpose

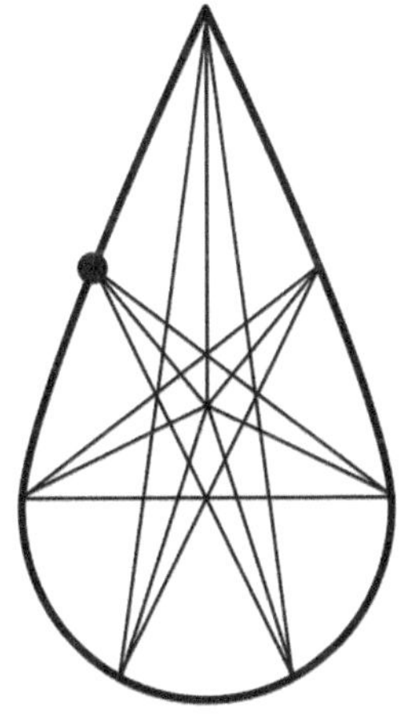

Delirium

22

Ylena woke up to the sound of a man singing. Her eyes popped open, and she scrambled out of her curtains. Standing on the stage was the boy, except he was no longer a boy. He was a teenager.

"Ylena!" He ran over to her. "Did you hear my voice? Don't I sound great?"

"Yes, you do." She studied his face. "You grew up a lot while I was gone."

He touched his face. "Do I look different?"

"Yes and no ... I could tell it was you. Although, the deep voice was shocking."

"To be honest, my voice shocked me, too."

"I'm sorry I wasn't here." He only appeared to be a few years younger than her, but she still felt responsible for him, as if he was a child. "Maybe I should try to spend more time here with you. Are you lonely when I'm gone?"

He smiled. "I'm never lonely. You're always here."

She brushed his hair back from his forehead. "Your hair is getting long ... Do I need to give you a haircut?"

He shrugged.

She frowned. "I'm sorry I don't know how to do this right."

"Do what right?"

"Be a mom. I never knew my mom. I'm not sure what moms do."

"You didn't have anyone to take care of you?"

"Well, I mean, I had my grandfather ..."

"He took care of you?"

She thought of all the lies he had told and the secrets he had kept from her.

And then she thought of sitting on a little stool while he trimmed her hair.

"Yes. He took care of me."

"Good. I'm glad you weren't alone."

"No. I was never alone." She sighed. "I'm sorry, but I've got to leave again. Thanks for the helpful talk."

He patted her on the shoulder and smiled. Then, he ran back onto the stage to test out his new voice.

Ylena took a deep breath and then knocked on her grandfather's door. The door opened a crack and then flung wide.

"Ylena!" His voice was barely a whisper. "Come in, please, come in."

She entered his small apartment behind the store. It looked much the same as the last time that she had been there.

"Can I get you something to drink?" He moved into the little kitchen. "Um ... not tea." He bit his lip. "I have coffee. I remember you like coffee ..."

"That would be nice. Thanks." She sat down at the little table while he heated the water. She could see him glance at her from the corner of his eye, but he kept his hands busy. When the coffee was finally ready, he joined her at the table.

She poured the coffee into the two mugs he had brought and took a sip. "Thank you."

They both spoke at once.

"Ylena, I should—"

"I wanted to say—"

They both cut off.

"Ylena, I'm sorry. There is so much I should have told you. I put you in danger by keeping secrets from you. I was a fool."

"Grandfather—"

"You have a right to be angry with me." He raked his fingers through his gray hair. "The night of the Spectacle ... What the Little Wardens did to you—" His voice caught. "I didn't know. I swear it. They told me we were raising our own Gifted children who could fight, but I didn't—I didn't know they would do that to you." His voice dropped to a whisper. "I thought they were going to kill you." He rubbed the tears out of his eyes.

Her grandfather had never shown those emotions to her before. But now, his face was open with grief and regret.

"What you did ... the way you fought them ... You know my feelings about the Goddess and the Priests. They are the ones to blame for your mother's death. For that, I will never forgive them. But you? You are something different. You are a wonder. You are the first true miracle I've ever seen."

She choked back a sob, closing her eyes as her tears fell. Her anger wasn't gone, but the edges had worn down so it no longer cut. She opened her eyes and studied his face.

"You might not forgive me for drugging you your whole life, or for never telling you about your parents, or for never mentioning a single damn thing about this City ... I completely understand. But I just want you to know that despite all my terrible decisions, the only two shining stars in my life have been your mother and you."

Ylena reached her hand across the table and grasped his rough fingers. "Grandfather, I am still hurt by the secrets you kept. I wish you had told me so many things, both for my sake and for yours. But no matter how angry I am at you, I have never for a moment regretted having you as my grandfather. You were always there for me. Always. I am the woman that I am because of you."

"Oh, Ylena ..." Grandfather rubbed his eyes again. "You always were such a good girl. I'm sorry I've ruined everything."

"It's not over yet."

"I think it is. The Wardens told me there would be a revolution. They said they were going to overthrow the High Priests, but they only replaced them. I lied and drugged you all these years for nothing. There is no revolution. Nothing will change."

"Something *has* to change. I refuse to settle for this. I'm going to continue to fight. The question is, will you?"

Grandfather studied his coffee for a few moments. His eyes flicked up to meet hers. "I've never been good at following anyone. But if you make a plan and need my help, I will follow you in a heartbeat, dear."

"I don't have a plan yet, but I'd love your help. I don't know what the two of us can do, but I feel like we have to try."

"When the time comes, Ylena, I can get you a lot more than just the two of us. There are many people down here who are desperate for a change. Maybe you will be the one to bring it."

23

Ylena left Grandfather and headed to the crystal in Delirium, where people both ecstatic and tranquil filled the area surrounding it. Ylena tried to blend in by adopting a sleepy, calm look. She strolled near the crystal and laid her hand on it. The low note vibrated the stone at her feet and throughout the Grotto.

The people looked around to see what was happening, so she kept her hand sinking into the stone hidden by her body. She looked toward the Den and waited for the guards to come out and head toward the stairs.

They never appeared.

It didn't make sense. Were there no guards in this Den? Did they not feel the vibration? Weren't they worried about what it meant? Why wouldn't they investigate it?

Unless they had talked to the other Little Wardens and expected it to happen. She was happy to avoid the guards that would have streamed by, but she was more worried about what it implied. If the Little Wardens and Wardens were discussing what was happening in their respective territories, then they might have already picked out a pattern. Breaking into the temple would be even more dangerous today.

Ylena turned to leave and found two white wolves staring at her. They sat on their haunches, and as Ylena approached, they hopped up and trotted down the street. She gathered her strength and followed them into an alley and wasn't surprised at who she found.

Wilder.

"Ylena." She could tell by his expression that he was surprised to see her.

"Wilder. I'm glad to see you."

"Um ..."

She frowned. "I understand if you can't say the same."

"I am glad that you are safe. I wasn't sure if you were going to be okay."

"I was in pretty rough shape for a while. Are you okay?"

"I've been staying busy." That wasn't quite an answer.

"Ah ... I saw Quinn and Tayeh. They seem to be well."

"Yes, they seem well."

The silence grew between them, and Ylena didn't know how to break it.

"Do you want your wolves back?" he asked.

"Want them back?"

"You sent them to follow us after the Spectacle, and they never left. I thought at least one of them might have followed Quinn and Tayeh when they went to Instinct, but both of them stayed with me for some reason."

Ylena looked at the wolves seated on either side of him. They stared at her with hard, blue eyes. "I don't think they want to come with me."

"Can't you talk to them or whatever you do? You can tell them I'm safe and they can go now."

The wolves never broke their stare. "They aren't here because of my command." Ylena looked back at Wilder. "I can convince them to leave you, if that's what you want, but it would be by force."

He frowned and looked at the wolves. "Well, no, I don't want you to force them." He leaned down and patted one of them on the neck. "Maybe they'll just get bored at some point and wander off?"

"Maybe..." Ylena eyed the wolves warily as they continued to stare at her.

Wilder looked around the alley. "I should probably go. Because of the Spectacle, I'm fairly recognizable. I need to avoid anyone who reports to the Little Wardens."

"Yes, I understand." She hesitated, but then her words spilled out in a rush. "Wilder, I don't have a right to ask you for any favors, but I don't know that many people, and even the ones I know, I'm not sure I can trust them, and I really need—"

"What do you need?" His voice was as calm as always, even if a bit colder.

"The baby Priests from the temples—the ones whose tears we poured into the basin—most of them are still being held by the Wardens, but a few were rescued. I could use some help moving them from their current hideout into the Heart where we can protect them."

His eyes widened. "I didn't realize any Priests had escaped. The word down here is that they have taken all the Priests captive. I guess they don't want any information getting out that sounds like someone could challenge the Wardens."

"I don't know how possible it is to challenge them. There are only a handful of Priests that are free." She bit her lip. "One of them is Caed."

"Of course he is." He took a deep breath. "What do you need me to do?"

"I will send word to you as soon as I know the plan."

"I don't exactly stay in the same place. The Little Wardens are extremely upset with me. How do you plan to find me?"

"I'll find them." She nodded at the white wolves. "They understand enough to let me find them, even if they are very displeased with me."

He chuckled and rubbed both wolves behind the ears. "I guess I'll keep them around a while longer."

She pulled the hood of her cloak back up and held his eyes as she said, "Thank you, Wilder."

He turned around, and the wolves followed him through the alley.

24

Ylena had plenty of time to reflect on her walk back to the Heart. It felt like she spent most of her days walking back and forth across the City. The trip to each crystal and back exhausted her, and she thought again it would be much more convenient if she could just use the staircases in the temples.

She made it back to the Heart, but there was no sign of the boy. The teenager. She wasn't sure where he went when she left. Would she come back to find him an adult? Would he continue to age this quickly and soon become an old man? How old would he get before he finally …? She tried to not worry about him and climbed up the staircase to the amphitheater.

As she exited the door beneath the stage, she found Lady Erenne. She sat in the front row of the audience in the High Priest seat she had been in the night of the Pageant. She stared at the stage, lost in her own thoughts.

"Lady Erenne." She startled at the sound of Ylena's voice. "Were you waiting for me?"

"I guess I was." She patted the High Priest seat to her left. "Join me, will you?"

Ylena lowered herself onto the throne with the tall back. She realized the High Priest who previously occupied this throne was who they found dead in a cage yesterday.

"Did you give him the poison dust?"

"He wasn't the first one I handed that gift to." Lady Erenne leaned her head back against the throne. "I'm not sure what to believe about them. Did they breathe the dust to end their own suffering? Or did they finally make a selfless choice by deciding to not let their secrets fall into the hands of the Wardens?"

"What else could the Wardens want? They already have the entire City."

Lady Erenne considered her for a long time before she answered. "The High Priests had many secrets, but the Wardens are torturing them for the secret of their long lives. Even when Perfection Priests heal people of every illness, they will eventually die from old age. But the High Priests have lived longer than anyone else alive, and no one outside of their circle knows why. If the Wardens discover their secret, there will be no end to the amount of suffering they inflict on this City."

"That's why you gave the High Priests the poison dust. You want them to take that secret to their graves."

"This City was created to work in balance, but the High Priests discovered an advantage and exploited it for centuries. The secret has to end here."

"But why would the Goddess allow something like that? Why wouldn't she stop it before now?"

She sighed. "That's a good question. I wish I had an answer, but I don't." She leaned her head back against the throne and closed her eyes.

Ylena considered her words in silence for a moment. Then, she leaned toward Lady Erenne. "You said that only the High Priests have lived that long, but I know someone else that old."

Lady Erenne cracked open an eyelid. "Really?"

"I met a man named Walter who said he was alive before the High Priests took over. Even the Priest who worked with him said he was older than anyone could remember."

"You met him recently?" Lady Erenne had closed her eyes again and appeared only mildly interested.

"I met him when I first visited Perfection. He was in the room when Wilder …" When he killed the Priest to protect her secret. "Well, I saw him again a few days ago. He gave me a notebook that belonged to my father."

Ylena studied Lady Erenne's calm face turned up to the sun and put some pieces together. "Walter was in the healing center at the same time as my father, and so were you. Do you know him?"

"I spent most of my time at the healing center in a fog of sadness. I remember little until I heard your mother sing."

Ylena realized that wasn't quite an answer. She imagined the kind, strange man sitting at his table, scribbling in his notebooks, while a shrewd-eyed Lady Erenne came to visit him. "I shouldn't have told you about him. Are you going to hurt him?"

Lady Erenne's eyes snapped open, and a fire burned behind them. "How many times do I have to tell you I do not want to hurt anyone? Even delivering the poison dust to those terrible High Priests was enough to send me back into despair!" She tried to catch her breath and dropped her voice to a whisper. "You saw me after I left the temple last night, Ylena. Do you think I enjoyed handing Jahan that poison dust?"

Ylena dropped her voice to a whisper to match. "I didn't ask if you would enjoy it. I asked if you would hurt him."

Lady Erenne stood quickly. "Goodbye, Ylena."

Ylena watched Lady Erenne as she walked out of the amphitheater. She held her head high, and though she walked fast, she still strode through the stone benches like she owned the place. Ylena shook her head. Sometimes, Lady Erenne felt relatable, but other times, she still had the attitude of a High Priest.

Ylena considered going to Perfection to hide Walter from Lady Erenne. She knew from last time that he did not want to leave. He would have to be restrained and carried off against his will. She couldn't think of a way to do that without traumatizing him and possibly injuring them both.

Lady Erenne was arrogant and a schemer, but Ylena had seen nothing violent in her. She didn't believe Lady Erenne would actually hurt him. Ylena took a deep breath and trusted her this time. She hoped she wasn't gambling on Walter's life.

25

Ylena paced on a rooftop near Temple Purpose. As she waited for Caed and Rose to arrive, she was second-guessing her decision about Walter. Maybe she should have gone ... She could have run faster than Lady Erenne. Maybe she should—

"What's wrong?" Caed's voice made her jump. He stood next to her beside the taller building that hid them from view, while Rose crouched down to peek over the edge of the roof.

"I'm just worried about someone ... How much do you trust Lady Erenne?"

He seemed taken aback. "I've worked with her to stop the Wardens, and before that, the High Priests, and before that, the High Priest of Purpose who killed my brothers and sister. I didn't join up with her because I trusted her, but our purposes have aligned so far."

"Do you think she would kill an innocent person to get what she wants?"

He tilted his head as he considered the question. "No, I don't. Her plans always seem to avoid hurting anyone. That's one of our major sources of conflict. I want her to take more risks to accomplish our goals, but she is unwilling to hurt even the worst people."

"She's the one who delivered the poison dust to the High Priests."

"Hmm ... That's interesting. We knew some of the other High Priests died, but we didn't know how. Rose and I decided to deliver the poison dust to the High Priests who were still alive but not mention it to her. We assumed she wouldn't agree to it."

"Are you two done chatting?" Rose tied her red hair back into a knot. "We've got another temple to break into."

They all crouched down and slid to the edge of the roof to plan their approach to the temple.

"I'd like to get closer to that stream." Ylena pointed to the water running through the buildings ahead. "I think I can work with that."

"I bet you can," said Rose. "It's not as cute as the dog, but I guess we will make it work."

They slid off the roof and made their way through the buildings. It was still daylight, and Ylena felt exposed in the bright sunlight. However, the streets were fairly quiet, at least until they approached the stream.

They heard the crying before they could see why the child was in distress. Ylena tried to dart out from behind a building, but Caed grabbed her waist and pulled her back.

He whispered into her ear. "Shh ... listen. The child is not alone. Be smart about this."

She froze in his arms and listened. She heard several other people talking. And a second child crying. Possibly more.

She turned to look him in the eyes. "Yes. You're right."

They both seemed to realize at the same time how close they stood. Caed dropped his arm from around her waist and stepped back.

Rose rolled her eyes at them both. She walked back to the door on the side of the building, opened it slowly, and then waved them both to follow her inside.

They followed her into an abandoned shoe shop. All that remained were a few mismatched shoes scattered among the broken shelves. They made their way to the window at the front of the shop, ducked down side by side, and slowly raised their heads to look out.

The Wardens had cleared the enormous park and turned it into a makeshift farm. Amid the patches of corn and grapes and wheat were children.

These were the children the Wardens had raised. Their Champions. And soldiers watched them as they caused the fields to grow over and over. As soon as they caused something to grow, the soldiers would send the people from the City to gather the food as fast as possible. These people looked in worse shape than the people building the walls. Dirt and sweat coated their skin and clothes, and they fell down as they carried basket after basket up to the soldiers who waited with carts.

She saw a child no older than five sitting in the dirt. He looked exhausted, and his fair skin was caked with dirt. The workers had cleared the surrounding field of potatoes, and the boy stared off into the distance in a daze. A soldier yelled at him, but his eyes remained unfocused. The soldier walked up and slapped him on the back of the head. The boy reached out to catch himself as he fell, and his touch, along with his fresh tears, caused the field to sprout all over again.

A fire rose in Ylena, and if Caed hadn't grabbed her arm, she would have stormed outside to take on all the soldiers herself.

"Please, Ylena." Caed's voice was calm. "You need to think about this. We need to make a plan."

"I've seen that look before," said Rose. "That's the way she looked when she rescued those Priests from the Warden's harem. That time, she ground half the temple into dust." Ylena's palms were gripping the edge of the stone windowsill, and she could feel the pulse of the stone spread through every building on the block.

"Ylena, don't do anything rash." Caed's whisper was desperate. "We need to make a plan. Please, let's work together on this."

Ylena took a few deep breaths. She slowly lowered her hands from the windowsill and clasped them at her waist. She spoke in a voice that was calm and fake. "What do you propose?"

Caed took a deep breath and rubbed his hands through his hair. "I think we should continue with our initial plan to get into the temple. Unless you have given up on reaching the crystal spire?"

She thought about her visions as rationally as she could. She believed they were leading her somewhere, but she wasn't sure where. Even if she had another vision, she might still have unanswered questions. However, if she entombed each of these soldiers in stone, that would be a definitive answer.

She sighed. "You're right. We should continue with the plan." She looked out onto the field again. "This isn't just happening here. The Wardens didn't divide their children up according to their Gifts, so this is exactly what is happening in every other Diocese. We have to stop this everywhere."

Caed nodded, and his shoulders relaxed slightly. "Yes, I agree. Now, do you have a way to get us into and out of the temple quickly?"

Her eyes followed the stream that had been her initial target. She saw a soldier holding a child. The girl was so young that she might have been a baby from the temple nursery. The soldier would occasionally lower the child into the cold water, making her cry. Her tears caused the water to flow into a series of pools that more workers were using to fill large containers.

Caed followed the direction of her eyes and said in a hesitant voice, "I believe they have closed off the water supply to most of the City so the people are forced to depend on the Wardens. But um ... will you remember to not get distracted by murdering anyone right now?"

She closed her eyes and tears fell on her cheeks. "No promises."

She walked out the side door, and Rose and Caed scrambled to follow her. She moved along the back of the building until she found the wagon they were loading with large containers of water.

She spoke to the workers. "We will put that in the truck so you can go get another container."

The two people lowered the container to the ground and shrugged. They shuffled back to the others.

Ylena twisted the top off of the container and plunged her hands inside. The water rose from the container as raindrops falling in reverse. They fell into the air and floated as a cloud over the heads of the children, soldiers, and workers.

The baby girl was the first to notice. Her sobs settled down as she put her thumb in her mouth and followed the raindrops across the sky. The soldier didn't notice until the first raindrop hit the top of his head. He looked around in confusion as the rest of the people cried out.

As the rain splashed down around them, Ylena realized they had never seen rain before. The crystals caused the inside of the City to be warm all year long, and the Priests watered all the plants using their Gift. The only exception had been when Ylena's tear had caused the crystals to flicker and go out. That night, it had been snow falling for the first time.

As the people ran into buildings to hide, she knew they remembered that night. She felt bad about scaring the workers, but the soldiers' fear, along with the delight of the children, made it worth it.

Each drop of rain that fell into the stream caused two more drops to fly into the air and then fall again. She reached her hand into the sky, and as she touched the raindrops, she caused the rain to spread all along the stream as it stretched into the temple.

She saw the baby girl stretch out her hand, and raindrops flew toward her to gather in a ball of rain in her hand. The guard looked at her and at the rain falling around them. His eyes widened, and he dropped her to the ground and ran.

Ylena started toward the little girl when Caed stopped her. Rain was dripping down his face and weighing down his white-streaked hair. "We have to go. She will be okay."

Ylena turned to see a worker scoop up the little girl and run with her into a building. Ylena nodded. "You're right. Let's go."

"Um ... Rose?" Caed looked at his sister. Rose had her face tipped up into the sky and was smiling as the water ran down her face. "We really should go now."

"You're right." She sighed. "I liked the dog, but this is the drama I have been expecting from you."

"Glad I could deliver," said Ylena. "Let's go."

The rain followed the stream and soon engulfed the entire temple. Everyone crowded inside to escape the storm. Soldiers and white-haired Priests huddled in hallways and every room in the corridor.

"It's more crowded in here than usual," said Caed. The

three of them blended in among the Priests, and no one realized they didn't belong. "Getting in here was easy, but as usual, getting out is the hard part. Luckily, this was Erenne's temple, so we don't need to make any deliveries first."

As they headed into the inner courtyard, it got even more crowded. Priests continued with their chores as the Warden's people listened to the stories about the rain. As the three of them moved toward the crystal, Ylena saw they had tables set up to mix various potions. At one table, they had dry tea leaves.

She looked at Caed in the crystal's glow. The light reflected off the rain on his face. She reached her hand toward him. "May I?"

He looked surprised but nodded. She brushed her fingers gently across his cheeks and pulled the rainwater away. She lowered her hand and held a puddle in her fingertips.

She held his gaze. "Be ready to run."

She heard Rose groan.

The drops of water in her small puddle dropped out of her hand and flew toward the ceiling. They floated for a moment before they fell. Rainwater that had collected along the doorways flowed inside, and once the trickle hit the raindrops in the courtyard, they floated back to the ceiling, where they fell again.

Water began pouring in larger and larger streams along the floor, where it rained up and then down again. The people stomped their feet, trying to make the water stop floating up. They grabbed potions off the tables and tried to find a dry room.

She looked at Caed one more time. "When you drag me out of here, try not to slip."

She winked and touched the crystal.

26

Ylena opened her eyes and found herself in a dressing room. Instead of the stone rooms in the current amphitheater, she recognized this room as part of the wooden building around the stage from the past. Costumes hung on neat racks, and props were stacked on a long bench. She sat at a table with a pile of makeup. It was in different containers than she was used to, but the scene felt very familiar.

"There you are!" The Director smiled at her as he set a few more props on the bench. "I can't wait for you to see everyone in costume tonight. The designers really did a fantastic job."

He pulled his shirt off over his head and stood in the middle of the room, scratching his beard.

Ylena nearly knocked the chair over in her haste to stand. "I should go ..."

"No, it's okay. I moved the mirror over here." He turned toward another small table with a mirror and a bowl of steaming water. He dug a stool out from underneath a pile of clothes and didn't notice her awkwardness. "This beard has been fun, but I want to look sharp for dress rehearsal."

He began lathering up his beard with foam, and she settled down to watch him in fascination.

She had always enjoyed watching her grandfather shave. She found it soothing. The Director chatted about various parts of the Pageant without expecting Ylena to answer, which was good because she had no idea what to say.

What was she doing here? She had hoped there was a purpose behind these visions and that she would discover something to help her overthrow the Wardens. She thought this early version of the City would hold a clue for her. What could she possibly learn from a shirtless man who was shaving in front of her? Was she just wasting her time?

The Director splashed his face with water and picked up a towel. "That feels so strange!" He turned to her with his arms out. "So, do you prefer the beard or clean shaven?"

Her eyes widened, and she stood. "You're the boy."

He grabbed her by the waist. "I might look younger this way, but I'm definitely not a boy."

She gasped and woke up.

"She's never taken this long to wake up."

"You need to relax, Caed. That girl is filled with miracles and weirdness. She'll be fine."

"But what if something different happened? What if—?"

She reached out her hand, and Caed took it into his own.

"Ylena? Can you hear me?"

She blinked her eyes open. The sun had set, and she was on the ground in the trees that surrounded the amphitheater. Her head was resting on Caed's legs, and now her hand was in his.

"I can hear you. I'm ... okay." Lying on the ground was

awkward, so she pushed herself up to seated, which unfortunately caused Caed to let go of her hand.

Rose stood above them and studied Ylena's face. "So, was that time extra productive when you do ... whatever it is you do? Or were you just hoping Caed would carry you all the way back home?"

Ylena looked back toward the glowing crystal of Temple Purpose. "You carried me the whole way?"

"You don't remember walking, do you?" Rose answered drily.

"It was fine. I'm glad you're okay." Caed ran his fingers through his damp hair, and Ylena realized how soggy they were.

"Sorry about all the water. I didn't want to draw attention by keeping it off of just us." She held her hand out, collected all the remaining water from their clothes and hair, and scattered it around the roots of the closest trees.

Rose shook herself. "That felt odd, but thank you. Too bad you couldn't do that as we dripped all the way here."

Ylena sighed. "Yeah, I'm sorry about that, too."

"What's the matter?" Caed tried to catch her eyes, but she was picking at a piece of grass without looking at him. "What did you see?"

"It's complicated."

Rose snorted. "Something complicated? Well, that's new."

Caed snapped. "Rose, please! Either sit down and listen, or leave."

She huffed but sat down in the grass to their side. She still looked cranky, so Ylena spoke to Caed.

"I saw the people rehearsing for the Pageant before the City was built." Rose made a sound, but Ylena continued. "All the visions have included the Director, and this time ... I recognized him."

"You recognized him?" asked Caed. "You recognized someone from before the City was built?"

"I guess I need to explain something else first. Before the Spectacle, I kept hearing a baby crying. I assumed it was one of the Wardens' Gifted children and that I could hear them somehow. But it wasn't." She took a deep breath. "When my tear fell in the basin, it caused something to be born. He became a boy, and he said he was the City. He's grown up so fast ... The last time I saw him, he was a teenager, but when I saw the Director's face tonight, I know it was him."

Caed was blinking slowly, and she couldn't interpret his expression. She looked over at Rose, and her expression was clear.

"You are crazy." Rose shook her head. "I can't believe we've been breaking into every temple and carrying you out so you could follow this—"

"Rose!" Caed's voice was sharp. "Go. Now."

She stood with a huff and stomped away.

Caed shut his eyes and took a deep breath. "That's a lot to take in, Ylena. I—"

"You don't believe me." Her voice was quieter than she wanted, but she couldn't find enough air.

"It's not that I don't believe you—"

"Why would I make this up?"

"I'm not saying that you made it up. You might really believe it."

"But you don't think it's real."

"Ylena, you experienced something really traumatic with the Pageant and then with the Spectacle. It makes sense that your mind would invent something to protect yourself from the memories."

She stared at him with a flat expression. "You think I'm sick. That I might belong in a healing center with people who have illnesses of the mind."

"Well, there aren't any Priests there right now, so—"

She stood quickly. "I have to go." She started walking across the field to the amphitheater.

"Wait!" he called. "Will you still come back to help us hide the children tomorrow?"

She didn't look back.

Ylena walked slowly down the stairs to the Heart. She sat down on her pile of curtains and unbuckled her boots.

"Hi, Ylena! Did you do anything fun today?"

She didn't answer as she moved her boots to the side of the curtains.

"I did a lot more singing today. Does my voice sound any deeper?"

She lay back on the curtains and stared at the ceiling of the Heart. The crystalline climbed up stone spires that surrounded the center crystal and spread throughout the ceiling leading up to the various lights spread through the City. From her position on the ground, she realized the liquid crystal flowed upward, like her raindrops had.

"Ylena? Are you okay? You are scaring me."

She closed her eyes, and tears leaked out the corners. She sighed and sat up.

"I'm sorry to scare you. I shouldn't ignore you, even if I'm not sure you are real."

"You aren't sure I'm real?" His eyes widened. She added him to the list of people that doubted her sanity.

"My mental stability is in question. Apparently, since no one else has seen you, and since you claim you are the City, those are enough reasons for people to question your existence."

He frowned. "I can understand why that's challenging."

She studied his face. He seemed older than the last time she had seen him, but not yet as old as he was in her visions. He had the same playful smile, and she was glad to realize that she still looked at him as her child, not as anything else.

She squeezed his shoulder. "I'm sorry to doubt you. It's not fair to you. You've been trying to show me something important, but I just don't know what it is."

"What have I shown you?"

"Your visions. I've seen you ... Well, I think it was you before the City was built. I'm not sure how it works, but I know it was you. I know you are real."

He gave her a comforting smile. "Thank you. I know you are real, too!"

She laughed. "Thanks." She wiped her tears from her eyes and considered them as they sparkled on her fingertips. "Um ... could I try something with you? I don't know if it will work, but can I try to share these visions with you? Maybe they will help you remember and you can tell me what's going on."

His face lit up. "Yes! Finally! Something I can do to help you!"

She smiled and took his hand.

She showed him the first memory of standing in front of the stage in the open field.

His eyes opened wide.

The crystal spire and all the crystalline flickered and went out.

She sat in the dark, unable to move for some time. As she settled onto her curtains to sleep, she realized either she had broken the City for a second time, or she was crazy and only imagining herself in the dark.

Harmony

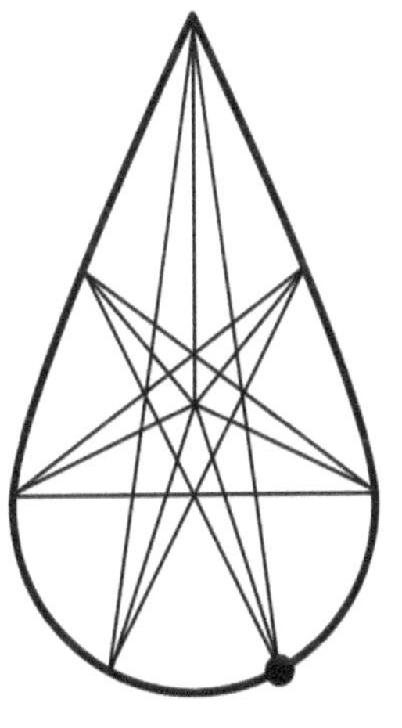

Rivalry

Ylena woke to footsteps clattering down the staircase. She sat up slowly and was relieved to see Quinn and Tayeh. She was even more relieved to see at all.

The crystal and liquid crystalline were glowing again.

"Hi, Ylena!" Quinn's cheerful voice clashed with her mood. "It's good to see you!"

Ylena looked around the Heart. The boy was gone. Was he hiding because Quinn and Tayeh were here? Or was he just gone? Or was he never there at all?

"Are you okay?" Quinn sat down on the bottom step across from her, and Tayeh stood beside him.

"I need to ask you both a question, but I'm scared the question alone will cause you to look at me like I'm crazy."

Tayeh raised an eyebrow. "I've met a lot of crazy people over the years. It's not really that surprising anymore."

"Did the crystals and crystalline go out last night?"

Tayeh and Quinn exchanged a look.

"Yes. Obviously," said Tayeh.

"We actually planned on coming back here last night,

but it really gets dark Upstairs without the crystals or any lamps. No one up there has even heard of a candle!"

Ylena sighed in relief. The boy had to be real. Using her Gift had shocked him, but hopefully, he would be back.

"The people Upstairs were freaking out!" said Quinn. "They aren't used to the dark, are they?" He shook his head. "People screamed nonstop until the lights finally came back on."

"How long were they out?"

Tayeh looked at the crystal in the center of the Heart and the tracery of crystalline flowing along the ceiling. "You didn't notice?"

"Um ... I was asleep."

Tayeh snorted. "They were out for a few hours. Enough to terrify every person Upstairs, including the Priests at the Library. I suggested we light a fire, and I thought they were going to murder me." She smiled as if she was proud of them.

"Do you know what caused it?" asked Quinn.

She wanted to explain about the boy, but she still didn't have any proof of his existence other than all the crystals going out again. They might think that she imagined the story with the boy to explain the crystals going out.

Then, she wondered if that's what really happened.

"Ylena?" Quinn was staring at her with concern.

"Oh, um ... no, I don't know what caused that. It sure was strange, right?"

Tayeh looked at her with narrowed eyes, but Quinn leaped up with excitement.

"We haven't told you why we came back!"

"I thought you came back because of the crystals going out."

"No, that was just curious, not our reason to find you. We discovered something." Quinn's eyes lit up.

"When he says *we* discovered something, he means that *he* discovered something."

"It's true." He grinned. "I cracked the code."

Ylena looked at him in confusion.

"The old languages! I can read them! Well, not *all* of them, and not every word, but enough to understand some things."

"Wow! That's amazing, Quinn."

"Thanks." He smiled modestly. "The librarian Priests were very helpful. They led me to the right books that helped me put the pieces together. Once I saw it, they saw it. They are still there now, digging through the books, trying to discover more."

"So, what did you find?"

"Well, the Priests are still debating if what we found is actually true. They aren't sure if it is heretical or not."

"That's perfect," said Ylena. "As if I'm not heretical enough myself." She shook her head.

Quinn rubbed his chin with a thoughtful expression. "Now that you say that, it actually might explain you."

"Explain what?" she asked.

"You! Where you came from. Why you have all the Gifts."

"It explains *me*? Wait, what?"

Tayeh sighed. "Quinn, please explain to her what you are talking about."

Quinn straightened up and nodded. "Yes, okay. Some books talk about the time before the City. And apparently before the City people had Gifts."

She thought about her visions. "I don't think they did ..." But she didn't finish after she realized she couldn't prove the visions were real.

"To be more accurate, there were people with what they called 'the Spark.' They didn't call them Gifts until after the time of the Goddess. These people with the Spark were extremely rare. There weren't large groups of Priests with Gifts like we have now. Their Spark was unusual, and it presented in different ways than we are used to."

"Like what? What could they do?"

"Some of that has been hard to interpret. Some of the magic is so different from what we know, and we can't find any clues to what the words even mean." He looked embarrassed. "I can only read a tiny fraction of the words in their language. There is so much more to study! Some of the books—"

"Quinn!" Tayeh's voice snapped him out of his excitement. "Please continue with the relevant information."

"Yes, okay. We don't know every type of magic these people manifested, but we do know that they used their magic without being bonded to the City. And as a result, they wouldn't die from using their power."

She touched the white streak in her hair. It was only white coloring given to her by the Little Warden from Peculiarity, but before her tears had fallen into the basin, her hair had faded white like the other Priests. "But my Gifts are all tied to the City. How does this explain me?"

Quinn stared at her white streak. "I'm not sure about your hair turning white, but it explains more about how you could have all the Gifts. Even though it was rare in the past, it was a common enough phenomenon that there are several books about it. I found a few books about the mathematical formulas of how many people with the Spark were expected in any population."

"So, my Gifts don't come from the Goddess? I was born with magic as some statistical inevitability?"

Quinn opened his mouth to reply but shut it again slowly. He looked to Tayeh for help.

Tayeh sighed. "Ylena, these books aren't about the

Goddess. They are just a way to figure out what's going on around here. That's what you wanted, right?"

"Yes, I did, but I am looking for answers on how we can fix this City. I didn't think I'd discover answers that would affect how I thought about myself. I'm finally understanding what my Gifts are, and now you tell me they might not be Gifts from the Goddess at all, but something completely strange called the Spark?"

Quinn leaned forward and patted her leg comfortingly. "But the Spark isn't so bad! It's possible that the Goddess was just a woman who had the Spark herself."

Ylena stared at him, blinking slowly. She lowered her head into her hands and tried to breathe.

Tayeh whispered, "Quinn! You are so smart and yet so stupid sometimes."

Ylena took a deep breath and sat up. "Okay. Thank you for telling me. I could use a drink, so I—"

"Oh! I forgot the most important part!" Quinn was bouncing with excitement.

Ylena sighed but braced herself for more life altering news. "What else is there?"

"We don't know about every type of magic they had, but I discovered one in particular. Some people could grant long life."

Ylena's head shot up. "The High Priests?"

"If one of them could grant long life, that could be why they lived so long. The books tell of people with a Spark similar to the Priests' ability to heal, and they differentiated the Spark to extend the length of someone's life as something unusual."

"So, the question is, which one of them had that ability?" asked Tayeh. "Let's hope it was one that is already dead. We don't need the Wardens getting their hands on that kind of magic."

"Most of the High Priests are dead," said Quinn. "But—"

Ylena closed her eyes. "It wasn't a High Priest." She bit her lip and tried to remind herself that she trusted Lady Erenne, but now, she wasn't so sure. "But if we try to find him, he will either be missing or dead."

28

Ylena led Quinn and Tayeh out of the Heart and through the tunnel to Grotto Rivalry. They didn't speak, sensing her need for silence. She couldn't stop thinking about Walter. She worried maybe she had misjudged Lady Erenne. If she had, then he was already dead.

She sighed as they continued through the streets. The three of them got a few looks from people looking for a fight, but Tayeh glared at them long enough to cause them to back down. The three of them didn't say a word until Ylena stopped in front of the crystal.

"Try to act casual." She raised her hand to the crystal.

The vibrations ran through her hands and through her feet. The note rang through the Grotto. Her hand sank into the crystal in a ripple.

The crystal flickered off.

Ylena gasped and stepped back. She heard Tayeh swear as she elbowed her in the chest.

That's when the screaming started.

She could hear the terror of people plunged suddenly

into the dark. Without the light of the crystal and the crystalline, the cave was pitch-black.

Until a light flickered on. And then another. Around the Grotto, people lit candles and lamps. There was still a lot of yelling, but Ylena saw shadows moving toward each of the little lights. Next to her, a small light flickered to life.

"We need to get away from here." Tayeh's face wavered in the light of her candle. "I don't think anyone should see us close to this crystal, do you?"

Ylena nodded, and she and Quinn followed close behind Tayeh. By the time they were several blocks away, most of the Grotto was lit with the warm glow of candles.

"Looks like the people down here adapted already," said Ylena.

"Down here, you can't always rely on the light from the crystalline lamps," said Quinn. "They either require a Priest to shape the stone for it to flow, or it takes a master stonemason to shape it. Everyone usually has a candle or two somewhere in their house, just in case."

"So, where are we going now?" asked Tayeh as she blew out her candle before it could melt down her hand. "Back Upstairs?"

"Yes, but we need to find someone else first." She closed her eyes and cocked her head to the side. When she whistled, Quinn jumped.

A gray cat sauntered into view. He sat down in the middle of the road and began giving himself a leisurely bath.

"Hey, buddy. Long time no see! You look well."

Tayeh stared at Ylena. "Is this who you were looking for?"

Quinn and Tayeh both stared at her like she was crazy. She rubbed her forehead.

"No. This is not who I am looking for. But he knows which way to go. So, if you are willing to appear as crazy as me, you can join me as I follow this cat down a few back alleys, okay?"

Tayeh gave her a flat stare, but Quinn shrugged with a smile. That seemed about all the agreement she was going to get, so she sank down to her knees to talk to the cat.

"Do you think we can go now?" she whispered. "You're embarrassing me in front of my friends."

The cat gave himself a few last licks before he stood with a long stretch. Eventually, he strolled down the alley. Following a cat wasn't the quickest form of travel, but as long as Ylena kept up a steady stream of admiration for the cat, he continued on to his destination.

"Your fur is so pretty ... Yes, it is shiny in the light of our candle ... Your legs are so long when you stretch them, but even longer when you walk a little faster ..."

Her constant flow of praise distracted her from realizing which direction the cat was leading. She thought it was possible the cat would lead them out of Grotto Rivalry and back to Delirium, but he continued to lead them deeper inside, toward the performing arts school they had stayed at last time they were here.

The path was familiar, and her breathing sped up. The performing arts school was where Wilder, Quinn, and Rev all met. Wilder and his wolves were at the end of the cat's path, but she knew who else she would find. Her chatter fell away as the panic rose in her chest. What would Rev do when she saw her? The last time she had seen Rev, she had been furious about what Ylena had done to Wilder. Rev hadn't known the specifics, but now that she knew, what would she do?

Her footsteps slowed until the cat turned around to stare at her in disgust. Ylena's feet slid to a stop a block away from the school.

"Thanks, buddy. I'll handle it from here."

The cat gave a little sniff. He stuck his tail into the air proudly and marched away.

"So, are we actually going in?" asked Tayeh. "Or will we continue standing here in the dark?"

"We're going in." She took a deep breath and started down the block. Once she was in front of the door, she shook out her muscles to relax. She raised her hand and gave the door three sharp raps.

The door flew open, and Rev stood framed in the doorway.

Ylena braced herself for the attack as Rev flew at her but instead felt the wind being crushed from her lungs by the power of Rev's embrace.

"Oh, Ylena," she sobbed. "I'm so glad you are alive." She pulled herself back a little and smoothed her hands through Ylena's hair. "You still have the white streaks, I see." She held Ylena by the arms and examined her body. "You aren't eating enough." She stroked her hands on Ylena's tear-streaked cheeks. "You also have dark circles. You haven't been sleeping." She crushed her in another hug. "I'm sorry I wasn't there to take care of you after all of that. I've got you back now, and I'm going to make sure you eat what I tell you."

"I hate to break this up," said Tayeh, "but is it possible to take this inside? Or do we need to stand out here all day?"

"Yes, come in!" Rev ushered them inside. A group of students sat on couches with a candle on the table between them. Ylena and Rev had prompted a few giggles and raised eyebrows, but they seemed fairly immune to dramatic moments.

Rev led Ylena over to a table at the side of the room. "Tayeh and Quinn, why don't you go find Wilder? I'm sure we will need to be on our way soon."

They obediently did as they were told and left Rev alone with Ylena.

"I thought you would still be angry at me for ... for what I did to Wilder."

Rev gave her a hard stare with her single eye. "Well, yes. I still might attempt to strangle you for breaking his heart, like I knew you would." She reached across the table to grab Ylena's hand. "But currently, my concern for you is outweighing that, so you better lean into it now while you have the chance."

Ylena gave the tiniest of smiles. "I've also been drinking way too much."

Rev threw her head back and laughed. "I'm sure you have! I'm reprimanding you for that and feeling equally sorry that I missed it."

"I should have come to you immediately, Rev. I've been moping around by myself when I should have found you."

She folded her arms across her chest. "Yes, you should have. I'm glad you've learned that lesson." She leaned closer across the table. "So, Wilder tells me we are going to rescue some babies. How exciting!"

"I'm sure it will be more than exciting. I recruited Wilder into this because we are honestly desperate for the help. But that 'we' includes Caed. And now, it includes you, who still wants to murder me a little. So, I'm really not sure how this is going to work."

Rev clapped her hands. "Oh, this is going to be so exciting!" She reached her hand across the table again. "And don't worry about me trying to murder you, Ylena. I like you enough to give you a head start." She patted her hand as she stood.

Ylena started to chuckle, but based on Rev's face, she wasn't sure if it was a joke or not.

"Come on! Let's find the others." Rev took her hand and

led her through the dark hallways into a room that was glowing with the light from a lantern high on a shelf.

"They have snacks!" called Quinn cheerfully.

Rev pulled Ylena down on the bench next to her. "Yes! Let's eat snacks before we go." She grabbed a cookie.

Ylena looked up and found herself across from Wilder. From the soft growling under the table, she knew his two white wolves were at his feet. She tucked her feet underneath herself, just to be safe.

"I guess you found us easily enough?" he asked.

"I know you are trying to lie low, but a guy with two white wolves is fairly easy to find if you know the right person to ask."

She saw a fraction of a smirk in the dim light. "I've never been good at being inconspicuous."

She smiled and ate all the food Rev put in front of her.

29

They spent most of the day at the school, eating and catching up on stories. At one point, Kieran, Wilder's former rival, joined them at the table. He wasn't as terrible as Ylena expected, so she counted that as a win. Eventually, it was time for them to leave, so they said their goodbyes and headed out.

Their group settled into their familiar formation as they walked. Ylena looked at Rev in awe. Wilder was still quiet and avoided standing close to Ylena, but Rev seemed like nothing changed.

Ylena felt a tear trickle down her cheek, but she wiped it away quickly.

"Are you sure that's safe?" asked Rev.

"Safe?"

Rev mimed wiping her tear.

"Oh, that. No, it's definitely not safe. But I guess I will need the tear at some point tonight, so I might as well let them fall when they occur. I'm sorry I never told you about, you know, all of it."

"That was your secret to keep, Ylena. I only wish that I hadn't been so distracted being bossy about your relationship with Wilder that I didn't notice there was more going on."

"You admit you were being bossy about Wilder?"

Rev narrowed her eye and gave her a sharp glance.

"Um ... never mind," said Ylena quickly.

Rev flipped her blond hair, then looped her arm through Ylena's and continued walking.

Wilder brought a lantern from the school along with them, so they had a small amount of light as they walked through the tunnel. They stayed close together all the way through.

When they made it into the Heart, Ylena was shocked at how large and empty it felt. She hadn't expected the boy to make an appearance, especially now that the lights were all off, but she still felt his loss. Their voices echoed through the space in a way that didn't happen while the crystal glowed. They walked past the crystalline, and in the reflected light of the lantern, the liquid crystal was dull and still.

They followed each other up the stairs slowly, holding hands. There were no railings, and the steps were narrow enough to be dangerous in the dim light. They made it off the stairs and into the small space under the stage, filing out of the stage door one at a time until Rev exited with a gasp.

The sun had set, and the faint purple glow on the horizon was fading. Without the bright light of the crystal spires, thousands of stars stretched across the clear sky. A small sliver of the moon hung in the air.

Rev wept.

The whole group stopped to give her time. Rev's tattoo was visible in the faint moonlight. Behind her ear, she had a crescent moon surrounded by seven stars. Rev had told her she'd got the tattoo to remind her of the hope that, some-day, she would leave the Underneath and see the sky. Ylena smiled up at the moon and imagined seeing it for the first time. From her cave on the mountain, she usually had an even better view than this, and she had seen the moon since she was a tiny baby. She couldn't imagine Rev's wonder.

Rev wiped her tears and smoothed her hair back into its ponytail. She took a deep breath and nodded. Without a word, the group continued on.

Once they left the amphitheater, Ylena took the lead. She led them through the dark streets until they came to the house Caed had described.

She gathered their group together and whispered, "In case I didn't say it clear enough before, this isn't our mission. We are just assisting. And I'll remind you, all the people we will work with are Priests. Please keep the sacrilege to a minimum, please?"

Tayeh elbowed Quinn, and he looked confused. Ylena sighed and knocked on the door.

Caed answered the door and shoved Ylena behind him. She heard several grunts outside, but it was hard to see with the light inside blinding her eyes.

Tayeh stood behind a man with white-streaked hair, and she had his arm twisted behind his back. Quinn looked confused as a woman with a single white streak in her hair held a knife to his throat. Rev looked irritated to have been overcome by the Priest who had locked both arms behind her back. Wilder and Rose stood face to face almost casually, except Ylena saw that they each held a knife at the other's throat.

"Caed!" Ylena gasped. "What are you doing? Tell them to stop!"

"They followed you out of the Underneath." Caed's voice was hard.

"Yes! I asked for their help!"

Tayeh shook her head. "That's the guy you picked?" Her nose turned up in disgust. "You chose a real genius there."

"Tayeh," Wilder growled. "You aren't helping."

"Wilder." Caed's voice was calm, but Ylena could tell he was one heartbeat away from an eye roll.

"Pleasure to see you again, Caed." Wilder spoke with his usual confidence. "I understand you've never been fond of me, but I'd appreciate it if you could ask your people to release my friends."

"Ugh. Release them." Then, finally, the eye roll.

"You only asked to release your friends?" Rose asked Wilder. "You don't want him to tell me to release you, too?"

"By the look in your eyes, I assume you are a woman who does as she pleases." Wilder sheathed his blade.

She proudly nodded her head once and put her knife away.

Everyone separated from each other and massaged sore arms and delicate necks. Caed ushered Ylena out the door, and they joined the rest of the group.

"Aren't we going inside to get all the babies?"

"They aren't here," he said. "This was just our meeting place."

"In case I accidentally brought four strangers along with me?"

He signaled the group to fall in line and began walking.

"I wasn't sure you would come at all." His voice was quiet in the dark night. "You seemed ... confused last night."

"I'm not confused, Caed. I know what I saw. And I know what I did to make the crystals go dark. Again."

He looked at her sharply but didn't stop walking. "You did this?"

"Of course I did this!" A few Priests turned at her sharp whisper. She dropped her voice lower. "You were there when I did it the first time. I did it again. And the boy was there this time. I haven't seen him since yesterday, and I hope he is okay."

"Oh, Ylena," he sighed. "Can you hear yourself? You sound—"

"Don't say it," she growled.

He ran his fingers through his hair. "I've told you before that I don't believe in the fantastical story about the Goddess. If I don't believe in her with the weight of history on her side, why would I believe that the City is actually a rapidly aging little boy?"

"Because I'm the one saying it! Why can't you believe in me?"

"I'm still not sure I can trust you, Ylena. I'm sorry." He glanced at Wilder, then continued ahead.

Ylena stopped and tried to catch her breath. Rev caught her by the arm.

"Come on, honey. We've got to keep walking."

They walked slowly until the rest of the group passed in front of them. Tayeh gave them a look, but Rev nodded her on ahead.

"I thought he was the one you picked. Did he ... um ... not pick you in return?"

Ylena sighed. "He picked me. And then I betrayed him the same way I betrayed Wilder."

"Oh ..." From her reaction, Wilder had explained what happened.

"Yeah. I ruined it terribly. And now when I need him to trust me, he won't."

"Give him some time. It's clear he still has feelings for you. He pulled you close to protect you even though he assumed you led strangers to their most precious treasure. He's still hurt, but he can't hide his feelings when they are written so clearly."

"But he thinks I'm crazy! He said it straight out. He

implied I might need to go to a healing center because I am sick. It's because what I have to say doesn't fit in with what he believes or, more accurately, what he doesn't believe. I bet Wilder would believe me—"

Rev grabbed Ylena's hand and twisted it until she bound it between the two of them. Rev stared up into her eyes and twisted Ylena's wrist until she bent over in pain to relieve the tension.

"Listen to me carefully, Ylena," Rev's voice was dead calm. "You will never use Wilder in any of your fights with Caed. Do you understand me? You will not do it." She twisted Ylena's wrist even further.

"Yes, I understand," she gasped.

Rev immediately let go. "Good." She walked at Ylena's side until they caught up to the group. And if Ylena flinched when Rev took her arm, Rev was kind enough not to mention it.

30

Their group quietly approached a building at the inner edge of Harmony. From the outside, it appeared to be a place to house animals, even though it was just as beautiful as the rest of the City. All the windows were dark, and there were no sounds from within.

Caed tapped on the door in a precise rhythm. The door cracked open. Caed whispered a few words, and a woman pulled the door open for them to enter.

The room was completely dark, but so was the rest of the City, so that was to be expected. Caed signaled for them to each take the hand of a Priest who knew the way through the obstacles in the dark room. Ylena couldn't see his expression in the faint moonlight, but he took her hand and led her inside.

The room smelled of animals and hay, but there were no sounds of anything living. She could hear the shuffling foot-steps of everyone behind her and the confident steps of Caed in front of her. Part of her reveled in the feel of his warm, strong hand, and part of her wanted to use the dried tear on her cheek to prove to him what she had seen. Forcing a memory on him was probably not the best way to prove he could trust her. Plus, she thought it possible to show him delusions just as easily as reality. She didn't want to test out that theory.

Once they had all filed inside the dark room, Caed knocked again. Several locks clicked open, followed by a bright sliver of light. Caed nodded, and the door opened fully for them to enter.

Rows of little children sat on blankets. They stared at the group of newcomers with wide eyes. Some of them held toys, and some had fingers in their mouths. They were all well under the age of two, some of them barely old enough to walk on their own.

"Ylena." An older woman with smooth, dark skin and white streaks in her hair walked squarely in front of her.

"Mims." Her voice came out as a whisper. Mims examined her even closer than she had the first time they had met. Ylena had a sudden moment of panic, wondering if Mims was actually her name or the familiar name Caed called his adopted mother.

"I see you've brought some ... friends ... to help us." Her gaze lingered meaningfully on Wilder.

"Um ... yes ... just friends." She didn't like the hard expression on Mims's face, but she was desperate to get back in her good graces. "I'll do whatever I can to help."

"Hmm," she answered noncommittally. "Most of them appear strong enough, but we will see if they can manage this without getting us all rounded up by the Wardens."

Ylena suddenly felt as if the outcome of this night would determine if Mims would forgive her for breaking Caed's heart. She looked at her crew and wondered for the first time if they had any experience with babies.

Mims addressed the group. "You will each be responsible for one child, two if you are skilled enough. We only have to make it through the trees and the field before we are inside the amphitheater and can make it down to the Heart. You must keep the children quiet, and above all else, you cannot let them cry. They are Priests, and their Gifts are completely untrained. If you don't have experience with young Priests, they could accidentally hurt you or, even worse, themselves. So, keep them happy and keep them quiet. Understood?"

"Oh, is that all?" murmured Rose.

Mims gave her a stern look.

"I apologize, Mims." Ylena had never seen Rose contrite before. Maybe with Mims around, Rose wouldn't be so rude to Ylena.

"They are all fed and well-rested, so we need to move right now," said Mims. "Don't frighten them by moving too quickly, but don't dawdle."

Happy, but quiet. Hurry, but not too fast. Ylena looked at the expanse of babies and wondered how they would save them all. She took a steadying breath and moved to the baby closest to her.

As she bent down, she realized she knew the little girl. She was one of the first babies she met when Caed introduced her to Mims in the nursery.

"Phoebe, right? That's your name?" The little girl didn't answer, but just stared at her with big blue eyes. Her dark hair had lost the white streak she had when they first met. Despite how terribly the Pageant had ended, Ylena was glad that she and Wilder had poured these babies' tears into the basin.

"We are going to go on an adventure! Can I pick you up?" Ylena reached out her hands, and the little girl held her arms out in response.

Ylena lifted the little girl and stood. Phoebe began playing with Ylena's sleek hair. She was quiet and happy. Ylena sighed in relief.

Around the room, the results were mixed. Mims pointed for certain people to take specific babies, probably based on the person's skill and the baby's fussiness. Rev seemed to be a natural. She had a baby on each hip, and they were tracing the lines of her tattoo and playing with her ponytail. Quinn looked like he was about to dissect an interesting specimen. The baby was still sitting on her blanket, but Quinn was in the middle of a very in-depth conversation with her. A Priest handed a baby to Wilder, and he looked unsure about the situation. The little boy smiled, which caused Wilder's face to break out in his wide grin. The little boy clapped his hands, and they were suddenly best friends.

Tayeh stared in horror as Mims put a sleeping baby in her arms. "All you have to do is walk calmly, and he will stay asleep the whole trip."

Tayeh's whisper was desperate. "But what if we need to fight? I thought I was coming along to protect you, not … this."

Mims gave her a hard glare. "If we have to fight, everything is lost. Do you understand? Keep them quiet and happy. That's the only option."

Tayeh bit her lip and nodded.

Rose had picked up a little girl on her own, but she looked only slightly less stressed than Tayeh did. She held the baby far away from her body, like the baby was contaminated. After a sharp look from Mims, she ducked her head and held the baby properly.

Caed held two babies in his arms, and they were looking around the room with excitement. He caught Ylena's eye but then looked away.

The secret knock came at the door.

Everyone in the room froze. Mims walked slowly to the door and cracked it open. Then, she let Lady Erenne slip inside.

"I'm sorry I'm late." She strode over and picked up the last baby off the floor.

Ylena walked over to her. "Were you checking on a mutual friend?"

Lady Erenne frowned at her, then walked up to Mims. They conferred quietly for a few moments before Mims spoke.

"Quiet and happy. That's the only option. Let's go."

31

As they headed out into the dark room, several babies whimpered. Ylena heard comforting hushing and cooing sounds from the ones carrying them. Once they were outside, the babies settled down again. The moon and stars gave enough light for them to see, and they calmed down as they walked.

They passed through the thin ring of trees and stood as one before the open field they had to cross before reaching the amphitheater. As they walked across the grass, Ylena felt very exposed. Even without the bright light of the crystals, if someone looked their direction, their group would be clearly visible.

A few babies began whimpering again. They had hidden in that location for days, and she imagined the new people and dark sky must be terrifying. The little girl in Quinn's arms looked around wildly, and despite his best attempts to calm her down, she appeared one step away from breaking out in tears. Mims noticed the little girl, but she had her hands full with two other scared babies and couldn't help.

Ylena began to sing.

She grasped the air of her song the moment it left her

lips and trickled it on a breeze, right into the ears of the girl squirming in Quinn's arms. The girl immediately stopped moving and looked at the sky in wonder. She leaned her head back against Quinn's chest to listen to the song.

Ylena split the breeze into multiple threads that she sent out to each of the unsettled babies. When they heard the song, they each snuggled into the arms of the person carrying them and relaxed.

Some people appeared confused when the fussy baby they carried suddenly relaxed in their arms. Lady Erenne shot her a glance. She sensed what Ylena was doing and nodded.

As she sang in silence, she caught Caed watching her. Both of his babies were calm without help from her, but he recognized what she did. She continued to sing, and he never took his eyes from her.

They crossed the entire field with quiet and happy babies, and once inside the amphitheater, Ylena gave a sigh of relief. They filed through the aisle beside the stone benches and headed to the entrance at the front of the stage.

"Look at this!" A loud voice floated to them from the stage. "It appears I've discovered the young, missing Priests from Discipline."

The small Warden of Rivalry stepped to the front of the stage, her dark skin shimmering in the moonlight. Their group froze halfway down the stairs. Tayeh looked around wildly, ready to strike but trying to figure out what to do with the baby in her arms.

"We don't have to mention any of this to the Warden of Indulgence. You will all make a delightful addition to Rivalry, and we will just keep your origins a secret between us."

"I don't think so, Warden." Wilder's voice was confident,

even though his arms were currently still full. "You will not take these children."

"Oh, Wilder!" she purred. "I didn't know I would get you, too! What a night!" She leaped off the stage and stalked closer to them.

Lady Erenne handed her child to Ylena. She took a deep breath and moved to confront the Warden.

As she walked forward, Ylena realized Lady Erenne was the only Priest besides the babies whose hair wasn't streaked with white. Lady Erenne was always drinking tea. Had she been drugging herself to keep from using her Gifts?

Lady Erenne's voice was firm, but Ylena was close enough to see her hands tremble. "Child, you need to walk away right now."

The Warden stepped in front of her. She was about a foot shorter than Lady Erenne, but her voice snapped. "I am not a child. And this is a battle I have already won. You can either walk peacefully to Rivalry, or you can do it the hard way." Her eyes glittered. "I really hope you choose the hard way."

Ylena watched a tear fall down Lady Erenne's cheek. She would choose the hard way.

One of the stone benches appeared to come alive. It melted into the shape of a tiger that leaped for the Warden. She only hesitated for a moment, surprised that the woman with dark hair was a Priest. But she quickly jumped onto one of the other benches and landed in a crouch. Her eyes landed on the stone tiger with glee. She waved it forward with a grin.

The Warden leaped from bench to bench, spinning and turning out of the grasp of the tiger as it moved nimbly through the air but landed with a crunch of the stone benches beneath it. Lady Erenne watched the tiger chase after the Warden with more tears streaming down her face.

The Warden laughed and gave a sharp whistle. Three lean fighters stepped out of the shadows across the amphitheater and headed toward the group of Priests huddled together behind Lady Erenne.

She reached out her hand, and three more stone tigers came to life. They chased after the fighters, who spun and leaped and dodged. The fighters tried cracking the tigers on the head with long, wooden staffs, but that only resulted in breaking them.

Ylena thought the tigers came close enough to hurt the fighters multiple times, but they appeared to pull back. Lady Erenne didn't look like she struggled to control the stone tigers, but her face was so sad, and Ylena couldn't figure out why. She looked like she could win at any time.

Ylena juggled both babies more securely in her arms and whispered to Lady Erenne, "Knock them out! Capture them! Do something! Stop them now so we can get the babies out of here."

Lady Erenne nodded with a sad frown. The tigers fell into a formation that backed the fighters against the far wall. As the Warden walked backward, she raised a hand to her side and snapped.

A young girl, maybe around nine years old, stepped out of the shadows. She ran to stand next to the Warden. A tear glittered on her cheek, and she touched the stone bench in front of her. The stone melted into a low stone wall that the Warden and her fighters jumped behind. The young girl stood in front of the wall and faced the stone tigers with hands raised in front of her.

The girl's face was determined but also scared. Each of the four stone tigers was taller than her, and by the simple look of the wall she built, her skills were nowhere close to Lady Erenne's.

Lady Erenne's breathing become shallow. Her hands

lowered to her sides, and she stared at the little girl as she prepared to fight. Lady Erenne's hands twitched, and her eyes darted around the dark amphitheater, trying to figure out a way to stop the girl without hurting her.

The girl took two hesitant steps toward the tigers, who were still poised to attack. Lady Erenne slowly raised her shaking hands.

The light returned.

Every crystal spire in the temples and the crystal in the basin at the front of the stage flickered back to life. Every drop of crystalline that lined the edges of stage and the rows of seats began flowing again. Everyone blinked their eyes at the sudden light and looked around, surprised at what they saw.

Soldiers and children stood lined up along every wall. The current battle was just a tiny fraction of the fighters they had available. The Warden was amusing herself by making the fight appear to be close. There were more soldiers than there were Priests, and each of the children had their hands raised in a way that proved they would use whatever Gift they had.

The tigers melted into a puddle of stone. Lady Erenne's hands dropped to her sides, and she staggered backward. "I can't do it. I can't hurt them." She chanted the words over and over in a ragged whisper until she sagged against the stone wall. Her eyes glossed over until Ylena wasn't sure she saw anything.

"That's disappointing!" the Warden's voice called across the theater. "I hoped we could play for a while longer, but now that you realize how pointless it is, I guess all our fun is spoiled."

As the Warden hopped across the stone benches toward their group holding the babies, Ylena saw Caed and Wilder and Tayeh and Rose counting the soldiers and calculating their odds. Ylena knew enough from gambling with Quinn that they were out of luck.

"We go with them." Caed's quiet whisper floated over their group. "We live to fight another day."

Ylena saw the tension between Tayeh's shoulders even as she held the baby who slept through it all. She obviously wanted to fight, but she nodded stiffly.

The Warden sent her soldiers over to herd them all out of the amphitheater. Ylena was scared they would try ripping the children out of their arms, but apparently, they were happy to let them carry the babies themselves.

As they marched across the open field, Ylena realized everyone was accounted for, except Lady Erenne was nowhere to be seen.

32

Ylena sang for the children on the way to the temple. She hid her face behind Phoebe's blond head so the soldiers wouldn't see her singing with no sound. Since the older children with Gifts surrounded them, she directed the sound precisely to avoid any children who could detect the music.

The walk from the amphitheater to each of the temples always felt long, but now that she carried two children, Phoebe and the child Lady Erenne had been carrying, the walk felt even longer. She couldn't imagine how Caed had carried her from the temple so many times.

She glanced to the side to look at him. His face was grim as he marched with two babies in his arms. The children had curled up against his chest and were sucking their thumbs. She couldn't imagine what these babies had already been through. Now that they were about to be held captive in the Warden's temple, she wondered what would happen to them.

They marched toward the glowing crystal spire. She wondered if the light returning meant the boy had returned to the Heart. What else she would discover about him? Would all the crystals go dark again at her touch?

The soldiers marched them inside and led them into one of the inner rooms. The captives blinked in the bright light of the empty room. The Priests holding babies looked exhausted and ready to give up. But Ylena's crew, Caed, and Rose adjusted the babies in their arms and looked prepared to fight if necessary.

"Where is the Priest who made the stone tigers?" The Warden looked from face to face. She glared at her soldiers. "How did you let one of them slip away?"

"No one left. We had them surrounded the entire time."

The Warden continued studying faces until she stood in front of Ylena. "You! The one from the Spectacle!" She took a step back. "Guards, grab her!"

They grabbed her harshly and shook the babies in her arms.

"Wait! I'll come peacefully! Don't hurt the babies!" She handed the children to Quinn and Rose and held her arms out to the soldiers.

"Put that one in the metal cage. The High Priest obviously doesn't need it anymore." Ylena wondered if that's why Lady Erenne had been late.

The Warden continued her survey of the room. "The rest of these are weak Priests or Wilder's cronies." She strolled up to Wilder and placed her hand on his chest, near the face of the boy sleeping in his arms. "I will be back for you soon. For now, you can rest with the babies. I think it's adorable." She winked and waved for the soldiers to follow her.

Ylena got one last glimpse of the others. Caed looked at her with fear in his eyes. She tried to communicate with a glance. *I'll be okay. Protect the children. Wait for me.*

The Warden slammed the door to the room and led her

down the stairs to the metal cage in the lower level. Soldiers roughly threw her inside, and the Warden locked the door and put the key in her pocket. She narrowed her eyes and studied Ylena.

"I'm not sure what you are, but I definitely don't like it. I'm keeping you alive right now, because someday, I might need you as an advantage against the other Wardens. However, if you make my life complicated, well then … puff!" She mimed blowing poison dust at Ylena. "So, you promise to be as sweet and submissive as the other Priests, right?"

Ylena nodded obediently.

The Warden smiled and closed the outer door with a click.

Ylena sank down onto the metal bars that lined the bottom of the cage. Her mind played through scenarios of ways to get the babies out of that room, but she couldn't figure out how to get them far enough away from the temple to escape. She imagined long tunnels and staircases and walls of water, and each plan ended with soldiers and child Champions capturing them immediately.

She sighed. They had to defeat the Wardens and free all the Priests. There were enough people in the Underneath and Upstairs who were tired of being ruled by tyrants, but they had to find a way to act all at once. She imagined baby Priests like Phoebe and the little girl in the rain spread throughout the City, and she was determined to stop the Wardens for good. Tears gathered in her eyes, and she was ready.

She listened for any sounds at the door. If the Warden left anyone guarding her, they were silent. That meant she had to be equally quiet.

She gathered one of her tears and lay on her stomach, reaching her hand through the bars of her cage to touch the stone floor beneath her. As she closed her eyes, she traced the layout of the stone in the entire temple. She sensed the room where the others were being held and drew a mental map of the rooms surrounding it.

Her eyes opened. She plucked a thread of stone from the floor and formed it into a thin rod, then snaked her hands through the bars to pick the lock. The stone rod snapped multiple times, and she had to melt it and try again. The metal tools Quinn gave her were back in the Heart, and she cursed herself for not remembering them. Eventually, she figured out a way to form the stone into the exact shape she needed, and it twisted like a key in the lock. She stepped out of the cage and dropped the stone key into her pocket for luck.

She avoided the door, since it was likely a guard stood outside, formed a small hole in the back wall of the room to peek through, then stepped into an empty storeroom. The Wardens had apparently raided everything from the storerooms, so she passed several empty rooms before she found the one she wanted.

She stacked a couple wooden crates and climbed up them carefully. She reached toward the ceiling and melted a small hole in the floor near where she remembered Caed had been sitting. The ceiling was the only thing she saw in the room above, but she heard the soft voices of people trying to comfort the babies.

She floated her whisper on a breeze through the hole.

"Caed! Are there any guards in the room?"

A string of unidentifiable words came from several people before she saw Caed's eye through the hole in the floor.

"Ylena! You're out! How did ...? Never mind. No, there are no guards in here with us."

"Step back."

They scrambled away, but she melted the floor slowly, just in case. She had soon opened up a large enough hole to fit through.

She put her hands on the edges of the floor and lifted herself up. Caed came to the edge and offered her his hand to help her out.

She dusted herself off as she stood. The Priests and babies stared at her like they couldn't decide if she was fascinating or terrifying. Caed, Rose, and her friends from the Underneath were looking at her like they expected nothing else.

Rose looked down the hole to the storeroom beyond. "So, what's the plan? How are we getting out of here?"

Ylena looked at the faces of the babies in the room. She whispered, "I can't get them all out. All of us together are too slow. I can't figure out a way ..." Her voice trailed off.

Caed placed his hand on her arm. "Ylena, it's okay. They know." He nodded at Mims and the other Priests who had laid their coats out on the floor as makeshift beds for the babies.

Rev focused on the babies with confused expressions on their faces. "We have to do something about this. You saw those children the Warden brought to fight. That's the future of every child in this room."

"That won't happen." Rose's voice was fierce. "We are going to end this."

"I think we can end it." Ylena sounded more confident than she felt. "But we can't do it separately. The City and the Underneath have to join and fight as one. But we can't do it if we don't trust each other." She gave Caed a meaningful look, but he looked away. "We need to know that when we show up, there will be someone waiting on the other side."

Wilder's voice was rough. "There are plenty of people in the Underneath who are ready to rise up and fight. But how do we know anyone up here would respond?" He looked around the room at the Priests talking softly to the babies. "It looks like most of the Priests will curl up in their cage and wait it out."

Rose grabbed him by the front of his shirt. "Do you see all those white streaks in their hair?" Her voice was low and angry. "They have been using their powers to protect those children at the cost of their own lives. We've already lost some who pushed beyond their limits. It's true that most of them don't know how to fight, but they will give their lives to protect the people in this City. If there is a call to action, they will answer it."

Wilder looked down at her fist clenched around his shirt and nodded slowly. "You're right. I apologize. There are many ways to fight, and we will need them all."

Rose released his shirt and seemed mollified. Ylena had already learned that apologizing to a Priest was the quickest way to disarm them.

"So, can we get out of here now?" asked Tayeh. "I don't think we can organize a proper rebellion while trapped in here."

"You're right," said Ylena. "We've got to split up and spread the word that revolution is coming. Everyone Upstairs and in the Underneath has to wait for their cue."

"What's the cue?" Quinn's face lit up with excitement.

"Um ... I'm not sure yet," said Ylena. "I'm working on it. But we need to get out of here, and I'll figure it out later."

Wilder lowered himself down onto the crates and helped Rev and Quinn jump down. Rose and Caed went to tell Mims goodbye. Ylena saw Caed hug her. Mims smoothed Caed's wavy hair away from his face, and she whispered something in his ear that Ylena couldn't hear.

Her words to Rose were loud enough for Ylena to pick up part of it. "... you'll never end up in a relationship if you keep rough handling every cute guy you meet ...” Rose swatted Mims hand away from her hair but leaned into the hug.

When Rose and Caed joined Ylena, she pretended she'd heard nothing. Once they were all together in the lower room, Ylena sealed up the stone floor. The sound of the babies was abruptly cut off, and it grew eerily quiet.

The seven of them set off to start a rebellion.

33

Ylena led them down empty hallways until they stood in a storeroom near the door that led to the Underneath.

"I've been walking to the Underneath through the Heart, but we don't have time for that anymore. We need to get you through that door."

"It's only guarded by five soldiers," said Tayeh. "We can easily make it past that many."

"It will only be you, Wilder, Rev, and Quinn getting past them," said Ylena. "Rose and Caed will gather people up here."

Tayeh looked through the hole Ylena had formed in the stone. "The four of us to five of them? I still like those odds."

Ylena grinned. "You'll be fine. Especially since I'm planning a distraction or two. Be prepared. The lights might go out again."

Caed turned toward her sharply. "Ylena. You can't be planning on touching the crystal again."

She purposefully didn't answer him. "I will get word to the four of you when I know the cue. I'm depending on all of you. Can you manage spreading the word without getting caught? If something happened to you …"

Rev caught her by the hand. "Ylena, it's okay." She tucked Ylena's white streak behind her ear. "We've got each other, and we've got you on our side. We are going to stop this, no matter what it takes. Let us do our jobs, and you do yours. We will meet up with you again soon."

Ylena nodded. "Yes, we will see each other soon." She looked out at the soldiers. "Wait in here for the distraction, and then, good luck."

Rev smiled. "Goddess blessing upon you, too, Ylena."

Ylena ducked her head and slipped out of the room, Caed and Rose trailing behind. She led them to an outer wall and pressed her hand to the stone.

"I am going to make a door for you. You should probably wait to run out until I cause the distraction. It should be dramatic enough to give you plenty of time to run away. Maybe you can find Lady Erenne somewhere out there. She didn't look well the last time I saw her."

Rose looked at her suspiciously. "What do you know about Lady Erenne?"

Ylena blinked. "Honestly, not as much as I would like. I still don't really trust her, but after her performance back there at the amphitheater, I'm worried about her. Her hair hadn't turned yet, but I'm sure it must be white now."

"Ylena, what Lady Erenne did back there …" Caed's voice trailed off. "Something wasn't right."

"What do you mean? She tried to protect us from the Warden, but she didn't want to hurt anyone."

"That's not it," said Rose. "Have you ever melted stone into the shape of an animal and had it attack anyone?"

"Oh," said Ylena with a sigh. "Heresy."

Rose crossed her arms. "Possibly, but that's not what I mean. Can you animate stone and make it jump around?"

Ylena touched the stone wall and considered it.

"I'm not suggesting you try!" Rose rolled her eyes. "You probably could actually do it. My point is, no other Priests of Purpose can. It's not what they do."

Ylena looked between Caed and Rose and tried to understand. "Is it because she was one of the High Priests?"

"No," said Rose. "That's not how the Gift works."

Caed's brows furrowed. "Ylena, you should just be careful if you see her again. She is hiding more secrets than either of us realized."

"Okay. Thanks for telling me." She sighed and opened a doorway in the stone. "Well, I guess it is goodbye for now. If I am successful tonight, I will contact you. Good luck."

She left them by the open doorway and headed back the way they came.

Caed caught her by the arm as she opened the door to the hallway. "Ylena, wait! Come with us."

Rose stared out the stone doorway leading outside, pretending she couldn't hear them.

Ylena's voice was firm. "I have to do what I came here for, Caed."

"You came here because the Warden captured us."

"No. I came here because this was my destination all along. I enjoyed not having to break in for once. They led me right in the front door." She smiled, but he didn't.

"Please, Ylena. Come with Rose and me. We will figure out the next step in the plan."

"I know the next step, Caed. I'm going to touch the crystal and gather the next vision. The City is trying to tell me something, and I have to figure out what that is."

He stepped closer to her. "Ylena, you aren't well. Touching the crystal again is dangerous. You pass out every time. That can't be good for you!"

She tried to keep her voice quiet, but it rose in frustration. "You saw the visions! I showed you what I saw! Why don't you believe me anymore?"

"None of it makes sense! The most reasonable explanation—"

"Is that I'm crazy. Yes, you've said that, Caed." She stepped away from him. "I realize you don't believe me, but I'm tired of trying to prove myself to you. You don't need to drag me out of here anymore. I believe in these visions so much that I'm willing to risk waking up trapped here. You and Rose should wait for the lights to go off and escape in the initial chaos. Unless you think I'm just imagining that my touch will cause the City to go dark. If so, I guess you might as well go now."

She opened the door and walked out.

She only had to run up a single staircase to be in the hallway outside the inner courtyard. She hid in a small closet and took a moment to catch her breath. How could he continue to not trust her? Her very existence defied everything he knew, and yet despite that, he had always believed in her. He believed in her before she even knew who she was.

There was a night he kissed her and the song that vibrated between them resonated through the entire temple. Was he willing to risk losing that by not listening to her? She didn't know how to make him trust her again.

Her tears fell as usual, and she wiped them away almost casually. She heard the sounds of fighters practicing in the inner courtyard and focused on them first.

She sang a couple of high-pitched notes and squeezed them under the closet door, snaking them around the crystal until it squealed in dissonance. The fighters training in the courtyard ran out with their hands clapped over their ears.

She sang another note as deep as her voice could get,

pouring the note into the stone floor and walls until the entire temple was vibrating and rattling her very bones.

In the confusion, she ran into the empty courtyard. She wrapped the notes further around one another but blew out a small breath so that the notes would eventually fade. She didn't want to cause permanent damage to the babies' ears if she passed out.

She touched her hand to the crystal. She didn't have time to notice if the light went out before she lost consciousness.

～

Ylena sat in the front row for dress rehearsal. The Director sat beside her, thankfully with his shirt on this time. She was going to speak to the boy about that. There was no need to remove your shirt while there was a lady in the room.

The couple on stage sang their hearts out. A small orchestra was immediately in front of her at the foot of the stage. The music in this Pageant was simpler than she had heard it before, but there was something so sincere about their performance. She loved to watch them.

The actors playing the Goddess and Companion moved in steps familiar to the ones she knew. She couldn't imagine how long ago this memory took place, but the fact that the music and the dancing were so similar fascinated her. She was enjoying the show so much she forgot why she was there.

She needed to discover something that would help her defeat the Wardens. She needed an edge. Something to help them get ahead.

"You're frowning," said the Director. "This is the best part! The love story! This is where it all happens!" His voice was as passionate as usual.

"You're right," she said. "I love this song. I'll smile like I am supposed to."

He chuckled. "Like you ever do what you are supposed to." He looked at the performers on the stage. "Maybe I made a mistake in the casting. I'm not sure that young boy is cocky enough to woo a Goddess."

"He's doing great! I'm sure it will be fine."

"Ugh ... We're back to 'fine.' I knew it. I should have sung it myself."

She laughed at his dramatic tone. "But then who would sit out here with me?"

He looked her in the eyes, and his love for her was clear to see. "You will always have people clamoring for your attention, Erenne. I'm just glad sometimes you choose me."

"What did you call me?" Her heart seemed to stop beating.

He tucked a lock of hair behind her ear and smirked. "Sorry, dear. Would you prefer I call you Goddess?"

Her eyes shot open in blackness.

34

Ylena's hands rested in soft grass, and the rough bark of a tree was at her back. As her eyes adjusted to the moonlight, she realized she was in a garden enclosed by a framework of stone and looping metal. Birds cooed softly in the branches of the surrounding trees. As she brought her attention to each bird, she realized these were the injured birds the Priests cared for. She was inside the aviary.

She had no idea how she got here.

Her body tensed, and she held her breath.

"Ylena." Caed dropped to her side. "We're safe, but we need to be quiet. There are soldiers patrolling outside."

A small glow of light shone through the windows of the aviary. Someone was walking by with a lantern. She mentally traced the lines of the large stone and metal cage in her mind and realized there was no mesh on the windows. The birds calmly rested in their trees thanks to the direction of the Priests.

Caed helped her stand, and they both held their breath as they hid behind the wide trunk of the tree. Footsteps shuffled outside, and the soldiers grumbled in low voices as they passed by.

The glow faded away, and Ylena sagged in his arms. She focused on the rise and fall of Caed's chest against her own, and as his breathing slowed, hers slowed in return. After the soldiers passed out of earshot, she sighed and leaned her head against his chest.

"I'm sorry, Ylena." Caed's whisper brushed through her hair.

"For what?" Her whisper caused a few birds to shake out their feathers.

"I hesitated." His whisper dropped even quieter. "I considered leaving with Rose while you headed to the crystal alone." His sigh was warm against her cheek. "I should have been by your side the whole time. If I had been there, I would have caught you when you fell and carried you out sooner." His breathing was ragged, and she felt his voice more than heard it. "I was still on the stairs when the temple went dark ... I stumbled my way into the inner courtyard. I couldn't find you." His voice caught. "I circled the crystal in the dark on my hands and knees, and I thought you were gone. I thought I'd lost you."

His voice was so sad it broke her heart. "You never lost me, Caed. I'm right here."

"I hate what's happening in the City. I thought if I denied what you were saying, it wouldn't be real. There are too many unknowns. And I can't fix any of it."

She lifted her head and rested her hand on his chest until she felt the rapid beating of his heart under her palm. "Everything seems like chaos, but this is the only thing that makes sense. I want you to believe me when I tell you about the visions, but beyond that, I want you to trust me when I say this: I love you. You, Caed. It's always been you."

Her heart stilled as he reached for her with deliberate

movement. His palms were soft against her cheeks as he tilted her face to meet his. His fingertips touched her tears, and he saw himself through her eyes.

Caed standing in front of the mirror for her first dance lesson.

Caed standing close to her among the bookshelves in the library.

Caed rocking one of the baby Priests to sleep.

Caed in moments both simple and sublime.

Caed.

He pulled her close, and their lips found each other in the dark.

She flooded his mind with every thought of love she ever had. Her soul was laid bare before him, and she trusted him with it all.

His arms wrapped around her like he would never let her go again. She leaned against the tree at her back and savored the sensation of his kiss, rebounding the thoughts back into his mind until she couldn't separate one moment from the next.

Caed stilled with his lips against hers.

She opened her eyes and heard the sound. Hundreds of birds cooed in an echoing love song that spread throughout the garden.

She felt Caed's lips turn up into a grin.

"Oops," she said.

He chuckled softly and pulled her away from the tree. They escaped hand in hand into the night.

Ylena and Caed walked quietly through the dark streets of Harmony. Ylena pulled him close to whisper, "This is something I have to do, but you don't have to come with me. I can do this on my own."

He squeezed her hand. "I know you can, but I'm not leaving you again."

She squeezed his hand in return, and they continued on.

They came upon the low stone wall draped with vines, and Ylena stopped before the path leading through the gravestones.

"I don't know where she is."

He gripped her hand tighter. "We will find her. Together."

They walked along the path until they arrived at the newest section. Her steps slowed as they walked through the rows. She knew she would find Pim's grave, but when she saw it, the sight still pained her.

"Oh, Pim," she whispered. "I'm so sorry." She kneeled down to touch the gravestone, and in the dim light of the moon, she found some carved animal statues in the grass. "Her family must come visit her grave. I never met them, but she talked about them a lot."

Caed kneeled down beside her. "She was such a sweet person. So many people miss her."

Ylena traced the shape of the wooden pony and tried not to imagine Pim's body in the ground beneath her. "Where do you think she is now?"

Caed blew out a gentle breath. "I don't know if I'm the best one to ask about that."

"We are basically on a date at a graveyard, Caed. There is not much else to talk about in this situation."

He smirked. "That's fair. But I don't have the answer. I'm probably not the most comforting Priest to bring with you to visit a graveyard."

"Well, what do the good Priests say? Is Pim at peace? Is she happy?"

Caed studied the moon as it shone through the trees. He weighed his words before he spoke. "A good Priest would say yes, that she is at peace and happy. A good Priest would say that Pim wouldn't want you to continue to blame yourself for her death."

She placed the little horse back in its place and stood. "You might not be the best Priest, Caed, but you are still pretty good." She gave him a kiss on the cheek and took his hand again.

She saw his smile in the moonlight as they left the graveyard together.

35

Ylena grabbed Caed's hand before he knocked on the door. "I can't go in there, Caed."

"Yes, you can. It's not safe for you to go back to the amphitheater tonight. Plus, you said you don't have any lanterns in the Heart. You can't just stumble down the staircase in the dark. Several of my brothers and sisters are currently staying in this house. It will be much safer."

"Are you sure about that?" Rose had been rude to her from day one, and Mims stared at her with hard, cold eyes. She couldn't guess what the rest of the family would be like.

Caed smirked. "Sure, a few of them might dream about injuring you, but they are all better Priests than I am, so I'm pretty sure they won't actually do it."

"Pretty sure?"

"I won't make any promises. I am their baby brother." He winked and knocked on the door.

An older man opened the door. His dark skin shone in the light of the single candle coming from within and his broad shoulders filled the door frame. He broke into a warm smile when he saw Caed. When he saw Ylena, he raised an eyebrow.

"Hi, Seb. This is Ylena. Can we come in?"

"Sure." Seb let them in the dark house. "I get the feeling that tonight didn't go as planned."

"No. It was stunningly terrible, in fact. Can we rest here tonight?"

"Of course. I'll go get us something to drink, and you can tell me about it."

Caed led Ylena over to the couch. She sank down on the cushions and realized how exhausted she was. She had hoped that the time she spent unconscious would have rested her body, but that was not the case. Seb came back in the room with some hot chocolate for the three of them. Ylena was relieved it wasn't tea.

She sipped on the hot chocolate as Caed explained what happened in the amphitheater. He skimmed over a lot about Lady Erenne's part in it. She guessed it was because he wasn't sure what he thought about her unusual skills yet. When he got to the part about leaving Mims and the babies in the temple, tears sprang to Seb's eyes. She eyed the white streaks in his short, dark hair with trepidation, but his Gift stayed under control.

"Rose and I split up at the temple. She's spreading the word through her contacts in different Dioceses to wait for the sign. The Underneath is also preparing. It's time for us to work together to end this now."

"So, what kind of sign are we waiting for?" asked Seb.

"Umm ... I'm working on that," said Ylena. "I'm close."

Seb raised an eyebrow but was kind enough not to question further.

Caed looked around. "Where are the others?"

He chuckled quietly. "They're asleep. You do realize it's pretty late, baby brother?"

Caed rolled his eyes. "How am I supposed to plan a revolution with so many of you old people? I'm going to see if I can find any comfortable clothes to change into. I don't feel like sleeping in leather pants if I don't have to."

As he stood, Ylena noticed how tight Caed's pants were, and her head tilted in a fascinated stare.

Seb noticed the focus of her attention, and she blushed.

Caed noticed her stare and the blush, and he winked as he left the room.

Seb cleared his throat politely. "It's nice to finally meet you, Ylena. I've heard a lot about you."

"That's unfortunate. Most of the things you've heard recently are probably terrible, though unfortunately true. I doubt you've heard much you can approve of."

"Despite his story about tonight's failure, I just saw Caed smiling. I approve of that."

She sighed. "Well, I have some other news that will upset him, so I don't know how long that smile will last."

Seb's face remained calm, but his eyes glittered with cold. "Are you going to break his heart again?"

"No!" Her voice rang out before she remembered the others were sleeping. "No, definitely not!" she whispered. "I just learned some things about the Goddess that he will have a hard time believing."

Seb's body relaxed. "You aren't the first one to tell him something about the Goddess he doesn't believe."

"I know, but we recently fought because he didn't believe me. I feel like our relationship is still balanced on a fine thread, and I don't want to do anything to wreck it again."

"So, what do you need from him? Do you need him to believe the same things as you do?"

"No, not really. Most of the time, I don't even know what I believe myself, so I don't expect any belief from him."

"So, if it's not the believing that you need, what is it?"

"I guess I just need to know that he will be there. That he won't run when he doesn't agree with me."

Seb smiled. "If that's what you need, he will deliver. He's part of an entire family of Priests, despite what he believes. He's never run from us. And this is where he came when he needed a safe place to hide. And he never runs from using his Gifts to serve others. I saw the two of you dance together. He taught you every step in a Pageant that he doesn't believe. A difference of belief isn't enough to make him leave."

She leaned back into the cushions and sighed. "You are right. I know that about him. I guess there is just one more tiny thing. What if he thinks my beliefs are crazy? That I am crazy?"

"He might think that at some point. And sometimes, he can be one smug little brat." He shook his head with a smile. "But the amazing thing is that even if you *are* crazy, that's not enough to make him run either. When he believes in you, he will be there through it all."

Ylena imagined her mother singing to her father during his time in the healing center and imagined that same heart in Caed. Tears sprang to her eyes, and she bowed her head. "Thank you, Priest."

Seb kissed her on the forehead. "Goddess blessing upon you, Ylena."

She lay down on the cushions to wait for Caed to come back, but her eyes refused to stay open, and she fell asleep.

Ylena blinked her eyes open to the soft glow of a crystalline lamp. Someone had covered her with a blanket while she slept. She turned on her side and examined the room now that there was more than just a candle light. The room was simply furnished with a variety of chairs scattered around the room. Caed had ten surviving siblings, so they would need a lot of chairs if they had a family meeting.

She wondered when the crystals had relit and exactly how long she had been asleep. Dark curtains covered all the windows, so she couldn't tell what time of day it was. The only hopeful clue was that she smelled coffee.

She sat up on the couch and found Caed draped across the chair next to her, still asleep. She felt guilty for taking the whole couch while he slept in a chair. Although, when she considered sleeping curled up next to Caed on the couch, her face grew warm, and she realized she never would have fallen asleep.

A guy she hadn't met entered the room. He was muscular with pale gold skin and tousled dark hair. His dark eyes were playful as he held a finger to his lips to keep her quiet, and with his other hand, he brought her a cup of coffee. She accepted it gladly.

"Wake up, Caedy! Introduce me to your friend!" He quickly squished himself onto the chair next to Caed, waking him up. The chair was fairly large, but there was not enough room for two full-grown guys to sit together comfortably.

Caed groaned and closed his eyes again. "Kai! Why are you so awful?"

"Come on!" He started poking Caed in the sides. "Introduce me so I can start gossiping with your friend!"

Caed spoke with his eyes closed. "Kai, Ylena. Ylena, this is Kai." He peeked through one eyelid. "Don't listen to anything he says."

"Don't listen to Caedy," said Kai. "He's super cranky in the morning."

"Caedy?" She took a quick sip of her coffee to hide the smile curling on her lips.

"Yes, my brooding baby brother is so grumpy in the

morning. That's why I brought you some coffee. You're going to need it." He winked.

Caed's eyes shot open. "Hey! Where's my coffee?"

"Good! You're awake! Can you grab a cup of coffee for me while you are up?"

Caed growled and shoved Kai while he wrestled his way out of the chair.

Kai blew Caed a kiss as he left the room.

Ylena watched the interaction with wide eyes. "I've only seen Caed in situations where he was in charge. Seeing him with his siblings is such a treat."

Kai snuggled up in the big chair by himself. "The Goddess put us in his life to keep him from getting too full of himself."

She chuckled, but it also reminded her she wasn't sure what to do about the whole Goddess situation.

Caed walked back in, carrying two cups of coffee. He gave one to Kai and then settled down on the couch next to Ylena.

"So, what are your plans today?" asked Kai. He leaned back in the chair and sipped his coffee.

"We need to spread the word that the Underneath and the City will join together to overthrow the Wardens. Rose left last night to talk to the people she knows. We should head to some of the other Dioceses today."

Ylena swallowed another sip of coffee before she spoke. "Um ... I have something else I need to do today."

Kai gave a fake gasp. "Something more important than inciting a rebellion?"

"It's possibly related. I need to find Lady Erenne."

"Ylena, you need to be careful of her. I don't know if I trust her right now."

Ylena looked between Caed and Kai and shook her head. "I have some information about her. I think it will be deeply troubling for both of you but in completely opposite ways. Before I talk about it, I need to speak to her."

Caed nodded. "Okay. We will go find her."

"You don't have to come. I'm sure you have other things to do—"

"I thought I lost you last night. I'm not leaving you again."

"Awww!" said Kai. "You two are so cute!"

Caed rolled his eyes, but Ylena smiled as she finished her coffee.

ORDER

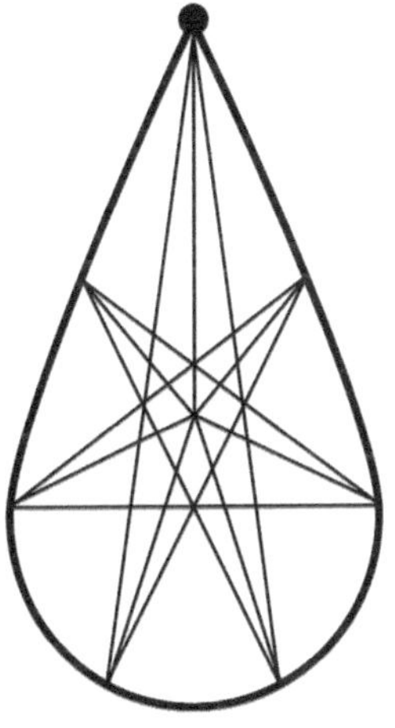

CHAOS

36

Ylena and Caed headed to the Heart together after his brothers made sure they'd had breakfast and packed food for later in the day. Ylena didn't have any siblings, and she loved watching how much they cared for Caed. And by extension, they cared for her.

"I can't believe I was so worried to meet your siblings. Seb and Kai are both amazing."

"That's because you've only met Rose. The two of you didn't start off well."

Ylena laughed. "The first day we met, she called me 'interesting, but kind of a disaster.' I mean, she was right, but still ... it's rude."

Caed laughed but quieted as they neared the amphitheater. "I'm not thrilled to be walking into this place again."

"I agree. But I don't know of another good way to get into the Underneath."

They decided not to walk through the amphitheater seating, but to try to sneak in through one of the stage doors at the back. They were slow as they moved ahead, but they made it underneath the stage without seeing any soldiers.

They walked down the stairs, and Ylena covered the top

with stone instead of the sliding planks. She could have secured it better long ago, except that she had left it open for Caed to come back.

At the bottom of the stairs, Caed stopped in front of the pile of velvet curtains. "What is this?"

She ducked her head. "It's my bed. I slept here to keep watch in case you ..."

He looked at the view of the stairs from her bed and frowned. "Oh, Ylena ... I'm so sorry I never came back."

"It wasn't your fault, Caed. It was mine. What you saw was a betrayal and a lack of honesty on my part. I knew what I wanted the whole time, and I was too afraid to say it."

"And who is it you wanted?" His lips curved in a smug yet sweet smile.

She wrapped her arms around his waist and whispered, "You. I wanted you, Caed." He pulled her close, and they melted into a kiss.

Someone was watching them.

She stepped back and looked around the open cavern. The boy wasn't there, but she knew it was him. She wanted to call out but was afraid that would firmly establish her in the crazy category.

"Ylena? What is it?"

"It's nothing. We should get going. I want to get in and out of Chaos as fast as possible."

"You don't want to go dancing in the club while we are there?" That smile was back.

She remembered dancing close to him with the music pounding through her veins. He pulled her close as if to dance.

She felt the eyes again.

"Nope. We don't have time for that." At his disappointed expression, she grabbed his hand. "But at least we're together. It's time for Chaos."

They walked together to the crystal. Except for the night out dancing, she found Chaos to be the most stressful Grotto. She felt on edge just walking through the streets.

They stood next to the crystal, side by side. "You've got this, Ylena. And I'm right here."

She let a tear fall and touched the crystal.

The light flickered off.

Lamps and candles came to life even quicker than last time. There were still quite a few people who screamed at the sudden dark, and she couldn't blame them. The complete dark was unnerving.

Caed pulled her closer and then dropped her hand. A lantern sprang to life in his hands. They walked calmly away from the crystal.

"Well, that's done. Next up ... Any idea how to find Lady Erenne?" Despite the pitch-black Grotto, Caed's voice was matter-of-fact, and Ylena laughed.

"Honestly, I was hoping you would have an idea."

"I only saw her when she came to help Mims with the babies. I don't know where she has been staying."

Ylena thought back to all of her interactions with Lady Erenne and realized she knew very little about her life. She said she had been in love once. She had spent time in the healing center. She loved music. She drank a lot of tea.

She stopped in her tracks and looked around the Grotto. "Which way is it to Delirium?"

Caed pointed.

"Let's go. I'll introduce you to my grandfather."

Ylena was glad Delirium was next to Chaos, because all the walking was exhausting. She'd explored every single corner of the City both up and down in the last few days. Caed told her stories of his brothers and sisters to pass the time.

"Someday, after all this is over, I hope we can all sit down for a meal together. Your grandfather, too."

Ylena tried to imagine her grandfather eating with a dozen Priests. She wasn't sure she was ready for that yet.

They arrived at her grandfather's house and found him behind the counter of the shop.

"Ylena! What are you doing here? Is everything okay?" He rushed out from behind the counter and examined her face to see if he could discover any wounds.

"I'm fine, Grandfather. I'm looking for someone and thought you might help." She grabbed Caed's hand and pulled him next to her. "And this is Caed. He's from Upstairs ... He's a Priest."

Caed laughed. "Yes, but I'm a terrible Priest, so don't hold that against me."

Her grandfather snorted.

Ylena coughed awkwardly. "Yes, well, Caed, this is my grandfather, Brynn."

"It's nice to meet you, sir. Ylena has told me a lot about you."

Grandfather narrowed his eyes at Caed. "Has she now? That's how you know about me?"

"Oh ... well, I also did my own research. I knew you lived here, and I sent Ylena to find you after the Pageant."

Grandfather nodded his head slowly. "Yes, that was good. I assumed someone must have told her, but I wasn't sure who."

Ylena coughed again. "Now that introductions are done, I have a question for you. Do you know Lady Erenne?"

"Yes, of course. She became the new High Priest of

Purpose after the old one died."

"True, but do you know her?" asked Caed.

Grandfather narrowed his eyes again. "I don't give out the information of my customers, so even if I did, I wouldn't say."

"Grandfather, this is important. I believe she can help us overthrow the Wardens. And I also believe she might be in trouble."

Caed gave her a confused look, and Grandfather frowned. "Ylena, I can't—"

"Please, just tell me, did she get the tea that suppresses her Gifts from you?"

He looked surprised. "Why do you need to know that?"

"I think she has been drinking that tea for some time now but has recently stopped. Now, she is missing and sad. None of us know where she is. I have to find her."

Grandfather bit his lip as he considered. "I don't know how it will help you, but yes, that is the tea she got from me."

"Has she been back recently?"

"No. It's been a couple of days."

"Is there anywhere else she could go to get the tea?"

He chuckled. "Not unless she climbed back up the mountain to get it."

She stopped breathing.

Caed looked at her. "What is it?"

"Grandfather, you told me my mother is the one who found the tea leaves on the mountain. How did she find them?"

He rolled his eyes. "She said the Goddess showed it to her. She found a patch of it growing to the north of our cave, near the tall formations you liked to climb."

She laughed silently. "Of course. Where I can find some warm clothes? I lost mine a while back."

37

Grandfather had a collection of warm clothes and fur coats in his shop for the people that traveled back and forth to the City to collect the tea they had grown on the mountain. Ylena found a pair of warm socks and sturdy boots that fit and gathered several other layers to put on when they made it outside the City. Caed stared at the clothing in confusion.

"Do we seriously need all of this?" He was lacing up boots over a pair of thick pants Ylena had picked out. Even in the coolness of the cave, a faint sweat broke out on his forehead.

"You've lived in the warm City your whole life. Trust me. The weather on the mountain isn't anything like what you've experienced before."

"Every time the crystals go dark, the City gets much colder. I know what cold air is like."

Ylena and her grandfather looked at each other with barely hidden smiles. "I'm sorry to tell you that it's going to be much colder than that." She watched him gather up the rest of the warm clothing. "You don't have to go with me,

Caed. I've climbed the mountain my whole life, but even for me, it's going to be intense. We have a long way to go."

He pulled her as close as the bulky clothes in his arms would let him. "I told you already. I'm going with you. We are doing this together. And even if it's hard, I know I can do this. You've seen me fight and dance. You know I'm strong."

Her eyes drifted over his body as she remembered watching him move. She had seen his muscles up close when he didn't have his shirt on. Her lips curled in a smile as she remembered the way his strong arms—

Grandfather coughed.

Ylena hurriedly grabbed the clothes from Caed's arms and turned away to hide her face. "I guess we should get going. We've got a long walk ahead of us. We have to go back to the Heart and then walk all the way to Order to take the same door that I entered through."

Grandfather frowned. "Why don't you just take the tunnel from the Underneath that leads to the mountain? That's how the traders always made it back and forth."

Caed laughed. "Yes, how about we do that!" He slapped her grandfather on the back. "Thanks, Brynn. You've been extremely helpful."

Grandfather looked at him with narrowed eyes but kept his grouchy thoughts to himself.

Ylena gave him a kiss on the cheek. "Thank you, Grandfather. Hopefully, we will back soon with a way to rally this City together, both Upstairs and the Underneath."

Grandfather tucked her hair up into her warm hat as he spoke. "You've always been such a clever girl. I'm not surprised that you are better at leading a revolution than I am." He turned, but she saw him wipe a hand across his eyes. "Come on. I'll take you to the tunnel."

The tunnel entrance hid inside an old wooden shack built next to the cave wall. The stone was cut by conventional means, not by a Priest. She wondered how long it must have taken them to clear it. The Wardens had been very motivated to give the tea to the babies with Gifts to keep them in the Underneath.

She walked with Caed through the dark tunnel. He still had the lantern, but it didn't light very far in front of them. The tunnel was pitched at a steep incline, and by the time they reached the simple, wooden door, Ylena was warm. Daylight peeked through the bottom and sides of the doors, and it was a welcome relief to see in the darkness.

"We should stop here and put the rest of our clothes on." She expected Caed to suggest they go outside into the light first, but he set down the lantern and began pulling on a sweater.

Once they were suitably bundled, she opened the door a crack. They both blinked in the bright sunlight. After her eyes adjusted, she saw that the area around the door was clear. She hadn't really expected to see any people outside the City, but she wasn't sure if wild animals roamed nearby. She opened the door fully, and they both stepped out.

Caed gasped. "Wow, that's cold."

She giggled. "It's going to get much, much worse. It's still not too late if you ..." She stopped talking when she saw the dead stare on his face. She raised her hands up. "Okay! Sorry for suggesting it again! You are coming with me. You will definitely climb this mountain. You are strong and manly, and you will defeat it."

He gave her a bow. "Thank you very much. Yes, I will."

They both laughed and began the long trek up the mountain.

～

Ylena remembered that her walk down the mountain had been long, but going up took much longer. Besides the extra time it would have taken her to go up, she was slowed down by Caed being an inexperienced climber. A few times, she used her Gift to shape the stone into an easier pathway to climb.

After a particularly rough climb, they came to a flat area, and Caed paused with both hands resting on his thighs. "I take back all of my cocky statements about defeating this mountain. It's a better man than I am, and he's bested me."

Ylena smiled. "Actually, I think this mountain is a woman."

"Ah, that makes even more sense." He took a deep breath to calm his panting. "You climbed this mountain all the time?"

"Well, I only ever went all the way to the bottom once. I usually spent most of the time going up."

Caed looked at the steep inclines near the top of the mountain. "So, you're saying this is the easy part of the mountain?"

She bit her lips to hide her smile.

He sighed. "I'm guessing we still have a long way to go, so lead on, my dear."

She took advantage of the marginally less difficult slope to talk. "If it makes you feel any better, climbing feels harder than I remember. The muscles you use when climbing differ from the ones you use when dancing. I learned that the hard way after my first few dance lessons. I was grateful to have access to a hot bath to soak in."

"So, you're warning me I'm going to be in more pain when we finish?" His laugh mixed in with his panting breath. "I guess we won't find a hot bath waiting for us up there, will we?"

Ylena looked up to the spires above. They looked close,

but she knew they were a long way off. "I'm not sure what we will find up there."

They came upon a steep section of rock and fell into silence as they concentrated on the climb.

The sun set, and the sky lit up with a rainbow of colors. Ylena watched Caed as he tried to sneak a glance of the view over his shoulder.

"Focus, Caed!" she teased. "I don't want you to fall. Healing you will slow us down."

He laughed. "That would be so inconvenient!"

She paused, clinging to the stone. "Do you hear that?"

"Um ... water?"

She smiled. "Home."

She wanted to rush ahead but stayed close to Caed to help him up the last few steps. She took his hand and pulled him up next to her on a flat piece of rock. He leaned over to catch his breath, but she pulled him by the arm.

"Come on! We are so close!"

He groaned. "This is punishment for how hard I made you practice in dance class, isn't it?"

"Maybe it is. Maybe I should snap 'Shoulders!' so you straighten your posture right now."

He hunched over under the weight of his pack and laughed as he straightened. "Okay, teacher. Lead on."

She pulled him along with her the last few steps until the roaring of the waterfall became clear and the area around the cave came into sight. He followed her behind the waterfall and into the cave.

She took the lantern out of her pack and lit it as the setting sun barely filtered in past the water. She hadn't been gone that long, but she was surprised by how unfamiliar everything felt. It looked like a pack of small animals had made a home in her blankets, but other than that, it was relatively unchanged.

Caed stared around in wonder. "This is where you lived your entire life?" He ran his hand over the rough table and looked at the fire pit they'd used for cooking and warmth. "This is so beyond my experience. I can't imagine what it must have been like." He walked over to the large copper pot. "What's this?"

"Um ... that's the closest thing you can get to a hot bath up here." She imagined Caed rinsing himself off with water heated from the fire pit and immediately blushed.

He laughed. "I think I'll pass this time." He looked at the darkening sky through the waterfall. "So, are we going to rest here until morning?"

Her blush was still cooling on her cheeks, and she answered quickly. "No. We are close. We should go."

She ducked under the waterfall, but he grabbed her and pulled her close. "Ylena." The way he said her name caused a shiver to trickle up her spine. "Thank you for bringing me here. I have no idea what is going on, but I'm glad to be here with you."

She couldn't meet his eyes. "I hope you still think that after we find Lady Erenne."

"You really think she is here somewhere? Why would she hide all the way up here?"

"I'd rather let her explain. We need to hurry before the sun sets. I don't think you should try this in the dark."

"I imagine that is much more difficult." He followed her out of the cave.

"And colder."

He groaned.

38

Ylena stepped back as Caed pulled himself onto her perch on the mountain. They both took a seat on the narrow ledge and leaned against the stone at their backs. Caed took a deep breath as he surveyed the City below.

"It really is beautiful, isn't it?" he said. The crystals were glowing again, and their bright purple lit up the sky.

"It looks so different with the crystals that color. The last time I was up here, the crystals were still amber. I stared at the City every day, trying to imagine what it was like inside. I honestly had no idea what to expect."

He looked at her. "I saw the mountains that surround the City every day of my life, but I never guessed there was anyone like you living up here."

She smiled. "Don't distract me." She smacked him on the leg before she stood. "I think we are close. We need to keep moving."

He groaned as he stood carefully on the narrow ledge. "You think we will find her somewhere that's inside? I'm about to whine about how frozen my toes and fingers are, and I'm afraid that will further destroy my manly image."

She laughed and continued around the ledge. They stepped into a slight indentation in the rock, and the wind cut off.

Caed sighed. "Much better."

Ylena pulled off her gloves and ran her hands along each of the walls. "I don't know if this is it, but I have a hunch."

"I trust you, Ylena." His voice was quiet in the still cave. She realized how close they were in the confined space, and her breathing slowed.

He pulled her closer. Layers of thick clothing separated them, but she still felt the warmth of his body pressed against her. Her lips parted, and he leaned into the kiss.

She never wanted to leave this small cave. She wanted to live in this single moment and in this perfect kiss forever. Once they found Lady Erenne, the knowledge would set them down a certain path, and Ylena didn't know where it ended. She didn't think she was ready yet.

Caed pulled away from her slowly and looked at the tears poised on her lashes, ready to fall. "Why is it that kissing me always makes you cry?" He gave her a wry smile. "It's enough to make a guy insecure."

She sighed. "I don't know if I'm ready to find her yet. I just want to be here with you."

He took her hand. "I'm here. No matter what we find."

She nodded and took a deep breath. Her free hand collected a tear, and she touched the stone wall.

Her mind reached out through the stone as it drew itself into a map in her mind. She felt the steep slopes and the narrow inclines. She traced the lines of the stone spires as they arched into the air above them. And in front of her, she sensed an empty space. A perfectly circular, empty space.

She gripped Caed's hand harder and melted the stone in front of her. It fell away from them in a river until they stood in a large cave lit with a single lantern resting on a table. It wasn't bright enough to light the entire space.

Lady Erenne's voice came from the shadows. "You could have knocked."

Ylena and Caed exchanged a glance. "May we come in?" she asked.

Lady Erenne walked toward the table and into the light. "You might as well since you've come all this way."

Ylena managed not to gasp at the sight of her, but she clutched Caed's hand even harder. Lady Erenne's hair was still the same chestnut color, but it was piled on her head in disheveled knot. Instead of her usual beautiful, well-tailored clothing, she wore several layers of ragged sweaters.

Lady Erenne picked up the lantern. "I don't get visitors." Ylena looked at the single chair tucked under the table. Lady Erenne led them over to a couch and set the lantern on the floor. The two of them sat down on the couch, and Lady Erenne pulled over the chair.

She sat up straight in the chair with her perfect posture. Despite her sloppy appearance, she looked at them like she still wore the High Priest crown. "Do you need something from me?"

Caed seemed even more surprised by Lady's Erenne's appearance than she was, so she took the lead. "Um ... possibly? But first I want to know how you are doing? After the whole showdown in the amphitheater, you seemed ... upset."

Lady Erenne raised an eyebrow. "Yes. That was upsetting. I decided to get away for a while."

Caed looked around the austere cavern. "This looks very relaxing."

Ylena elbowed him in the ribs. "I understand why you might want to get away, but we could use your help in the City."

Lady Erenne crossed her arms. "I think I'm done helping the City for a while. My help has not been very productive."

"Maybe there is something more you can do ... I have a feeling you can do a lot more than you've demonstrated."

Lady Erenne narrowed her eyes at Ylena. "Really? What *more* would you have me do? Animating stone tigers was only going to result in hurting children. What else should I do?"

Ylena's frustration rose at the woman's cool indifference. "I don't know! Something *more*!"

Lady Erenne stood so that she towered over the two of them seated on the couch. She looked down on them with a haughty glare. "I am done with the City, Ylena. I have nothing left to offer."

Ylena stood and stared Lady Erenne in the eyes. She was usually shorter because Lady Erenne wore heels, but today, they were the same height. "This is *your* City. You can't just leave."

"I believe that's exactly what I did." Her voice was calm, and she settled her shoulders to stand her ground.

"You left before, didn't you?" Ylena knew her accusation was true by Lady Erenne's slight flinch. "How long were you gone? Is that how the High Priests took over in the first place? Because you just left?" Ylena could see Caed shifting anxiously on the couch. He clearly wasn't sure what was happening, but he didn't interrupt.

"How dare you judge me!" Lady Erenne's voice was pure fury. "You have no idea what I have been through, Ylena."

"Actually, I do." Ylena grabbed Lady Erenne by the hand. Lady Erenne tried to shake her off, but Ylena held tight.

Caed reached his hand up to Ylena's. "Ylena, maybe you should—"

Ylena plunged them into the City's memories.

The Director watching the rehearsals. The Director singing

*the racy song around the bonfire. The Director dancing with her.
The Director shaving.*

He called her Erenne.

He called her Goddess.

Ylena let go of their hands, and Lady Erenne and Caed both pulled back with a gasp.

Lady Erenne staggered back into her chair. Her strict posture was gone, and she slumped over with her face in her hands. Her body shook with sobs.

Ylena sat down slowly on the couch next to Caed. He stared at Lady Erenne with wide eyes. They sat in silence for so long, and Ylena felt guilty about showing them the memories so quickly.

Lady Erenne's voice came from her hands in a ragged whisper. "Where did you find those memories?"

"Each time I touched a crystal, one of his memories was revealed."

"Whose memories do you think you have?"

"It's the City. Somehow, when my tears fell into the basin, the City was born again as a baby. I've been watching him grow up. The last time I saw him, he was old enough that I recognized him as the Director when he shaved. Somehow, he is alive."

Lady Erenne looked up at her with tear-filled eyes. "You know nothing, Ylena." She shook her head, and her breath caught on a sob. "Those memories don't belong to the City. They belong to me."

Ylena felt silly when she realized it was true. Of course they were Lady Erenne's memories. She had been seeing the Director from her eyes.

"You must have drawn my memories from the crystals somehow. I don't know what it is you created with your tears, but it is not Nelson. It is not him."

"But he looks just like the Director! It's him!"

Lady Erenne dropped her voice to a harsh whisper. "Did he remember any of that? Did he remember his name? Did he remember *me*?" She must have read the answer in Ylena's expression, because she pressed on. "Whatever it is you created, *it is not him*."

"But what if it is? Won't you come and—?"

"No!" Lady Erenne's voice roared through the cavern. "I will not lose him again!" She stood and grabbed Ylena and Caed by the hands. "You need to leave."

"Lady Erenne, please!" Ylena begged as Lady Erenne pulled her and Caed toward the exit in the stone. "We need you!"

Lady Erenne stopped dragging them but held tightly to their hands. "Ylena." Her whisper was as soft as a butterfly's wing. "I gave the City everything. I have nothing left."

She closed her eyes as the tears ran down her face. Ylena blinked and was no longer in the cave.

She stood on the grass at the far end of the first amphitheater and looked down at the hand on her arm. It was the woman who played the role of the Goddess.

"Erenne! Goddess! Please hurry! He needs you!"

The woman pulled her forward, and wild anxiety began hammering in her chest. Up at the front of the stage, she saw a ladder that had fallen over. Beside it was a twisted body.

She shook off the woman's hand and ran toward him. Her bulky skirts slowed her down, and she skidded to a stop in front of him.

The Director... The City... The Companion... The boy... A pool of blood was seeping into the grass around his head. His eyes were unfocused as they stared off toward the stage.

She knew it was too late ... much too late. But still, she wiped a tear from her eye and pressed it against his forehead. She begged and pleaded to the Goddess, to herself, to anyone who would listen ... *Please let him live. Let him live!*

She listened, praying she would hear him take a breath, that she would hear his heart beat again, but the only sound was the quiet sobs of the woman.

Ylena pulled her hand back from his forehead. She studied the blood on her hand and tried to understand. "How did this happen?"

The woman struggled to speak. "He was here alone ... Goddess. I'm sure he was trying to adjust something to make it perfect. You know how he is ..." She gulped. "How he was."

Ylena screamed. All of her rage from Pim's death, her helplessness at the babies being taken, the unending despair that she could never make the City whole ... She screamed it all to the sky.

She opened her eyes and saw the woman looking at her in terror. Ylena spoke to her in a calm voice. "You should leave. Now."

The woman gathered up her skirts and sprinted away.

Ylena's hands moved as if she was in a dream. She knew what Erenne did next. And the fear and sadness in her own heart answered in return.

Ylena bent down and kissed the Companion on the forehead. Her tears trickled down her face and splashed onto his clean-shaven cheeks. She sat up and rested both of her hands on his chest. She gathered up every scrap of the Spark that pulsed through her veins, and she *pushed*.

She imagined the City she had dreamed about building with him at her side.

And she built it.

From him.

She drove his body into the earth, and his bones became crystal that shot into the sky. His blood became crystalline, pulsing through the ground. She pulled the stone from the ground, leaving great caverns behind, and used it to build temples around his crystal bones. She built the entire City out of *him*. Out of her grief.

She kneeled beside a crystal basin at the foot of a great stone amphitheater she built for him. The basin glowed with an amber light.

But it was not him.

She looked around at the great City she had constructed, more beautiful and perfect than any city she had ever seen. Her people would grow to fill it. Some of them would inherit her Gifts because of what she imbued in the City. They would fall in love and marry and grow old together.

And the Goddess would live the rest of her long life walking through the streets of a City that was his grave.

Lady Erenne let go of their hands, and Ylena and Caed dropped to the cavern floor. They both gasped for breath, and by the tears falling down Caed's cheeks, Ylena knew he had seen the same vision.

Lady Erenne stood with her head bowed. Exhaustion and sadness lined her face. Ylena wanted to speak to her, but she had no words.

"I built the City." Lady Erenne's whisper was gentle. "I gave my people everything I had. Everything *he* had. I can't do anything else. Please don't ask me."

Ylena looked up at her from where she kneeled. "But if you could just help us remove the Wardens ... After that, you can just leave the City on its own."

"Just remove them? Should I bury them alive in stone,

Ylena? Drown them? Steal every drop of air from their lungs? I've done it before. In another life." Her matter-of-fact tone made Ylena shiver. "But the people of this City are mine, no matter how terrible they might be, and I can't bring myself to hurt them. I know countless ways to use my Gifts for evil, but no matter how hard I try, I can't fix anything."

"If you come back to the City with us, we can talk about it. I'm sure we can fix this together."

Lady Erenne looked down at them with a sad smile. "You both should know by now how much I truly have enjoyed your company. And if you ever cared for me at all, please do as I say. Never come up here again."

She placed a palm on each of their foreheads like a benediction.

They blinked and opened their eyes in the amphitheater.

Ylena and Caed looked in each other's eyes and saw their same shock reflected back. They walked in silence through the quiet amphitheater until they made it to the stone-covered entrance to the Heart. They walked down the staircase and removed their heavy coats and boots. The Heart was glowing brightly, but the boy was nowhere to be found. They curled up on the velvet curtains together and fell asleep without a word.

39

Ylena woke in the curtains alone. She wondered if she had dreamed of sleeping next to Caed until she saw him standing in the middle of the Heart. He stared into the crystalline that flowed around the spire at the base of the crystal basin Upstairs.

He didn't turn as she approached. "She made all this from his blood and bones? What is she?"

She hugged her arms around her chest. "Quinn discovered some of the old books that said that, before the City, there were rare people who had Gifts they called the Spark. It wasn't as common as it is with Priests, and the magic they possessed was much different."

"Like suddenly transporting us here?" He shook his head. "Not that I was looking forward to walking back down the mountain, but I would have preferred a little warning."

"I completely agree with you on that."

"So, what now?" He turned to face her. "I get the feeling that you were hoping she would be the answer to our current situation. Now that she is out of the picture, I guess we need to make a new plan."

"She was my whole plan, Caed. Everything I planned is ruined. How can you move on to something else so quickly?"

"Despite all my beliefs getting turned upside down, I'm used to acting like the Goddess doesn't exist. It's good to know at least my behavior doesn't have to change."

His lips turned up in a smirk, and she couldn't help but smile. "Okay. A new plan. I'm out of ideas at the moment. What do you have in mind?"

"My first plan is to stop underestimating you. I doubted your visions, but everything you saw led us to Lady Erenne on the mountain. Even if she isn't willing to help us, I believe your visions still hold a lot of potential."

"But those were her memories she implanted in the crystals when she created the City. I don't know what else they can do." She shrugged.

"Maybe nothing, but the question remains. Who is the boy? Even if he is only the form of the Goddess's Companion, what is he? I believe you saw him. I think we need to talk to him." Caed looked around the cavern like the boy might suddenly appear.

"I haven't seen him since the night I shared the memories with him. And since then, every time I touch a crystal, the City goes dark."

"Yes. You are affecting him somehow. We need to find him. Have you ever been able to call for him?"

"No, but I felt like he was watching us the last time we were in the Heart. It was ... um ... when we kissed."

Caed got a smug expression on his face. He put his hands on her waist and pulled her close. "Really? Do you think he was jealous?"

"No! He's like my child, Caed." He raised an eyebrow, but she continued. "It's true, he's probably older than us by now, but despite that, I brought him to life, and he's my responsibility."

"Ah ... So, a different type of jealousy. He wants his mom to give him all the attention and stop kissing some strange guy." He leaned closer to her until their faces were almost touching, and his voice was a warm whisper against her cheek. "When I was a kid, I would occasionally interrupt my older brothers and sisters as they were about to kiss their dates. It's a very 'kid' thing to do." He brushed a finger along her cheek. "I'll do whatever it takes to tempt him to stop us."

Ylena closed her eyes and melded her body to his muscular form. His lips brushed a soft caress across hers, and she sighed, longing for more.

"Hi!" The voice of the boy, the man, rang out behind them.

Caed pulled away from her with a self-satisfied grin.

"You're back!" She rushed to the boy's side and reached up to brush his long hair from his face. "How are you? I've been worried about you."

"I'm okay. Where were you? I couldn't find you in the City." His face looked like the age of the Companion from her vision, but his eyes seemed much more innocent.

"I had to leave the City to search for someone. I'm sorry if I worried you."

"I'm just glad you are back. It was strange to not feel you here."

She realized Caed was staring at them both in fascination. She pulled him close. "I'd like you to meet Caed. He's my ... boyfriend." She wasn't sure what she felt about the word, but Caed's expression grew even smugger.

"It's nice to meet you." Caed extended his hand. "And you are?"

"My name is Nelson." He answered with a smile.

"What?" Ylena grabbed him by the arm. "How do you know that?"

He looked confused. "I'm not sure."

Caed studied him. "Maybe he is linked with you somehow and when you heard his name, he learned it."

She looked up into Nelson's eyes. "Do you remember any of the memories I shared with you? Do you remember anything from before?"

He rubbed his chin like he did when he had a beard. "I remember you sharing your memories with me, but they are fuzzy. Do you want to try it again?"

"No! The last time, you disappeared. I don't want that to happen again."

"Are you going to call my name again?" he asked.

She tilted her head. "What do you mean?"

"When you call my name, it rings out through the whole City. The last few times you've called, I've fallen asleep and had strange dreams."

"It's when I've touched the crystals. That sounds like me calling your name?"

"Yes, I think that's how I know my name is Nelson. I heard you call it."

"I didn't know your name the last time I touched the crystal." She looked at Caed. "I know where we are going next."

He sighed. "I guess we've broken in to all six other temples. We might as well make it an even set."

She turned back to the boy. "We are going Upstairs, and I will call your name again. Maybe you'll finally remember who you are."

They put their boots on quickly and started toward the staircase.

"While you are up there, will you look for the woman?"

Ylena's foot paused on the stair. "The ... woman?"

"Yes. The other one. She's not in the City anymore. Will you see if you can find her?"

She carefully arranged her face into a calm expression. "Yes, Nelson. If I discover a way to drag that woman back to the City, I will do it."

40

Ylena and Caed hid outside Temple Order. They had broken into the last few temples at night, so it seemed strange to look at the temple in the bright daylight. There were more soldiers than at some of the other temples, and all of them were armed with swords at their waist and knives sheathed all over their body.

"Well, this should be fun," said Caed. "So, what's your idea for sneaking in this time?"

"I'm tired of sneaking. We're going to storm the place."

Caed looked at her with a smile. "I like it when you are fierce."

She ducked her head to hide her blush and placed both hands on the stone building they were hiding behind. The stone melted off the walls and formed into the shape of a stone tiger. The tiger tossed its head in a silent roar, then sat back on its haunches to wait for her cue.

Caed stared at the tiger with wide eyes.

"I was curious if I could do it." Ylena shrugged. "I guess I can."

Caed laughed out loud, then slapped his hand over his mouth to cover the sound.

She smiled at his reaction and created a dozen more.

"This will be quite the distraction to get us in," he said in astonishment. "What's the plan to get out?"

"Can you ride a horse?" she asked.

He raised an eyebrow.

She touched one of tigers and melted it into a horse. It pawed at the ground, and Caed looked at Ylena in wonder. He looked like he might speak, but instead, he pulled her into a wild kiss. He pushed her against the remaining portion of the wall, and she was glad the stone held her up, because her knees were suddenly weak. She wrapped her fingers through his white-streaked hair, and his hands were hot against her lower back.

She didn't want to let him go, but the stone animals grew restless the longer they kissed. Caed pulled back from her, and she struggled to catch her breath. He gathered up the lock of hair that had come loose from her ponytail and tucked it behind her ear. "I love you, Ylena. I never stopped loving you. Not even for a moment."

She leaned in and pressed a gentle kiss on his lips. "I love you, too, Caed." She whispered against his lips, "Now, are you ready to storm this temple with me?"

He grinned, and she released the tigers.

The tigers bounded up the front of the temple, cracking stone steps on the way. Soldiers tried to fight them, but their swords slid off the stone. One soldier fell to the ground with a sharp scream as a tiger swatted him with a heavy stone paw. Another tiger barreled into two soldiers, knocking them down before spinning its head around to see who was next. The soldiers formed into groups to try to battle the tigers one by one.

Ylena and Caed ran up the steps with the stone horse following behind them. The hallway to the inner courtyard was empty. Most of the soldiers were outside battling the tigers, but she ran quickly into the inner courtyard before soldiers rounded up the Warden's children with the Gift of Purpose.

The inner courtyard was empty of people but filled with row upon row of weapons. Knives glittered in the crystal's light, and swords shone with a polished gleam. Caed followed Ylena between the shelves until they stood at the crystal at the center.

"This is the last temple, Ylena. Find what we need. I believe in you." He gave her a comforting smile.

She wiped a tear from her eye and reached toward the crystal.

"Aren't you the sneaky ones?" A laughing voice came from her back.

Ylena turned slowly to see the Warden of Chaos skipping into the room. "I knew you would try to sneak in here, but I thought you'd be quieter about it. I guess I should have known that you'd want to put on a show."

Ylena's breath slowed as her mind ran through her options. Three soldiers followed the Warden, and Ylena thought that if Caed was ready to catch her, the stone horse would charge over anyone in their way.

"I see you calculating, dearie!" The Warden giggled. She shook her finger at Ylena. "You need to recalculate. Unless you are okay with what I will do with them."

At the Warden's word, three more soldiers entered, holding three white-streaked Priests with knives at their throats. One Priest looked no older than a thirteen-year-old girl. Ylena flexed her hands at her side and reconsidered.

The Warden's deep laugh raised the hair on the back of Ylena's neck. She felt Caed's comforting presence at her side. She knew he was itching to step in front of her, but she held her arm out to hold him back.

The Warden noticed Caed twitching. "Oh! I see you have

a new boy now! Did you tire of Wilder and get rid of him already?"

She heard a low growl rise in Caed's throat and knew she had to act quickly. She couldn't let this spiral out of control while the soldiers were holding those knives.

"I surrender!" She raised her arms in front of her.

"Ylena!" Caed slid in front of her. Despite his back to the soldiers, he fixed his eyes on hers without fear. "You can't surrender now."

"It's okay, Caed. I'll escape, or you will rescue me. Either option is fine with me."

"I don't think you understand," said the Warden. "He's not walking out of here."

Ylena stared Caed in the eyes. "Oh, I understand. He is definitely not walking out of here."

"Ylena, no!" He raised his arms, but he was too late.

She touched her hand to his forehead and sent him to his brothers' house.

Then, she touched her hand to the crystal and passed out.

Ylena sat alone on a stone bench in the middle of the new amphitheater at the center of the City she had built. Since she was the only one in the audience, she could have taken a seat closer to the stage, but there was a part of her that imagined she would smell his blood if she sat any closer to the crystal basin.

The actors who played the Goddess and Companion were on stage. They were singing a song, and Ylena realized with a start that she had never heard it before.

The Goddess and Companion sang of their undying

love, and they vowed to stand by each other's side until the end of time. The other actors draped them in flowers and tossed rose petals at their feet.

It was their wedding.

There was no wedding in the Pageant. Ylena had always assumed the Goddess was above marriage, that marriage was just something for simple mortals. But the actors smiled at each other with love and danced with passion, and she knew they did every move the Director taught them.

She remembered his face as he watched their rehearsals. He was always so concerned with them doing it correctly. She initially thought it was because he was as particular as Madame Director or Maestro, but now, she realized what this Pageant really was.

It was his love letter to the Goddess. To the woman he loved.

Tears poured down her face, and she wept for the loss of him. He died in such a meaningless way! It was a simple accident, and he was suddenly gone. She never said goodbye.

Ylena wondered if this scene recreated a wedding that already happened or if it was a sign of a wedding that had been to come.

She couldn't breathe. The song was so beautiful, and each note was like a knife to her core. She stood and tried to catch her breath.

The singers and musicians stopped abruptly as she stood. They looked at her with pity and a fair amount of terror. The woman playing the Goddess was the first to overcome her fear and speak.

"We apologize, Goddess. This isn't right ... We'll change it, Goddess. We will rewrite the scene."

Ylena stared back at them but couldn't bring herself to

speak. The performers would change it. They would add the death of the Companion as a scene in the Pageant. The wedding scene would be forgotten. And that would be the version they would hand down through the centuries.

She sat down and rested her head in her hands until she woke from the vision.

41

Ylena woke in the dark with the taste of her grandfather's tea in her mouth. She stretched out her hand and touched the bars of a metal cage surrounding her. Her body was in a crumpled heap, so she tried to roll on her back and stretch out, but the cage wasn't large enough. She stared into the dark, waiting for her eyes to adjust, but there was absolutely no light. Her eyes wouldn't adjust.

She pressed her palms against her eyes. Her head ached from shedding so many tears. She felt guilty for asking Lady Erenne to remember such a traumatic memory. And she was angry that Lady Erenne refused to come down from the mountain. She didn't know what she should do next. Except escape, of course.

She couldn't tell how long she had been asleep. She wondered if it had been long enough for Caed to walk all the way back to the temple from his brother's house. He'd probably uttered a string of curses when he suddenly found himself transported there. Until she'd touched him, she hadn't been sure if she could do it. She had a feeling the Wardens would want to keep her alive for whatever nefarious schemes they still had planned, but she couldn't guarantee they would feel the same about Caed. No matter how much he cursed her, she was glad she'd sent him away.

She rolled into a seated position and dug into her pocket until she found what she needed. A key made of stone. She wondered if the Wardens had searched her. Maybe they only looked for weapons and didn't worry about a lucky rock in her pocket. She hoped the lock was just the same, because that would make her life so much easier. She reached her arms through the bars and felt around for the lock but stopped when she saw a faint light coming from under the door across the room. She tucked the key back in her pocket and sat back down.

A soldier and a woman with white-streaked curls entered. The Priest held a lantern in one hand, and in the other, she held a cup containing what Ylena suspected was tea. As she approached the cage, Ylena recognized her as a Priest the soldiers had threatened with a knife. The soldier remained at the door and studied them both with a glare.

The Priest kneeled down in front of Ylena. "Are you well?" Her soft voice was kind.

"As well as can be expected, all things considered."

The Priest nodded. "I'm glad you are awake. It will make it much easier for you to drink this tea."

"I'd rather not drink that, but thanks."

The Priest looked confused. "Don't you understand what this tea does? It's actually beneficial." The Priest dropped her voice to a whisper. "Honestly, I'm surprised the Warden allows you to drink it."

Ylena raised her eyebrows. "Beneficial? I'm going to have to disagree with you on that."

"The tea prevents you from using your Gifts." She reached her hands through the bars and tucked a white streak of Ylena's hair behind her ear. "There are a lot of tears around here lately, and the tea protects from any unintentional use of your Gift. So, please, drink it. We've lost too many already."

Ylena wanted to explain to the Priest that her white streak was different, but she thought the story was a bit too long. "I appreciate your kindness, but I'm going to decline."

The soldier shifted his position, and the Priest flinched. Ylena could now make out in the dim light the bruises and cuts that lined the woman's bare arms.

She dropped her voice into a low growl. "They are hurting you."

The woman ducked her head self-consciously. "They occasionally allow us to be healed, but the only ones who can safely use their Gifts belong to the Warden." She met Ylena's eyes, and tears shone on her lashes. "They are just children. Being forced to heal us upsets them, so I try to avoid it if I can."

Rage simmered in Ylena's chest. She imagined pulling the entire temple down on the Warden's head. But the temple was also filled with fading Priests and children. She started plotting a dozen different ways to take out a Warden without harming any children.

"Time to go," the soldier's voice grated from the shadows. "Drink the tea. Now."

Ylena stared at him with narrowed eyes and imagined a dozen different scenarios for him as well.

He took a single step toward the Priest. The woman flinched and ducked her head. He sneered and stared at Ylena with dead eyes. "Drink. The. Tea."

Ylena reached through the bars of her cage and drank the tea. She had never noticed it as a child, but she felt the tea spread through her body, causing her blood to slow.

"Let's go." The soldier turned toward the door.

The Priest took the cup back from Ylena and dropped

her voice to shaking whisper. "I'm Adhira. You are just as beautiful and kind as your mother was. Goddess blessing upon you, Ylena."

⁓

Ylena sat frozen in the dark. She hadn't considered the fact that many of the Priests in this temple would have known her mother. When she had been in Temple Order during the Pageant rehearsals, she hadn't even known her mother had been a Priest. This was the first temple she ever entered, and now she was back again at the end of a long series of discoveries. She could barely recognize the girl she had been when she first stepped through the small gate in the City wall. She had grown so much, and yet she still didn't know if she was enough.

She considered digging her key out again when the lights came back on. She blinked several times to adjust to the sudden light. There were two crystalline lamps on the wall, and when they relit, she could see that she was in an empty storeroom like the one she had been in before. She stood up in her cage, but before she found her key, the door opened.

Two soldiers entered, followed by a boy of around seven years. She assumed he must be one of the Warden's Champions and wondered what his Gift was. A healer in case the soldiers got injured? Or had they trained him to use his Gift to injure?

The soldier rattled a pair of shackles in his hands. "You are going to do this the easy way, right?"

She looked at the young boy with wide, dark eyes. "I won't cause any problems. I promise."

The soldier chuckled grimly. "Too late for that." He put the shackles on her hands while she was still inside the cage, then opened the door and pulled her out. "The Warden wants to see you. I'm warning you now because I'm a nice guy. Don't cause any problems, and we won't have to hurt anyone."

She understood that the threat wasn't against her. She nodded and followed him up the stairs. He led her to a room that previously belonged to the High Priest. She remembered sneaking into a similar room with Lady Erenne while Caed climbed onto the balcony. She mapped the location in her mind in case she found a chance to run.

The Warden sat in a throne covered with flowering vines, her hair piled on her head in a purposeful disarray. Her smile didn't reach her eyes. As she watched Ylena approach, she absently scratched her black fingernails across a vine on the arm of her throne. Ylena wasn't sure if the throne belonged to the High Priest or if it was a recent addition.

The soldier pushed Ylena's shoulder until she kneeled in front of the Warden. Ylena looked around the room and found several Priests serving food or cleaning. A few of the white-streaked Priests were younger than Ylena. She sighed. There were plenty of people the Warden could use against her.

"Good to see you are finally awake. I thought you might pull some clever trick before, but apparently, you were so incompetent you knocked yourself out when the crystal went dark. You're not the smartest girl, are you?"

Ylena thought through the event from the Warden's perspective and realized that's exactly what it looked like. She found no reason to correct her.

"And the boy that was with you?" She threw her head back and laughed. "Once the lights were out, he ran off and left you here all alone. I barely know you, but it appears you have phenomenally bad luck with men."

She wanted to growl out a response but vowed to not let the Warden get to her.

"Don't worry, though. Even though you can't keep a man around on your own, I am going to help you. I've got people searching, and I'm going to bring him back for you."

She tried to school her expression, but the Warden smirked when she saw the fear in Ylena's eyes. She hoped Caed would just stay hidden for a while. Hopefully, his brothers would keep him out of trouble.

"We have a little assignment for you both. We don't have enough Champions to produce enough food for everyone. And yet, I'm sitting on a whole pile of Priests who could work out in the fields every day. Unfortunately, they all seem to be a limited resource. I've already used up several."

Ylena thought of Adhira's comment about losing too many Priests. Her eyes glittered with rage, but she bit back her angry words.

"We need to get these Priests back to work! And once we do, I'll be the richest Warden. I plan on making a lot of profitable trades with the other Wardens in exchange for my Priest farmers."

Ylena imagined the Priests being bought and sold by the Wardens. Her body trembled, and she breathed through her nose in quick puffs, locking her jaws shut.

"That's why I'm bringing your boy back. We need you and Wilder to perform another Pageant."

Her breath escaped in a rush. "Wilder?"

"Yes. This time you will finish the Pageant, add these Priests' tears to the basin, and get them back to work!" She laughed and shook her finger at a Priest as he walked by. "Lazy, lazy Priests!"

Ylena's mind worked furiously. She wanted to save the Priests' lives by bonding them to the City again, but with the full power of the Priests' Gifts behind them, the Wardens would be even more difficult to overthrow. And where was Wilder? Was he hiding? She cursed those two white wolves that made him conspicuous.

"I'm assuming you need little practice, considering how strict the High Priests were about everything. Once we find Wilder, we will bundle you off to the amphitheater and get this all worked out." Her smile looked unhinged. "That was a really pleasant chat! Soldiers, take her back. And make sure she drinks the tea."

Ylena staggered to her feet as the soldiers pulled her up. They shuffled her back to her cage and locked her in. She briefly considered trying to escape, but instead, she settled down in the corner of the cage and thought about the Pageant.

Reprise

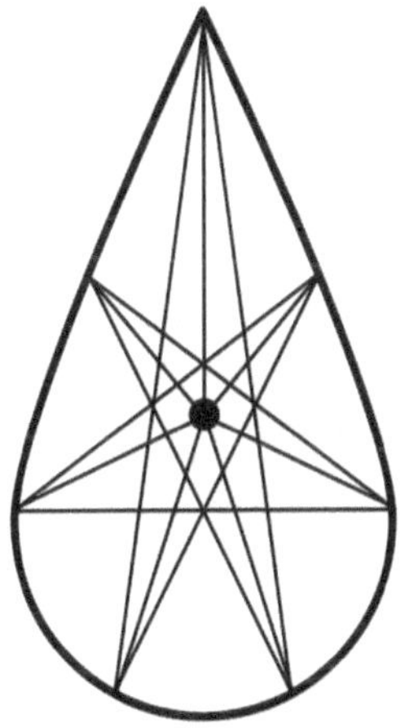

42

Ylena measured time by the frequency of tea delivered. Different Priests and soldiers brought her the tea, and she didn't see Priest Adhira again. She was grateful for one Priest who smuggled a chunk of bread in his sleeve for her. Other than that, they had given her nothing but tea.

She was considering how to best phrase her awkward request for a chamber pot when a soldier arrived with shackles. "It's time to go."

Her heart stuttered. Did they find Wilder? Was he okay? She thought he would fight being captured. Would they risk hurting him?

After her awkward request to stop by the bathroom, they marched Ylena out of the temple and toward the amphitheater.

She walked in the middle of an escort of seven soldiers and seven of the Wardens' Champions. A group of Priests shuffled along at their side. Most of them looked defeated. Ylena thought that the only reason they invited the Priests was so the soldiers could have someone to threaten to make her compliant.

Along the path to the amphitheater, soldiers and people from the City paused in their work. Ylena remembered the bright and colorful people of the City when she first arrived. Now, the people stood in brightly colored rags, exhaustion written on their faces. She straightened her shoulders back and down like Caed had taught her in her first dance lesson and walked with her head held high. She wanted them to see that just because she was captured, she wasn't defeated.

When they arrived at the amphitheater, Ylena found teenagers repairing the stone benches. They were reshaping the pieces that Lady Erenne's stone tigers had broken apart. Ylena wondered how many people the Warden was going to invite. Usually, the entire City was invited to the Pageant, and during the Spectacle, the Wardens required everyone in the Underneath to attend. What were they planning this time?

The soldiers escorted Ylena into a dressing room. It was the same one she had been in during the Pageant, and she could still see the feathers imprinted in the stone on the floors and walls. A soldier stood outside the curtain that provided privacy, and they assigned her two Priests to help her change.

One Priest was Adhira. Now that they were in the bright, crystalline light, Ylena could see white streaks in the woman's lush, corkscrew curls. Her deep brown skin was unlined, but Ylena guessed if she was friends with her mother, she was over forty. The other was a young teenage girl named Katya. Her dark hair fell lifelessly around her shoulders, and she looked ill from not eating well. They were both covered in bruises that Ylena longed to heal despite the tea slowing her blood.

They helped her change into her costume, which required clever maneuvering since the soldier refused to remove Ylena's shackles. As Ylena stepped into the familiar costume of the Goddess, her heart began pounding hard in her chest. She had to sit down to keep from passing out.

The young Priest looked disturbed by Ylena's reaction. Her hands shook, and she backed against the wall.

Priest Adhira's comforting voice spoke. "Katya, dear. Ylena is weak from not eating. Will you go find her some food? The Wardens don't want her passing out on stage."

Katya nodded quickly and rushed out of the dressing room.

Adhira kneeled on the floor in front of Ylena. "Are you okay, child? I'm sure you are hungry, but I sense this is more than just hunger."

Ylena gripped her chest and tried to still her racing heart. "I can't do this. I can't go out there again. The last time … I lost so many. I stood backstage with Pim and wished the Goddess's blessing upon her, and by the end of the night, she was gone forever."

Adhira took hold of Ylena's hand and met her eyes. "Pim isn't gone. She's clearly still in your heart, even now."

Ylena whispered, "But I miss her." Tears spilled down her cheeks, but there were no miracles. They were just ordinary tears.

Adhira held Ylena's hand in silence and let her cry. Once her tears slowed, Adhira cleared her throat.

"Ylena, I need to confess something to you."

Adhira's words caused Ylena to look up. If a Priest was confessing, it was something notable.

"I knew your mother. We were friends. You look so much like her when she was your age. You remind me of those simpler times." She sighed. "You probably already know this, but she loved your father very much. She twisted her ankle one day when she was out in a field, and Ylain was the one who healed her. After that, they were never apart. I knew he was … sick. He struggled with overwhelming sadness from time to time. Mae was always by his side. One day, it was too much. He didn't make it out." She carefully wiped her tears. "Mae came to me and told me she had to leave. I didn't know why, but there was a part of me that suspected that she was with child. It shouldn't have been possible, but I could see you in the way she held her stomach, in the way her face glowed despite the tears." Adhira bowed her head and took a piece of paper from an inner pocket of her robe. "And my confession ... before she left, she asked me to place this on Ylain's grave. I told her I would ... But I didn't. I've never been sure what caused me to tuck this letter away, but maybe the Goddess's hand can be found, even though I broke my word."

She placed the letter in Ylena's hands. "I don't know what will happen tonight, but I believe you are the Goddess's hidden gift, Ylena. You will make all things right." She kissed Ylena on the forehead and left her alone with the letter.

Ylena's hands shook as she unfolded the page. Her tears dripped down as she read.

Dearest Ylain,

I can't believe you are gone. Our lives have been intertwined for so long that without you, I feel like a piece of my own soul has fled. If I close my eyes, I can almost grasp hold of you, but when my eyes open, I lose you all over again.

There is a part of me that wants to lie down and never rise back up, but I can't. Because of her. Our daughter. I have to keep moving forward because of her.

The part of my soul that is you says, "Mae, 'she' might actually be a 'he,' you know?" And yes, dear part of my soul, you might be right. But humor me like you always have.

She will be kind and empathetic and artistic, just like her father. I will tell her about you every day of her life. She will have such a clear picture of you in her mind that it will be like you are right here.

When the loss of you threatens to break me into pieces, I will remind myself that I still believe. I believe in our daughter, and I believe in us. I believe the Goddess blessed our love story and that this isn't the end. I believe that our love stretches beyond the stars and beyond time, and I know that we truly will be together again.

Always yours,

Mae

Ylena read the letter three times before she folded it back up and tucked it into the top of her dress. She wiped the tears off her face and looked at herself in the small mirror on her makeup desk.

Her mother believed in her. Ylena would not let her down.

She took a deep breath and began applying her makeup for the show.

43

Katya came back with some food, and Ylena ate every bite as Adhira twisted Ylena's hair on top of her head and let gentle curls frame her face. Both Priests fluffed her gown as she stood.

"You look like the Goddess herself," said Adhira. She spun a white lock of Ylena's hair around her finger so that it fell just right. "I've seen some phenomenal Pageants over the years, but watching you on stage was a true blessing."

Ylena wanted to curl inward at the thought of the last Pageant, but she was determined to remain strong. "Thank you both for your help. Do you know when we will begin?"

A familiar voice answered. "The Wardens aren't as punctual as the High Priests were."

Ylena turned to find Maestro at her door. "Maestro! What are you doing here?"

"I seem to have gotten myself 'recruited' again." He rolled his eyes. "So much for living in obscurity in the Underneath. Although, I have missed the accommodations." He ran his hand over the stone door frame. "This is a bit more impressive than our setup for the Spectacle. The velvet curtains don't compare to this architecture."

She remembered the velvet curtains that were now crumpled on the floor as her makeshift bed and thought he would find them even less impressive now.

"So, we aren't starting soon?" she asked.

He shrugged. "I guess we are still waiting for your Companion to arrive."

She closed her eyes and hoped that Wilder was safe.

Maestro continued. "But I've got the orchestra all tuned up and ready. I've assigned a few experienced Priests to the Wardens' Champions to coach them through the scenes that require blooming trees and fountains. I don't know what the lighting will be like, though. The kids working with the light Priests from Purpose might melt the stone and crystalline all over the stage." He sighed. "If they would have given me more than a day to prepare and Priests who could actually use their Gifts, maybe I could have made something adequate. I just hope this doesn't end in disaster."

Ylena raised an eyebrow. "I wouldn't know anything about a Pageant ending in disaster."

"Oh, well, I guess that's true." He straightened his vest and nodded at the Priests. "Will the two of you also assist the young Champions on stage?"

Adhira cleared her throat. "No, thank you, Maestro. We will stay backstage."

He shrugged. "Nice work on her costume and makeup, though. At least we've got a decent Goddess going for us. I sure hope they remove your shackles first ... I'll see you onstage soon." He ducked out of the room.

Ylena paced from one end of her small dressing room to the other. The two Priests shifted out of her way each time she passed. She was about to make another lap when a soldier walked in with a cup of tea.

Adhira and Katya relaxed once she took the cup with no complaints. Ylena sighed but dutifully drank the tea. She'd always enjoyed drinking tea when Grandfather made it for her, but now, she could barely choke it down. She handed the cup back to the soldier. He made sure it was empty before he backed up to let the Warden of Chaos enter.

She looked at Ylena's dress and clapped her hands. "How quaint! This is going to be fun! You'll be glad to know that we found your Companion. He was hiding, but luckily, we found someone who knew him."

Ylena's eyes went wide as her grandfather stepped up beside the Warden. "What have you done?" she whispered.

He tried to move closer to her, but she stepped back. "I had to do it, Ylena." He was desperately trying to meet her eyes, but she couldn't even look at him. "I'm … protecting you. I didn't know what else I could do."

She shook her head. Wilder trusted Grandfather. Their entire crew had stayed at his house. Wilder would have looked to her grandfather for help, but instead, he found betrayal.

She closed her eyes. "Get him out. I don't want to see him."

The Warden chuckled. "I don't quite believe you are as through with him as you claim, so we're going to keep him close to ensure your good behavior." The Warden nodded at the soldier. "Once you are onstage, he will remove your shackles. We don't want them spoiling your costume. But just remember, we will have your grandfather, plus a couple dozen helpless Priests at our sides, to make sure you perform everything as planned. You'll pour the tears in during the usual spot, but I expect you to finish the Pageant in its entirety." She grabbed the bodice of Ylena's dress and pulled her forward. "This show needs to go as perfectly as the High Priests drilled into you. I need these Priests to start growing food. I won't allow you to ruin this for me. If you do, I will rain chaos down on you, your grandfather, and every

Priest I can get my hands on. Then, when I ruin this Pageant as badly as the last one, I will start over with a completely new cast until someone gets it right. Do I make myself clear?"

"Yes, Warden. I understand." Ylena understood the Warden sounded exactly like the High Priests. Instead of scaring her, it put fire in her veins. She would defeat them.

The Warden's smile flickered to life. "Terrific! I'm heading out to my seat. Let's get this started!" She snapped her fingers and motioned for Ylena's grandfather to follow.

He stared at Ylena with desperate eyes, but she turned away. She tasted the bitter tea in her mouth and felt betrayed all over again.

Adhira and Katya straightened Ylena's dress where the Warden had grabbed it. Ylena smoothed her hair back and strode onto the stage.

44

Ylena stood backstage in the dark, waiting for her cue. The soldier had removed her shackles, and she tried not to fidget as she waited. She could hear sounds from the audience and tried to guess how many people were out there. They were much louder than they had been during the previous Pageant. It sounded more like what she heard before the Spectacle. She wondered if they had brought the same amount of alcohol this time. She peeked around a curtain when she heard the first notes from the orchestra.

The music transported her back to the other Pageant. She'd stood in the wings with Pim and Wilder, with no idea what the night would bring. It was terrifying, but she was more excited than she had ever been in her life. The memories crashed over her like a wave, and she closed her eyes and relived each one. She needed those memories tonight. The good and the bad, everything she had learned, everything she had broken. She wrapped all of those moments together and placed them gently in the center of her chest. She could feel the memories burning like a fire, and in the warmth of their glow, she walked to her position on the dark stage.

The Pageant, like the City, began with chaos.

The music itself was frenetic. The orchestra played the wild notes that sounded like anarchy barely contained. She heard the voice that called out the first lines of the Pageant and recognized the girl from the school Wilder attended. Obviously, Maestro knew where to find trained singers ready to perform with no rehearsal.

She hid in the darkness behind the curtain and saw the Wardens seated in their place of honor in the front row. Seated to the left of the Wardens was her grandfather. He looked small compared to the Wardens in their thrones. He stared directly at her in her shadowed position on stage, and she looked away.

The chaos of music quieted for a single breath, and the voice sang out:

"The Goddess was born, and SHE shaped the chaos into order."

Ylena was revealed amid water and flowers and light. The Priests did a good job directing the young Champions in the moment. Even if it wasn't as elaborate as her first Pageant, the stage still shone with everything she needed to reenact the Goddess's moment of creation.

Her hands moved, and structured gardens formed. She lifted her arms, and fountains of water sprang to life. She gestured, and birds took flight. Even though the tea stifled her own Gifts, she pretended these miracles were her own.

She thought she might have a hard time remembering, but every line, every song, every step was imprinted in her mind. Her body reacted without hesitation as her mind picked up and discarded ways to defeat the Wardens.

The girl from the school sang out:

"SHE gave them her magic to build and mend.

But the Goddess was still alone."

Ylena sang her line and waited for Wilder to come.

"Who in all creation is mighty enough to be my Companion?"

But instead of Wilder, Caed walked onstage.

Ylena shot a confused look at her grandfather but quickly schooled her face. He gave her a slight nod and the barest hint of a wink.

Caed approached her with the confident swagger required of a Companion to a Goddess, and he sang the words just for her but loud enough for the audience to hear.

"My Lady,

My heartbeat pulses with the rhythm of a fiery lute, and I will strum your spirit to life.

My fingers pluck the strings of a delicate harp, and I am gentle enough to awaken your soul.

My lips curve around tender notes of love, and I will breathe a new fire into your heart."

He put his hand on her waist, and warmth spread through her. She took his hand, and they waltzed as the chorus sang.

He twirled her around the stage in a flurry of skirts, and for a moment, she forgot all about the Wardens. She hadn't danced with him in so long, and she'd missed the confident way he held her. He spun her to a breathless stop and pulled her close to his chest as the other performers moved forward to dance.

His soft voice tingled against the back of her neck. "Don't blame your grandfather. I made him deliver me to the Wardens."

He was smart to say it while she faced the audience. That made it much harder for her to murder him.

He spun her around, and they danced to their next position. She could see by the twinkle in his eye that he knew she was furious with him. And that he also knew how relieved she was to have him by her side.

They finished the first act, then rushed backstage for a costume change. She could see a soldier waiting outside Caed's dressing room, just like her own. The Wardens had learned the lesson to monitor the performers to make sure they didn't wander off like Wilder had the first time.

She couldn't find time to speak to Caed until their break in Act Two. As they waited for their cue, Caed whispered in her ear, "So, are we really putting the tears into the basin? Are we prepared to give the Wardens that much power?"

Ylena twisted her finger through one of his many white-streaked waves. "We are pouring in as many tears as they have gathered. I won't allow any more Priests to die if I can stop it."

He nodded, and it was their cue to go back on stage.

Ylena danced with Caed and fell in love with him all over again. She remembered their first performance together. Even though the night had ended horribly, the time she spent dancing with him was the happiest moment of her life. They had each used their Gifts to tease and surprise the other, and the memory of their dance was lit with a golden glow in her mind.

During this Pageant, though, neither one of them could use their Gifts. She thought that their dancing might be boring or simple without them, but it was steady and strong. They couldn't rely on a breeze to twirl faster. Instead, they had to put in the effort required.

They poured the bowl of tears in together. Ylena looked at Caed's hair to see if it would immediately return to its dark sheen. Even after they changed into their costumes for Act Three, it was still streaked.

Ylena grabbed him by the arm. "Caed, please tell me you put your own tears in there."

"Of course I did," he said. "I might disagree with the entire system, but I don't have a death wish. I don't think the change is immediate, but I'm not sure. Usually, the only ones with white hair are the babies who stay at the temples. I don't know the timing."

Ylena bit her lip and brushed Caed's hair back from his brow. "I hoped the change would be immediate. Then I wouldn't feel guilty trying something so risky."

He narrowed his eyes. "Risky? Ylena, what are you planning?"

"I'm planning on putting on a show." She planted a firm kiss on his lips, then walked onto the stage for her solo.

45

———

Act Three began with Ylena in the dark. Every other time she sang this solo, she relied on her Gift to carry her voice through the amphitheater. She tried to remember that her voice was the same as it had been her entire life while being drugged by her grandfather. But without her Gift, her voice felt small.

She gathered up the warm, glowing core of memories within her heart and used it to power her song. When Caed joined her after her solo, she allowed her joy of dancing with him to fan the flame into a blaze. She took every drop of love and delight and crafted it into a bonfire burning in the night. Her song rang through the night without her Gift, carried purely on the wildfire in her chest.

She created a beacon. And when the time came, she was ready.

Act Three, Scene Four began with the Goddess kneeling over the fallen form of the Companion. She'd sung the beautiful, mournful song dozens of times, but she didn't truly understand it until she saw Lady Erenne's memory. The Pageant ended with the love of the Goddess lost.

That's not where it would end tonight.

256

Ylena and Caed started the scene in the dark. Caed lowered himself to the ground, but Ylena pulled him to her side.

"Will you let me lead this dance?" she whispered.

She could barely see his smile in the dark. "Of course. Your surprises always fascinate me."

She took his hand in hers and began her song.

The lights came up on her first note, but the orchestra whispered among themselves that she was singing the wrong song. Not a single person in the amphitheater had ever heard this song before.

The song of the Goddess and Companion's wedding.

The song in Ylena's vision was actually a duet with a full orchestra, but she didn't know how to teach Caed or the musicians their parts without sharing the vision. So, instead, she sang the solo a cappella, with the full wildfire burning in her chest.

The other performers were still as they listened. They knew their planned choreography, but the slow, melancholy moves didn't fit with the joyous melody she sang.

She risked a glance at the Wardens. They were confused, but instead of focusing on Ylena, they stared at the fumbling musicians. The Wardens weren't as familiar with the Pageant as everyone Upstairs, so they thought that the lack of music was the orchestra's fault, not hers.

Maestro should have been afraid, but he stared at Ylena in awe. One of the string players tapped his arm, and he finally turned to look at the Wardens. His eyes opened wide, and he turned back to the string player and whispered in her ear. Her lips turned up in a grin. She brought her violin to her chin and played a harmony to Ylena's song.

The other players slowly trickled in as they figured out their parts. Like most of the songs in the Pageant, the melody was direct and powerful. Very much like the

Companion himself. The orchestra grew stronger and stronger as they played.

Ylena repeated the chorus again, and the other singers around her filled in with harmony. She'd heard most of these students sing at the performing arts school, and they certainly knew their craft. She smiled as their song rang into the night.

She turned to Caed, who held her hand silently. He stared at her in wonder, like he had never truly noticed her before. His face was such pure delight, she nearly laughed with joy. He locked his gaze on hers like he would never let her go.

A tear landed on his cheek. She reached up to wipe it away, but he caught her hand and brought it to his lips. He brushed her knuckles with a kiss, and as he lowered her hand, he grabbed the notes of her song. He wrapped the notes in a breeze, and the song flew away from the City. The melody curled itself around the lonely mountain of the Goddess, seeking her ears.

Ylena gasped as she realized what he was doing. She studied his hair and found another white streak among the dark locks. He caught hold of her eyes and added his song to hers.

His song differed from what the Companion wrote, but it was like Caed—brooding and playful, thoughtful and daring. His song wrapped around her heart and spread its roots through her body until a flower garden bloomed in her veins.

He brushed his thumb across the tear on her cheek.

Her Gifts leaped in response.

Her song intertwined with his until they were one. She grabbed hold of the orchestra's accompaniment and the fullness of the choir. She took every note she could find, wrapped it all up in a whirlwind, and hurled the song at the mountain.

She felt it travel through the City, rattling windows and shaking buildings. It burst over the City wall and hit the mountain with a roar. The notes spilled over and around and up until the melody coated the mountain. The song didn't diminish as it hit the stone. It grew stronger.

The wedding song traveled through every crevice and cave and cavern until the entire mountain pulsed with its rhythm.

The Goddess appeared at center stage.

She was stunning. Gone were her ragged sweaters, and she stood in a simple, white, long-sleeved dress that trailed the ground. Her warm brown skin glowed faintly under the lights of the stage, and her chestnut hair fell in soft waves down her back. Though Ylena dressed for the part, there was no denying who was the true Goddess.

The musicians cut off and stared in silence. Some people fell to their knees. Some ran. The Wardens stood from their thrones and watched in outrage.

The Goddess studied Ylena with narrowed eyes. "As usual, Ylena, you are far too clever for your own good." Her words were angry, but Ylena could see the tears shining on her cheeks.

"It's time to fix this," said Ylena. "I would like your help."

The Goddess looked at the Wardens gathering up the Gifted children to attack. "I already told you. I won't hurt them. Any of them."

"I'll handle them. What I need from you is something only a Goddess can give." Ylena's voice dropped to an urgent whisper. "Give them a sign."

"A sign?"

Ylena stepped closer to her. "The people in the City and the Underneath are waiting for their cue to band together to fight. You don't have to hurt any of your people. Just bring them together." Her voice dropped to a low growl. "Do something that proves you haven't forsaken them. I don't care what you do, but make it big. Can you do that?"

The Goddess studied Ylena, and the fire that had been missing rekindled in her eyes. "Child, you aren't the only one who knows how to put on a show."

She looked out into the City and disappeared.

The Wardens' attack faltered as they looked around wildly for the missing Goddess. Soldiers shuffled nervously, unsure who or what they should fight.

The Goddess reappeared at the top of the white cliffs at the back of the amphitheater. She pointed at the stone at her feet and spun in a slow circle. Stone swirled in waves around her, and crystalline flowed up to the surface until she stood in the middle of a bright circle of light.

She turned to face Temple Order and held up her hand, palm outward. For a moment, there was nothing. Then, every stone building in the City *rippled.*

Ylena sensed through the framework of stone mapped in her mind what the Goddess created. A hole opened in the middle of one of the wide streets outside Temple Order until the people below would see the night sky shining through. The stone bedrock between the City and Underneath flowed at her command, melting into a giant stone bridge connecting above and below. White stone flowed in graceful curves until the bridge hardened, forever connecting the City and Underneath.

The Goddess turned toward Temple Purity and raised her palm.

The Wardens didn't have the Gift of Purpose to sense what the Goddess did, although a few Gifted children looked up at her with stunned expressions on their face. The Priests stared at the Goddess in awe. Some were openly weeping, and Ylena trembled with the realization of how white their hair had turned.

The Wardens looked between Ylena and Caed on stage and the woman glowing like a beacon high on the cliffs and chose the most threatening target.

The Warden of Rivalry pointed at the Goddess. "Get her!"

46

—————

S oldiers and the young Champions shook themselves from their daze and looked to their individual Wardens for directions. The Warden of Rivalry signaled two of her soldiers to guard Ylena and Caed while the child Champions focused on the Goddess.

Ylena realized the Wardens didn't know that she had her Gifts back. They thought the tea had worked, that she would be easy to contain.

She would enjoy proving them wrong.

The guards strode confidently to subdue them, and Ylena braced for attack. The Warden of Delirium signaled one of her guards, who stepped to Grandfather's side with sword drawn.

Ylena sucked in a breath and relaxed her stance. Her eyes flicked between and Caed and Grandfather.

She reached for Caed's hand, and he turned to her with a fierce look. "You better not even think of blinking me out of here," he growled.

She snapped her mouth shut, not wanting to admit that's exactly what she had considered.

The Wardens yelled at the children to stop the Goddess.

Some children stood frozen in fear, but others complied. Unlike Ylena, the Champions had to touch vine or water to use their Gift, so groups of children sprinted into position. An older teen girl grabbed a vine on the edge of the stage and sent it racing through the amphitheater to the Goddess high on the cliff. A young boy plunged his arms into a stream on stage, and water poured in a steady river along the stone benches toward the Goddess.

The vines and water sizzled as they touched the glowing crystalline barrier she constructed. She turned toward Knowledge with an outstretched palm as she continued reshaping the City.

Three fierce, young girls raised their hands, and wind gathered around their palms. They pulled their arms back and then flung the wind up at the Goddess. The crystalline couldn't stop the wind. Her long hair blew wildly around her face, and the trailing sleeves of her dress flapped against her outstretched arm.

But the Goddess's feet remained firmly set against the stone cliffs.

A skinny boy with bright blond hair sank to his knees and pressed a palm against the stone floor. A ripple of stone shuddered along the stone benches and slid up the stone cliff where she stood. Stone melted and reformed, and the crystalline shifted in response. The glowing crystalline circle at the Goddess's feet flowed away, and she stood unprotected.

A vine curled up her leg, and she flinched.

The Priests reacted.

A golden-haired Priest straightened her spine and raised her hands. A storm flowed from her flexed fingers and formed a wind tunnel around the Goddess. The children's wind couldn't compete against the older woman's strength. A limping Priest clapped his hand to the vine that trailed through the theater. It uncurled from the Goddess's ankle and grew in a sprawling pattern around her. Flowers bloomed in a wild array of colors, standing out in bright contrast to the Goddess's white dress. The flowers weren't necessary. It was simply beautiful.

It was worship.

Priests redirected the wind and water and held the stone in place. They countered every move by the children until the Goddess stood ringed in a flower garden, blowing with wind and water.

The golden-haired Priest's hair turned completely white. She staggered and fell.

Ylena screamed. She had to stop them, but she couldn't fight them all, not without hurting children and not without risking her grandfather. She needed to end it.

She grabbed Caed's hand and spoke to him with Knowledge.

"I'm about to use my Gifts in some unconventional ways. Are you prepared for that?"

His eyes widened in confusion, and he looked down at her hand in his.

She frowned. *"I guess this isn't the way Priests traditionally use this Gift?"*

A smile formed on his lips, and he shook his head.

"Are you ready to trust me again?"

His eyes blazed with faith and desire in equal measure.

She grinned. *"I'm glad to see that."*

She blinked another tear from her eyes and let her power sink into him.

Her thoughts raced through his body, healing every ache and scratch. His white-streaked hair was beyond her touch, but she healed every other weakness she could find. She used the Priests' trick of creating youthful appearances and took it a step farther. She breathed life and energy into every inch of his body until he was practically bursting with vitality.

He gasped with the rush of power. Neither Caed nor Ylena uttered a single word, but the guard at his side shifted his stance at their strange behavior.

Caed whispered, "Wow." He tilted his head, cracking his neck bones into place as the enhanced strength settled into him.

She focused her thoughts on him again. "*I know you don't want to leave me, but I can't bear to lose Grandfather here like I lost Pim. Please get him out of here.*"

He must have seen the terror on her face, because he nodded.

"*I'll send you directly behind the guard at Grandfather's back. You will only have moments to get him away before I put an end to all this.*"

In his face, she saw his love and fear for her written clearly. A tear trailed down his cheek, and she narrowed her eyes. She sent a warm breeze to brush it away with a gentle caress. "*I'll take this with me. I don't trust you not to use it.*"

His eyes were intense, and he nodded that he was ready.

She sent him directly behind the guard at Grandfather's side but didn't have time to watch them escape. She had to trust Caed and focus on her own task.

The two guards at her side were still blinking in shock, wondering where Caed went, when she grabbed them both by the hand and sent them outside the amphitheater. Alone at center stage, she focused on the scene in the audience. Children stood with hands raised against the Goddess, and Priests trembled as they tried to hold them back. Some of the younger children were so frightened by the chaos that they stood frozen. The Warden of Chaos slapped a young girl until she fell against one of the stone benches. Her tears flowed, and the bench melted beneath her hands.

Ylena roared in fury. She outstretched her hands and gathered every scrap of wind swirling in the amphitheater. The wind raced through the crowd, blowing hair and clothing and sending icy drafts down spines. The Wardens struggled to stand in the strong wind, but they didn't know its source.

Next, she collected each stream and fountain, stealing it out of the hands of child and Priest alike. She pulled every drop of water in the amphitheater until it floated in a shimmering lake in the night sky.

The whirlwind surged below the shining disc, two forces narrowly balanced. She clapped her hands together, and they collided.

Wind and water blended into fog and mist and rain. The storm raged throughout the amphitheater, except for a dry patch of sky surrounding Ylena. She raised her arms above her head, carefully moving wrists and fingers until the wind followed a pattern that was only known to her. Priests and children with Gifts would see no better than anyone else.

She desperately hoped Caed and Grandfather had already escaped.

Her circle of clear sky followed her as she walked to the edge of the stage. She placed her hands on the crystal basin and called, "Nelson!"

"Hi, Ylena." He appeared inside her dry space. His voice was calm, as if he wasn't standing in the middle of a hurricane.

"Remember how you asked if you could help fix things? I know what you can do."

He grinned, and she could still see the boy inside the grown man with a beard.

She looked directly into his eyes, dark as the night. "Take it back. Take all the Gifts back. Mine and everyone else's. Right now."

He lifted his head and looked around the City. "All of them?"

She could hear Wardens screaming at the children in the storm.

Ylena grabbed hold of his arm. "All of them. Now!"

Nelson took a deep breath in and closed his eyes. His face was peaceful, like he breathed in the cool air of the mountain. He opened his eyes.

Ylena's storm hovered for one more moment, then crashed to the ground in a flood.

The Wardens screamed at the children to fight, but they only stared at their small hands in confusion. The Priests fell to their knees and sank onto the stone benches, their mouths open in shock. Each Priests' hair had returned to its original color, except for the fake streak of white still in Ylena's hair. The Priests turned their attention one by one up to the cliffs to seek an answer, but they found none.

The Goddess was gone.

47

The Wardens quickly realized they had lost their biggest advantage, so they scrambled to mobilize their soldiers. Without the Goddess to distract them, their attention turned fully to Ylena. Without her Gifts, she was defenseless. She wasn't a match for even a single trained fighter, and the Wardens had dozens. Her eyes searched for a way to escape when she heard a scream.

Charging down the aisles of benches were dozens of fighters from the City and Underneath. At their head was Wilder. His white wolves grabbed hold of a soldier and pulled him to the ground. Tayeh battled two soldiers in a storm of movement. Rose had two blades in her hands as she fought a soldier, and Rev and Quinn teamed up to fight another.

The children still stared at their hands in shock. A little girl started crying with a confused look on her face. The Priests were still in a daze, but when they saw the children in the middle of the battle, they leaped into action. Priests grabbed hold of children's hands, gathered them up into their arms, and shuffled through the pockets of fighting.

Ylena reached for her Gifts, but the emptiness inside

was different than the effects of the tea. Her Gifts weren't just slowed. They were gone.

Screams and clashing weapons echoed across the stone. She scanned her eyes around the amphitheater for Caed and her grandfather. Caed must have him, but she didn't know where. Men and women from the Underneath and Upstairs fought together side by side. They swarmed the soldiers with their overwhelming numbers, and every soldier brought down was a weapon gained.

Without her Gifts or any fighting skill, she felt useless as she stood alone on stage. The Wardens summoned their remaining soldiers to their side, and they fought in a shrinking circle near their thrones in the front row.

But she only saw six Wardens.

"Ylena! Call them off!" the Warden of Delirium yelled at her from backstage. Ylena turned around to find the Warden walking across the stage with a knife pressed to her grandfather's neck. "Call off your fighters! Do it now!"

"No! Don't do it!" Grandfather's voice was fierce. "This is the revolution I wanted, Ylena! Win it!"

Caed held a sword and fought two soldiers backstage, but his eyes flicked to her grandfather with concern.

The hurricane had soaked the Warden, and her auburn hair dripped water in her wild eyes. Ylena knew her grandfather would die if she didn't call off the fighters. She didn't even know if they would listen to her, but she opened her mouth to yell.

Her grandfather pulled away from the Warden, and her blade slid across his neck.

He dropped to the ground as Caed tackled the Warden.

Ylena ran to her grandfather's side. Blood poured from his throat onto the wooden stage. She pressed her hand against the wound, but blood continued to stream.

"No, no, no ... Hold on, Grandfather! Maybe someone

still has their Gift! Maybe ..." His eyes glossed over. "No, I won't let this happen!"

Ylena screamed at the sky, and angry tears poured down her cheeks. Her scream echoed through the amphitheater and reverberated throughout the City. She reached inside for her missing Gifts. Nothing stirred. The Gifts given by the City were gone.

Too many lives had ended in this amphitheater. She would not allow another death.

She found the empty place inside and reached beyond.

She dove into the Abyss within and swam so deep her lungs burned. Time slowed around her, but she clawed and pulled and tore until she reached the space beneath.

She found the place beyond the stars and beyond time ...

The bright, glowing core at the center of all things...

She stretched out a trembling hand and brushed her fingers along the very edge ...

Her parents reunited in an embrace.

Pim laughed with face turned to the sun.

The fallen Priests sang as flower petals floated on the wind.

She awoke with a gasp.

The Gifts came from the City, but her Spark ran deeper than that. And with her Spark, she was alive.

Flesh re-knit itself beneath her hands. Grandfather stirred, and the glimmer of life returned to his eyes.

"Ylena," he breathed in a ragged voice.

"Shh ... Don't try to speak yet."

He reached a shaking hand up to her cheek. "I've always been proud of you, Ylena. And your mother would be proud, too."

Ylena choked on a sob.

"Go finish the fight," he said. "I'll be fine."

Ylena hesitated to leave him, but Quinn kneeled down beside him. "I'll look after him. Do what you need to do."

Caed had disabled the Warden of Delirium, and Rev kneeled on her back, tying her arms with a thick rope. Caed's eyes caught on Ylena in panic.

She looked down at her blood-soaked white dress. "It's not mine." She wanted to touch him, but her hands were still covered in blood.

He ignored the blood and pulled her firmly to his chest. "I thought ..." His words were a breath against her neck. "Oh, Ylena ..."

A cheer went up from the front row at the Wardens' defeat, but Ylena only cared about Caed's arms wrapped around her. The world narrowed until it was just the two of them standing center stage.

"Thank you for protecting him," she said. She could still sense the heightened vitality she had Gifted him running through his veins, but he was also covered in bruises and cuts from his fight with the soldiers.

"You're the one who saved his life." He brushed her white lock of hair behind her ear. "Even though I don't know how. I felt when my Gift left me. I was so disoriented that the Warden slipped past me."

His hair had returned to its original ebony waves. She swallowed down her guilt that Nelson had taken the Gifts from Caed and every other Priest but she'd regained hers.

He pulled her closer. "Don't blame yourself. I told you I would sacrifice my Gift to see this City change." He looked at the people from the City and Underneath working together to tie up the Wardens and lead them away. "And you did it. You changed everything, Ylena."

She wondered how the City and Underneath would adjust to the bridges now connecting above and below. There were people seeing stars for the very first time at this moment. And without Gifts, no one could destroy the bridges the Goddess had created. They would forever be joined. The City would never be the same.

"What's going to happen now that there are no High Priests or Wardens to lead?" she asked.

"I don't know." His eyes softened and trailed across her lips. "But I can't wait to discover it by your side."

She relaxed into his embrace. His lips met hers, and her Spark sang like a symphony in her blood. She sent healing and vitality through his veins until his heartbeat thudded against her chest as loud as thunder.

Her lips curled in a playful smile. "Don't expect that to happen every time we kiss."

His voice was breathless, but his eyes were completely serious. "It always feels like that when we kiss, Ylena. Always."

She pulled him into another kiss—in a crowd of people, but alone at center stage.

Beyond

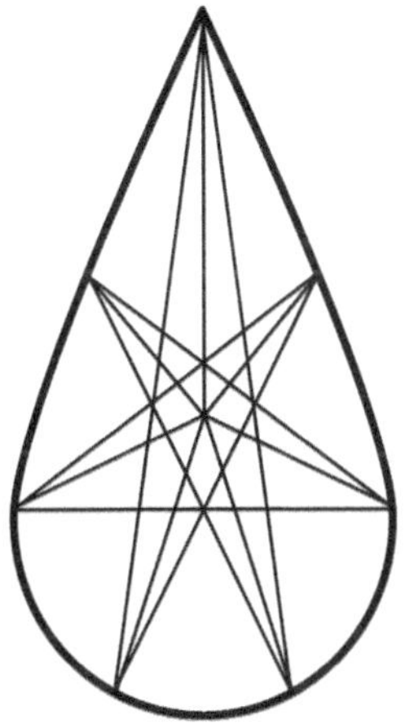

48

Ylena and Caed were the only two left in the amphitheater. People from the City and the Underneath had led the Wardens away and cared for the injured. Now, only one thing remained.

Ylena touched the crystal and called for the Companion.

He appeared next to her. "Hi, Ylena."

"Hi, Nelson. Thanks for your help earlier."

"Is everything fixed?"

"There's just one more thing. I'd like for you to perform for us."

"Really?" Ylena saw the cocky grin of the Director shine through. "You like my voice?"

"Yes, I do. Do you know the wedding song from the Pageant?"

He tilted his head and closed his eyes. "Hmm ... Is that the song still floating through the air?"

Ylena closed her eyes and listened. "Yes, I guess it is. You go ahead. I'm going to sit here and listen." She sat down beside Caed in a throne that belonged to no one.

Nelson hopped onto the stage like an expert and began to sing.

His voice was warm and strong and filled the amphitheater. Ylena settled back on the throne to watch.

Caed took her hand. "Ylena ... what if it's not really him? What if he never remembers?"

Ylena looked at him with clear eyes. "It's him, Caed ... It's him."

Caed took a deep breath and nodded once.

Nelson's voice continued to wind its way through the amphitheater. Ylena sought the same place she found when she healed her grandfather, gathered his voice inside a breeze, and sent it seeking through the City.

There were no reports of the Goddess since she had formed the final stairway connecting the Underneath to Upstairs, but Ylena had a feeling she was still in the City. And Ylena was determined to find her.

She sent the breeze with Nelson's voice twisting down every street and alley. It crawled through cracks in windows and under doorways. His voice crept into every house and shop and storage room and closet until there was nowhere in the City to hide from the song.

The Goddess appeared.

She stood on the stage next to Nelson, looking defeated. Shoulders stooped and head bowed, she refused to look him in the eyes.

Nelson stopped his song. His eyes never left the woman before him as he said to Ylena, "You found her." He took a step closer and addressed the Goddess. "I know you ... You're the Goddess."

Tears leaked from her downcast eyes. "I'm not a goddess."

He took another step and raised a trembling hand to her cheek. "You're right ... You're *my* Goddess. Erenne." Her eyes met his, and he mouthed another word so quietly Ylena couldn't hear.

She sucked in her breath in a sob. "Nelson?"

He pulled her into his arms and kissed her with a desperate fury. Her hands grasped his back, and she clung to him like she was drowning. He ran his hands through her hair and traced the line of her neck as if to remember her shape.

She pulled back from him with a gasp. "How?"

He shrugged. "I'm not sure."

She rubbed her fingers against his beard. "You're back to the beard?"

"I know you liked it." He gave her a smug smile.

Her lips curved. "Of course I liked it. Without the beard, it looks like I'm married to a child."

He smirked and pulled her close. "I'm definitely not a child."

Ylena coughed politely.

Lady Erenne pulled her eyes away from Nelson to study Ylena standing at the foot of the stage. "How did you do this?"

"I was hoping you could tell me."

Lady Erenne chuckled. "Well, you clearly have more Gifts than any I ever bestowed." She clutched Nelson's hand, and they both walked to the edge of the stage. He hopped to the ground and then grabbed her by the waist to set her gently on her feet.

She turned to Ylena with kind eyes. "Not only did you bring Nelson back to life, but you brought me back from the darkness as well. In case I don't see you again, I want to say thank you." She grabbed Nelson's hand again and walked toward the basin.

"Wait!" Ylena ran to their side. "In case you don't see me again? Where are you going? You can't leave the City now!"

She smiled and grasped Nelson's hand tighter. "I'm never leaving the City again."

"But I have so many questions!" She stepped closer to Lady Erenne and dropped her voice to a whisper. "My Gifts are beyond what the Priests have. Does that mean I'm like you? Am I ... a goddess?"

Lady Erenne grinned. "Do you want to be a goddess?"

Ylena looked at her with wide eyes. "I don't even know what that means. What are we? Is all of this because of a Spark?"

Lady Erenne seemed impressed that she knew the word. "My Spark is the ability to replicate the Spark of anyone else I meet. I suspect yours is similar."

"But where does the Spark come from? Why do we have it?"

"That's a long story. You'd have to travel to the Origin to ask the prophets. They are much smarter than I am."

Caed stood silently during their conversation, but at this, his eyes lit with hungry fascination. "The Origin? Prophets? You can't throw out words like that and not explain."

Lady Erenne smirked. "Intrigued by a new mystery, Caed? The Origin was our home before we arrived here. It was a dangerous place, so we escaped." She looked around at the amphitheater damaged in battle and sighed. "We couldn't escape ourselves, though." She pulled herself up taller. "I can't thank you enough for bringing Nelson back to me, but I can give you a small gift." She reached for them, and Ylena and Caed each took a hand.

Images shot through Ylena's mind. Mountains ... snow ... a treacherous pass ... water ... water for days ... The path to the Origin laid itself out precisely in her mind. Her thoughts screamed in protest at the new information crashing down. The world was so much bigger than she imagined.

And at the end of the avalanche of images, an unfamiliar sensation raced through her veins. It was like being healed.

Except instead of a cold splash of water, it felt like a lightning strike to each drop of her blood.

She and Caed snatched their hands back from Lady Erenne with a gasp.

Lady Erenne chuckled. "Tingles a bit? Just a little Spark I picked up from our friend Walter. It doesn't fix everything, so please, try to avoid ladders." She gently elbowed Nelson in the ribs, and he laughed.

"Walter? Where is he?" asked Ylena.

"He's safe. Two hundred years ago, the High Priests tricked him into extending their lives. I rescued him from their prison and hid him inside the same healing center I called home for a time. Fortunately for both of us, the High Priests avoided the healing centers and the 'imperfect' people inside. But I think it's best if he remains hidden for now, so I found a new place for him to live."

Caed studied his hand, and Ylena thought it must sting like hers did. "That's all out there? Another world beyond the City?"

She looked at him with maternal eyes. "Yes. That and so much more. There is beauty to rival the Shining City, with danger and violence to match." She looked at the blood that still stained the floor of the amphitheater and frowned. "I wanted the City to be a place of refuge. I turned out to be a very poor goddess."

Caed smiled warmly. "I've never worshipped you, Erenne, but I'm glad to call you a friend."

Her face lit up. "Likewise, Caed."

"And that's how you created this City? You saw someone else do something like this, and it became part of your Spark?"

Lady Erenne faced one of the purple, glowing spires, but her eyes unfocused as she looked within. "I didn't create this

City with a Spark. In my grief, I drew from a deeper source. It was ... something else. Something ... beyond."

Ylena whispered, "Beyond the stars and beyond time."

Lady Erenne's eyes snapped back into focus. "Exactly. You understand."

Ylena frowned. "Not exactly. It's something my mother believed. It's why she believed she would see my father again. I felt it when I healed my grandfather."

She smiled. "Perhaps you are a goddess after all."

She took Nelson's hand and walked to the crystal basin. They raised their outer hands to the crystal as one.

Lady Erenne spared one more look for Ylena. "And while I appreciate you remedying the problem of children with Gifts, you don't get to take them away from everyone. I'll decide who gets them from now on." She turned loving eyes on Nelson. "This City is mine."

They touched their hands to the basin, and every crystal in the City flared to a bright white. Ylena and Caed covered their eyes with their hands. When they could blink their eyes open, the crystals had settled into a soft, white glow, and the Goddess and Companion were gone.

49

———

Ylena sipped her coffee with a smile as her friends bickered noisily in a cozy coffee shop in Order Diocese. During the week following the battle, the crew had grown to include Caed and Rose, so their group of seven took up most of the furniture and made the little shop feel full. Caed and Ylena sat snuggled together on a love seat, and Tayeh relaxed as she leaned back in a wooden chair. Rose looked uncomfortable wedged between Quinn and Rev on the other couch, with Wilder lounging along the back, his wolves on the ground by his feet.

"I'm just saying that they should take more weapons," said Tayeh.

Rev frowned. "They have plenty of weapons. What they need is more warm clothing. They can fight off any wild animals with Ylena's ... skills. But they don't have any defense against the freezing temperatures."

Caed leaned forward. "Ylena knows how to survive in the mountains. We won't freeze to death."

"He's right," said Wilder. There were a few raised eyebrows at hearing Wilder agree with Caed. He continued in a lazy drawl. "It's not the cold that will kill him. It's the cardio."

Caed gave him a flat look. "My stamina is more than sufficient."

"I think you are both idiots," said Rose. "Why would you risk your lives by going on this ridiculous expedition?"

"For Knowledge," said Quinn dreamily. "Imagine the new things they will learn." He sighed. "I wish I could go, too."

Rev reached across Rose to give him a comforting pat on the knee. Rose scowled at the invasion.

"We'll come back." Ylena smiled at Quinn. "And we'll bring books when we return."

"I almost forgot!" Quinn pulled a small notebook from his pocket and handed it to Ylena. "It's a few of the words and phrases I translated from the old languages. I don't know what language they will speak where you are going, but maybe it will help."

"Thanks, Quinn. You are very considerate." Ylena put it in her backpack next to her father's sketchbook and her mother's letter.

"It still doesn't make sense," said Rose. "Ylena, you are the only person in this City that still has a Gift. How can you leave the rest of us to rebuild the City ourselves?"

Tayeh gave her a flat look. "They are going on a quest to discover a world that was so deadly the founders of the City escaped and purposely forgot all knowledge of the place. They will cross deadly terrain and have to count on each other to survive."

Rose huffed in exasperation. "Exactly! Why would they do that?"

Tayeh groaned. "Because it's Goddess-damn romantic, okay?"

Rose rolled her eyes.

"You aren't alone here, Rose," said Ylena. "The Goddess is still here ... somewhere. She said she would return her Gifts to whom she chose. She claimed the City for her own. I believe her when she says she will never leave again."

Caed stood. "It's time for us to go." He held his hand out to Ylena. "Are you ready?"

Her heart skipped a beat as she took his hand and stood. "I can't wait to go on an adventure with you."

Rose muttered, "The cold won't kill you. It will be the wild animals sneaking up on you when you spend all your time making out."

Wilder sat up on the edge of the couch to study Rose. "You really are a feisty one, aren't you?"

Rose puffed up her shoulders. "So what? You can't handle a feisty woman?"

Wilder smirked. "I can definitely handle a feisty woman. I'll show you anytime."

Rose's mouth dropped open.

Ylena covered her grin with her hand. She wondered if anyone had ever spoken to Rose that way before. There was something about their interaction that made Ylena happy. She enjoyed seeing Rose flustered, but more than that, she hadn't seen Wilder's flirty smile for some time. Seeing it directed at someone else pleased her more than she expected.

Tears and final goodbyes followed. Ylena hugged everyone, including Wilder, but they cut the embrace short thanks to the two white wolves growling at his heels. Rev agreed to check in on Ylena's grandfather from time to time. Ylena knew he was self-sufficient, but she relaxed knowing that someone as kind and as bossy as Rev would watch out for him.

Once there were no words left to say, Caed and Ylena picked up their packs and left the coffee shop alone. They headed to the edge of Order Diocese and soon arrived at the same gate in the wall that Ylena entered on her first day in the City.

She hesitated before opening the gate. "What do you think we will find out there?"

"I have no idea." His eyes were bright with anticipation. "It's thrilling."

She took comfort from his enthusiasm. "You're not worried about what we will find?"

He brushed her white lock of hair behind her ears. "I was a bad Priest because the simple answers the other Priests gave never satisfied me. The stories say it is chaos out there, and it might be. But I want to see it myself. I want to *know,* not just believe." His voice was low and just for her. "If you are having second thoughts about leaving, we don't have to go."

Tears prickled on her lashes at the thought that he would give up the answers he desperately wanted for her. She shook her head. "I have to know where it all began. I want to know what it means to have a Spark. And there is no one I would rather go on this adventure with than you."

He pulled her into an embrace made awkward by their bulky packs. As his soft lips pressed against hers, a warm breeze twirled around them, ruffling hair and tickling skin. Her tears dried in the wind, and the breeze settled into a warm cloak around their shoulders.

Ylena opened the gate and took his hand. "Let's go see what lies beyond."

ACKNOWLEDGMENTS

Some people spend years researching topics to write about. I have never enjoyed research, so I have no choice but to let the strange inner workings of my mind carry the load instead.

So I write what I know.

I know that music can enchant and dance can heal. I know about powerful women and men strong enough to love them. My books overflow with faith and devotion and dark nights of the soul.

And sprinkled on top will be coffee, curry, and cats.

People die and suffer from mental illness, but running through the center is a common thread.

Love, Magic, and Happily Ever After.

Thank you to my friends and family who have supported me through a lifetime of this type of "research." I have had more cheerleaders on this journey than I deserve. Without your encouragement, I never would have put my fanciful ideas onto the page.

To all the authors whose books I have devoured through my lifetime, thanks for creating a mental playground for me to process the beauty and terror of the real world. I will never stop reading, but now I'm ready to contribute.

And to those of you drowning in despair, you are not alone. Find a healing center. Seek your crew. Tread water until the storm passes, and you can catch your breath. Your story is not over yet.

Keep writing.

Sign up for the newsletter, discover more books, quizzes, and extras at www.susannahwelch.com.

ABOUT THE AUTHOR

Susannah Welch lives in sunny South Florida with her brilliant husband and a magically hypoallergenic cat. She enjoys singing and dancing and showing off. She likes her stories with a little bit of drama, and a whole lot of sparkle.

facebook.com/susannah.welch.author
instagram.com/susannahwelchauthor

DUCKETT & DYER

The Mystery of the Murdered Guy

ISBN: 978-1-7338943-8-8
PI: 3.14159265358979323842. . .

10 9 8 7 6 5 4 3 2 1

For Trudy, who let me use her likeness with implied consent

DUCKETT & DYER

The Mystery of the Murdered Guy

TABLE OF CONTENTS

THE STRANGE LITTLE LIFE OF ADRIAN PANCAKE

Adrian Pancake had no idea what happened.

One moment, he was setting up clever chalkboard art outside his bar. The next, he was waking up in the Armitage Pembroke Bodily Reconstruction wing of City Presbyterian in a full body cast, with his arms and legs strung up in a complicated pulley system. The two doctors hovering over him tried to catch Adrian up on things. They talked about The Future Group and a giant monster—*Krobu* or *Korthuu* or something—and then they said something about it fighting a flying octopus, which is where he really got lost.

What Adrian *did* understand was that he had been directly in the path of a piece of falling debris and was "very lucky to be alive." Of course, the doctors didn't hesitate to tell him he'd pretty much been flattened.

Like a pancake.

Adrian tried to sigh, but his ribs hurt so much it came out as a half-snort half-wheeze. Even though most of his bones had been shattered and his body damaged beyond all reasonable repair, they had been obligated to make the joke. After suggesting his only way forward was months of bed rest, an intensive regimen of physical therapy, and a frightening abundance of painkillers, the two doctors left him to his limited devices.

One thing was for sure: life would never be the same for Adrian Pancake. He'd be lucky if he ever lifted a pinky again. Hell, who knew if he'd even be sane after months in a full body cast with only eye-holes cut out. Adrian never thought he'd miss his old, boring life, but here he was, wishing he was back washing down the bar and slinging whiskey to strangers before slinking back to his crappy apartment at 4am. It wasn't anything special, but it was sure as hell better than this.

Maybe his family would come to see him. His friends. Co-workers from the bar. Hopefully, they knew he was still alive. Although, Adrian couldn't bear the thought of his mom weeping at his bedside while his limbs stuck out in front of him like a shitty, inanimate mummy.

He could have spent a few more hours lamenting the loss of his old life. Instead, Adrian decided to lapse into unconsciousness.

He awoke a short while later. Or a long while later. He didn't really know. A clock ticked on his bedside table, but he couldn't move his neck—or anything—to see. But it was dark now. Nighttime. He couldn't rule out having slipped into a coma. It could have been days, weeks, or months since the doctors visited. His condition hadn't improved, though, so it couldn't have been too long.

To maintain his sanity, Adrian scanned the room, locking onto identifiable objects in the dim light and saying their names in his head.

Door.

Plant. Fern.

Chair.

Chairs.

TV. Television.

Shadow Demon.

Window.

IV Drip Stand.

Wait. What was that last one?

Oh, yeah. Window.

* * *

The next time Adrian awoke, it was still night. But this time, he was sure it was a different night. For one, a cast no longer covered his chest and it no longer hurt to breathe. His ribs had somehow healed, but his arms and legs were still stiff and suspended. How long had he been asleep? Adrian tried to look at his bedside clock, but his head was securely bandaged, a thick plastic brace preventing him from moving his neck. But his face was free! Adrian relished the feel of the bland hospital air on his skin. Smacking his lips, he practiced a few lines of *Don't Stop Believing*—a karaoke favorite at the bar. He sounded terrible, but it was nice to hear his own voice again, rough-hewn as it was.

Knock knock.

Adrian's eyes darted to the hospital room door. He could see the distorted shadow of a man through the glass but couldn't place the silhouette.

Knock knock. Again, the man rapped on the door.

"Uh. . . come in?"

"Good evening, Mr. Pancake. How are we feeling tonight?" The door creaked open and a rich voice full of glee lilted its way through, followed by a man so tall and slender, he looked like the victim of a surprise taffy pull.

"Doing. . . just fine, I think." Adrian couldn't make heads or tails of who this person was. A doctor, clearly. But not one of his doctors. He was bald and pale, with a slight hunch to his back.

"Good, good!" With a smile as sharp as the rest of his features, the man hiked up the sleeves of his white coat. "That's what I like to hear."

"Excuse me, but who are you?"

"I'm Dr. Keene." As if to prove it, the man materialized a stethoscope in his hand and pressed it to Adrian's newly freed chest, nodding along to the *lubs* and the *dubs*. "Oh, fantastic. Fantastic!"

"I'm sorry, but I thought Doctor"—he reached into his memory for their names, but found it harder than usual to retrieve them—"Lee and Dr. Perrins were going to be taking care of me."

"Oh, I wouldn't worry about them. They have a large caseload, and asked me to fill in on your situation. I am a total body reconstruction specialist, and I just happened to be doing a visiting residency. You're quite lucky, you see. I'm the reason your ribcage is no longer shattered."

"Uh. . . huh," Adrian squinted as Dr. Keene shone a small penlight into his eyes. "So what should I expect in terms of physical therapy?"

"You are doing fantastic without it, I'd say!" Doctor Keene grinned.

"No PT?" Adrian looked at his arms and legs, still encased in plaster.

"Yes! Barring any . . . unfortunate circumstances, you'll just need a few more weeks' bed rest. Wouldn't that be nice?"

"Well, yeah," Adrian would love to be back to normal that quickly, especially since PT would've been hell on his wallet. He wasn't sure his insurance covered it. He wasn't even sure if he had insurance anymore. Had anyone called his bar? "Uh, Dr. Keene?"

"Oh, no more out of you. It's settled. Rest up, and we'll see you through this yet!" The smile never left Dr. Keene's face as he waltzed through the door from whence he came. Adrian hoped the ticking of his clock would help put him back to sleep, but he couldn't hear it anymore.

The batteries must've run out.

* * *

"Wow, you seem to be making a speedy recovery!" the large nurse beamed as she opened the curtains, letting a torrent of afternoon sunlight into the room. "I remember when you came in. It was like you'd been flattened like—"

"A pancake, yes." Adrian squinted in the new light, raising his one healed hand in front of his eyes to shield them. A few days ago, he awoke to a cast-less left arm, though everything else was still immobilized. He hadn't remembered Dr. Keene taking him into surgery, but he must have. Either way, he wasn't complaining. That guy was a miracle worker!

"Oh, I'm sorry." The nurse covered a giggle with her hand. A dark birthmark on her thumb gave her a temporary Hitler mustache. "Flattened like a pancake. You must get that a lot. Annoying, right?"

"Well, it's not every day I get my body crushed, so luckily, I've only had to deal with it for two weeks," Adrian lied. He had his share of middle and high school bullies who put that insult into very good practice.

"I suppose so," the nurse chuckled as she began to make her exit. "Well, if you don't need anything further, I've got a few other patients to check before my shift ends."

"Oh," Adrian said. "If you see Dr. Keene around, tell him I'm feeling much better already! He hasn't stopped by in a while."

"Dr. Keene?" she cocked her head.

"Yeah. Tall guy? Rail thin? Bald?"

"I don't know a Dr. Keene. Does he work on this floor?"

"He should. I saw him last Tuesday night."

"Oh, he might be on the night shift. I don't usually mess with this place after 6pm." She offered a sweet smile. "Kinda gets spooky, y'know?"

"I'm sure it does."

"You enjoy your nap, now!"

And she was gone.

Adrian placed his one working arm—still a bit sore—behind his head, while the other remained strung up. It wasn't the most comfortable position, especially with his head and neck still forcibly secured, but he had to hand it to Dr. Keene. He felt much better. Before Adrian drifted off to sleep and dreams of going home, he realized he should have asked the nurse what day it was. For some reason, he couldn't remember.

* * *

The rapid beat of frantic footsteps woke Adrian. It wasn't quite night, but the afternoon had passed Adrian by, leaving the red and purple fire of sundown streaming through his window. The runner pattered down the hall outside. The footfalls increased in volume and frequency as they drew closer to his door.

Whatever it was, it certainly wasn't his problem, so Adrian shut his eyes and pretended to go back to sleep. The footsteps stopped outside his room, replaced by the heaving breaths of two very tired people.

SLAM.

Whoever they were, they were now in the room with him.

"Oh my god, oh my god, oh my god." The first one—a man—repeated his anxious mantra as his shoes scuffed back and forth across the tiled floor.

"Take a breather, man. We're alright." The second—a woman—spoke. Adrian heard the soft slaps of her hand patting the man's back.

After catching his breath, the man continued, his words a torrent of fear. "That room was full of dismembered corpses, Steph! That is so far from good it's not funny. All the blood? Did you see all the blood? Even thinking about it is giving me dry heaves."

"Good point." The girl—Steph—paused. "You think he's building a Frankenstein?"

"A Frankenstein?" The mere suggestion seemed to offend him. "You think this guy is building a Frankenstein."

"Yeah, yeah, I know! It's Frankenstein's *monster*, you big friggin' nerd. But it's the only logical explanation."

"I can think of a hundred other logical explanations."

"Name two."

"I . . . uh . . ."

"Thought so." Steph clucked her tongue. "Now why were all the body parts old and wrinkly? Who wants to build an old Frankenstein?" Adrian heard the clicks of the girl's steps approach the foot of his bed. He resisted the urge to peek. "Hey, Mike. Look at this guy's name. A. Pancake. Haha!"

"That's"—Mike snorted, covering a laugh—"that's not funny."

"You love it."

"Alright, maybe it's a little funny."

"You know I can hear you guys, right?" Adrian broke his façade, scowling and opening his eyes. He'd heard just about enough.

"Agh!" Mike—timid, lanky, and drenched in slop sweat—looked like he was going to jump into the girl's arms, which were drowning in a raggedy green jacket. Neither of them looked much older than Adrian.

"Oh, hey, uh . . . Mr. Pancake." Steph tugged on her ear, tucked behind a thick fringe of floppy hair. "You're awake."

"Sorry about that," Mike regained his composure and apologized. "Mr. Pancake."

"It's Adrian. Just—just don't worry about it." Adrian shook his head. "Who the hell are you and what are you doing in my hospital room?"

"We're, uh . . ." Mike cleared his throat. "Duckett and Dyer."

Steph jumped in front of him in a dance-like flourish and finished the sentence. "Dicks for Hire!"

"No!" Mike barked at Steph before turning back to Adrian with a pleading look in his eyes. "Don't call us that. Please. It's not our name and I hate it. We're . . . we're detectives. P.I.s."

Adrian felt his eyebrow arch involuntarily. "You're detectives?"

"That's right!" Steph jerked a thumb toward her chest. "You might've heard of us. We helped save the city."

"Uh . . . no. Not familiar."

"Are you kidding me?" Steph shot back.

"Steph, leave him alone." Mike put his hand on her shoulder.

"No, I'm sorry. We had to defeat a mind-controlling interdimensional kaiju. I was hoping for a little more respect!"

"Sorry. She gets like this."

Steph approached Adrian and her mood shifted from upset to enamored so rapidly, she should have suffered whiplash. "Aw, how could I stay mad at this handsome boy?" She grabbed and squished Adrian's cheeks. He was powerless to stop her. "Look at this punim."

"Steph, stop that."

She relented. "Sorry, you're just so cute."

"Wait, back up." Steph's rapid jostling of Adrian's head shook something loose. A vague memory surfaced somewhere in the back of his brain, something unsettling he couldn't quite place. "Did you say *monster*?"

"Yeah." Mike sighed. "It was a whole thing. The less said about it the better."

"He's trying not to relive it," Steph whispered. "He got fired."

"Do you guys deal with monsters?" A fleeting shadow passed over Adrian as he spoke. Maybe this was something best left unremembered.

He pushed the thought away and pressed on. "Because I think I saw a one."

"I mean, we don't 'deal' with monsters. We just kind of try to investigate smaller stuff like—"

Steph interrupted. "You saw a monster? Here?"

"Yeah, I dunno. It was like . . . some sort of shadow, the night I first woke up. After my doctors saw me."

"Those doctors wouldn't happen to be Albert Lee and Richard Perrins, would they?"

"Uh. . ." Adrian blinked. "Yeah, actually."

"Huh." Steph rubbed her chin. "We were hired to find them. They disappeared a few weeks ago. Any idea what might've happened to them?"

"Not really." Adrian bit his lip. "Unless . . ."

"Unless what?" Mike asked.

"My new doctor. Dr. Keene. He replaced them. Said that they had a full caseload. He's a specialist."

"Keene, huh?" Steph rubbed her chin. "This guy a creepy son of a bitch?"

"I mean, I've only met him once that I can remember." Adrian said. Now that Stephanie mentioned it, "creepy" was exactly the adjective he'd use. "But he's a miracle worker. When I got here I was completely busted, and in just a few weeks, he fixed up my chest and arm!"

"Uh-huh," Mike nodded. "You said Keene was a specialist. What kind of specialist is he?"

"Body Reconstruction."

Steph broke out into a wide grin and she extended a finger at Mike. "Frankenstein."

Mike didn't have time to process a reaction as the night nurse, a stout, heavy set woman with fire in her eyes, burst into the room. The light she turned on momentarily blinded all of them. "Excuse me, but who the hell are you two?"

Steph, in the midst of rubbing her eyes, attempted to jump again to the forefront. "We're Duckett and Dyer: Dic—"

"Visiting hours have been over since *five*. Get the hell out!"

"They weren't actually bothering me." Adrian's objection fell on deaf ears, or at least ears too enamored with the power of their job to listen.

"Wait, we just need to—" Mike attempted to dig something out of his shirt pocket. He fumbled as the nurse began to shove the two of them out, and a small card fluttered to the floor.

"Go on! Get! Mr. Pancake needs his rest!"

Mike made a "call me" gesture on the way out, while Steph simply smiled and pointed a gun finger. "See you soon, my beautiful boy!"

The door swung shut behind them and the nurse—her arms akimbo—stood guard to ensure the two dicks would not return.

She turned back to Adrian.

"Sorry about that, sweetie. I won't let it happen again."

"Well, uh, thanks. But it wasn't any trouble, really."

"Nonsense," the nurse tutted, wiping some sweat off her brow with her arm. A tattoo of a misshapen tiger peeked out from beneath her shirt sleeve. "Can I get you anything? A blanket? Maybe some Jell-o?"

"No, that's alright. I'm good." Adrian bit his lip. "But could you maybe tell me when the doctor's gonna be in to see me?"

"Sure. Who's your doctor again, sweetie?"

"Uh, Dr. Keene?"

"Doctor . . . Keene?" The nurse's small face scrunched even smaller.

"Yeah. The Body Reconstruction Specialist. The day nurse says he probably only works nights?"

"I don't know any Dr. Keene off the top of my head. But I'll check at the desk and get back to you." She nodded and made her way out the door.

"Oh, and if you could just—" Adrian reached out with his good hand as the business card was swept into the hallway, out of reach.

* * *

The next week felt interminable, as Adrian lay immobile on his bed. He had seen neither hide nor hair of Dr. Keene—nor the night nurse who promised to get back to him. All the while, his condition remained disappointingly stagnant. Sure, Adrian's arm and chest were fine. Better than ever, really. But he was expecting the rest of him to be fixed just as quickly so he could get back to normal. If Dr. Keene was who he said he was.

That was the problem with Adrian's empty days; they could only be filled with thinking. A barrage of questions assaulted from the back of his own head. Dr. Keene couldn't be some sort of mass murdering psycho, could he? He saved Adrian's life through some sort of miracle cure. But what if he was a mad scientist? A real Frankenstein. The doctor. Not the monster, of course.

Adrian blamed those two goofball P.I.s for putting nonsense in his head. What did they know? They didn't even look like detectives. They looked like the out-of-work hipsters he used to sling drinks to at the bar. God damn, he never thought he'd miss working there. But now he'd give anything for things to go back to the way they were. To go back to his normal life.

Adrian's train of thought stalled in the station. A multitude of facts he had somehow forgotten about got on board.

His friends. His parents. Surely they missed him? They should have been here, or at least called and asked after him! Hell, why hadn't Adrian called them? It must have slipped his mind while he was wrapping it around the possibility of being a paraplegic. But now he had an arm back. The ability to call them was quite literally within reach.

Still peripherally blind due to his braced neck, Adrian felt around his bedside table, finding what felt like an old touch-tone phone. He moved the entire set over to his lap and began dialing his parents. Bringing the handset up to his bandaged ear, Adrian was greeted with a piercing tone.

"No outgoing calls are allowed from this phone. Please hang up."

Adrian barely had time to raise an eyebrow ear before the handset cracked in two in his grip.

"Stupid cheap hospital crap," he grumbled, smacking the plastic debris off his blanket. "What the hell kind of—"

A dark spot caught Adrian's eye and stayed his tongue. It was a large discoloration just below the thumbnail on his left hand, like a birthmark. Maybe a scar as a result of Keene's surgery? It had to be that.

Didn't it?

Adrian shoved the pieces of his phone into the drawer in the table beside him and tried not to think about it. He failed.

* * *

That night, Dr. Keene graced Adrian with his presence. He flowed through the door as usual, opting to limit the room's light to the pale moon through the curtains. But even the thin slashes of moon cutting across his face were enough to show the doctor's weariness. His severe features were saggy, his skin paler than usual.

"Wow, doc. You look like shit. Where have you been?" Adrian didn't want to make it sound like he was grilling him. He'd get to the more pressing questions in due time. And he had a lot of them.

"Mr. Pancake. I do appreciate your concern. I've been feeling under the weather lately and opted not to come in, lest I infect you or any other patients."

"Oh, I guess that makes sense." Adrian cleared his throat. "But I was hoping to get out of this bed pretty soon."

"Yes, I did make a promise to you, and I intend to fulfill it." Keene tented his hands and grinned. "Thus, tonight I'll be performing an emergency surgical procedure that will leave much more of your body mended by the morning."

"Uh . . ." Adrian glanced around the room, wary. "What kind of procedure?"

"An emergency surgical one. Come now, there's no time to waste!"

In one swift motion, all of Adrian's limb pulleys were severed, and his head thudded down as the bed flattened. Adrian was seeing stars, and they didn't disappear until Dr. Keene was already wheeling his bed down the darkened hospital hallway with impossible speed.

"Whoa, doc. Slow down!" Adrian struggled to crane his neck, but to no avail. All he could see were dead fluorescent bulbs rushing by, accompanied by what sounded like Dr. Keene foaming at the mouth. "Where are you taking me?"

They rushed into the patient elevator. Keene stabbed a button before stepping back and bouncing up and down on his feet.

"Aren't you excited?" He whispered back to Adrian. "I'm excited."

Adrian didn't have time to ask exactly what he was excited for before he was rushed out of the elevator into the dank hospital basement. Pipes snaked around unfinished cement walls and around corners. If the surgery took place here, it certainly didn't seem very sterile. But it did seem familiar. Had he been here before?

"Uh, doc, where are you taking me?" Adrian repeated.

"Oh, my operating room is just down this way. I like to keep it cool and dark."

"I see." Adrian didn't know what else he could say. "Well, uh, in that case . . . help?"

"What?"

"HELP!" Adrian shouted. "HELP! HELP! HELP! SOMEBODY HELP ME! PLEASE!"

Adrian continued yelling, but no one could hear him. Dr. Keene just kept pushing his bed faster and faster. All Adrian could see was the underside of his manic grin as they burst through a set of metallic double doors. The room was as dark and cool as Dr. Keene had said, but was filled with the acrid stench of rotting meat, mostly due to the disused body parts heaped in dripping, congealing piles.

Adrian tried to scream, but it caught in his throat. A sharp pain in his neck sent him directly into blackness.

* * *

Adrian bolted upright in his hospital bed. The bright morning light kept him squinting for a minute before he realized he shouldn't have been able to bolt upright at all. As his eyes adjusted, the hospital room around him crystalized into view, and he caught sight of his legs. Adrian wriggled his toes to be sure. And yes, they were normal, unbroken legs. A bit stiff, but they were working. He let out a whoop of pleasure, immediately discovering he could not raise his right arm. It was still in a cast, though much smaller one, held up in a sling close to his body. But it was better than nothing. He looked around for a nurse to share his good news with but found none. When was the last time he'd seen a nurse anyway? Last night? No . . .

Adrian tried to recall more, but he could not for the life of him remember anything past last night's initial conversation with Dr. Keene. Any further attempts to probe his memories were immediately thwarted.

BRINNGGGG

Adrian whipped around at the sound of the phone ringing, but his stiff neck brace and bandaged head still limited his movement. He almost fell out of bed, but managed to steady himself and catch sight of his bedside table for the first time since he'd gotten here.

It was empty.

BRINNGGGG

The sound was coming from within the table. That's right. Adrian remembered shoving the broken phone in the drawer. He slid it open and extricated the remains of the handset, holding them to his ear and mouth as if he was making a call in 1920.

"Um . . . hello?"

"Hello?" A tinny voice vibrated through the speaker. At least the wires of the phone were still intact.

"Yes, this is Adrian. Who's this?"

"Adrian! My beautiful boy!" A vaguely familiar woman's voice wafted through the earpiece. "How's every little thing?"

"Uh . . . who is this?"

"Oh, c'mon. It's me. Stephanie Dyer. From Duckett and Dyer, Di—"

"Don't say it." A man's voice from further away.

"Ahem. From the detective agency. We met two months ago."

Oh. Yes. Mike and Steph. He remembered them.

Wait.

"Two months ago?"

"Yeah. Don't you remember?"

"No, it's only been a week." Adrian's mouth went dry. He couldn't have lost track of time that badly.

"Yeah, no. Pretty sure it's been months. We've been on this case for what's felt like forever," Stephanie said. "Anyway. We've got some bad news for you, Adrian. You're dead."

Adrian's jaw dropped as far as the bandage would let it. When the ringing in his ears began to fade, he caught wind of some harsh whispers on the other end of the line.

"Oh, sorry. I meant *legally dead*," Steph finished. "Someone's gone into the public record and erased all trace of you. Even your parents think you died in the monster attack. They had a funeral put together for you. It was all very sad. We were there. It was a nice service. And when I say 'we were there,' I mean hiding in the bushes."

"Wh—what?" Adrian's hope of returning back to his normal life had been dashed in the space of seconds. Everyone thought he was dead? Is that why his phone didn't allow outgoing calls? Why he could never find out what day or time it was? Who would do this? And why would they want to keep him isolated?

"Sorry. I'm getting off track. We'll shore up all of that later. Mike and I need your help. On top of your missing doctors, there have been bodies disappearing from morgues all across the city. Classic Frankenstein maneuver. We think your Dr. Keene is connected."

"Yeah, yeah." Adrian found his words. He'd do anything to be able to get back home. Back to normal. "I'll help you. But you need to help me, too. I don't think I'm safe here. There's things I . . . I can't remember."

"Oh, you my boy, Adrian! Don't worry. We'll help you out. That's what we do. All we need is for you to let us into the hospital tonight. Basement. Boiler Room. Back Door. 2:00 am. Can you do that?"

"Uh, yes. Yes. I can do that."

"Good. You're the only one we can trust, my beautiful baby boy. Over and out."

"Wait," Adrian said, just before Stephanie hung up. "How did you get my number?"

"Oh, I just dialed every extension in the hospital over and over. I was bound to get you some time. See you tonight!"

"Wait, did you say 2:00 am?" Mike's voice filtered through the background. "I don't want to stay up until 2:00 am!"

The line clicked silent. Adrian shoved the broken pieces of his phone into the side drawer and waited.

* * *

It was dark, and Adrian was tired, but he willed himself awake. He just had to stay awake until 2:00 am.

Whenever that was.

Lacking any sense of time, Adrian thought it best to pick an approximate time based on an educated guess and count the seconds forward. It wasn't the best strategy, but it was all he could do. Plus, it took his mind off the implications of his situation.

At what he figured was 1:30 am, Adrian rubbed his eyes and forced himself up, dangling his feet over his bed. He felt the cool touch of the floor on his left foot a bit before his right, but he paid it no mind as he stood up for the first time in what had apparently been months. Aside from his right arm, his body was fully functional again. Adrian felt good, and . . . somewhat taller, if that was possible.

He began to move and immediately tripped over himself. He had to get the hang of walking again, Adrian supposed. Without much more struggle, he made it out into the dark, empty hallway, grasping the wall to inch himself closer to the elevator. His steps felt odd. Staccato, like he was limping. Adrian chalked it up to some muscle atrophy.

Soon, the cold metal doors of the elevator loomed. Adrian squinted at the faded, warped reflection in the metal for a second, then jabbed at the button. He slunk in, slumped against the wall, and hit the "B." The elevator shuddered and descended, and with it, Adrian's mind fell into a crevasse of déjà vu. He'd been in this elevator before. And it wasn't pleasant. His head pounded, as if something in the back of his mind begged for release.

He clutched at his bandaged head to get it to stop, but when the doors dinged open into the rough concrete hallways and twisting pipes, Adrian could practically hear himself screaming for help. Closing his eyes, he trudged forward, stumbling awkwardly—angrily—down the basement corridors while struggling to make sense of it all. When the pounding in his head became unbearable, he steadied himself against a cool metal door. The bright red paint glowed against the gray concrete, searing the words into Adrian's eyes.

FIRE DOOR.

Adrian recoiled internally, but couldn't figure out why. There was nothing bad about a fire door. But the thought of fire itself felt like acid in his veins. Worse than the drumming in his mind, the burning was so intense, he could barely stand. He slumped with his back to the door. It gave way and creaked open, letting in a cool, calming breeze. It felt wonderful.

But that wasn't all he let in.

"Adrian, you cutie patootie! You did it!" Stephanie Dyer rushed in and helped him back to his feet. "Wow, you're heavy. And, uh, taller than I expected."

"Whoa." Mike slipped through the closing door. "You look terrible."

"Thanks," Adrian muttered. "I think I had a panic attack or something."

"What do you mean?"

"I dunno. Flashbacks. Stuff I can't—but should—remember. I think I've been down here before."

"Hm. That might be real helpful." Steph narrowed her eyes. "Why don't you come with us?"

"Steph," Mike chided. "That might not be safe. We don't know what we're getting into. Besides, he's still recovering."

"Oh, come on. My baby boy's nearly better. Looks as strong as an ox. An ox with one broken arm."

"Yeah, okay, it's fine," Adrian said. "I'll come with you. I need to know what the hell's been going on with Keene. He's messing with me somehow, but I don't know why."

"Alright, it's your funeral." Mike pulled a bat out from behind his back and thrust it towards him. It was like he'd had it the entire time as insurance. "Might wanna take this."

Adrian nodded and grabbed the business end, cradling the bat against his chest as the three of them proceeded down the basement corridors. He stayed behind Mike and Steph since they seemed to know what they were doing—at least, a little bit. Fortunately, he could see clear over the tops of their heads by about an inch or so. They were shorter than he thought.

Rounding a few corners put them smack dab in front of a set of familiar metal double doors. Adrian raised his bat, governed by some faint, near-forgotten instinct. Maybe he just had a thing against doors?

"This is it," Steph said, her hands on her hips. "Your one-stop-shop for gently used body parts. If Mike will try not to throw up again, maybe we can do some proper investigating this time."

"I didn't throw up, Steph. It was dry! Dry!"

"I've . . ." Adrian tried to grasp the words. "I've been here before."

"You have?" Mike wheeled around. "Why?"

"I don't remember."

"Well, let's find out, shall we?" Steph burst through the doors and left them swinging in her wake. Mike and Adrian had no choice but to follow.

The first thing that struck Adrian about the room was its familiarity. The second was the persistent chill. The third was the mountainous piles of dead body parts. All of it caused a reverberation in his head. It only intensified when he spotted the cold metal table in the middle of the mess. He'd seen this before. Adrian let the wooden bat clatter to the floor as the memories of Dr. Keene's outrageous surgeries rushed into his head, threatening to burn his brain out of his skull.

He would have cried out in anguish had he not noticed the fourth thing: medieval style wood torches hanging in sconces on the wall, each ablaze with flames failing to warm the room. A spike of fear pierced Adrian's stomach, switching him into flight mode.

"No!" He screamed. "No fire!"

"Whoa, Adrian!" Steph crouched down beside him.

"What's the matter?"

"Fire!" The words flew out of Adrian's mouth instinctively. "Fire bad!"

"Mike, put out the torches!" Steph yelled.

"But we won't be able to see anything!"

"Just do it!"

Peeking through his fingers, Adrian watched Mike grab each individual torch—reluctantly climbing upon piles of desiccated arms and legs to do so—and extinguish them on the cold ground. Soon, the room was dark. A bright rectangle emerged from the void as Mike turned on his phone to provide some visible light.

"There," he said. "Better?"

"Yes . . . uh . . . a lot, actually." The spike in his abdomen subsided and the icy fear running down his spine was replaced by the less intense cold of the room itself.

"What the hell was that?" Steph asked.

"I . . . uh . . . just felt . . . that fire . . . bad. I guess."

The following silence was almost worse than the fear. Almost.

"Uh, Mike . . ." Steph's voice trailed off. "I think I might have been right."

The doors burst open, and the weak industrial light of the hallway bathed the room, throwing the shadows of disembodied arms and legs into terrifying pantomimes on the high walls. And there, in the center of it all, swirled the dark form of Dr. Keene.

"Hello, Adrian," the words slithered past his teeth. Shedding his white coat to reveal a cloak of pure black, he turned an annoyed glance at Mike and Steph. "And you are?"

"Duckett and Dyer: D—"

"Not the time, Steph!" Mike hissed.

"Fine. Well, we're here to kick your ass for what you've done to Adrian." Steph growled. This was the first time Adrian had seen this weird wispy girl get angry. "You turned my beautiful boy into a

Frankenstein!"

Keene's sharp grin widened. With each revealed tooth, Adrian grasped piecemeal bits of reality. His blood coursed through foreign veins. Dr. Keene had been replacing each and every one of Adrian's limbs with dead body parts. That's why he was taller, stronger, more uncoordinated. The birthmark beneath his thumb. His new arm had belonged to one of his nurses. His limp. One of his legs was now longer than the other! Stephanie was right! He was a Frankenstein!

"Technically, he's a Keene's monster," Keene said.

"Yeah? Well we're not exactly 'keen' on it!" Mike yelled.

Steph patted Mike's chest with the back of her hand, "Terrible. But nice try."

Then Adrian heard the screaming. A sustained, anguished cry, it caused everyone—even Keene—to cover their ears. Only after a few seconds did Adrian realize he was the one screaming. His mind finally caught up, everything washed over him in an instant. He had lost time. Family. A life. Not to mention all his limbs! Any hope of going back to his normal life was now as dead as the disembodied parts around him. He was now a literal monster, so why not act like it?

Adrian's scream turned into a roar as he lunged at Keene, single-handedly lifting him off the floor with a surprising show of strength. He swung the doctor into a pile of arms and legs, the dead limbs flying apart on impact. As Keene stirred, dazed on the floor, Adrian rushed over to grab and pin the doctor to the wall using the cast on his right arm.

"Whoa, Adrian, whoa, relax!" Mike shouted.

Adrian could barely hear him as he stared into Keene's still grinning face. Cracks snaked through his cast, and the plaster began to fall away in chunks, revealing a thick, tanned arm with a tattoo of a deformed tiger. Adrian knew it was not his own.

"Why?" He roared. "Why did you do this to me?"

"Well, if you must know," Keene snarled, his teeth morphing into thin, pointed blades, "I was hungry!"

With a hiss, Keene bit down on Adrian's arm. The cast took most of the blow, and the remainder of it shattered. In shock, Adrian dropped Keene and stumbled back before the doctor could reach him.

Keene twirled and hissed. The shadows around him pooled at his feet, revealing his true form: a pale monster with bloodshot eyes and dagger-like yellowing teeth and nails.

"Wait, hold on," Mike said from somewhere behind Adrian. "What the actual hell is going on here?"

"Are you telling me," Steph started, "that Keene is a Dracula? And he *made* a Frankenstein?"

"It's only logical, my dear." Keene crept toward them, teeth out, back hunched. "Why go through the trouble of sucking people dry and covering up their deaths, when I have a strong heart that can replenish the blood supply of hundreds of disposable limbs?"

Adrian's eyes went wide as Keene's clawed hand indicated him. That's why all these limbs were wrinkled and aged. Keene had been sucking the blood out of them. Adrian's blood. And he'd do it over and over and over again. Adrian's lip trembled in a disgusted sneer.

"That's friggin gross, man." Stephanie had adopted a similar sneer. But this one was a bit more defiant, even though they were all being backed into a corner by the advancing vampire. "You're turning people's arms into your own personal Capri Suns?"

"I wouldn't use that term, but the idea is sound. But now you two will be added to my collection since you couldn't leave well enough alone." Keene's gaze snapped to Adrian. "And Mr. Pancake is going back to bed . . . for an extended stay."

"You stay away from my beautiful boy!" Steph dove to the floor and snatched up two limp, rubbery arms—one in each hand—and crisscrossed them, thrusting the result in front of Keene's face. "Back! Back!"

Keene scrunched up his face, but only in confusion. "Whatever it is you're trying to do, it's not working."

"It's a cross," she said. "You guys don't like that stuff."

"Well, yes. But this is more of a sideways X than anything. And those arms aren't remotely holy. And crosses aren't made of arms."

"All good points." Steph glanced down at her creation. "Well, then I guess it's just a distraction."

"A distraction?"

Steph slapped Dr. Keene upside the head with the arms, sending him flat on his back on the cold floor. For someone of her build, she had a surprising amount of power.

"Run!" she shouted.

Mike obeyed immediately and was already out the door. Adrian, on the other hand, stood frozen in shock.

"You, too, Adrian! Let's go!" Steph's hand circled Adrian's wrist and he let himself be dragged, stumbling, after her.

* * *

They ran too fast, nearly colliding with walls and pipes several times. Steph's haphazard brand of leadership wasn't doing them any favors. So, favoring his left leg, Adrian picked up the pace. Soon, he was dragging Steph through the maze of corridors at an impossible speed. Around an upcoming corner, Adrian heard Mike's ragged breathing. He'd stopped, but Adrian was moving too fast to adjust. He and Steph collided with Mike as they rounded the bend.

"Goddamnit." Mike sat up and rubbed his head. "That hurt!"

"Well, why'd you stop?" Steph frowned. "I gave us a real good head start!"

"I'd be a lot more comfortable if your plans didn't come out of the Three Stooges handbook."

A shrill screech echoed down the maintenance corridors, transforming into an angry yell as it bounced off each hard edge. Keene was up and he was on the move. They had lost precious seconds sprawled on the floor.

"Split up!" Steph said almost immediately.

"What?" Mike scrunched up his face.

"He can't catch all of us. He's only one dude. He can't multiply himself. That's not a thing Draculas can do, right?"

"He's a vampire. Not an X-Man!"

"Would you two stop bickering?" Adrian whispered, though it came out as a shout. "Keene is on his way!"

"Sorry," Steph said. "It's kind of our thing. Anyway. I'll distract Keene. Lead him up the stairs or something. Mike, you take Adrian, find something we can use to kill a Dracula. There must be something in this place."

"Okay, fine. Then what?"

"Come find me, and hope he hasn't turned me into another Dracula. Break!" Steph jumped up and turned back to Mike as she jogged away. "And make sure you take care of that cute little face!"

"Is she always like this?" Adrian asked.

"Hey, Count Chocula!" Steph's voice carried down the hallway, chased by an indignant hiss. "Come get some of this balanced breakfast!"

"You get used to it," Mike said in a tone that implied that you really didn't. "She's probably shaking her ass at him. Let's go."

Adrian followed Mike as they sprinted around the opposite corner to the sounds of hurried footsteps and angry screaming. They found themselves back in front of the elevator Adrian used earlier and rushed inside, Mike slamming the "Door Close" button repeatedly.

"Okay. Okay. Okay. Okay. Okay. Okay." Mike tightened and loosened his fists with each repetition of the word. "Okay. What kills vampires and where can we find it in this hospital?"

"Um . . ." Adrian started. "Crosses."

"Tried that. Need a real one."

"Holy Water."

"Hm. Not bad. Is there a hospital chapel? We could get both there."

"Yeah, but it's two in the morning. It's probably closed. Besides, as a monster, I'm not sure if I can even cross the threshold."

"Fine, fine. What else?"

"Wooden stakes," Adrian counted off on his—well, not *his*—fingers. "We could use tongue depressors?"

"If you want to give him a splinter, sure."

"Oh, how about the sun!"

"It's 2:00 am! Where're we going to get *the sun*?"

"Would you stop being so negative?"

"Oh, what about garlic?" Mike snapped his fingers. "We could get some in the cafeteria."

"It's a *hospital* cafeteria. Have you tasted the food here? They think steam is a spice."

"And you're calling *me* negative."

Adrian thought for a few more seconds, then an idea dinged into his head. Actually, the ding was the elevator beginning to rise, but he still had the idea. Something he read ages ago.

"Vampires like to count. It's like a compulsion. If you spilled a bunch of rice, they'd have to count every grain."

"What? Like Rainman?"

"I guess." Adrian shrugged his asymmetrical shoulders.

"So that's why Count from Sesame Street likes math so much! Did you know his full name is Count Von Count?"

"I think we're getting off track."

"Right, right. Sorry." Mike shook his head as the elevator doors opened. "We gotta find a supply room. There's bound to be something we can use."

Mike barreled out of the elevator and Adrian followed suit, slipping and sliding on the slick floors. After a few haphazard turns, they managed to find a supply closet halfway down the cardiology wing. After ensuring the coast was clear, they slipped inside. Unfortunately, the closet didn't have room for both a man and a large monster, so it was a tight squeeze while they turned the place inside out.

"Catheters? No. Masks? Not enough to distract him." Mike tossed boxes to the floor as he crossed each option off.

Adrian, frozen in an awkward position, did his best to hunch over and stay out of the way. But he couldn't help but start thinking aloud, which was not helping his mental state.

"What am I going to do? I can't go back to work. I can't go home again. Everyone thinks I'm dead. Hell, maybe I am! I'm not even myself anymore. I'm a monster. A literal monster!"

Mike stopped tossing boxes and turned to the hulking, quivering mass Adrian could no longer recognize as his body. He reached up and placed a firm but gentle hand on a tan, chubby shoulder.

"Adrian, listen. I know monsters. I fought a bunch of monsters. And you're not a monster."

"Really?" Adrian looked down, his eyes blurry with slight tears.

"Oh, yeah. I used to work for a bunch of actual shape-shifting demons. In an office building! And not one of them had as much humanity as you do."

"You . . . you think things will be okay?"

"Not gonna lie. Things'll be different. Hard. But they'll be better if you just embrace it and learn to enjoy the ride. I mean, just a few months ago I was doing data entry. And now I'm fighting monsters and solving crime."

"That's . . . quite the pivot."

"Tell me about it. But once I leaned into it, things got easier. And that's something I had to learn the hard way." Mike sighed. "Don't tell her I said this, but Steph's the best at that stuff. She can find a new normal—even in the craziest times. She doesn't let the crappy stuff define her, she just keeps pushing forward." Mike pointed at Adrian's heart. "With this."

"Thanks, Mike. That helps." Adrian nodded, sniffing.

"Unless Keene replaced your heart, too. Then all bets are off." Mike turned his attention back to the shelves.

Adrian chuckled. He reached up and cracked the plastic neck brace holding his head upright, tossing it to the floor. He unwound the sticky bandage encompassing his head and let his long hair finally breathe free. Wiping his bleary eyes with an oversized hand, Adrian got a clear view of a box sitting on a shelf in front of him. "IV needles. 2000 count."

Mike's eyes widened when he spotted the box.

"Fantastic!" He yanked it off the shelf and the two of them spilled back into the hallway. Mike dug his phone out of his pocket and hit the speed dial. "Steph! We got something! Where are you?"

After a few huffs and puffs, Steph's voice croaked through the speaker, "Almost to the roof! I don't know how much longer I can shake this guy."

"Don't worry, Steph. We're on our way!" Mike shoved his phone back in his pocket and ran towards the closest elevator, Adrian in tow.

* * *

By the time they reached the roof of the hospital and burst through the doors, Dr. Keene already had Stephanie on the ropes. The doctor's shadow stretched out behind him as Steph teetered on the roof's edge. The only thing between her and a deadly drop were the giant illuminated letters spelling "City Presbyterian Hospital."

"Steph!" Michael yelled. "We're here!"

"Great timing, guys!" she shouted with a scowl that suddenly softened. "Oh, Adrian. Nice hair!"

"Adrian Pancake," Keene hissed, his eyes burning as he stared back. "You ungrateful whelp. I could've given you phenomenal power, but you had to stick your nose where it didn't belong. Once I'm done turning your little girlfriend here into my unholy bride, we'll turn you into a mindless blood factory."

"Bride? Gross!" Steph grimaced. "Mike, whatever you're going to do, do it fast, because I'm not doing the horizontal mambo with a Dracula!"

"Hey, Keene, check this out!" Mike reared back and launched the box of needles into the air. They crashed to the floor by Keene's dark feet, spilling their glittering contents across the entire roof.

Keene hissed, as if he'd been burnt, and immediately crouched down to pick up and count the needles one by one. Steph let out a breath and dashed over to safety by Mike, wrapping her arms around Adrian's waist.

"Wow. That was close." She looked up. "How're you doing, my big beautiful boy?"

"I'm . . . actually, I'm good. Trying to get used to things."

"Oh, that's good." Steph squeezed him tighter.

"Alright, that's enough." Mike shooed her away.

"How'd you know that'd work?" Steph asked.

"Adrian told me vampires have a compulsion to count."

"Like on Sesame Street!"

"That's what I said." Mike smirked.

"Did you know his name is 'Count Von Count'? How nuts is that?"

"Ahem." Dr. Keene cleared his throat as he rose up in front of them. He held the needle box aloft in his clawed, shadowy hands. "2000 count."

"Ah, crap," Stephanie muttered.

Keene hissed and reared back, his fangs growing ever longer. It was barely a second before he struck, but Adrian's increased reaction time and speed allowed him to put himself right in Keene's path. Grabbing the doctor's wrists in his new mismatched hands, Adrian pushed back. The two of them growled and snarled, wrestling their way to the edge of the roof.

Keene tried to claw and slash, but Adrian held him at bay. He wasn't about to let Keene turn him into some sort of vampiric Frankenstein. Things were already crazy enough.

With one swift jerk, Adrian whipped Keene's body aside, sending him spiraling toward the edge of the rooftop. Keene caught himself in time, of course, crouching on all fours for balance, like an animal.

"Fight me all you want. I am immortal." Dr. Keene floated to his feet, licking his chops. "If I don't kill you tonight, I'll have plenty of other days to do it. And by hook or by crook, I will turn your other little friends over there into monsters just as terrible and savage as you."

"I'm not a monster!" Adrian growled, which somewhat undercut the point, but now wasn't the time to nitpick. He wasn't about to let Keene define who he was. He was going to do what he knew – in his heart – that he had to do. "My name is Adrian Pancake! And I won't let you do this to anyone ever again!"

Adrian lunged at Keene, catching him right in the stomach. His hodgepodge body was massive, its speed great. Adrian's momentum was more than enough to send himself and Keene flying off the roof, crashing right through the framework of the giant Presbyterian sign.

Dr. Keene clawed at Adrian's back, hissing and yowling with malice, but Adrian closed his eyes and silently accepted his fate as they plummeted to the ground.

* * *

Adrian Pancake had no idea what happened.

The warm light of the morning sun caressed his face just before Stephanie Dyer slapped it. Repeatedly.

"Adrian! Wake up!" Steph had been cradling his head and neck in her arms. "Oh, my boy!" she cried. "Look what they did to my boy!"

"Ugh. Steph. I'm awake. I'm alive. Let me go!" Adrian coughed the words out of his mouth and found the strength to push himself up. It took a second to regain his bearings. Taking stock of their surroundings, Adrian discovered his little selfless sacrifice caused the hospital's illuminated signage to dislodge and tumble to the ground. Adrian himself was lucky enough to be in the middle of a large O. The other damaged letters were strewn across the street, twisted and almost unrecognizable—aside from the giant lower case T from Presbyterian sitting neatly atop a circular black pool of detritus formerly known as Dr. Keene. He had quite literally been flattened.

Adrian didn't need to complete the thought.

"That's as holy a cross as we were going to get, I guess," Mike winced, rubbing the back of his head.

"He's dead," Adrian said, mostly for himself. "He's finally dead."

"Yeah," Steph said. "But you gotta get out of here quick."

"What? Why?"

"Because you're a Frankenstein, man! If hospital management and the cops get wind a Frankenstein did all this"—she indicated the alphabetical warzone around them—"there's gonna be trouble. They're going to wanna lock up and study the monster."

"But I'm not a monster. Doesn't it only matter what's in my heart?"

"I mean, yeah. In an ideal world." Stephanie shrugged at Mike, who seemed confused by the words coming out of her mouth. "But in another, more technically accurate world, scientists are going to try to dissect you. So you'd better hightail it."

Adrian struggled to his feet. "Where am I going to go? What am I going to do? I'm technically dead and I don't think my friends and family would want to see me like this. And they might not be happy about my fake death."

"You'd be surprised at what crazy shit friends and family will put up with," Mike said. "You could try to go back to normal."

"Maybe." Adrian nodded, looking down at his hands. "Or maybe I could do something good for the world with what I've been given. Maybe a different—better—normal. Kinda like you guys."

"Yeah." Mike bit his lip. "I dunno if you could classify what we do as good."

"Whatever you do, first—find a big and tall shop. Get something nice." Steph slapped Adrian's butt, which was a little too exposed by the thin hospital gown. She winked at him as approaching sirens wailed in the distance. "We'll cover for you. We've got a lot of experience dealing with the cops."

Mike sighed. "She's right, unfortunately."

"Goodbye, my adorable little boy . . ." Steph smiled and caressed Adrian's cheek, before delivering another slap to his butt that spurred him to get going.

Adrian let out a long breath and loped into the rapidly fading night. Once he had made his way into the small copse of trees and shrubbery surrounding the hospital, he allowed himself one look back. Mike and Steph were fielding questions from the cavalcade of red and blue lights orbiting around them. Adrian nodded to himself before slipping into darkness and distance.

For better or for worse, his life was never going to be the same. But maybe that'd be okay.

THE HUNT I

The fabric of the multi-verse was an intricate wonder with the capacity to drive most sentient beings to madness. If their minds were not crushed by the very concept of its structure—simultaneously a multi-leveled tower with countless floors, an intricately woven web of delicate, spindly branches, and a horrific globular mishmash of raucous, infinitely churning fluidity—they certainly would not survive the assault on their sense of self by the near immeasurable variations on even the most miniscule of things manifested or choices made, rendering questions of free will—real or perceived—all but moot.

Here, in the space between decisions, was where Korthuu hid. Being a giant, interdimensional monster that fed on the energy of dying universes, it was not accustomed to hiding. Case in point, its recent attempt to hide its presence on a backwater strand of the multi-verse ended in utter failure. Now, not only was Korthuu in danger of crossing paths with a dark, malignant entity bent on destroying all existence, it was also being hunted by a giant, flying octopus.

Although the octopus was the most immediate threat, Korthuu could not ignore the more devastating impact of the so-called "Black King." For lack of a better term, Korthuu was scared. Even now, through the corners of its many cyes, it could see—and indeed feel in its intangible bones—a small, faraway branch of the multi-verse darkly withering before breaking off and crumbling to dust.

Another universe dead before its time, erased from existence.

While Korthuu did not weep for the lives lost or the beauty squandered, it did regret the loss of one more good meal. But this meant the King was relatively near. Even a distance of billions of universe spindles was too close. The King struck at random, destroying universe after universe regardless of the metaphorical distance between them. Korthuu now had a choice: edge itself out of its hiding place and take its chances in a less populated swath of the multi-verse, or remain here and risk drawing the attention of the Black King.

Korthuu shifted its bulk—a mere fraction of which it had manifested in the universes it fed on—and slowly crept out, hoping to shield itself from detection behind a universe of cyberpunk samurai and electric horses. Moving past that layer, Korthuu emerged into an open gulf of the multi-verse, over ten trillion universes wide. Once, even more burgeoning realities had filled the space—to use an inaccurate term—but the Black King had come and razed them all in a storm of fire and shadow. Now there was nothing left except non-existence. And, unless he doubled back, this was the last place the King would come looking.

But the octopus found it first.

It blasted out of the confines of the closest universe and covered the vast distance between the two of them with one contraction of its body musculature and its mighty tentacles. Korthuu sprouted more of its own spindly arms in an attempt to counter, but the Cloud Octopus slammed into it with such force that it sent them both tumbling through the empty sector.

The creature's rubbery appendages latched on to Korthuu's loose green skin, the suction cups somehow performing their intended function in the absence of any air. They grabbed and tore at its folds, causing Korthuu to leak bodily fluids that floated away in dark globules.

Korthuu locked its many jaws and gritted its respective rows of teeth against the pain, finding enough leverage to lash out with gnarled, yellowing claws that it willed out of its appendages. The Cloud Octopus merely narrowed its bulbous, panoramic eyes and tightened its grip, thrashing their bodies around violently through empty nothingness.

Korthuu's blood-red eyes widened as it realized it had little recourse but to take the fight to solid ground. It pushed back against the almighty cephalopod's aggression, hoping to steer them past the gulf in the multi-verse and put them within breaching distance of a singular reality. It was impossible to say how long the tug of war lasted between the two, as their battle was wholly outside the realm of time.

Eventually, though, Korthuu was able to reach out toward the nearest passing universe, latching on with a tentative grip of its wiry arms. Stars, nebulae, and planets coalesced around them as they exited the blurry, bluish monocolor of the multi-verse and were dragged into the vibrant, time-dependent hell of existence. Gravity, mass, and causality asserted themselves, and the grotesque bulk of green and red entangled limbs fell toward what looked like the dry landscape of a desert planet. Heat seared Korthuu's skin as it and the octopus entered a rapidly decaying orbit around the planet, propelling them hypersonically to the arid red ground below.

Still, the octopus did not dislodge.

Bracing for impact, Korthuu screwed its arrays of eyes shut. The two monsters struck the ground with such force that it shattered. Korthuu's eyes shot back open to something unexpected.

It was not the ground that shattered.

It was the boundaries of the universe itself.

The octopus and Korthuu, still in their death embrace, were now falling through the skies of a technologically advanced Arabesque kingdom, with sparkling glass and steel minarets pointing up at them like beautiful daggers. The frightened citizens, too, pointed, screaming, at the horror descending rapidly upon them. Flying cars and rickshaws only added to the cacophony. But Korthuu had other things to concern itself with.

Wresting a set of arms free, it dug into the octopus' leftmost tentacles, rending large wounds into its flesh. The octopus let out a pained shriek—its first audible cry since entering an atmosphere—and its black beak nipped at Korthuu's underbelly. This gave Korthuu the chance to adjust their trajectory. It had hoped to spear the octopus on one of the minarets, but instead it was only able to shift slightly, causing the glass spear to graze both their sides as they slammed to the ground, crashing into a third universe stacked beneath this one.

Korthuu and the octopus emerged 70,000 feet above another Earth. Taking advantage of the distraction that comes with shifting one's reality, Korthuu wrenched off two of the octopus' wounded tentacles and beat them against its expanding and contracting head. It emitted yet another screech, and Korthuu could feel the creature's grip loosening. Doubling its assault, Korthuu struck out with more of its claws and jaws, rending and tearing at whatever piece of octopus flesh came its way. Finally, it was winning this battle of attrition.

But it was a pyrrhic victory and a hollow one, as the octopus—finally too tired and hurt to continue—released its prey and, with a deafening squawk, used its last bits of strength to contract its body into nothingness, escaping back into the void of the multi-verse, leaving a stinging, lightly acidic blast of ink in its wake.

Korthuu was free, but partially blind, and clawed at its eyes to remove the mucousy dark ink. Its unobstructed eyes could still see a blurry image of what was coming up fast from below, but before Korthuu could react, it slammed into the ground, not with enough force to crack through reality, but enough to finally cause the multi-dimensional demi-god to succumb to its countless wounds. Korthuu felt its body contract and relax, as some bits cracked and others oozed. It could not make out where it had landed. Some place bright and warm and golden and wonderful.

This was not how it imagined it would die. In fact, dying had never seemed a distinct possibility to Korthuu. But now that it was here, it felt peaceful. Whatever this place was, it felt right, almost warming. It felt like where it wanted and needed to be.

Korthuu closed its eyes, and for the first time in a long time, it felt its ever-present hunger fade.

227 MINUTES TO EXPLOSIONTOWN

The harsh blare of his morning alarm shattered Michael Duckett's dreams into tiny little pieces. His dry, bleary eyes cracked open and were met by the soulless, perpetually cheerful gaze of the anime schoolgirl body pillow demarcating the center of his and Stephanie Dyer's single Murphy bed.

"Ugh." He recoiled and swung his legs over the side of the bed, smacking the bland taste of sleep out of his mouth. He blinked. "Blargh. What time is it?"

Flailing blindly toward his nightstand, Michael grabbed his phone and swiped the alarm away, but it wasn't until he donned his glasses that he could see it was 10:45 am.

Michael leapt out of bed and sprinted toward the closet. "Aw, crap! I'm late! How the hell did this happen?"

From the opposite side of their kawaii Maginot Line, Steph rolled over with a yawn and a stretch. She tousled her own hair and peered over the pillow in her pajamas, adorned with little yellow ducks. "Morning, Mike. What up?"

"I needed to be up by 8, but my alarm only rang at 10:45!"

"Oh, uh . . . wow. That's a . . ." Steph ducked back behind the body pillow, using the blonde schoolgirl as a human shield. ". . . that's a real humdinger."

Michael stopped tripping over attempts to pull on socks and put his hands on his hips. "What did you do?"

"Hey, man, I just wanted to sleep in, and your alarms always go off way too early. So I . . . uh . . . just nudged 'em forward." She cleared her throat to mutter. "About four hours."

"Steph!"

"What? It's not like you have a job you need to commute to anymore! We live in the office! We have everything we need right here." Steph extended her arms to indicate their 750 square foot combination apartment/detective agency. The lightbulb in Michael's bedside lamp popped, sending a small shower of sparks across the side table. Steph blinked. "I'll make a note to fix that."

"For your information, Steph," Michael said, the words forced through gritted teeth. He resumed his sock offensive. "I'm going out of town today and I'm going to miss my train! It's a good thing I packed all my stuff last night."

"A train? Pshaw!" Stephanie issued a curt wave of her hand while Michael dashed into the bathroom. "This isn't 1934. Who takes a train? Trains suck!"

"For your information, this isn't just any old train. I scored a ticket on the maiden voyage of a brand new, high-speed express line." Michael's voice echoed off the midnight blue bathroom tile as he prepped his toothbrush.

"Maiden voyage? Huh. Maybe this *is* 1934." Steph leaned in through the doorway, waving a small, shiny piece of paper in her hand, before fumbling about to read it. "*The Exo-City Express. Come aboard and experience the ride of your life!* Is this what you're talking about?"

Michael caught the glint of the paper out of the corner of his eye and snatched it away from her, slipping it into the waistband of his boxer-briefs. "Don't go through my wallet!"

"Well, don't leave it lying around."

"It was in my pants!"

"Whatever. Why do you have an actual golden ticket? Is this some Willy Wonka shit? Is Gene Wilder going to be there? Is it going to be like that scary part of the movie on the boat? Is the train made of chocolate? Can I come? Why didn't you tell me the train was made of chocolate?"

"Steph, shut up," Michael shot back through the foam of his toothpaste. "It's not a chocolate train. It's just a very exclusive event, and I happened to be invited."

"Why you?"

Michael stopped brushing and blinked at himself in the mirror. This was the first non-ridiculous question Steph had asked, and he didn't have an answer.

"They didn't invite me, too? Do you think my ticket got lost in the mail? That's not fair!"

"You wouldn't like it, Steph. You would think it was boring. Besides, you were just telling me trains suck two minutes ago."

"Yeah, well, I'm still pissed."

"Well, I'm sorry," Michael said through his still foaming mouth. After a rinse and spit, he continued. "I'll let you know how the ride is. They say the train'll only take 227 minutes to get from here to North Brockville."

"I thought this was a super-fast bullet train." Steph counted on her fingers. "That's, like, four hours."

Michael frowned as he emerged from the bathroom.

"Nevertheless. I'm still going."

"Suit yourself, Mike! Call me when you get there." Steph leapt back into bed and was snoring before Michael had a chance to put on the rest of yesterday's clothes.

* * *

It was about 11:30 when Michael's cab rolled up to the City Train Station. The *Exo-City Express* was due to depart at noon, exactly. He nodded to himself as he grabbed his bag from the trunk—self-satisfied he'd preemptively set his alarm early enough to rout Steph's shenanigans with time enough to spare.

Slinging the duffel over his shoulder, Michael rapped on the roof of the cab twice, and it sped off. He hadn't needed to do that, he just kinda liked it. As the dust from the cab cleared, Michael could see the station was crowded. More than normal. Not that Michael knew exactly how crowded it was normally. But he couldn't imagine it was always drowning in this sea of people. Were they here to gawk at the *Exo-City Express,* or was this maiden voyage less exclusive than his literal golden ticket had led him to believe?

Michael jostled through the throng of people, juggling his duffel bag and the sport coat hanging over his arm. "Sorry. 'scuse me." He pushed past a reporter and his photographer, fumbling with her camera. To his left, a single mother attempted to wrangle two unruly boys with the only weapon in her arsenal—loud, sustained yelling. As he reached the front, toward the entrance, he saw a small stage erected beside the ticket booth. The lone ticket agent eyed the crowd with the judging glare of some haughty nineteenth-century tycoon. How the station still had a human ticket agent was beyond him. Maybe if the *Express* was successful, they'd get enough revenue to finally pivot to automation.

Michael glanced to the right and caught a glimpse of an attractive, lady about his age who did not seem like the target audience for a luxury commuter train experience. Her raven hair was cut short, and its deep black matched her messily applied mascara, not to mention her shirt with its fishnet sleeves, and dark jeans. She looked like a black hole of a person, which would explain why Michael was inexplicably drawn to her.

He coughed, his version of making a move when anxiety rose in his chest like a lungful of pine needles.

She glanced in his direction and her stoic frown turned into something a bit lighter. Success!

"Sorry, mate," she said in a delightful Australian accent. She squinted at him. "Do I know you?"

She was talking to him. And she recognized him. Double success!

But Michael had found little success parleying the newfound fame of his and Steph's P.I. business into social situations. Perhaps it was because he ended up saying things like, "I mean, maybe? I guess people know me now. Because I do things. They've heard of me. I think."

"You . . . do things?" With a smirk, she cocked a playful eyebrow and crossed her arms. "Pray tell. What are the 'things' that you do?"

Michael reared back a little; he hadn't expected her to be so receptive to his awkward stumbling over simple words. Unconsciously, he doubled down. "Uh . . . I detect things."

"Oh, shit." Her eyes widened and Michael could finally see the whites of them. "You're that guy!"

Michael offered a weak smile.

"Wait. Aren't there supposed to be two of you?" she asked, betraying a hint of disappointment.

"What?"

"Two of you. Detectives," she clarified. "Drucker and Dryer?"

"Duckett and Dyer, actually. We're, uh, P.I.s for—"

"Oh, yeah! Dicks for Hire. I love that name."

Michael cleared his throat. "Well, I'm not partial to that branding myself. But, I guess, if you like it . . ."

"So where's the other one?"

"We're not joined at the hip, y'know." He frowned. "We have our own lives."

"Right, of course, sorry."

"So, this train, huh? Supposed to be pretty cool." Even Michael was offended by how lame he sounded. "Are you gonna be on it?"

"Yeah, actually."

"How'd you get a ticket?"

"Funny story. I'm the—" She was interrupted by the crowd, who had begun to cheer as a tall man in a polo shirt and khaki sport coat took the stage, followed by a mousey woman in a pink pantsuit.

"Hello, everyone!" With a wave of his hand and an artificial smile too big for his face, the man addressed the excited foofaraw. "Yes! Thank you, yes! I'm so glad you could all make it." He clapped a little bit himself, inviting the crowd to simmer down. "Thank you, thank you, thank you everyone for coming to the unveiling of Barnes Investments' latest technological venture. *The Exo-City Express* is our proudest accomplishment, and we hope it will help bring rail travel into the 21st Century, with all the romantic beauty of the 20th!"

Another cheer went up from the crowd. Michael raised his arms in a half-hearted 'woo' despite not knowing exactly what was going on.

The black-haired girl leaned over to him, without taking her eyes off the stage. The man continued his charismatic diatribe. "You don't know who the hell he is, do you?"

Michael could do nothing but grimace.

"Don't worry. It's Dalton Barnes," she whispered, her accent setting his heart aflutter. "Hedge fund guy. Recently started investing heavily in tech and infrastructure. Being a rich guy and investing in shiny toys for the unwashed masses made him pretty popular in the city."

"Uh . . . huh," Michael said, unsure of how he'd never heard of this Dalton person before.

"He kinda came out of nowhere after the Future Group collapsed.

They were his single biggest competitor in the tech sphere."

"But, uh, they were a cult," Michael said, drawing on his experience. "They didn't actually *produce* anything."

"Either way, I think Dalton basically ate their lunch."

"Right, and how do you know this?"

"Another funny story. Same funny story, actually—"

"And thanks to my business acumen and eye for talent"—Dalton's voice boomed as if he'd commandeered a megaphone—"we were able to hire one of the most promising civil and mechanical engineers of our generation to design the *Express*. Helena, get up here!"

Michael could only stare bewildered as Dalton offered his outstretched hand to the fishnet-sleeved girl beside him—Helena, apparently—and boosted her up. As she mounted the stage, she gave him a coy shrug and smile, and Michael felt his heart skip a beat.

"Thanks to Helena's tireless efforts—and our money—Barnes Investments is proud to present *The Exo-City Express*!" Camera flashes exploded around Michael as golden confetti shot up through the floor of the stage, twinkling as it fluttered its way down. "Now, for those of you lucky enough to have scored a ticket on this beauty, please line up to your left and soon you'll be able to experience the future of rail travel side by side with us! All aboard!"

The crowd surged around Michael, thrusting him into a vortex of confusion. Most people dissipated away, but others—fortunate to have a ticket—lined up as they were told before the sole ticket agent. As he overcame his disorientation, Michael saw that Barnes, the pink pantsuit lady, and—most importantly—Helena had vanished somewhere into the station proper, and his only means to reconnect with her was to join this line, right behind the yelling mom and her two terrible boys.

Fortunately, and to the credit of the ticket agent, the queue moved swiftly. After the troublesome kids disappeared into the station, Michael stepped up to the booth.

"Ticket please?" the agent drawled.

Michael handed over the ticket as he glanced at the man's nametag. *Donneger*, it said.

Donneger snatched the foil ticket out of Michael's grasp and turned it around in his hands, as if baffled by its very existence. He blinked rapidly. "What the hell is this?"

"Um." Michael cleared his throat. "It's my ticket."

"Is this some sort of joke?" Donneger thrust the ticket back at him. "This isn't a ticket."

"What do you mean? This was sent to me specifically. It even says so." Michael pointed at his name, which was embossed on the foil. "See? I'm Michael Duckett."

"Excuse me, sir?" Donneger craned his neck to look over Michael's shoulder.

"Yes?" said the portly man in the line behind him.

"Could I please see your ticket for a second?"

The man obliged and handed his ticket over to the agent, who turned it around and displayed it to Michael. It looked like normal glossy card stock printed off a machine. "*This* is a ticket," Donneger said, before bringing the gold foil back into Michael's eyeline. "*This* is some Willy Wonka shit."

"But why would someone send me this ticket? I'm sorry. That doesn't make any sense."

"No, *I'm* sorry. Because someone must be playing an elaborate prank on you." Donneger looked Michael up and down. "And from the looks of you, this *cannot* be the first time."

"But—" Michael's syllable of protestation fell on deaf ears as the ticket agent held up his hand.

"No ticket. No ride. Please leave immediately without making a scene, or I'll be forced to call security."

"I—" Michael started, but he backed off as soon as he saw Donneger reach for a radio on his belt. "Fine."

"Sorry, kid," the portly man behind him frowned as Michael slunk past him back onto the wider promenade of the City Station entrance. He dropped his duffel bag and plopped down onto a bench. The occasional other traveler flitted by on their way to another track as Michael hung his head in self-pity. Not only was he missing his exclusive train ride, but he was also missing out on a shot with an interesting, smart, weird girl with her shit together. That type didn't blow into his life that often—much to his chagrin.

He had to get back in the station somehow. He had to get on that train. Michael chewed his lip in thought.

There was one option.

Did he dare step slightly outside the rule of law for a shot with this girl he'd just met?

Ah, screw it, he thought. *Why not?* Maybe he'd been spending too much time with Steph. Her breezy attitude was starting to rub off on him.

Michael snatched his bag up and rushed back to the station gate. Avoiding the firm gaze of Donneger the ticket agent—who was still dealing with the dregs of the *Exo-City* queue—Michael skirted around the gate and line entirely and proceeded around the side wall of the building looking for a back way in. He found one in a fire door. After looking over his shoulder, he rapped sharply on the faded red metal. Hopefully someone would hear him.

Michael had to knock two more times before he heard a thunk and the door scraped open. An older man peeked out with eyes as fiery as the remaining hair on the sides of his head.

"Who're you? What do you want?"

"Uh, I, uh . . ." Michael adopted his trademark awkward 'I need to pee' stance—a jig with crossed legs. "Bathroom?"

"Really?" The man narrowed his eyes. "You're not trying to sneak onto the *Exo-City Express*, are you?"

"Uh . . ." Michael hadn't expected such a direct and accurate line of questioning. "No?"

"Good." The man nodded and opened the door the rest of the way. Judging by the dark blue jumpsuit that had seen better days and the wrench in his off hand, he was some sort of maintenance guy. "Ain't nothing good going on with that train. The whole operation's just a greedy scam, if you ask me."

"Uh-huh, yeah, okay, whatever." Michael waved away whatever rambling nonsense this guy was spouting. It was just more crap standing between him and Helena. "Where's the bathroom?"

"That-a-way." The man angled his wrench down the hall behind him. "Past the rail offices and into the main track promenade."

"Thanks," Michael said as he shuffled past, out of the daylight and into the darker hallway.

"I'm tellin' ya, kid. I don't know whatcher up to, but whatever you do, don't get on that train!" The maintenance guy's call—which Michael again elected to ignore—echoed after him, even after he turned a corner.

With the man out of sight, Michael resumed his normal walk and dashed down the corridor. The lightly tinted, frosted windows of the offices and beige walls made Michael feel like he was running through a sepia filter. Turning another corner, he could see the literal light at the end of the tunnel where the hallway opened up into the main promenade. He was about to pick up his pace—lest he miss the train— when the sound of yelling caught his ear.

"—what you're trying to do!" It was a woman, and her voice unrecognizable, but tinted heavily with outrage. "I don't care about all that weird nonsense you're obsessed with. This is my thing. Mine! And you can't take this away from me!"

Michael inadvertently slowed down as the small, nosey part of his brain kicked into gear. He didn't stop, but he kept his eyes and ears trained on the office where the shouting was coming from as he moved forward.

"You've gotten to be too much, you know that?" An older man

said, his voice roughly filtered through a speaker phone. "You're not entitled to this at all. I made you and I can break you if you don't return what is rightfully mine."

"Oh yeah?" the woman continued, her voice fading as Michael passed the office. "Well, I'd like to see you try, you creaky old bastard! See you in hell."

The call was cut off with a beep, and Michael shrugged, chalking it up to something he wasn't meant to hear. His attention was better focused on getting to the train. Had he actually been focused on that, he wouldn't have immediately collided with someone after entering the promenade. Michael pitched forward and his duffel bag, still moving quite quickly, took the opportunity to swing around his neck and send the two of them crashing down to the floor.

"Dammit!" Michael yelled as he shook off his daze and scrambled around for his glasses. "Why don't you watch where you're going?"

His scolding was met only with a frantic shuffling, as the other traveler jumped to their feet. Donning his glasses, Michael only saw the person, clad in a swirling black greatcoat with a cloak-like hood, dashing off toward the train platform.

"Hey!" Michael shouted. "What the hell!"

The person zigged through other passengers heading toward the platform, pausing only once to glance back his way. His gaze would have met theirs, had they not been covered in an odd iron mask of incongruous shapes. The black, inset lenses felt like they stared at him for hours. Before Michael could gather his thoughts on the matter, the cloaked passenger ducked behind a pillar and disappeared.

"A simple 'sorry' would've been nice," Michael said. He bent down to pick up his dropped sport coat and re-align his duffel bag.

"Hey!" an unfortunately familiar voice yelled—there seemed to be too much yelling going around today for Michael's taste. "You! Yeah! I see you! Stop right there!"

Michael snapped around to see Donneger, the surly ticket taker, pointing right at him, before breaking into a run.

"Crap!" Michael gathered himself as quick as he could and dashed off in the direction of the platform.

"Get back here!" Donneger blew a whistle. "Stop him! Stop that man!"

Michael, a stitch rapidly forming in his side, ran through the promenade and burst onto the platform, unintentionally aping the cloaked passenger's route from earlier. Rounding the corner gave him his first real look at the train he was—or was not—to be boarding.

The Exo-City Express was enormous, bigger than any subway or train he'd ever seen, and it was modeled in a deliberate art deco style that evoked the heyday of rail travel. Its rounded, aerodynamic engine popped with dark violet paint that verged on black, interrupted only by a single glowing headlight mounted in the center. Behind it trailed nine luxurious cars, which Michael observed only in passing as he ran alongside them.

At about car three, Michael took a sharp right onto another promenade before ducking into a restroom. Resting his sweaty neck against the cool tile, he slumped down and let out a breath as he heard Donneger's aggressive whistling pass by outside.

He almost regretted lying his way into the station. Ironically, now he really did have to go to the bathroom. But before he could execute on that thought, he was interrupted by another whistle. This one a few decibels louder, and followed by a labored chugging. *The Exo-City Express* was on the move.

Michael donned his sport coat and made preparations for another mad dash. He bolted back out the restroom door just in time to find the last two cars of the train gliding past the arched entryway to the promenade. He picked up the pace and rounded the corner back onto the main platform. As the eighth car pulled past him and the train began to accelerate further, the stitch in his side grew. He was losing ground.

Why was he so dead set on getting on this train anyway?

"C'mon, mate! C'mon! You can do it!" Leaning out the back door of the second to last car, it was Helena, her hand outstretched. "I gotcha!"

Oh, yeah. That was why.

Using his last burst of energy, Michael sped up, no thanks to the duffel bag repeatedly smacking his side. He grabbed onto Helena's hand so forcefully, he almost dragged her off the train.

"Urgh!" They both strained as they finally got Michael onto the train proper, just before he ran out of platform.

"Hoo boy," Michael wheezed, splayed out on the cold metal floor. "That was . . . that was a rush."

"What the hell happened?" Helena asked. "I thought you ditched me."

"No!" He said between breaths. "I had an issue with the ticket guy. Wouldn't honor my ticket."

"Who? Donneger? Yeah, that guy's got bugs in his brain. I hate interfacing with him."

"Oh, yeah." Michael smirked weakly. "I almost forgot. This is *your* train."

Helena averted her gaze sheepishly, rubbing the back of her head. "Well, yeah. Kinda."

"When were you gonna let that little tidbit slip?" Michael caught himself being more forward than he'd ever used to be with the opposite sex. Maybe it was a good thing that Stephanie was rubbing off on him.

"I was trying to tell you, but then Dalton . . . did what he always does. It's hard to stop him once he's on a roll." She rolled her eyes. "Anyway, it's his money. I was just glad to get the opportunity."

"Well . . ." Michael looked around the transitory corridor they were sitting in. "Looks like you did a hell of a job."

"Oh, hush. You haven't seen any actual part of the train yet." Helena chuckled. "Would you like a tour?"

"Sure!" He beamed. "But, uh, could the first stop be the bathroom? I kinda . . ."

"Of course." Helena stood up and gestured to the restroom. "There's one right over—"

A frazzled woman shoved her to the side, dragging her two unruly sons behind her. They were jumping from wall to wall and running around like maniacs. It was the same family that had been in front of Michael in the ticket line.

"Will you two just quiet down! Hey, wait." The woman spun around, putting a finger in Helena's face. "Aren't you that lady that's working with Dalton Barnes?"

Helena, now cross-eyed staring at the tip of her finger, said, "Yes?"

"We're supposed to—stop that!—we're supposed to meet with Dalton—put that down! I said *now*!—in the afternoon! We're on his schedule, right?"

"Well, I'm not really in charge of his day-to-day. You're going to have to talk to Ms. Meadows about that."

"I don't care! The children need to see him!"

"Okay, well, I understand that, Mrs. . . . ?"

"McMurray," she declared. "Anne McMurray."

"Mrs. McMurray. I'll try to ask him about it the next time I see him."

"Well, I . . . uh, think that's acceptable." Mrs. Murray's mask of anger dissolved quickly as she turned down to the two boys that were running around her ankles. "What do you think, boys?"

One ignored her entirely, while the other only stopped his escapades so he could kick Michael in the shin.

"Thank you, ma'am," Mrs. McMurray said over his sharp intake of breath.

"Mommy." One of the rugrats—the non-kicking one—tugged at Mrs. McMurray's pant leg. "I needta go to the bafroom."

"Alright, alright," she said, guiding them carefully. "Let's go."

With a soft click, the bathroom door shut behind the family, and a tiny label shifted from "vacant" to "occupied."

"Maybe we can get you into one on the next car." Helena shrugged. "Where are you supposed to be seated, anyway?"

Michael glanced down, taking the golden ticket out of his pocket. "Looks like Car Four, Seat 34B. But I'm not sure this ticket is even real."

"Well, don't worry about that, mate! You're with me!" Helena strode to the sliding door and it hissed open, allowing them into the main cabin area of Car 8, if the placard above it was to be believed.

The car was double-decked and surprisingly spacious, even with most of the seats occupied. Michael could see this being a pretty nice way to travel. He had expected to hear the thunderous noise of the air rushing past, and to feel an uncomfortable swaying, but instead, Michael was met with nothing but a soft hum. And he could barely feel any movement at all, as if he was gliding on a cloud. This was great news for his occasional motion sickness. Helena had designed this thing right.

Michael whistled in appreciation.

"Nice, right?" Helena asked, stopping at a pair of empty seats. "Check out the view."

Michael leaned down to peer out the window. They were far beyond the city limits now and had reached a steady clip, with the landscape whizzing by in a brown-green blur. He couldn't really discern how fast they were going, but he knew it was impressive.

"Seeing that always gives me goosebumps. But it looks like no one else really appreciates it," Helena said as they walked up the stairway to the second floor. The passengers were indeed distracted, mostly minding their own business, reading newspapers, playing on their phones, or sleeping. "Not to toot my own horn or anything, but I guess that's just a testament to how well-designed it is. Plus, when you reach your seat, you'll be amazed at the amount of legroom you'll get."

"I'm sure I will," Michael nodded. He had a healthy respect for how good legroom could be a gamechanger for the travel experience. "But I'm amazed already."

"We've also got individual internet-ready tablets in the back of each headrest." She indicated one in an empty seatback as she passed. "Plus, a set of huge LED screens up at the front of every car that broadcast news, weather, and other helpful information." Helena motioned to the far end of the car. Two screens embedded in the bulkhead currently showcased a commercial for hemorrhoid cream.

"Helpful information?" Michael smirked. The ad faded into a more appropriate display of *The Exo-City*'s route and transit time.

"Hey, mama's gotta raise capital somehow." She smiled back, and Michael's stomach exploded in butterflies. "C'mon, let's keep moving."

Michael followed Helena like a lost puppy as they approached the front of Car Eight's top deck. But as they descended the stairs to move onto the next car, the map and schedule display faded from the screen before fizzling out entirely and giving into black and white static. Before Michael had a chance to wrap his head around the idea of static on a digital television, it resolved into a clear silhouette of a person in front of a stained, off-white background.

"Oh," Michael leaned back to get a closer look. "You even have a little host for your train programming. That's neat."

"Uh. . ." Helena, who had been two steps ahead of Michael, jogged back up to take a look for herself. "What? That's not ours."

The dark figure moved forward, throwing into relief the thick, iron mask over its face. It was the same cloaked stranger Michael had collided with in the station. The other passengers behind them tapped at the tablets in their headrests. The broadcast had taken over every screen on the train.

"Oh, that doesn't bode well," Michael whispered.

"Hello, everyone. I trust you are enjoying your trip, and I hope you are all sitting comfortably." The masked person's voice was modulated into deep, digital baritone. "Because we are about to play a little game."

Michael looked around as a low undercurrent of whispers permeated the car, floating amongst the sea of cocked, confused heads.

"Oh, don't worry," the deep, partially garbled voice thundered. "The rules are quite simple. Number one: there is a bomb on this train."

The curious whispers shifted immediately to gasps and screams as the passengers jumped up and frantically looked around—first at each other, then beneath their seats. If they hadn't been moving at hundreds of miles per hour, Michael figured they'd have tried to jump off. At least, he would have, anyway.

"Oh, please," the masked bomber scoffed from the safety of the LED screen. "I'd be a real shitty terrorist if I left it lying around in plain sight. But rest assured, there is a bomb on this train, and it is rigged to blow."

Michael bit his lip. This was really not good. He glanced at Helena, who was stumbling forward, to plead for some sort of sanity from the passengers. Needless to say, it wasn't working.

"Rule number two. If anyone disembarks from this train before the bomb is found, it will—yes, you guessed it—explode."

Michael had to call someone. Maybe 911? Would local cops have jurisdiction on an inter-state train? Or maybe the FBI? Michael dug his nails into his palm to stop his anxious overthinking. At this point, he had to call someone. Anyone. He reached into his pocket and grabbed his phone, hitting speed dial for the first person he could think of.

"Now that brings me to rule number three," the bomber continued. "Don't try to contact anyone. I'm monitoring all the wifi and cell signals coming from this train. Not to mention all the cameras."

Michael's stomach dropped.

"I understand there might be a bit of a lag, so you have a few minutes to turn off your devices. But after that, if I see anyone even pull out their phone. KABOOM. Hahahaha!"

Michael's suddenly sweaty palms fumbled his phone, and it slipped. Luckily, he managed to grab it before it hit the floor, but not before swiping awkwardly across the keypad. He shut it down and tucked it back away immediately.

"Now, here's the deal. We have quite a bit of time left on our ride together, so let's make this fun. I've got the remote to shut down the bomb. Find me and make me hand it over, and you'll all be safe. But if we roll into North Brockville before we meet . . . KABOO—well, you get the idea. I'll check in on your progress in just a little bit. Until then, ta-ta!"

The masked terrorist disappeared off the screen, leaving only the splotchy, cream background behind them, before the monitors shut off. The panicked public freakout intensified.

"Please, everyone!" Helena tried to yell over the noise of the crowd. "Don't panic! This will just make things harder."

"Aw, crap," Michael muttered.

Suddenly, the train jerked hard, throwing him to the floor and all the passengers forward, tumbling over the seats in front of them, before lurching again and speeding up. Michael rolled back down the corridor, while the other passengers were thrown back into their seats. Helena herself was thrown halfway down the aisle.

The bomber and their garbled voice returned to the screen. "Oh, by the way, I can also control the speed of the train. Sorry. Forgot to mention that. I guess that's pretty important."

"Double crap," Michael said.

* * *

"Hey."

. . .

"Hey!"

. . .

"Wake up!" A gruff voice with an even gruffer hand shoved

Stephanie Dyer out of bed. She woke up just as she hit the ground.

"Yo! What's the big idea?" Stephanie shot up, still wrapped in her comforter but brandishing her fists, ready for a fight. But, when she saw who had disturbed her slumber, she let the blanket slough off as she leaned casually on her bedside table. "Oh, hey Maureen. How you livin'?"

Maureen, their large stodgy secretary—and former assassin—glared at Steph with her hands on her hips, blowing a loose hair curl out of her eyes.

"Uh . . ." Steph bit her lip. "You having a good morning?"

"It's past noon," Maureen grumbled, tossing a small sheaf of papers her way. "By the way, here's your mail."

Amidst the pile, Steph spied a flash of gold she recognized. Immediately, she grabbed at it, letting the rest of the stack of envelopes splat to the ground. It was, as she'd surmised, a personal ticket to the maiden voyage of *The Exo-City Express*. But it was late, and, therefore, now so was she. At least she no longer felt excluded.

"And the only reason I'm here today is because it's payday." Maureen drew Steph's attention with a series of snaps before her eyes. "And you owe me a month's back pay."

"Listen, Maureen, baby. It's a simple explanation." Steph stuffed the ticket into her pajama pocket as she backed her way to the office's main desk. She didn't want to anger Maureen, who probably knew seven ways to kill her with objects in this room alone. But how could Steph in good conscience admit she spent all of Maureen's salary money on old packs of baseball cards with expired sticks of gum in them?

Luckily for Steph, she wouldn't have time to admit anything. The dulcet tones of the Monster Mash emanated from her cell phone, which she yanked off the top of the desk. The photo on the caller ID was one of Mike mid-sneeze. "One sec. Gotta take this." She held up a finger to Maureen. "Hey Mike. How's the train thing going?"

But Mike did not answer. Instead, all Steph heard was a series of touch tones. Her jaw dropped as something clicked in the back of her head. This could only mean one thing. And it was bad.

"Mike's in trouble," she blurted out as she hung up the phone.

"What do you mean?" Maureen scrunched up her face. "What kind of trouble? What did he say?"

"He didn't have to say anything. Trust me. I just know. We've got to go help him."

"I ain't moving from this spot until I get my money."

"Well," Steph looked away, trying to figure a way out of this. "Mike, uh, has the bank details, so . . ."

"Alright, let's go." Maureen grabbed Steph by the collar and they were out the door and down the stairs in the blink of an eye. As they emerged into the daylight, Steph was sure they looked like an odd pair: a twenty-something slacker still in her duck-themed pajamas, and her older, angrier mom.

Her angry fake mom turned to her. "Okay, so where is he?"

"He's on a train," Steph said. "Heading to North Brockville."

"North Brockville is a dump. Why's he going there?"

"He got a fancy ticket on some newfangled train. This one." Steph handed her the golden ticket. "Real fast. He had a real hard-on about it. It's the kind of lame thing he likes."

"Great." Maureen groaned, turning the ticket around in her hands. "How're we gonna catch something like that?"

Steph glanced across the street where a 1982 Mercury Zephyr sat quietly rusting, with mismatched doors and a top speed of 35 miles per hour. Mike had never let her drive the Garbagemobile before, but, given the circumstances, she was sure he wouldn't mind this time.

"Maureen, grab your shit."

* * *

The bomber had forced the train to slow to a crawl. They were still moving, but at the merest fraction of a mile per hour in some sort of cruel taunt. The mass panic had subdued, which was good, but there was a palpable nervous energy brewing among the passengers, knowing they had nowhere to go lest they be blown to kingdom come. Meanwhile, Michael and Helena had descended the stairs and shut themselves away in the throughway between cars so they could freak out semi-privately.

"This is not good." Helena paced back and forth as Michael did his best not to look like he was terrified beyond belief. "What're we supposed to do?"

"I—I don't know!" His stutter was not helping his image. "Maybe—maybe Dalton knows what to do?"

"Dalton?" Helena snapped. "Dalton's useless. He's just a—wait. No. Sorry. I shouldn't be upset at you. It's worth trying. Let's go." She nodded and stormed through the doors into the next car. The slowly creaking wheels were silenced as the door hissed closed. Michael, as unsure of himself as ever, looked around and spun on his heel before speed walking directly toward the bathroom. He would rather not have his bladder explode before the bomb did.

He sighed in relief as he approached the gray metal door and saw the tiny green "vacant" sign above the latch. Michael reached for the handle—but then he felt his stomach yanked to the side as the train accelerated to top speed once again. He flew back, his shoulder slamming into the bulkhead before he slid to the ground in pain.

"Ow! Goddamnit!"

Through the wall, Michael heard the muffled laughter of the bomber echoing across the info screens of Car Eight. He struggled to his wobbly feet and regained his bearings, stomping back toward the bathroom.

Michael felt a sudden onrush of wind and heard the loud thundering of the train across the tracks as the causeway between the cars hissed open. A man slipped in. It was the portly guy he'd met in line, gingerly reaching for the bathroom door.

"Hey! Hey! Hey!" He ran over, waving his hands. "What're you doing? I was here first!"

"Well, why didn't you use the bathroom then?" The man looked down his upturned nose at Michael as if his actions were beyond reproach.

"Because the train sped up and knocked me on my ass!" Michael dragged his fingers through his hair, whining. "Why can't you take any of the bathrooms on the other cars?"

"Because they are all occupied. Excuse me." And with a swiftness Michael hadn't expected from a man that size, he disappeared through the narrow door and shut it, turning the sign to an infuriatingly bright red "occupied."

"RRGH." Michael struggled to keep his scream internal. Biting his lip, he tried pushing forward through the train to find Helena. There was one upside to his potential kidney damage. He was distracted enough to ignore the roar of rushing countryside battering against him as he moved from car to car. At these speeds, he typically would've been too nervous to make the short leap between them.

Cars Seven through Two were mostly identical to car eight, double decked with quietly panicking passengers and frustratingly occupied restrooms. It was only when Michael yanked open the door to Car One that he saw a vast difference. Instead of a passenger car, this was a single-level, high-ceilinged office, with a hardwood desk positioned by a large side window. Michael even felt the difference as his feet traversed from the cold metal of the other cars and onto the lush carpeting of this one. It was like stepping into a luxuriously mansion after living in a sterile office building. The only thing that felt out of place was the array of ultra-widescreen monitors mounted on the opposing walls, all displaying what looked to be live stock market graphs and tickers.

Helena, her back to him, was standing by the desk conversing with Dalton Barnes. Meanwhile, his pink pant-suited assistant silently tapped notes into her tablet and tried to be inconspicuous.

"This is a public relations nightmare!" Dalton screamed. "How the hell is this guy taking control of your train, Helena?"

"I don't know," Helena waved her hand. "I don't know who he is or what he's doing, but we're moving at top speed right now, so we have very little time to figure this out."

"Well, you better figure it out quick, because I am not paying for another one of these!"

"Don't worry, I think we've got the right people on the job."

"Like who?"

"Like me." Michael stepped forward. Then, realizing his undeserved boldness, shrunk back a bit and waved. "Um, hi."

"Who the hell is this?" Dalton snapped at his secretary. "Ms. Meadows, please kick the riff raff out of my private car."

"He's not riff raff!" Helena jumped in front of Michael and shielded him dramatically. "He's a detective. He's here to help."

"A detective?" Dalton furrowed his auburn eyebrows.

"Yeah." Michael cleared his throat. "Um. I helped take down the Future Group?"

"Oh yeah." Dalton rubbed his chin, narrowing his eyes in vague recollection. "Beavis and Butthead, right?"

"No, that's . . . that's not right."

"Whatever. We'll run with it. But where's Beavis?"

"She's not here," Michael explained. "I was the only one who got—wait, why am I Butthead?"

"So if you're so good at being a detective," Dalton asserted, though Michael whole-heartedly disagreed with his assessment, "what're you going to do about this whole bomb situation?"

" I . . . uh . . ." Michael rubbed the back of his head and avoided eye contact with anyone in the room, causing him to stare at a painting of an crooked-nosed old man—probably a Barnes ancestor. "I thought you might know."

"Me? I don't know shit! I just provide the money, you idiot! What do I even pay you for?"

"You're not paying me."

"That's right I'm not. You're fired." Dalton turned back to the quiet Ms. Meadows with a flip of his hand. "Get this guy out of here."

"Wait," Helena piped up. "Just give him a chance. Michael, there's gotta be something you can do. Did you notice anything suspicious?"

"Well, uh . . ." Michael grasped at the straws in his head. "I'm pretty sure I ran into this bomber person just before I got onto the train."

"What?" Dalton blinked. "Why didn't you stop them?"

"Well, I didn't know they were a bomber then! I don't go around tackling people *just in case.*"

"Did you get a clear look at them?" Helena asked.

"No, not really. Just their cloak and their silver mask. It really could've been anyone under there. And there was this weird station maintenance guy who told me not to get on the train. I thought he was just crazy, but maybe he knew something."

"Maybe he's the bomber!" Dalton turned back to his assistant. "Ms. Meadows, I hope you're writing all this down."

She nodded curtly, silently continuing to take notes.

"Let's not jump to conclusions just yet," Helena cautioned. "Michael, did you see anything else suspicious?"

"Not really," Michael said. "But this chubby guy stole the bathroom from me, That was kind of rude. And so did this single mom with two kids. Wait, didn't she also say she wanted to see Dalton personally?"

Dalton straightened up and cleared his throat with a waggle of his thick neck. "This, uh, single mom. What'd she look like?"

"Frazzled, mostly. Reddish blonde hair. Streaks of grey. Her two boys were making such a racket it was hard to concentrate, actually. One of them kicked me."

"Is her name McMurray?"

"McMurray, yeah!" Helena said.

Dalton pivoted to his assistant, his off-white coat swishing in the air. "Ms. Meadows, triple the security in this car. If this detective can just waltz in here, so can Anne."

"You know this lady?" Michael arched an eyebrow.

"She's been after me for a while, says her kids are . . . well, mine."

"Crikey, Dalton. Another one?" Helena sighed.

"It doesn't matter." Dalton waved it away. "She's been after me for years. Maybe *she's* threatening my train as revenge!"

"You think a single mom has time to be a high-tech terrorist?" Michael scoffed. "She can barely handle her terrible kids."

Dalton glared at Michael before changing the subject. "Well, what if one of the kids is the bomber?"

Helena and Michael both rolled their eyes.

"What?" Dalton shrugged. "You said the kids were assholes."

The already derailed conversation was forced further off the tracks as they were interrupted by the crackle of static. The stock displays on the widescreen monitors blinked off one by one, replaced by a mosaic of the bomber's chilling metal mask and dark hood.

"Oh, hello again, my pretties. It seems like no one's even come *close* to finding my bomb. So, in the interest of fairness, I'm going to give you a bit of extra time."

The train rapidly slowed again and Michael, Dalton, Helena and Ms. Meadows lost their balance, tumbling into a large pile atop the soft carpeting.

"Now maybe that'll level the playing field for you," The bomber said, before the monitors went black.

"This whole variable speed thing is getting really annoying," Michael grumbled from the floor.

Helena, on the other hand, jumped back to her feet, pointing down at Dalton's assistant. "Ms. Meadows, does that tablet of yours connect to the television feed in this car?"

She nodded and wordlessly proffered the tablet to Helena.

"Fantastic," Helena's fingers whizzed across the screen, as she walked over to Dalton's desk and placed the tablet down to type. "I can backtrace where the broadcast is coming from and get the general location of the IP address."

"I don't know enough about the internet to know if that makes sense," Dalton said, looking at Michael, who could only shrug back.

Helena gasped.

"What?" Michael rushed to her side, peering over her shoulder. "What is it?"

"The bomber's on the train with us," she said.

* * *

"*That's* why you think Michael's in trouble?" Maureen scoffed from the back seat as Stephanie kept her full concentration on the road. "That's ridiculous. It could have just been a butt dial."

"Nuh-uh." Steph's grip on the steering wheel tightened as she yanked the Garbagemobile sideways around a slow-moving hatchback. They had long left the city limits and were now on the freeway in an attempt to follow the train, despite being nowhere near any actual train tracks. "You don't know Mike like I do. This was definitely a cry for help. Something's wrong."

"Fine. I'll take your word for it, but I still don't understand why we had to bring this thing." Maureen slapped the anime body pillow seat belted into the passenger's side seat.

"What? Oh, Oshinko? For luck." Stephanie leaned on the horn until an SUV relented and switched lanes out of her way. "And so we could use the carpool lane during the lunch rush."

Maureen rolled her eyes and returned to tapping away at Stephanie's phone. "I can't find any schedule for this . . . *Exo-City Express*. Are you sure this thing really exists?"

"This isn't Thomas and Friends, Maureen. This train really exists." Stephanie forced her words through her teeth as she laid on the horn at a passing minivan. "Those idiots think they own the road."

"Now I see why Michael doesn't let you drive."

Steph rolled down the window. "No, up *yours*, asshole!"

"Anyway, why doesn't the web have any info about this train, or even a place to buy tickets?"

"I dunno! It was some fancy big event. Like a grand opening at the City Station. Invite only. Maybe they didn't make it public on purpose."

"Well, if it left from the City Station and was heading up to North Brockville, the only tracks that can support a train that big go through Brinton. But if it's supposed to be fast, it should be a hundred miles away by now. This heap of crap isn't going to catch it."

"I've had it with your naysaying." Steph returned Maureen's glare. "We need to save Mike. Just tell me which way to Brinton. Maybe we can at least find the tracks."

"Alright, alright, kid. Relax." Maureen threw her hands up. "We need to peel off just south of the interstate viaduct. Next exit. That's the quickest way to Brinton."

"Well, then let's go!" Steph slammed her foot on the gas and the Garbagemobile grunted forward, nearly sideswiping a fruit truck.

* * *

"Why would anyone want to blow up a train that they're on?" Michael asked no one in particular.

"Because this person is insane!" Dalton shouted. "Did you really have to ask that question? Helena, can you trace where on the train their broadcast is coming from?"

"Give me a minute." Helena tapped at Ms. Meadows' tablet. "Car Nine. The signal's coming from the end of the train."

"Alright, detective," Dalton spun around on Michael. "You heard the lady, get your caboose down to the caboose and nab our bomber."

"Me?" Michael squeaked before glancing at Helena and clearing his throat. "Oh, yes, me. Of course. Of course I'll do it."

"Michael." Helena moved toward him and laid a soft hand on his shoulder, sending a jolt of electricity up his spine. "You don't have to go alone."

"Don't—uh—don't worry about me," Michael said, channeling as much false bravado as he could muster. "I can do this. I only need one thing."

"What is it?" Dalton asked.

"I really need to go to the bathroom."

"Hah! Bathroom. What a notion. You're a barrel of laughs, kid." Dalton began to chuckle but stopped in his tracks. "Actually, come to think of it, I really need to go to the bathroom, too. Excuse me. I'll be right out." He spun around and clicked open a hidden door. A white porcelain palace gleamed beyond, just ever so slightly out of reach. Dalton pointed at Michael as he slipped through the door. "Solve the mystery!" Then he was gone.

Michael squeezed his thighs together and winced. Ms. Meadows stared at him but offered no support or solace.

"Good luck, Michael," Helena said.

Steeling his fists, and his bladder with whatever muscles he had down there, Michael bit his lip and powerwalked his way out of Dalton's private car and back through the other coaches. The passengers he passed seemed quieter now, almost resigned to their fate, though they shared glances of fear—and maybe even a bit of hope—with Michael as he stormed by their seats.

Of course, the bathrooms in each car were still distressingly occupied. That was, until he reached the end of Car Eight, the last car before the caboose. Michael's eyes—not to mention his kidneys—were torn between the thick metal door to where the elusive mad bomber might be hiding, and the slightly ajar sliver of bulkhead that led to a cramped restroom. He could use the element of surprise, or he could tarry and possibly let the bomber hear him peeing like a racehorse, giving them ample time to flee. Would he choose his duty or his—well, if Steph were here, she'd say "doody," despite the inaccuracy.

A sudden spike in his bladder forced Michael's hand, and he leapt toward the restroom door.

"Yarrrgh!" was the only thing he heard as something large and very heavy barreled out of the restroom and took him full force in the torso.

"Noooooo!" Michael cried as the bathroom door retreated away from him. He felt himself being slammed backwards through the car doors, across the narrow gap, and down onto the darkened floor of the caboose. Michael looked up to find the wild-eyed maintenance guy from the station staring down at him, breathing heavily. "Why?" Michael groaned. "Why are you doing this to me?"

"I told you not to get on this train, goddamnit," the man barked. "But you didn't listen. You have to get off immediately! We're going slow enough now that you can jump off at the Brinton Station."

"Come on!" Michael whined. "I just wanna pee!"

"You can pee when you're off the train," the man growled as he got to his feet, surprisingly helping Michael up.

"But if anyone leaves the train, the bomber will make it explode!"

"Oh, you goddamn bloody-minded fool. You don't know a goddamn thing, do you?"

"What am I supposed to know?"

"Ah-ha!" the angry, jumpsuited man forced out a laugh that

sounded more like a cough. "You think the 'people' here are in real danger? That's how good they are! I mean, you didn't notice. And you're the detective."

"I mean, kinda. I'm not really a—"

"Of course you're not. You never even questioned why the bomber keeps slowing down the engine and giving you more time! This train isn't going to explode. Did you even ask yourself who's driving it?"

"Driving the trai—" Michael couldn't finish his thought as the train once again slammed to a halt, tossing Michael back into the caboose door. He grabbed hold of the railings to steady himself. The crazy maintenance guy was not so lucky, as the train immediately picked up speed again, causing him to lose his footing. He screamed as his flailing body smashed into the rear door of the caboose and rocketed out onto the track with a sickening crunch as the train blasted away.

"Oh Jesus!" Michael caught his breath as he forced himself to his feet before tumbling back onto the floor of the caboose. He felt bile rise in his throat. "Shit! Holy shit!"

"Michael, what happened?" Helena dashed through the doors behind him. "Are you okay?"

Michael stifled his retching and looked back over his shoulder. "What're you doing here?"

"I didn't want you to have to confront the bomber alone." Helena scanned the empty, dirty caboose, filled only with a few stray boxes and dusty, old tarps draped over what could only be other stacks of boxes. "Did you find anything?"

"There was—there was a guy here. The same weird maintenance guy I saw at the station. He said I didn't belong here, and the people on this train weren't in any real danger. That the bomber wasn't going to blow up the train."

"That . . . uh . . . doesn't make any sense." Helena blinked before something diverted her attention. "Wait," she said, moving toward one of the bigger tarps draped over a massive crate. "Every time the bomber was on screen, the background was a sort of dirty, stained off-white."

"You don't think . . ." Michael pushed himself to his feet and moved to the smaller tarp immediately behind Helena. Yanking it away revealed a small video camera set-up with wires feeding directly into the structure of the caboose. "They were filming right here."

"Then where did they go?" Helena's question was answered almost instantly by the hollow clomping of footfalls directly above them. Her eyes widened as the footsteps receded.

"Aw crap," Michael rushed to the front door of the caboose and caught a dark shadow flitting overhead, the trails of its black cloak slipping out of sight over the lip of the roof of Car Eight. "I should've expected this."

"We need to flank them." Helena stated. "You climb up there and drive them forward. I'll try to get ahead down here and corner them when they get closer to Dalton's car."

Michael looked longingly through the car doors at Car Eight's magnificently vacant restroom. He held back a single tear. "But, I . . ."

"Just go!" Helena slapped the metal ladder to the roof hanging between the cars. "We don't have time!"

Michael sighed and leapt onto the ladder, struggling his way up rung-by-rung. As he reached the top, the wind whipped mercilessly at his mop of hair, sending black strands of it flying into his face and, really, all over the place. He was going to look like a complete mess after this.

Michael heaved himself onto the roof of Car Eight and flattened his body to the ground in the face of the overwhelming wind. He still couldn't tell how fast they were going, but, judging by the way the countryside was rushing past, it was . . . fast.

Across the bright white metal roof stood the bomber, their formless black greatcoat flowing around them wildly like some sort of wind specter. The cold eyes of their iron mask focused squarely on Michael, and it bobbed. They were trying to say something. Michael couldn't hear anything over the consistent rush of air, but he did see the dark tiled roof of what might've been Brinton Station fly by.

"What?" Michael yelled, still flat on the ground.

The mask bobbed again, this time accompanied by a sweeping gesture of the bomber's gloved hand.

"Sorry! I—I can't hear a word you're saying." Michael strained against the air resistance to point at his ear and indicate this situation was a no-go. "I can't hear you because of the wind! *The—the wind!*"

The bomber expressed what looked like a sigh, and a small trigger mechanism appeared in their hand. They pressed the bright red button atop it and, to Michael's relief, the train didn't explode, but instead slowed to a more manageable speed, eventually inching along the tracks.

"How about this? Is this good?" The bomber's voice, still deep and distorted in real life, carried much better over the relatively still air. "Can you hear me now?"

"Yeah, that's, uh, that's great," Michael said as he picked himself up and dusted off his jeans.

"So we meet again, Michael Duckett."

"You know me?"

"I know a lot of things. But mostly I know how to blow up this train."

"Hey, look. Could you just stop?" Given Michael's desperate need to use the restroom, he didn't think tackling the bomber would have been the most . . . sanitary of ideas, so he opted to reason with them, instead. "Blowing us all up isn't going to get you anything. I don't know what you even want!"

"Oh, Michael Duckett." The bomber's garbled chuckle sent shivers down Michael's spine. "You're so close to the end. You just have to put together all the *clues.*"

"What the hell are you talking about, dude?" Michael shook his head, gesturing to the train and slow-moving countryside around them. "What clues? You're trying to blow up this train, and you're not making any sense."

"Then I suppose I'll have to beat some sense into you." The bomber shifted their body weight backwards.

"Listen, man." Michael planted his feet, wearily and reluctantly. "Could we not do this? I *really* need to go to the bathroom."

The bomber leapt across the train with surprising agility, arm outstretched in a fist. Michael barely had time to duck and roll out of the way as the cloaked bomber clanked to the metal floor.

A flurry of punches came Michael's way, and he did his best to dodge them, but one eventually connected with his shoulder and sent waves of pain reverberating across his body. He cried out and fell to the floor, grabbing his arm. He'd never been hit like that before. It felt like a sledgehammer had slammed into him. One thing was for sure, if the bomber landed another hit, he'd be done for.

The cloaked figure towered over him, their mask an expressionless steel visage of terror. "Now, Michael Duckett. I'll let you be the exception to the rules of my game and let you off this train myself."

The bomber grabbed Michael's foot and dragged him across to the edge of the carriage roof. Michael peered over. There, between the edge of the train tracks and a paved service road, was a deep gulf in the landscape. Since the bomber had slowed the train, the speed wasn't going to kill him, but the fall sure would.

With a surprising show of strength the bomber hoisted Michael up by his foot, and a surge of blood rushed to his head. Up until this point, Michael had managed not to piss himself, but he was seriously considering it if it meant the bomber would let him go.

"Goodbye, Michael Duckett," the bomber rasped.

Michael screwed his eyes shut and prepared to maneuver his body into a tuck and roll. Maybe he could still salvage some of his bones before he died.

A deafening crack shattered the air, followed by a thunderous clang.

"No! Arrgh!" The bomber cried in garbled pain as he loosed his grip on Michael's foot and let him thud to the floor. "This isn't what's supposed to happen."

When Michael finally managed to see past the stars swimming before his eyes, he spotted the cloaked bomber bounding away and dipping into the crevasse between the next two adjoining cars. Sitting upright, he rubbed his aching head. He thought he'd heard someone shout his name, but he chalked it up to his ears still ringing.

"Michael!"

"Mike!"

But it wasn't. Two different voices were calling out to him. There, chugging along the service road over the gulf was his decrepit 1982 Mercury Zephyr. Stephanie was waving at him from the driver's seat and attempting to honk—though the horn sounded more like a dying goose. Meanwhile, Maureen, leaning out the rear window side, had stabilized her high-powered sniper rifle across the car's roof.

"Steph?" Michael yelped. "What the hell are you doing here?"

"You looked like you were in a bit of a jam." She smiled, yelling back across the gap. "Good thing you got the train to slow down, otherwise, we'd never have caught up to you."

"How'd you manage to slow down high-speed rail, kid?" Maureen asked.

"It's . . . a long story." Michael said. "Listen, is there any way you can get on the train?"

Maureen ducked back behind the scope of her sniper rifle and shifted her view forward. "Looks like there's a crossing a few miles ahead. If you make sure this thing keeps chugging at this speed, we can pull up behind you and get on."

"Alright, I'll see what I can do!" Michael shouted back.

"Good luck, Mike!" Steph waved.

Michael nodded, before turning and jogging forward across the tops of the train carriages. The only way to make sure the bomber couldn't speed the train up again was to figure out how they were controlling the engine in the first place. So that was where he had to head. The bomber themselves was a secondary concern. Michael could only hope Helena would be able to corner them by Dalton's private car.

Once Michael reached the front of the train, he could see the crossing Maureen had mentioned up ahead. He slid down the rungs of the ladder into the narrow causeway between the first car and the engine. The deafening chugging of the pistons and wheels nearly drowned out his thoughts, but he pushed forward into the main cab.

The engine was much more complex than Michael had imagined. Why did he ever think he could figure out the mechanism that allowed the bomber to control the train? He wasn't an engineer. All his untrained eyes saw were walls and consoles crammed full of gauges and switches and levers he did not understand. But there, at the front of the cab, arched over the train's main controls with their back to Michael, sat a figure ensconced in an unmistakable black cloak.

"Oh, what the hell," he whispered to himself. "How'd they get here so fast?"

It was at that point Michael realized he hadn't come up with a proper plan. Panicking, his eyes darted around the cab, eventually settling on a bright yellow case conveniently left open. Inside sat the bulbous orange form of an emergency flare gun. Michael snagged it and, inching forward, pointed it at the back of the bomber's head.

"Alright, hands where I can see them. And turn around, slowly!"

The bomber did as they were told and began to turn. Out of the corner of his eye, Michael noticed the harsh edges of the bomber's metal mask resting on the console beside them. He could only blink as he took in the bomber's true face—one Michael recognized from not so long ago.

"Donneger?" Michael reared back at the ticket taker's stern visage. "You're the bomber?"

"Ah," he flashed a rictus grin. "So we meet again . . ."

"Again? I just saw you like five minutes ago! You punched me in the shoulder!" Michael shook his head. "This doesn't make any sense. Why would you want to take this train hostage?"

"I have my reasons!"

"Which are . . ." Michael led, waggling the gun in an effort to get him to spill the beans.

"I'm an old school railwayman." Donneger sneered. "The very idea of this *Exo-City Express* is a mockery of everything I believe in. Clean, sterile, soulless modernity hidden within the trappings of the gorgeous heyday of rail travel? It makes me sick."

"That's it? That's your reason?" Michael scoffed.

"What? That's not enough?"

"To threaten to blow up hundreds of people because you don't care for an *aesthetic*? Even Scooby-Doo villains have better motives than that. Y'know what? I don't care why you're doing this. You're coming with me." Michael grabbed Donneger by the collar, keeping the flare gun firmly pressed against the small of his back to prevent any funny business. Steadily, he dragged him out of the engine, back through the rear doors, and across the small gap in the cars.

"Knock," Michael ordered, his hands full of black cloak fabric and gun, respectively.

Donneger sheepishly rapped on the door and it slid open, revealing the familiar opulence of Dalton's private train car. Michael shoved the ticket taker through and onto the carpeted floor.

"Here's your bomber, eve—" Michael's words caught in his throat as he found Helena pinning a black cloaked figure to the floor with her knees. Dalton, meanwhile, had drawn an expensive looking golden gun and trained it at the figure's head.

"Ah-ha!" Helena said as she tore the figure's metal mask off and sent it clattering against the wall, revealing the fearful, mousey face of

Ms. Meadows—Dalton's personal assistant. "So it was you all alo—" Now it was Helena's turn to stop in her tracks as she registered Michael's presence with wide eyes.

"Uh . . ." Michael droned. "Wait. What? There are two bombers? I don't get it. What's—what's going on?"

Helena blinked twice before she unleashed a bedraggled sigh, dragging her fingers through her hair. "God *damn* it!" As she yelled, her voice instantly lost its charming Australian timbre, and descended into a frustrated, and admittedly less attractive, American accent. "This isn't what was supposed to happen! This isn't how it's supposed to work at all! Computer, shut down automation!"

On that cue, the train, still moving at about a half a mile an hour, ground to an easy halt. Simultaneously, Dalton Barnes slumped over and collapsed, as if his bones could no longer contain his weight. Both bombers, Donneger and Ms. Meadows, had no need to collapse as they were already on the floor, but the lights immediately went out of their eyes, replaced with a deep, unnerving black.

Michael jumped back. "What the—?"

"You screwed it all up! You messed up my entire business plan, you goddamn *moron*!" Helena shouted. "You and my goddamn father can't just let me do what I want!"

"Whoa. Where is *this* coming from?" Michael asked. He backed away from the slowly advancing Helena. She was acting like an entirely different person than she had been two seconds ago—except for one familiar thing he couldn't quite place.

"All I wanted to do was create an innovative, next-gen interactive experience that would change the entertainment industry forever! It shouldn't be that hard."

"I'm sorry." Michael squinted. A lot of words were coming at him at once, and he wasn't sure how to interpret them. "I'm not following."

"No, of course you don't. You and my father just want to take everything away from me!"

That's where he recognized Helena's unaccented voice from. She had been the woman yelling over a conference call in the station office. But before Michael could put more of these pieces together, he found Helena holding up the gold-plated gun that had belonged to Dalton Barnes—or whatever it was he was.

Michael's hands went up instinctively, as he backed up toward the wall. There was still a bit of distance between him and the deranged Helena, but what did it matter when a gun was involved?

"I swear, goddamnit. This is the last time," she said, almost sobbing. She pulled the trigger.

As the bang of Helena's pistol reverberated around the room, Michael reared back, wincing, but felt a large mass tumble through the air before him, absorbing the bullets with a dull thud and leaving him unscathed. When Michael opened his eyes, he saw the fluffy body of a scantily clad anime schoolgirl slumped on the floor, with two entry wounds three inches to the side of her comically large chest.

"Oshinko, no!" Steph dashed in and knelt at the side of the body pillow. "You're too barely legal to die!"

"Huh," Maureen said as she finished following through on the throw. "I guess that thing did come in handy."

"Oh my god." Michael let out a long breath, as their secretary/assassin handily tackled Helena, pinning her to the floor and containing the threat.

"Breathe, Mike." Steph patted him on the back. "It's okay. You're still alive. Although the way you stress out about stuff, you might prefer to be dead. Now, what's going on with this lady?"

"Actually, Steph, could you give me a few minutes?" Michael didn't wait for her answer and instead dashed his way toward the wall, slammed on the corner of the hidden door that led to Dalton's private restroom, and slipped inside. Three minutes later, he returned with a refreshed "Ahhhh."

"You better?" Steph smirked.

"You have no idea," Michael said.

"You'll pay for this," Helena said from her position on the ground. "You'll all pay! Don't you know who I am?"

"I'm really starting to think I don't," muttered Michael.

"I am Helena Pembroke!" She shouted, as if volume alone could convey the gravity of her statement.

Michael and Stephanie shared a look and a shrug.

"I'm sorry, I, uh, I don't—" Michael looked over at Maureen who still had her knee on Helena's back. "Maureen, do you. . . uh?"

"Don't look at me, kid. You're on your own with this one."

"Wait, hold on," Steph squinted at her. "Were you in that traveling production of Rent I saw back in 2011?"

A low growl escaped the back of Helena's throat. "No."

"Okay." Michael gave in. "Then who are you?"

"Helena Pembroke!" She repeated. "Daughter of Armitage Pembroke and heir to the Pembroke fortune. I'm an entrepreneur!"

"I thought you were an engineer."

"Well, I was, but after I had this train constructed, I realized there was very little money on the technical side," Helena spat. "So, I took my talents to business, because I realized there's no better investment than getting rubes to shell out cash for repeatable experiences with existing capital assets and cheaply rotable equipment. Like the artificial actors."

"Artificial actors?" Maureen snorted. "Like robots?"

"Yes, like robots!" yelled Helena. "My father invested heavily in artificial intelligence and life-like automaton reconstruction. He was steps away from transferring human consciousness into their memory banks, but I commandeered the technology for more lucrative purposes."

"Acting out some sort of train bombing interactive mystery?" Michael cocked an eyebrow. "It's basically an overly complicated escape room."

"Yes, and it would've made millions!" Helena insisted from the floor. "If it weren't for you screwing it all up."

"So . . . what?" Michael asked. "Everyone on this train is a robot? Is that why I'd never heard of 'Dalton Barnes' before?"

"Every single passenger was a construction. Dalton, Donneger, Mrs. McMurray and her kids. Everyone! Each instructed to play their parts according to the detailed script that I wrote."

"Oh." Michael coughed. "Well, sorry to tell you, but your script didn't make any sense. Donneger said he wanted to blow up the train because he didn't like what it looked like? That's super lame."

"He was an alternate contingency ending!" Helena said through gritted teeth. "Both of you were supposed to be here. The story was written to have the city's two most famous detectives participate in the mystery of the century! But when only one of you showed up, I had to retool everything on the fly." She looked away as Maureen began to zip-tie her wrists. "And there were loose ends that kept growing exponentially. You were supposed to chase the bomber to Dalton's car to find that it was Ms. Meadows the whole time."

"It still doesn't add up," Michael said. "Part of the fun of solving the mystery is piecing random stuff together. I don't think you put any reasonable clues in there. Ms. Meadows was with us when the bomber broadcast their announcements! And she didn't even have any dialogue. What was her motive supposed to be?"

"Ms. Meadows was fed up with—whatever! I don't need to explain the plot to you. I'm an entrepreneur, not a writer!"

"Well, that much is clear," Michael scoffed.

"I wasn't here for any of this," Steph said, "but it sounds like you pigeonholed yourself into this whole train premise without actually figuring out how everything should fall together."

Maureen guffawed as she picked herself off Helena and raised her by her collar. "Shit, lady. You just got called out."

"The one thing that worked was that crazy maintenance guy," Michael admitted. "He scared the crap out of me. But I guess that's a relief. I thought he died when he got thrown onto the tracks."

"Oh, he wasn't a robot," Helena said. "He was a real guy from the station and he was a pain in the ass from day one."

"Uh, wow. So then everything else was just a shoddy attempt at launching a business, Helena?" Michael frowned. "Nothing between you and me was real?"

"Of course not," she sneered. "Don't be an idiot."

He sighed. "Was there ever even any bomb?"

"Oh, that was real, too. Check your jacket."

Michael felt the inside pocket of his sport coat and extricated a small blinking unit no larger than a credit card.

"I had one of the bomber robots plant it when it ran into you in the station. It would've made the whole experience of the ending feel real."

"Oh, man, Mike." Steph laughed. "The real bomb was *in you* all along!"

Had Michael not relieved himself earlier, he certainly would have now. "Jesus Christ." He handed the device to Maureen who tucked it away in a pouch on her belt.

"Now will you release me, please?" Helena demanded. "I have done nothing wrong, and need to recoup my losses for a relaunch."

"I, uh, don't think there's gonna be a relaunch," Steph said. "We'll have to turn you in because you technically did kill that one weird guy."

"Oh," Helena hung her head. "Right."

"I'll call the cops and let 'em know there's someone they oughta pick up," Maureen said, and with a brusque nudge, herded Helena out into the next car.

"Case closed, then!" Stephanie dusted her hands. "That was easy."

"Wait a minute Steph." Michael raised a finger. "How did you know to come here?"

"Why wouldn't I? You called me."

"Did I?" Michael remembered speed dialing Steph earlier but thought he had hung up after fumbling with his phone. Now, upon closer inspection, he found that he indeed had accidentally placed a three second call to Steph. "But I didn't say anything." Michael narrowed his eyes. "How did you even know that I was in trouble?"

"Well . . ." Steph smirked, clearly proud of herself. "You pressed the keypad to the tune of 'Help Me Rhonda' by the Beach Boys as a call for help. Just like in Short Circuit 2—your favorite movie!"

Michael blinked.

"Steph, I've never seen Short Circuit 2."

"Oh." Steph bit her lip and glanced away. "Then who am I thinking of?"

T'was three weeks before Christmas and through the police station,
Rex Calhoun was heard voicing frustration.
"What d'ya mean the city's been shut down by the mayor?
It's just snow and there's a goddamn maniac out there!"

For years Calhoun had chased an anonymous schmoe
Who'd only ever struck under cover of snow.
Now, in the midst of a blizzard, he might strike again.
And would escape if Rex couldn't marshal his men.

Calhoun slammed down his phone with a guttural growl,
Then picked it up again with his traditional scowl.
"Yes, Chief?" said the desk cop as she got on the line.
Times like this made Rex want to resign.

Rex needed help, though he was loathe to admit it.
He was knee-deep in bureaucratic horseshit.
Pinching his eyes shut with consummate ire,
"Goddamnit," Rex groaned. "Get me Duckett and Dyer."

DUCKETT & DYER:
ST. NICKS FOR HIRE

Michael Duckett stuffed a second pillow down the front of his furry red suit, adding a bit of heft to his belly. Having lost his job months ago, and with the detective agency money going mostly to repairs for the Garbagemobile, Michael had decided to earn some extra scratch as a Santa at the Pembroke Mall, though he didn't really look the part. The red fur suit hung off his gangly, awkward frame with very little flesh to fill it out, and the pillows looked weird and rang false.

Michael glanced at the floor mirror leaning dangerously against the wall by the bed and took it all in. He frowned past his wispy cotton beard. The kids weren't going to buy it one bit. Why'd the mall even hire him?

"Steph!" he called. "Could you c'mere a minute? I could use a little help."

"Sure thing!" The muffled voice of Michael's best friend, roommate, and amateur co-detective Stephanie Dyer vibrated through the frosted window of their bathroom door. "Give me a sec."

Michael sighed as he angled himself for a side view. Maybe a few more pillows would manage to push him out of the uncanny valley.

The door to the closet-sized bathroom creaked open and Stephanie stepped out, dressed in a similar set of Santa Claus regalia.

"Ho ho-hold up." She eyed Michael up and down. "Great. Now one of us has to go home and change."

"Steph, we *are* home." Michael pulled down his beard. "And why are *you* dressed as Santa Claus?"

"I'm going Extreme Clausing," she said, as if the concept was self-explanatory.

"I'm sorry," Michael breathed. "What?"

"Extreme Clausing," Steph repeated slowly, extricating a camera from her fur-lined pocket. "I dress up as Santa Claus and explore abandoned buildings with a GoPro strapped to my head. Then I upload the footage to my YouTube channel."

"If the GoPro is strapped to your head, how do your viewers—if there are any—know you're dressed up as Santa Claus?"

"I guess they just take it on faith, Mike." She placed a saccharine hand on his shoulder. "After all, isn't that what Santa's all about?"

Though the whole thing was irritating, Michael was most perturbed by how much better Steph's Santa costume looked. She pulled it off way too well, despite the fact she was going to drag it through the city's seedy, distressed underbelly.

"Whoa!" Steph's cry evaporated Michael's cloud of jealousy. "It's really coming down out there."

She had moved to the window behind their shared wooden desk and pressed her nose up against the glass. Over her limp red stocking cap, thick snowflakes hurtled diagonally to the ground.

"Aw, crap," he said. "That's not good. They're gonna cancel my gig. I was really counting on this cash."

"Well, you can always come Clausing with me," Steph replied, her nose streaking up and down the windowpane.

"Yeah, no, I don't think I'm going to do that. There's no way I'm stepping out in this mess."

One of Michael's cavernous red pockets buzzed. Shoving his hand in there, he fished around until he managed to locate the offending phone. He bit his lip as he looked down at the screen. "Okay. That's weird."

"What is?"

Michael twisted the phone so Steph could see the three numbers on the caller ID. "911 is calling *me.*"

Steph grimaced. "What is this, Soviet Russia?"

Michael placed the phone on the desk between them and switched on speaker mode. "Uh, hello?"

"Hold, please," said a stoic voice.

"But you called me!"

"Hold, *please.*" This time, it was clearly an order.

The line went silent except for a flat beep repeating every five seconds. Once the beeping stopped, the phone rumbled with a growl only produced by one man: the current Chief of Police, with whom they currently shared a relatively amicable détente.

"Rexy!" Steph beamed. "How's it going? You seeing this snow outside? Crazy, huh?"

"Yeah, uh, hello, Rex. What's . . . uh . . . what's going on?"

The phone emitted a low rumble, which Michael eventually figured was Rex mumbling something underneath his breath.

"Sorry?" Steph said. "Didn't catch that."

A slightly louder rumble.

"You're going to have to speak up."

"I. NEED. YOUR. HELP." Michael could practically feel Rex's voice gurgling up the back of his throat and straining its way through his clenched teeth.

Steph broke out an unabashed grin.

"Stop smiling," Rex snarled. "I can hear you smiling."

"Right, right, okay." Steph cleared her throat and pulled herself together, straightening her Santa suit and deepening her voice. "What can we do for you, Chief?"

"Don't call me that," he shot back. "I've got a problem."

"We're all ears, Rex." Michael leaned closer to the phone.

"There's a killer on the loose who I've been trying to nail for years. Thing is, guy only comes out when the snow is fierce enough to cover his tracks. Given this shitstorm, I'll bet you dollars to doughnuts he's coming out tonight.

"Now, normally, I wouldn't ask you yahoos for anything, but because of this blizzard, our idiot mayor decided cops are only to be deployed for extreme emergencies, and this doesn't count. So now we're just sitting around here like idiots with our thumbs up our butts!"

"So like, what?" Steph cleared her throat. "Like . . . each other's butts? Or is it more of an 'every man for himself' kind of situation?"

"This isn't a joke!" Rex roared.

"Uh-oh, Steph." Michael smirked behind his ratty false beard. "Better not make him mad or he'll put his thumb up your butt."

"Listen, you morons. If you keep jerking me around, someone might die tonight."

"Alright, alright," Michael nodded to Steph, who was stifling her laughter. "Who is this guy and what's his MO?"

"We call him the Santa Claus killer. He has a thing for Mall Santas. There's been at least one or two abducted—possibly killed—every winter for the past few years. All from the Pembroke Mall."

"Oh." Michael bit his lip as he glanced at his and Steph's current attire. "Great."

"Now, all I need for you to do is to ID the perp. Maybe snap a couple of pics. Or track them back to their hidey-hole. But whatever you do, *don't* engage."

"You called the right people for the job, Rexy," she said. "In fact, I'd say we're uniquely qualified for this case."

"I don't know what you're getting at, but don't make me regret this more than I already do."

"Just one question before we hop on out of here."

"What?" Rex barked.

"You need to fire whoever came up with the 'Santa Claus Killer'. The 'Santa Slayer' is sitting right there. This is why I always insist you come to me first so we can workshop these things. Otherwise, you end up embarrassing yourself with a subpar product." Steph was met with a click and silence. "Hello? Hello?" She turned to Michael. "I'm sure he's taking it under advisement."

Michael picked up his phone to find he was getting no bars. Nor was Steph's. "Well, that's just great. The blizzard's knocked out cell service in the area. Now what're we gonna do?"

"Don't worry, Mike," she said. "I've got just the thing."

* * *

The wind was so fierce, Michael had to keep his Santa hat jammed on his head with his right hand. The other shielded his face from the thick flakes of snow stinging his skin and eyes. In a more ideal world, they would have taken the Garbagemobile to the Pembroke Mall. But, since the engine decided to freeze to the top of the hood, Michael and Stephanie's only option was to trudge their way through a mile and a half of ankle-high snow in their Santa costumes.

The ultra-low visibility conditions weren't helping much, either. Aside from the cloudy green eye of an upcoming traffic light, everything else blurred into a grey and white haze. Michael had even lost sight of Stephanie about an hour in. He knew she was close by, given her constant radio contact, but he had no idea exactly where. As if on cue, her crackling voice burst out of his pocket. "Echo 3 to Echo 7. Han ol' buddy, do you read me?" Then, after a brief pause, "Ah? Eh? Empire Strikes Back."

Michael's gloved hand abandoned his face to the onslaught of snow as he fumbled the handset to his ear. "I *know*. Now, would you stop saying that?"

Another brief pause.

"No."

"Where even are you right now, Steph? I can't see anything."

"I bet you're happy I got us these neat walkie talkies, then," she crackled back.

Michael turned the pastel blue and pink handset around, staring at the smiling sunflower on the speaker. "You mean these *baby monitors?*"

"They were on sale."

"Do you even know which way we're supposed to be going?"

"Left," she said, with a long pause. "I think."

"Great job. This disaster is going swimmingly."

"Hey, this was your gig. You should know where the mall is."

"I don't even know where *I* am," Michael shot back.

"Well, I'm on the corner of . . . 46th and Culver Street."

Michael recognized the name. "The mall's only two blocks from where you are. Stay right there. I'll come to you."

Shoving the baby monitor into his pocket, Michael continued to struggle his way through the empty streets, eventually making it close enough to read a street sign. He didn't have too much further to go.

The rest of the city had heeded the mayor's warning—apparently to Rex Calhoun's chagrin—and wisely stayed indoors to avoid the brunt of the storm. There were no cars on the road, allowing Michael to inch his way toward the mall, slogging from traffic light to traffic light, colorful beacons in the otherwise frozen darkness.

Soon, through the quiet torrent of falling snow, he spotted Stephanie beneath the now all white awning of an antique shop. She was enthusiastically vamping into her GoPro, audible from ten feet away, despite the muting power of the blizzard.

"Yo, what up! It's X-treemClauzSixNine—that's Claus with a Z—and welcome back to my channel! Now I know I said I was going to head down to the abandoned mine outside of town, but things have gone a little sideways, and I'm helping track down a criminal at the mall. Now, the mall looks like it's all lit up, but there ain't no one in there, so that still counts as abandoned, right? C'mon, let's check it out."

"Steph! Put the camera away," Michael said as he approached. Despite her nonsense, she did get one detail right: the Pembroke Mall was lit to the nines. The boxy, beige edifice looming over the streets beyond was draped in multi-colored, blinking Christmas lights, topped by the garish, glowing script of the Pembroke Mall logo. Its neon pink tinted the falling snow.

"Finally," Steph said. "What took you so long?"

Michael waved his hands around to exasperatedly gesture at, well, everything. "Will you put your camera away so we can get on with this?"

"No way, man. My followers are expecting quality content!"

"Gimme that." Michael yanked the GoPro out of Steph's hands and shoved it in his pocket. "There's nothing 'quality' about this content."

"That's not very Santa-like." She frowned. "I'm starting to think the only reason they gave you this job was because the other guys kept getting killed."

Though the thought had crossed Michael's mind, he refused to dignify it with a response. Instead, he grabbed Steph's sleeve, dragging her toward the mall's main entrance.

"It's locked." Michael frowned as he jiggled the array of front doors in succession before peering through the glass to confirm nobody was home. "What're we goin—aagh!"

Michael leapt back as Stephanie hurled a large rock through the doors, sending tiny bits of glass flying into and pockmarking the snow.

"What the hell are you doing?"

"Mike." Steph stepped gingerly through the empty doorframe. "All the cops are stuck at the station. And security probably went home. Nobody's gonna be around to stop us."

"I guess that's technically true." Michael shrugged and followed Stephanie inside. "But it's the principle of the thing."

"Principles schmrinciples."

"Schmrinciples?" Michael shook his head. "Never mind. We're in the mall. Now what?"

"I dunno. Bide our time until our Santa Slayer shows up." A grin spread across Steph's face. In a blink, she snatched her camera from Michael's pocket and broke into a sprint. "Yoink! Race you to the video store!"

"Steph! We don't have a DVD player. Or a TV. Steph!" Michael groaned as he tried, in vain, to keep up with her. His Santa suit had taken on too much snow. Now, he was dripping wet in the relative warmth of the mall, making him soggy and uncomfortable. Steph, on the other hand, had wisely weatherproofed her suit. She had already rounded the corner, out of earshot.

Michael dragged his booted feet across the rough brown entryway carpets while wringing the grey water out of his hat and beard. Past the ads for assorted perfumes and clothing lines, the mall's lobby opened into a bright, magnificent temple to consumerism. Emerging into the atrium from the bleakness outside felt like a revelation—though one stuck in the excess splendor of the eighties and early nineties. Still, with the stores devoid of and life and movement, the entire place left Michael deeply unsettled.

"Who left all the lights on? This is a tremendous waste of energy and money. Especially for a rapidly failing business model," Michael muttered before realizing he was only talking to himself. Now where had Steph gotten to? He certainly didn't want to corner a Santa Slayer alone.

Michael supposed he'd head in the direction of the video store, but he hadn't set foot in a mall in years. He trudged his way over to the upright map, hoping to feel the odd nostalgic rush of a YOU ARE HERE indicator. But it had been replaced with a digital touchscreen.

"Oh, that's actually kinda neat." Michael swiped his finger across the glass surface to remove an ad of a shirtless Ryan Gosling promoting breakfast cereal for some reason. It was replaced by the weather forecast. Unsurprisingly, it was full of snow for the rest of the night before the storm broke at dawn.

"No, I don't want that. I want the map." Michael looked down at the black icon bar on the bottom of the screen and hit the graphic that looked the most like a map—but more like a fried egg on a newspaper. The word MAP lit up the screen in bright pink letters before displaying the continental United States. "Goddamnit. This is why no one goes to malls anymore.”

Technically, that it wasn't why no one went to malls anymore. But now was not the time for that discussion. Sighing, Michael took a step back to see if there was a part of the display he could hit or kick to make it display what he wanted. There wasn't. But what he did find was a trail of slushy, brown boot prints.

“Aha.” Michael clucked his tongue and followed the thin clumps of melting snow leading to his friend. Passing an array of perfume, clothing, and electronics stores, it crossed Michael's mind that he could come back here to grab Steph a surprise gift—especially since she made it a point to open every package that came to the detective agency. But what do you get the girl who wants everything? There was that weird old movie series she liked. Maybe a DVD of one of those would make Steph's day. Michael shrugged. He'd probably have better luck just asking her.

Soon, despite climbing three floors, Michael couldn't tell if he had passed by the same Cinnabon three times or three entirely different Cinnabons. But, in any case, he only found Steph after he passed the third one. She was a far off splotch of red and black in a sea of shining white.

“Steph!” He called out, but she turned the corner around the fourth Cinnabon and was out of sight. “Hey! Wait up! We're not here for your dumb video store.”

Michael swung around the corner and straight into what felt like a brick wall. He shook his head as he found himself sprawled across the smooth floor, slipping as he tried to sit up.

“Goddamnit,” he grumbled. He felt around the floor for his glasses. When his fingers found the dull plastic frames, he jammed them back on. “Steph, why don't you watch where you're go—” Michael's words immediately caught in his throat as he peered up at what wasn't Steph, but rather a mountain of a man, looming over him.

He was dressed all in fur, from his head to his feet,
With red robes all torn, and soaked by the sleet.
The black coals of his eyes burned in a rage,
And his once-snow white beard had been yellowed with age.

His face was pale grey, and covered in wrinkles,
Which merged with some scars, not to mention the dimples.
He swung a broad axe and a distended belly,
Well-rounded and speckled, like meat from a deli.

Now, Michael had seen some strange things of late.
Insane phenomena were no longer up for debate.
But this odd occurrence still gave him some pause.
"Aw, crap," he said gruffly. "It's a goddamn Santa Claus."

"Pretender!" The disheveled and clearly crazy Santa impersonator roared as he swung his axe into the marble floor, cracks snaking from the area where Michael once lay. To his credit, Michael had managed to compose himself and roll away before being cut in twain. Any doubts he had that this was the Santa Slayer Calhoun had been hunting dissipated into the air like the man's whiskey-tinged breath. Michael just didn't realize the guy would've taken the name so literally.

"Hey, man. Just relax." Michael jumped to his feet and gently motioned for the fat man to calm down, which, of course, had the exact opposite effect, treating him to another axe swing. So he took a page from Steph's book and attempted to keep the Santa Slayer talking. "Why don't you put down the axe and let's talk a while? Where did you get it anyway? Does this mall have an. . . uh, axe store?"

"Quiet! You're just like all the other pretenders. Unworthy of the name Claus!" The Slayer swiped his axe at Michael again. "You don't want to spread joy or good cheer. You're all just weak, greedy prostitutes for the invisible hand of consumerism and soulless profiteering."

"Huh." Michael dropped his hands and bit his lip. "Well, I can't really argue with that, but I think killing me is treating a symptom instead of the disease."

"RRAAAGH!" the Santa Slayer lunged at Michael, who leapt out of the way. Stephanie's talking method hadn't solved the problem, so Michael opted for his go-to solution: running really fast in the opposite direction.

The Santa Slayer gave chase, his heavy, brutish footfalls thudding and squeaking against the mall floor. No matter where Michael ran, the Slayer followed close behind, showing few signs of slowing down. If the fat man wasn't going to give up, Michael would have to fight back. Clasping his moist Santa hat to his head, Michael scanned the storefronts for something he could use to defend himself, eventually finding the window of a sporting goods store. Turning on a dime, Michael sprinted inside and grabbed a golf club from the bag on display in the window. He didn't know squat about golf, so he picked the biggest one he could find. 8-iron? 5-wood? Whatever. It didn't matter. As long as it was blunt and heavy.

The Santa Slayer slid into view just outside, his breath fogging the glass. Their gazes locked, the eyes of the crazed Slayer filled with a misplaced, malicious fury, and Michael's full of confused fear. With no other options, Michael took drastic action. He reared back and launched himself forward, aiming to crash through the glass and catch the Santa Slayer by surprise with a club to the side of his head, tackling him to the floor in an epic takedown.

Instead, Michael slammed his entire body into the window with a dull thud before bouncing back, flying into the store's floor display of winter sports equipment. Skis and poles clattered to the ground as he pushed himself up with a groan, only to come face-to-face with the Santa Slayer and his axe.

"Ahhh!" Michael shrieked and swung his club at the man's face, sending the Santa Slayer stumbling back. But not for long. He recovered and swept his axe through the air. Michael ducked and dodged to get out of the way, but several nearby mannequins in windbreakers were not so lucky. As their hollow plastic heads bounced across the floor, Michael found he was unfortunately positioned between the Santa Slayer and the store's exit. He turned back and grimaced as he found the man barreling toward him, screaming something unintelligible.

"Aw, crap."

As the two collided, all of Michael's breath escaped his mouth in a loud "oomph." Trapped in the Slayer's thick arms, Michael could only watch as they hurtled out the door and into the thin, third-level guard railing. It gave way, sending their awkward, two-body system sailing into the air in a prodigious arc.

Everything slowed to a crawl. Michael's eyes widened, allowing him to take in every detail of his impending doom. The Santa Slayer did not seem to care about the three-story drop. No, his face remained contorted in a determined, angry roar. The veins on his head, barely covered by his own red stocking cap, bulged with pressure, as if his skin was the only thing keeping them from bursting. The rush of the crisp recirculated air passing Michael's ears managed to drown out the man's bellowing, as well as what was surely Michael's own sustained screaming.

As the two of them rotated in the air, Michael caught the lopsided sight of what awaited them below. Their landing zone was home to the pillowy fake snow surrounding the Pembroke Mall Santa's empty throne, alongside a plump, candy cane-themed bouncy house. Right next to it was the hard, pointy black roof of a mall information booth. Michael screwed his eyes shut and hoped God would not ignore his obvious personal preference.

Time resumed its normal speed of one second per second as Michael and the Santa Slayer crashed into the roof of the information booth, which gave way with a thunderous crack. When Michael finally cleared his head and regained his bearings, he realized he was lying atop the fat belly of the Santa Slayer, who had taken the brunt of the damage. The man was now splayed across a pile of broken wood, bent metal, and useless information pamphlets.

Michael struggled to his feet, exhaling past a strange pain in his torso. He sucked in another breath as he touched his ribs and winced. Peering into his Santa costume, he could see a bruise forming, with a little bit of bleeding. But at least he was alive. It was more than he could say for the Slayer, who didn't seem to be moving or breathing.

Limping back over, Michael snatched his golf club from the ruins of the information booth. Using the handle he stabbed at the Santa Slayer's now-motionless stomach.

Michael bit his lip and wondered for a split-second if this could be considered murder. The crazy weirdo was the one trying to kill *him*, right? It had to fall under the umbrella of self-defense. Besides, it was the booth that killed the guy. Not him. Yeah. If it wasn't self-defense on his part, it certainly was on the part of the information booth. Hopefully Calhoun and any subsequent jury of his peers would see it that way.

As he continued to trip over his own anxious thoughts, Michael failed to notice the Santa Slayer's movements until the man's thick sausage fingers were already around his neck. No more roaring, snarling or even angry gibberish. The Slayer had transitioned to silent rage, a terrifying thing to see in a face resembling Ol' Saint Nick.

Raising Michael off the ground with one hand, the Santa Slayer ripped the golf club out of his grip before throwing him to the ground and using it on him. The pain in Michael's ribs exploded in rolling waves across his body. His vision sparked in a multitude of colors before surrendering itself to an altogether more peaceful black.

* * *

Christmas had come early, and Stephanie was psyched.

The video store hadn't made it easy to get in—what, with its metal chain link shutters—but the lock picking kit Steph secreted away for Extreme Clausing purposes made short work of it. Having taken care of that annoyance, she made her way toward the Used and Donated section in the back. It took Steph nearly twenty minutes of searching, but past bootleg VHS copies of *Fritz the Cat* and *The Star Wars Holiday Special* and beneath a pile of *Dr. Demento* records was a perfectly shrink wrapped copy of *Leroy Noire: Professional Badass* on an oversized LaserDisc.

Gracing the cover was the titular badass himself: Leroy Noire, draped in his blue karate gi and brown trench coat. A no nonsense man of action, Leroy's profession changed multiple times through the movie, depending on what the situation called for. He was a spy, a detective, a soldier, and a priest, all at the same time. Plus, he drove a kickass Bronze Mustang.

Every family had a Christmas movie they bonded over every year, and Leroy Noire was the go to for the Dyer household—despite it being the furthest cry from anything resembling a Christmas movie. She didn't know who started the tradition, or when, but Steph recalled watching Leroy Noire kick ninjas and Nazis—and Nazi Ninjas—in the face on countless Christmas morns alongside her father and brother. Even her mom, despite accurately calling it sexist, misogynistic and racially exploitative trash, occasionally found some fun in it.

Memories flooded back, and Steph's eyes watered as she hugged the giant sleeve tightly in her arms. The Dyers were all long gone now. Her parents dead. Her brother missing, but for far too long to not have suffered a similar fate. Now, though after years of searching, Steph finally had a piece of them to warmly reminisce over. She didn't know where she'd get a LaserDisc player in this day and age, but there was no other way she could get her hands on this film in the original unaltered and uncensored widescreen. Leroy Noire was so niche and unpopular, nobody had bothered to digitize it—and all the torrent downloads Steph found ended up being weird porn she shunted into a hidden folder in case they ended up stirring anything in her.

She couldn't wait to show Mike. He hadn't grown up with Leroy Noire, and couldn't really see past the dated dialogue and effects, but Steph never stopped trying to convert him to the movie that defined a large part of her childhood before they met. Not that he'd know anything about that. Still, Mike would at least be ecstatic she wouldn't be dragging him to thrift stores to search for it anymore. Feeling generous, Steph left a twenty on the counter and sauntered back out into the mall.

"Mike!" she called out, hoping he could hear her voice echo down the empty halls and atria. There certainly wasn't anything else to hear. "Mike! You'll never believe what I found!"

Steph didn't get a proper answer, instead she was treated to an elongated scream, punctuated by a sudden, thundering crash. Her smile dropped. If she heard right, it had come from the other side of the mall. Clutching her spoils to her chest, Steph raced across the tiled floors as fast as her black Santa boots could carry her, despite the occasional slip.

As she turned the corner around a Cinnabon, she caught a glimpse of what was going on. Down on the ground floor, Mike was trapped in the clutches of a large hulking man atop a pile of debris next to a candy cane-themed bouncy castle. The man, of course, was decked head to toe in bright red with a long, raggedy beard.

The Santa Slayer.

When she suggested the name to Calhoun, she hadn't thought the actual guy would have gone so literal with it.

"Mike!" she cried, but it was too late. The Slayer struck Mike with a golf club, knocking him out of commission. "No!"

Steph's voice carried, and the large man's ears perked up and swung his head in her direction. Luckily, she was four floors up, and she managed to duck behind a pillar before his gaze trended upwards.

To avoid being spotted, Steph used her GoPro to peer around the side of the pillar. Checking the video on her phone, she zoomed in on the floors below. The Santa Slayer had grabbed Mike's comatose—she hoped—body and was dragging him across the floor, his head squeaking against the tile.

Steph grimaced. She couldn't let this guy out of her sight, lest he do something terrible to Mike.

Well, *more* terrible.

But where was he going?

She leaned her LaserDisc gingerly up against the pillar, knowing she couldn't carry it with her. The stoic figure of Leroy Noire met her gaze with a squint as if to say, "You know what you gotta do."

"Yeah. You stay here. I'm gonna go get Mike." She nodded. After a few steps, Steph paused and turned back to salute her childhood hero. "I'll come back for you." She sped away down the nearest staircase, doing her best not to squeak across the mall floors.

Following the Santa Slayer was easy. What Steph had a problem with was maintaining her distance. The Santa Slayer was making odd turns and winding through the labyrinthine mall in such an erratic way, Steph was constantly afraid she'd lose him around the next corner. Not until he slowed down and stopped in the food court did Steph allow herself room to breathe.

In the midst of the empty tables and chairs, the Slayer sniffed the air, like a wolf aware someone was tracking him. Steph kept herself hidden, still using her camera to keep him in her sights from behind a nearby escalator.

The Slayer, satisfied he was alone, proceeded to drag Mike by his booted foot into the long-abandoned Orange Julius stall. The two vanished into the darkness behind the counter, and Steph crept forward into the light.

"Orange Julius." Steph swirled the words around in her mouth. They tasted just as acrid and horrible as the product they described.

The Pembroke Mall's Orange Julius had been closed for as long as Stephanie could remember. A slate of rat infestations, a particularly poor orange harvest, and an inexplicable rise in the popularity of grapefruits had finally done it in back in the late nineties, and here it sat, collecting dust and dirty looks from whomever passed it. Why no other fast food company snapped up the location was one of the city's oldest enduring mysteries, and everyone was happy to leave it unsolved.

Steph nodded to herself and tightened her Santa beard as she inched toward the stall. Peering over the counter, she saw nothing except a few discarded paper cups, a still sticky tiled floor, and the black void into which her friend and his captor had disappeared. Steph vaulted onto the opposite side and proceeded into the unknown, pushing past an array of rusting blenders and tray racks.

What Steph found resembled the tiny, oppressive kitchen expected in a mall food court, but the enormous obsidian door at the far end was what really caught her eye. Steph approached it, her gaze magnetized to its blackness, and ran her hand across its surface. It was cold—almost freezing—to the touch. And though it looked like wrought iron, it was clearly something else entirely.

It was something not of this world.

It was also open.

Steph shrugged to no one in particular and slipped her thin frame through the crack in the doorway and into the dark entryway beyond. She could barely see five feet in front of her, since the only light was the thin stream filtering its way past the door. But she was equipped for just this kind of situation.

"Extreme Clausing." She smiled to herself as she strapped on her headband and clipped her camera to it. Steph clicked on the light attachment and the darkness dissipated. What she found was a stone hallway more at home in a castle than the back end of a defunct Orange Julius. Twenty feet away, it disappeared into darkness and mist.

"Hey, what up?" Steph began narrating at a whisper, hoping the one-sided conversation would dispel her fear over what happened to Mike. "This is your girl X-treemClauzSixNine—again, that's Claus with a Z. Turns out the mall is a pretty great place to spelunk. Ever wondered what's behind the old Orange Julius? Well, just smash those like and subscribe buttons below and join me after the break!"

Steph proceeded into the mist, her extra plush Santa costume, with its insulating lining, keeping the drastically decreasing temperatures at bay.

"Brr," she said to her fifteen-strong subscriber base. "Super cold. Whatever this place is, it looks like it's been carved into the foundation of the mall. Been here for at least 30 years. But I'm not sure I like the décor. Whoa!"

Steph reared back, stopping herself from walking into thin air. Right before her, the floor dropped away into a seemingly bottomless pit, with two long ropes disappearing into the cold dark, dangling just out of reach.

"Well that was a close one." Steph turned her head, the spotlight on her head swinging between the walkway's edge and the ropes. "Now it looks like there's only one way down." She took a few steps back and set up for a running jump. "And that's to take a leap of fai—ow!"

Stymied by the thin layer of ice developed on the floor, Steph slipped and fell on her face. Blinking the pain out of her eyes, she managed to peer through the space between the mist and the floor, which gave her—and her audience—a clear view of a spiral staircase carved into the walls of the pit and illuminated only by her headlamp.

"Okay. Maybe there's two ways."

Hugging the slick stone walls, Stephanie descended the staircase, eventually breaking clear of the mist. It was a very deep pit and a very long staircase, and it would be difficult to fill the dead air with content.

"So, while we're here. Any of you guys ever hear of Leroy Noire?"

It was about twenty more minutes of waxing nostalgic—most of which would be lost in the editing room—before Steph reached the bottom, where she could see frost forming on the cracks in between each stone. At the foot of the staircase, the floor was blanketed in white, powdery snow, including the pit's ropes, which were attached to a large wooden platform as part of a pulley system. An elevator.

"Well, that would have been super useful." Steph grimaced before turning around to see which way she could go next. Unfortunately, the circular atrium at the bottom of the stairwell was lousy with arched stone doorways. An array of ten or so surrounded her, with freezing air howling through each of them and delivering steady clouds of snow flurries.

Steph bit her lip and looked to the ground to see if there were any signs pointing to the door the Santa Slayer had dragged Mike through. Bootprints, maybe? A trench dug by Mike's head scraping against the floor? But there was nothing except fresh driven snow. "Nuts. Well, loyal viewers, if this were a livestream, I'd put up a poll, but I guess we're gonna have to do this the old fashioned way."

Steph clucked her tongue and raised a finger.

Eeny.

Meeny.

Miney.

That one.

Steph hoofed it down her chosen hallway. It was claustrophobically narrow, only lit by a series of blue wall sconces particularly out of place in an underground castle. As the hall stretched on and on, Steph began to question if she had indeed made the correct decision. But eventually she stumbled upon something that proved her right.

No, she hadn't picked the right path. Far from it. But she found herself face-to-face with a barred door one would only find in some sort of dungeon. As the light of her head lamp filtered through the bars, she could barely make out a few figures held within. Had Steph not been primed by recent events, their ragged suits, dark with soot and dirt, and their famished, wasted bodies would have led her to believe they were zombies. Or at least an Edgar Winter tribute band. But right now, there really was no mistaking them for anything else.

"Santa Clauses," she whispered to herself, biting her lip. "Or is it Santas Claus? Show me some love in the comments below and let me know what you think."

* * *

Michael awoke cold, dizzy, and shackled to a slab. If anyone had informed him this was where he'd be, he would have decided to remain unconscious. The room around him was dark, freezing, and blurry. When it remained out of focus after a few rapid blinks and searing breaths, Michael realized he no longer had his glasses on.

The one thing Michael could see was an ominous, yet oddly familiar, blue light pulsing absently against the far wall, illuminating what seemed to be machinery around it. The cold air was coming through it, carrying thick white snowflakes.

Beside the machine, something stirred.

From the sheer size and heft of the shadow, Michael knew it was the Santa Slayer. The hulking dark mass coalesced into a hulking red mass and then into angry, grey bulbous features as the Slayer stomped over to the slab. Despite knowing better, Michael tugged at his metal restraints.

"Struggling is useless, Michael Duckett."

Oh, great. He knew his name. Why did he know his name? It was usually a bad sign when people you didn't know knew your name.

"Hey, uh . . . man," Michael gritted his chattering teeth. "I don't know what you want, but I can tell you I don't have any money. That's why I'm dressed up like an idio–" His eyes darted down to his crappy Santa costume, then back up to the Slayer. "Uh. . . dressed up like you?" Michael offered a smile and cleared his throat. Despite the cold, he was sweating bullets. "But, like, if you let me go, maybe I can help you get what you want? Eh? Yes?"

"I want to go home!" The Slayer roared and swept his arm across a nearby table, sending several items clattering to the floor.

"Home? Uh, where's that?"

"Don't you dare. You're just another poor pretender. Like all the others. Many of them didn't even *try* to look the part. Everyone knows Santa Claus is supposed to be an old white male!"

"Ohhhhkay, I'm not sure what kind of vaguely racist point you're trying to make here, but let's put a pin in that. How about instead of trying to kill me, you let me try and help you find your way home? Would you, uh, be amenable to that?"

The Slayer began laughing. It was a guttural laugh, rising up from deep in his belly. "Ohohohoho—oh no. You cannot help me. I am not from here. You insolent, greedy monsters can't do anything for me. Only he can." The Slayer thrust a finger toward the pulsing, swirling blue presence at the end of the room.

"Yeah, uh." Michael bit his lip. "Who is *he* exactly?"

"Ohohoho. Of course. You can't hear his voice. He speaks only to me." The Slayer let out a long sigh, before hanging his head, changing tracks entirely. "They brought me here—ripped me out of my own magical universe. God only knows how long I've been here."

Michael's stomach dropped. ". . . you're not from this universe?"

"A feeble mind such as yours, poisoned by despair and greed, couldn't possibly understand." As the Santa Slayer—the Santa—whipped around, Michael barely noticed a specialized shiny bracelet clamped across his wrist. If he was telling the truth, whoever dragged him into this world knew what they were doing. Such a bracelet would keep him physically stable in-universe. Mental stability, though, was a different story.

"I was a hero there! A saint!" He roared in Michael's direction. "But for years, I've been trapped in this hell hole. This world of yours chafes at me. At my skin. There is no pure magic. There is no hope here. I have to return home. The children of my world need me to spread love and joy."

"Oh no." A slow cloud of realization coalesced in Michael's chest as he came to a conclusion which would have irritated him if he wasn't in mortal danger. "You're the real Santa Claus, aren't you?"

"I goddamn used to be!" Santa bellowed. "For years, your scientists ran experiments on me. Tortured me. Tested me. Hoping to extract the secret of my immortality. I kept telling them! My powers came from the magic within us all. Within our hearts."

"Yeah, that kinda sounds like bullshit."

"Of course it does. Here, in a world devoid of *true,* pure magic, like that of my home. That's why I couldn't prove it to your *scientists*." Santa looked away as he spat the word out. "They kept prodding and poking away, until one day they just gave up, disabled their machine, and locked me down here like some sort of pathetic monster. They didn't listen to me! Nobody listened! Except him."

"Being intentionally vague isn't helping either of us. Who the hell are you talking about?"

Santa's head whipped back to Michael, and a hopeless darkness consumed his face. "The Whispering Shadow. The Midnight Storm. The. Black. King."

Michael's jaw dropped for a second before returning to its original position. "I have no idea what that is, man."

"Of course you don't. But *he* knows *you*. Ever since I was strapped to that very slab, I could hear his voice. Floating gently through the tear in existence they created. He was a source of comfort. Of reassurance. He told me he alone knew how to get me home. But that it would take time. And today, he told me I would need to find you." Santa perked up, his gaze darting toward the fuzzy blue light. "See? I hear him. Even now, he beckons."

Michael had no words. Try as he might, he couldn't hear a goddamned thing.

"He told me everything I need to know about you, Michael Duckett. All your sins. You've been a naughty boy indeed." The words dripped out of Santa's mouth alongside some stray saliva.

Michael shuddered, searching for something to say that could atone for whatever sins this madman thought he'd committed. But all he managed to squeak out was "I'm not a boy, I'm a man."

It certainly didn't help his case.

"He wants you," Santa whispered. "You are my ticket back home. To my old life full of joy and cheer. I don't know why he wants you, Michael Duckett. But you are a sacrifice I am very willing to make."

"Then why are you trying to kill me?"

"Oh, I'm not going to kill you." Santa flashed a disconcerting grin. "I'm sending you to him. The Black King will deal with you. And then he'll take me home."

"What?"

"The machine the scientists built to bring me here still works." Santa gestured to the blue glow behind him. "It just has a habit of overheating. It works best on the coldest of days, and I have tuned it to a cold, lifeless dimension to speed its operation."

Michael gulped. If these scientists had managed to actually construct a machine that could pierce the veils of the multi-verse, he had a whole lot more to worry about than a murderous Santa and his imaginary friend.

"Well," Santa dusted his hands. "Once I finish up a few last tweaks, this will be a very merry Christmas for me indeed."

* * *

"Hello? Is someone there?" One of the imprisoned Santas—a dark-skinned man—croaked from the far wall.

Stephanie swung her head in his direction, and he squinted, turning away from the light of her headlamp. She could see his once red Santa suit was dark and splotchy, as was his skin. Both hung loosely from his skeletal frame that was shackled to the wall. The man could move around, but only slightly.

"Whoa, man. You don't look so good," she said. "Let's see if we can't get you outta there."

"Oh, thank god," rasped another Santa—this one equally thin, but Asian—who was lying on the floor, with his legs in manacles. "I didn't think the police would send anybody."

"Well, I'm only . . . loosely affiliated with the police," Steph whispered through the bars. "But don't tell them I told you that. How long have you guys been down here?"

"Judging by how many of us he's dragged down here, I'd say three years," said the man on the far wall. He nodded his head toward the Asian Santa. "He's been here for two."

"Wow. How're you guys still alive?" Steph asked.

"That guy thinks he's the real Santa Claus. He takes the role very seriously and brings us toys every year." Asian Santa motioned over to a heap of moldy, plastic junk in the corner. "Sometimes there's an advent calendar or dreidel in the mix and we get to ration the chocolate. And any Super Soakers we find are good sources of water."

"Well, get ready, guys, I'm about to bust you out." Steph knelt down by the giant door's keyhole, examining it while thumbing through her lock picking kit. "Looks like an older model, but I think I have the right picks for this door. Just give me a minute."

"Why do you have a lock picking kit?" asked the thin, black Santa.

"Ever hear of Extreme Clausing?"

"No," said Asian Santa. "That sounds like not a real thing."

Steph frowned. "Yeah, well, I bet you thought Santa wasn't a real thing, too. Now look where you are." She scoffed. "Whatever. Just stand back."

"We're chained to the wall and floor. This is pretty much as far back as we can stand."

"For a couple of Santas, you guys sure suck the fun out of everything." With a few clicks and clacks, Stephanie released the lock of the heavy wood door, allowing it to swing open before its rusted hinges gave way and it crashed to the cobblestone floor, throwing up a cloud of dust. "Well, that was a waste of time."

"Yeah." Thin Black Santa waved his manacled wrists at her. "But maybe you can take these off?"

"Sure thing, Thin Black Santa."

"Don't call me that. My name is Alan."

"Oh, uh." Steph looked away before turning back down to the manacle locks. "Sorry. I didn't know."

"Well, you didn't ask."

"Yeah, I just got caught up in the whole 'Santa' thing that seems to be happening around here." Steph popped one of Alan's wrists free. "Speaking of which, what the hell does the Santa Slayer want with you guys?"

"Ooh. 'Santa Slayer'. That's a good one," said the Asian Santa. He probably also had a name, but at this point, Steph was too self-conscious about her mistake and decided to just avoid referring to him directly.

"He says he wants to go home." Alan rubbed his manacle sores in a sort of weird ecstasy as Stephanie released his second wrist. She moved on to Asian Santa's leg chains.

"Yeah, to some weird magic world. I thought he was crazy until he showed me the device."

"Device?" Stephanie nearly dropped her lock pick. "What device?"

"It's some sort of trans-dimensional breaching device," said Alan.

"How do you know that?" Steph asked.

"I used to be a Quantum Physicist, but that didn't pay the bills, so I mall Santa-ed to make up the difference. In any case, all of that stuff is theoretical at best. There's no way his device actually works."

"Right . . ." Stephanie trailed off as she finished releasing Asian Santa, her mind aflutter with the implications of what she was hearing. The Slayer must be a Santa Claus from an alternate universe. An evil universe, maybe? But who built the device? And why would an evil universe even have a Santa at all?

As the second leg shackle clanked to the floor, she was thrown back into the present. Whatever the Slayer's point of origin, Steph needed to keep him from harming Mike. "Okay, all done. Let's get out of here."

"Wait," said Alan. "What about him?" He pointed off to an alcove of the cell Stephanie hadn't yet noticed. Within, a third Mall Santa was hanging from shackles on both his arms and his legs. This Santa wasn't nearly as emaciated as Alan and Asian Santa, and his suit still retained most of its distinctive red, but Steph supposed he hadn't been here as long.

"Huh," said Steph. "How'd I miss him?"

"Well, he's never been the talkative type."

"Alright, buddy," Steph moved toward the Third Santa, lock pick at the ready. "Let's get you down from there."

His eyes, closed until now, opened and, despite the dire circumstances, Steph could make out the distinct presence of a faded twinkle as he smiled weakly but warmly at her. His voice was a soft boom. "Hello, Stephanie Dyer."

"Wait." Steph reared back. "How do you know my name?"

"It's on your name tag," Alan said.

"Oh." Steph looked down at the piece of masking tape affixed to her chest, displaying her scrawled name for anyone who needed to identify her body in the event of an Extreme Clausing accident. "Right."

Soon, Third Santa was free and looking a good sight more cheerful than when Steph had found him. He offered her a warm and hearty handshake. "It's been a long year. Thank you for your help, Stephanie. If it weren't for you, I'd've almost lost all hope in the magic of this world."

"Yeah, well." Steph shrugged. "I was always told the real magic was supposed to be in you all along."

The Third Santa scoffed, "Who told you that?"

Steph paused for a second, her head nodding slightly. "My parents. After I told them I didn't believe in Santa anymore."

"Hm." He stroked his luxuriously curly beard.

"But that's neither here nor there." She waved away the memories. "Now I need all of you to do a favor for *me*. My friend Mike is a Mall Santa like you three, and the Slayer has him somewhere in this evil lair of his and I need to find him before he uh. . . dies."

"Well, sorry," said Asian Santa. "This place is a maze. You must've seen all the doorways. None of us are even sure where we are."

"I have to admit," Third Santa said, "even my sense of direction is confused."

"Ugh!" Steph scrunched her face and paced toward the cell's exit. As she approached the arch where the door had fallen, she heard a burst of fuzzy, staticy noise. "What the hell was that?"

"Sounds like it's coming from your robe," Alan said.

Steph reached into the inside pocket and pulled out her still functioning baby monitor.

"Oh, BZZZZZT you're the BZZZZZZZT BZZZTn't you?" it said. The distorted voice carried the frenzied anxiety of Michael Duckett.

"Well, boys," Steph said with a wry grin. "You might want to grab some of them toys, because I think I know how we can find Santa's workshop."

* * *

With clanks and whirs, the parts of the portal machine slid into place, inducing the swirling blue blur into a slightly larger blur. Michael shuddered. He'd been tossed through inter dimensional portals before, but not at the behest of an insane Santa Claus.

That was a new one for him.

"The machine is almost ready." Santa declared. "For years, I've bided my time, careful only to power it on when its energy needs would remain undetected—and when the winter months provide adequate cooling. But tonight, in this perfect storm, the Black King can finally triangulate our multi-versal coordinates, and I will be free of this godless, hopeless place shackled to the almighty dollar."

The portal crackled and, even with his blurry vision, Michael watched it widen and fill its mechanical frame. Bolts of bright energy shot at odd angles. Contained by the machine, they were repurposed to strengthen the portal.

"He comes," Santa said with a monotone fascination. He strode toward the glowing tear in the fabric of the universe. "I can feel his presence. I do not envy what must happen to this world. But it is for the greater good. For my children."

"BZZZZZT."

"What was that?" Santa spun around.

Michael strained to look down at his Santa robe, where the harsh snowy static had emanated from. "BZZZT-ho 3 to BZZT-ho 7. Han ol' buddy, BZZZZT read me?"

With a thunderous slam echoing across the room's stone walls, a set of doors far behind Michael swung open. He couldn't see who strode in, but he had an inkling.

"Hey, Santa! How's about you jingle these bells?" Steph's voice soared over his head.

"Jesus Christ." Michael sighed. He could picture the motion she was certainly making with her body. Taking a deep breath, he shouted,

"STEPHI'MTRAPPEDOVERHEREANDTHISGUYISTHEREAL
SANTACLAUSFROMANOTHERUNIVERSEANDHE'SUSING
MEASASACRIFICETOGETHIMSELFHOMETHROUGHAMUL
TIVERSEPORTAL."

"None of that should make sense, but it does!" she called back. "Don't worry, Mike! I've brought help."

"Help?" Michael raised an eyebrow as two gaunt men in heavily distressed Santa Claus gear rushed past his slab, brandishing wiffle ball bats and long, floppy lengths of orange Hot Wheels tracks as weapons. They held the line between the deranged Santa and Michael while Steph appeared at his side with an array of lock picks in her teeth. "How'd you find me?"

Steph waggled the baby monitor in his face. "Just kept walking until the signal got clearer. Still couldn't catch most of it. He say anything important?"

"Uh . . ." Michael thought for a second. This was neither the time nor the place. He'd bring up the whole 'Black King' concept with her later. "Not really. Who are these other guys? More Extreme Clausers?"

"I guess you could say that." Steph grinned as she popped Michael loose from his shackles. "They're the missing Mall Santas."

Michael sat up, rubbing his wrists as a third Mall Santa, who looked the part and was in much better shape, stomped past, planting himself at the front of the vanguard.

"You." The Santa Slayer's eyes narrowed. "You're worse than any of these pretenders. You're complicit."

"Ho!" The third Mall Santa said. "That's some talk coming from you. What happened to you? How dare you use this boy for your nefarious purposes!"

"Man," Michael muttered. "I'm a man."

But no one heard him as the room rumbled. Small bits of rock and debris fell from the ceiling as the portal flared. Overflowing the bounds of the machine, its color shifted from blue to purple to a not-to-friendly red.

"Okay," Steph said. "That's not good."

The rumbling escalated into a persistent shaking. Not just in the stone bowels of this underground facility, either. Rather, it was as if the fabric of the world itself trembled. A heretofore unused mechanical arm of the evil Santa's portal machine slammed into place, stabilizing the rift further. A tempestuous swirl of red energy burst forth, as if a portal to hell itself had opened. The arches of the room above them cracked and crumbled as fissures snaked their way along the dark walls. A large chunk of rock crashed into the slab where Michael had been sitting just a moment ago, shattering it into pieces.

"We've got to get out of here!" Michael yelled over the din.

"Guys, c'mon!" Stephanie was already at the exit, beckoning her newfound friends to follow her. Both of the decrepit, unkempt mall Santas dropped their makeshift weapons and hightailed it away from the vortex of fiery energy. But the third one employed a remarkably different strategy: taking the fight to the Santa Slayer with a dramatic lunge.

"You won't get the best of me again, you twisted monster!"

"Uhhh . . ." Michael stood frozen to the ground, partly in confused fear and partly in surprise the heavy-set man could achieve such graceful horizontality.

The two Santas crashed to the ground and traded a barrage of mighty blows as they rolled along the floor. "You don't know what I've lost!" The Santa Slayer jabbed at the Third Santa's ribs before attempting to claw his eyes out with his scraggly fingernails.

"You've lost your damn mind, from what I can see!" The Third Santa ducked down and landed a devastating uppercut on the Santa Slayer's chin, sending him flying back. The Slayer's rotund, somehow muscular body bounced across the stones, coming to a halt against the frame of his portal machinery just below the crackling and sputtering red rift.

"Mike," Steph yelled from the door amidst her two distressed Mall Santa friends. "I know it's really cool and you wanna watch, but we need to move!"

"Just a minute!" Michael didn't know what compelled him forward, but he dashed to the aid of the Third Santa, who, despite his resilience in the fight, was beginning to show his age with a wheeze and a limp. "Hey," Michael whispered, draping the Third Santa's arm around his shoulder and propping him up with his back. "We need to get you out of here."

"No," he pushed Michael away and stood up straight, albeit with a bit of a waver. "I know what he's planning to do and I can't let him succeed. Otherwise, it's the end of everything as we know it."

"What? How do you know?"

"I'm smarter than I look." The Third Santa offered Michael a wink. "Now go with your friend. Everything will be okay."

Despite his inherent cynicism, Michael could do nothing but nod.

"Oh, and Michael, just remember." He raised a finger and placed it squarely on Michael's chest. "The real magic is in here."

It was the kind of schmaltzy thing Michael would have expected to hear in a poorly written Christmas Special. But there was no time to dwell on it, as the room was falling apart, with pieces of the structure flying past him into the portal. The Santa Slayer, once prostrate on the ground, struggled to his feet, a crazed look overtaking his eyes. He felt around the wall beside him and grabbed his battle axe.

"Hahahaha!" The Slayer's manic laugh could have collapsed the entire structure if the process wasn't already underway. "He's coming! He's coming!"

"Go!" The Third Santa said. Michael felt himself pushed across the floor, right out of the path of a large cascade of rocks and a curtain of dust that separated them. "Be careful!"

Michael nodded before turning tail and running. Typically, it would have been his first tactic, but now he felt bad about it, especially since he was abandoning a Santa Claus. He caught up to Steph and wrapped his arm around one of the more delicate mall Santas.

"What the hell were you guys yapping about?" Steph said. "And why's he not coming with us?"

"I'll tell you later. We gotta go."

"You're not kidding," said Steph. "There's an elevator up ahead.

Let's roll!"

"An elevator?" asked the Asian Santa.

"Well . . ." Steph shrugged. "It's more of a pulley system."

* * *

With the four of them working the ropes, the motley group ascended the entrance pit faster than Steph had descended it. But they had barely made it out of the back of the Orange Julius before the entire mall began to crumble around them. Whatever was happening downstairs between the two Santas and the angry dimensional rift was destroying the very foundation of the building. Steph had a lot of questions and, though she'd never admit it, worried about the situation and its implications, but she'd have to think about it later. The floor was literally falling out from beneath them.

"Crap, crap, crap!" Summoning a surprising amount of strength, Steph slung Alan the thin, black Santa over her shoulder. Equally scared, Mike grabbed the Asian Santa's wrist and dragged him along, trying to stay as close as he could to Steph.

Tearing through the hallways as each of the floor tiles were swallowed up by the encroaching bottomless darkness, Steph swung around the final corner in the main atrium and spotted the entry lobby. With one final jolt of adrenaline, the haphazard team of disheveled, misshapen Santas leapt through the shattered glass doors and into the breaking daylight just as the mall's façade began to crack in two. The entire building thundered down, collapsing in on itself, leaving just clouds of dust, chunks of concrete, and the scent of approximately twelve Cinnabons in its wake. The majority of the distinctive neon 'Pembroke Mall' sign cracked into pieces. Now, it was mostly buried, aside from the single flickering word BROKE, peeking from the rubble.

Mike was breathing heavily, doubled over on his knees, and the two Mall Santas collapsed on their butts in the dust. Steph finally let out a breath she realized she'd been holding for minutes.

"I bet we get blamed for this," Mike muttered.

"Eh," Steph shrugged between puffs of air. "Everyone orders their shit online these days anyway. Besides." She yanked her camera off her head. "We have it all on video."

Mike smiled.

"Oh, wait." One glance at the LCD display changed her entire tune. "I ran out of batteries 5 hours ago."

Mike's smile fell.

"Don't worry, Mike." Steph perked up as she remembered her great find. "I've got something cool to show you! I found it at—" Her face collapsed as she remembered the LaserDisc leaning against a pillar by a now non-existent Hot Topic. Her white whale—her one connection to happier memories of her family-had been crushed to absolute dust. Quickly, she turned away, desperate to hide the sudden, uncontrollable heaviness in her chest, and, worse, the slight trickle of tears from the corner of her eyes. She felt weak, hurt, and helpless for the first time in a long time, and she certainly didn't want Mike to see. This wasn't his problem to deal with. It wasn't even one he'd understand.

"Uh, Steph?" Mike asked. "Are you okay?"

"Fine, fine," she sniffed desperately trying to cram these feelings back in. Steph turned back around, hoping her eyes weren't too red. "I'm good. I'm always good."

"Listen, Steph, I don't know what's going on with you right now, but if you want to talk about it later, I'm always here." Mike's hand touched his chest, and he stopped, recoiling a bit. He reached into his Santa robe and pulled out a rectangular box he seemed surprised to see. He squinted uncomfortably as he whispered to himself. "The real magic is in here?"

"What?"

"Um," Mike bit his lip and extended the box toward her. "It's your early present?"

Steph gingerly took the box and turned it around in her hands. It was an old, recordable DVD box with a homemade slipcover. Despite the blurry print-job, Stephanie immediately recognized the logo and the dashing, mustachioed figure of her childhood hero, beneath the bold, declarative words 'UNCUT' and 'UNCENSORED'. A torrent of emotions came rushing back.

She spoke not a word, but went straight for the hug,
And Michael, uncertain, gave a smile and a shrug.
Stepping back, the two of them admired their work.
While the Mall Santas managed a weak bemused smirk.

Steph smiled and whispered, at dawn's first light,
"Merry Christmas to all, and to all a good night."
Then in a voice flat and cynical that everyone heard,
"Steph," Michael said. "It's December Third."

WHAT IS YOUR EMERGENCY?

The following is transcribed from the City Police Department's 911 Call Logs. It is not to be released to the public.

[4:15pm Monday December 9th, 2013]

911 Operator: Hello, 911. What is your emergency?

Caller: Yes, can I speak to Police Chief Calhoun, please?

911 Operator: Uh, ma'am. This line is for emergencies only. Using it for other purposes is illegal.

Caller: Yeah, yeah. I've seen enough Matlock to know the law, but this is an absolute emergency. I need to speak to Chief Calhoun immediately! Can you connect me with him?

911 Operator: I really shouldn't.

Caller: Well, if he finds out that you didn't let this situation come to his attention, I can guarantee you that he's going to be royally pissed off. You know how he gets.

[Silence]

911 Operator: One moment please.

[Line ringing]

Chief Calhoun: Calhoun.

Caller: Rexy! Do you know how hard it is to get ahold of you these days?

Chief Calhoun: Oh, goddamnit. Dyer, is that you? Who the hell gave you the number to my direct line?

Caller: Yeah, I know you forgot to give it to me, but after a while I realized: what's the best way to reach a cop?

Chief Calhoun: If you say—

Caller: Nine. One. One! And I have to say, it worked like a charm.

Chief Calhoun: You're not supposed to use it for that!

Caller: Hey, you used it to call *us*! And I should get to use it too. I pay my taxes!

Chief Calhoun: [unintelligible grumbling] I doubt that you do.

Caller: That's neither here nor there. But I do have an emergency, and I know you're a very busy guy now. Lots of thumbs to stick up people's butts. I get it. So lemme get down to brass tacks: have you given Carrie McDermott my number?

Chief Calhoun: What?

Caller: Your CSI girl? Carrie McDermott. Red hair. Beautiful eyes. Nice, tight—well, you know. Anyways, back when we faced off against that giant disgusting monster, I felt a little spark between us, and I think there might be something there. So could you give me her number? Or pass mine to her?

Chief Calhoun: [exasperated growl] You've *got* to be shitting me.

Caller: Oh, I know. I get it. Maybe I'm being old fashioned. How about my email address?

Chief Calhoun: I'm the goddamn Chief of Police. Not your rolodex!

Caller: Rolodex? Now who's being old fashioned?

Chief Calhoun: I'm not responsible for facilitating your hookups! Especially with my staff!

Caller: Sure, sure. But maybe just jot this down. Got a pen? My e-mail address is Stephzilla—all one word—69. Six. Nine. You know. Like the sex number? At gmai-

[Line disconnects]

[Dial Tone]

THE HUNT II

Versailles burned.

Fortunately, it was just the palace. The majority of the city of Versailles itself remained relatively unscathed. But the towering flames had been raging through the Chateau for well over a week now, and the people were rightly worried. To be more precise, their worries started when the headless corpse of Louis Quatorze was dumped unceremoniously outside the palace gates by a hulking, cloaked figure in armor as black as soot.

When the Sun King's wigless purple head followed his headless body, that was when they knew they were in trouble. At this point, the endless fire was just another item on the increasingly long list of ill portents.

The world, however, seemed to go on just fine, despite the fact that one of its most prominent monarchs had been murdered and replaced by a mysterious being that—by all accounts—was composed entirely of shadow. The people only ever saw a silhouette against a background of dancing flames. And that's all he wanted them to see.

"Le Roi Noir," they called him, often yelling his name when they caught him lurking at the palace windows.

The Black King. He had to turn the French around in his mouth for days before he grew to appreciate it. It reminded him of something lost to him long ago, before he was violently dislodged from his home.

The quiet, fear-driven compliance of the purple-skinned, goblin-like citizenry of this version of 17th century France was quite nice, too. Though he never deigned to walk amongst them, he put out lists of items he desired from his seat on the golden throne. Useful things and technologies that would help him craft his staging ground for his leap to a new reality. And the citizens obeyed, scouring this Earth to please their new dark master.

Why wouldn't they? They adored him. Even through their fear, he'd managed to subtly manipulate their psyches using the techniques wrested from beings of other universes he'd wiped from existence.

But now, as far as these purple French goblins were concerned, the day the Black King strode upon their Earth was the most important day of their life. But for him, it was Tuesday.

Or was it Thursday?

His repeated crossings through the multi-verse had rendered the passage of time utterly meaningless to him. He had lost count long ago of the number of realities he had razed. But, despite his best, most brutal efforts, he was still no closer to the universe he belonged in. He needed to find a way to navigate the multi-verse. He was sick of blindly leaping from universe to universe, never sure where he would end up, and hoping each time that his next leap would be the leap home.

But, now, the Black King had a plan.

He needed to build something that would allow him to use his considerably strong mind to pierce the veil between dimensions so he could identify where exactly he was aiming to go.

Using his control over his new subjects, he gathered materials from across this strange, goblin Earth. As they assembled his requisite, he took a brief respite. He believed he had earned it.

It took decades, centuries even, for the people of this primitive time to assemble the various supplies he needed, and then longer still for them to reach a level of advancement enough to fashion the technology required to allow the Black King to project his voice and will through the multi-verse.

Sitting down upon the once golden throne, now altered into a black seat of wispy shadow, he attached the red and black visor-like device to his dark, horned helmet and placed his hands on the computer console. Drawing on his considerable energies, the Black King struggled to get the device to work. He strained against the bonds of his throne, projecting his thoughtwaves out with such ferocity that people who purported to have psychic abilities keeled over dead in the streets for days—but only after filling the sky with their anguished screeches.

This was a process he repeated again and again over many years. The bodies continued to pile up across the planet, but to no avail. He could not breach another reality with his mind alone. He was missing something.

The Black King was loathe to admit it, but he was just at the point of giving up. He was minutes away from alerting the forces he had culled from dead universes, now waiting in a pocket reality—a Singularity—of his own design. They would rally with him to raze this universe for the energy and parts he would need to make the blind leap to the next world. But, then, he heard the sound of glass breaking.

At 70,000 feet above Versailles.

Curious, he rushed out of the palace and into the courtyard—whose flames still burned eternally. Looking up, somewhere far in the distance, beyond the perception of any normal human, he could see the cracks in the framework of this universe begin to heal themselves. But below thee receding cracks was an incredible mass of bloody red and green tangled limbs and gnashing teeth.

He squinted in an attempt to make heads or tails of it. The reddish, blobbish portion separated from the larger grey-green mass and flew off, winking into non-existence. A being that could travel through dimensions such as himself. So surely this other small thing—

No.

Big thing.

Tremendous thing.

Enormously huge thing plummeting down at terminal velocity.

He could feel his eyes widen in terror—something he'd not honestly felt since his interminable years in the black, sightless prison of his youth. Were he a lesser man, he would have succumbed and run. But he was the Black King. He bowed to nothing except his own desire to put things right.

Using the telekinetic knowledge he had reaped from the minds of Tibetan Mystic Physicists of Kathmandu-23b three realities hence, the Black King reached out with tendrils of his mind and slowed the fall of the great green thing so that its impact would not destroy the world—but merely half the city. And, of course, he made sure it would leave his palace unscathed.

Once the dust had settled, the Black King strode past the golden, fiery gates of Versailles for the first time and admired the bloated corpse of the giant green monster—with patches of jet black burns across its skin—that had decimated the city. It was a curious thing, hundreds of stories tall with multiple eyes and jaws, now closed, and tiny arms lying limply at its side in a perverse sort of peacefulness. But even in death, its psychic aura was more powerful than anything the Black King had experienced. And, more importantly, what remained of its presence stretched across dimensions. The Black King could feel it. As if this was a mere protrusion of this being into the realm of physical space.

"Hm," the Black King said to no one in particular.

AN AMERICAN WEREWOLF ON THE MOON

Marla Stavros awoke cold and afraid. To be more precise, she awoke cold. The fear only began to creep in when she realized she did not know where she was. She remembered falling asleep in her warm, cloud-like bed with her husband, Gregor. But now she lay on a cold slab in a room made of a sterile black metal.

"Hello? Gregor?" Marla blinked and wiped the crust from her eyes. Swallowing the persistent lump in her throat, she called out again. "Hello? Where am I?"

The walls and floor ran together in a mobius strip of otherworldly metallic confusion which refused to echo. Her breathing quickened as she scrabbled at the walls in an attempt to find some purchase. Perhaps some seam led to a door or another means of egress. Because wherever this was, it was certainly not a place she wanted to be for even a second longer.

A glint on the far side of the room caught her eye. It was only a quick flash, but it allowed Marla to spot the single inconsistency in the otherwise uniform black room. A bit that was a little lighter black than the rest of the black. A sort of gray, even. It was the source of the light that allowed Marla to see the walls of her prison. Without it, she would have been effectively blind. Still, she hesitated to investigate.

The trembling in her legs was fierce, but Marla fought and achieved balance. After inching her way toward the gray, she found a circular window, lit from behind. Marla thumped her palms against the glass to make sure it was real. In the spaces between her fingers, Marla could see the stars. And there, hanging amongst them, was the Earth.

It glowed softly as Marla began to scream.

Behind her, a wall slid into the ceiling with a rapid whoosh and an influx of blinding light. Boots clanged against the metal floor, and rough arms grabbed Marla by her arms and shoulders, whisking her out of her prison and toward something altogether more terrifying.

* * *

"Yes, Gladys. We've met all your cats on more than one occasion." Michael Duckett slumped down in the plastic-covered wingback chair. The curtains had been drawn, so the old woman's apartment was dark and cool, allowing the mothball scent to really mingle with the lingering aroma of what was certainly feline urine. "We found Mr. Toots for you a few weeks ago!"

"Oh yes." Gladys Haberman shifted on her love seat and smiled. She had a grandmother's warmth but a two-year-old's attention span. A calico—the aforementioned Mr. Toots—appeared as if conjured by name and leapt onto her lap. "Thank you for that. I don't know what I would do without her!"

"Her?" Stephanie Dyer, who had opted to lean on Michael's chair, raised an eyebrow. "MISTER Toots is a girl?"

"Yes!" Gladys grinned. "She's a mischievous one, so I decided to teach her a lesson."

"Right." Michael cleared his throat as a clowder of cats encircled his ankles. "Anyway, so about payment . . ."

"Yes, all in due time, yes." Gladys shook a bony finger. "But first I have another case for you."

"Another one?" Michael sighed. "Gladys, you still owe us for the fifteen missing cats we've already found."

"Yeah, your cats don't pay the bills, Mrs. H," Stephanie added.

"Of course! Yes, yes!" Gladys answered a question that hadn't been asked and shoved Mr. Toots off her lap as she creaked to her feet. "Would you like some tea while I'm up?"

"No." Michael scratched the side of his face. "Thanks. That's . . . that's fine. Just the case, then. Please."

"Ah, yes." She straightened out her flower print dress, which looked as if it had been fashioned out of drapes. Shuffling over to the side table, Gladys picked up a heavily worn copy of the City Herald and placed it gingerly on the glass-topped coffee table between them, then sat back down. The entire process took about seven minutes. "There. Have a look at that!"

Michael slid the paper across the table toward him, shaking the glass bowl of non-descript candy undisturbed since the Kaiser had been in power. Steph cast a shadow as she hovered over his shoulder to read. The paper was a familiar one. Too familiar. The banner headline proudly proclaimed:

A Couple of Dicks Save The City

"You are the Dicks for Hire, correct? It's you in the picture? My eyes don't see so good anymore."

Michael rested his face in his palm. "Don't . . . call us that. That's not—y'know, never mind. Yes. That's us in the picture."

"Well, then take a look at this." Gladys retrieved the paper from

Michael and laid it flat again, flipping open to page 3. Below the fold was a smaller headline.

Full Moon Killer Strikes Again

The picture below the headline was so unconscionably grisly, Michael questioned why the Herald would even print it in the first place. There, rendered in stunning grayscale, was the mutilated body of a body lying face down—or up, it was hard to tell—in the middle of a city park while uniformed cops cordoned off the area.

"Jesus Christ, Gladys." Steph frowned. "You want us to catch this guy?"

"Yes, of course!" The old woman pointed to the lower left side of the picture. Michael leaned over her to get a closer look. Gladys rapped her finger on a fuzzy ball in the grass that was nigh unrecognizable. It could have been a bush or a smudge in the picture. Michael turned to Steph who only offered him a shrug. "You see him don't you?" the woman crowed. "Madame Pamplemousse?"

"What?"

"Another cat?" Michael scowled. "Gladys!"

"Your eyes 'don't see so good anymore' and you managed to spot that smudgy blur of a cat?" Steph asked.

"I'd know my sweet Pamplemousse anywhere. That naughty little tabby has been missing for weeks!" Gladys looked at them, her already watery eyes beginning to tear up further. "So will you take the case?"

"Yeah, yeah, whatever. We'll take the case." Michael grumbled, picking two cats off his shoulders.

* * *

The waxing moon hung low over the skyline as Steph and Michael descended the stoop of Gladys Haberman's apartment.

"How many times are we going to go back there?" Michael stuffed his notebook—unused—into his messenger bag and slung it over his shoulder.

"She's our most consistent customer, Mike."

"She also owes us $1,800. And besides, don't you think all these cats are running away for a reason?"

"Oh, yeah. They're definitely escaping. It's like a cat clown car in that apartment."

"We're supposed to be detectives. Not guards of a kitty jail."

Steph clucked her tongue. "Point taken. This'll be the last thing we do for Gladys. And then we cut her off."

"I'll believe that when it happens."

The angular shadow of the Garbagemobile—Michael's 1982 Mercury Zephyr which sometimes did double duty as a paperweight—flickered in and out in sync with the streetlight hanging above it. It was as if the damn thing influenced everything in the immediate vicinity to malfunction, as well.

"Back to the office?" Steph grinned as she swung herself through the passenger side window. This was her only means of entry, since that door—a canary yellow one from an entirely different make and model of car—had been welded shut.

"I guess." Michael sighed as he reached for the rusting door handle, but something stayed his hand. As the orange glow of the lamp strobed off, he caught a glimpse of the community garden across the street. A hulking shadow stalked between the trunks of fruit trees, its piercing yellow gaze igniting the air. The chill barely had time to make its way down Michael's spine before the thing disappeared after the streetlamp's next staccato flash.

Michael blinked. He rapped on the top of the Garbagemobile, careful not to hit the rusted out portion. "Uh, Steph?"

"Yeah, what up?" Steph leaned up and out of her window. She was halfway through a candy bar, the rest hanging out of her mouth.

"Did you see that?"

"See what?" She shoved her words past lumps of chewed up

peanuts and nougat.

Michael pointed in the direction of the community garden. "There was a thing!"

"You're gonna have to be more specific."

"It was a big thing. It was moving. It had eyes!"

Steph simply shrugged and slid back in through the window.

Michael let out an exasperated breath and ducked inside the car. "Just . . . never mind."

"Might've been another cat," Steph said as Michael began the arduous task of cranking the ignition. When the car didn't start, he removed the key and blew on it like an old Super NES cartridge before reinserting it. That seemed to do the trick, and they were off.

* * *

It was about a half hour later when the Garbagemobile chugged to a halt in the middle of the neighborhood known only as Squalor's Wallow. The streets were dark and quiet, since nobody with a lick of sense would be caught out past 8pm. Even the convenience store was closed, despite its sign insisting it was open 24/7. Any less precaution was basically an invitation to be robbed, murdered, or both.

Yes, the area had shut down, but a single window remained illuminated on the third floor of a dilapidated building losing more and more bricks by the day. It was the office—and apartment—of Duckett & Dyer: P.I.s for Hire.

"Why is our light on?" Michael slammed the driver side door shut, but not too hard, lest it fall off or crack clean in two . . . again.

Steph levered herself out of her window. "I dunno," she said, picking the peanuts out of her teeth. "Maybe Maureen forgot to turn it off.

"Ugh," Michael grumbled. He'd expected an ex-government assassin to be more conscientious of her duties as secretary. Electricity wasn't cheap—even if Squalor's Wallow's power plant was a set of daisy-chained gas generators run by a naked man who wrapped all his inoffensive bits in rat pelts. "What are we paying her for?"

"Well, we're *not* paying her. So . . ."

"Point taken. Let's just go. I'm tired and I need to sleep."

Steph leapt forward, bounding through the front door and the hallway beyond before taking the stairs up two-by-two. Michael had barely stepped onto the curb when he heard the loud clatter of a falling trashcan echo through the alley by the convenience store.

"Uh . . . hello?" He called, not wanting to move. Michael crept his way to the side of the building and peered into the inky blackness of the alley. All he could make out were the shapes of the upturned trashcan and a few empty cardboard boxes. Nothing was moving or shifting. Perhaps he was still on edge from that . . . thing he saw earlier. Michael shuddered and pulled his jacket tighter as the stiff night breeze rushed through the air. He hurried inside. There was no sense lingering around out here.

Michael reached the third floor landing to find Steph in the hallway, alongside Maureen Whelan, the 60-something assassin they'd hired on for secretarial and bodyguard duties.

"Oh, Maureen," Michael said. "You're here."

"There's a large, angry man to see you." She grunted. Her mask of stoic indifference showed no sign of cracking.

"Mike, do we know any large, angry men?"

"No." Michael paused. "Well, maybe. Maureen, it's ten at night. Why didn't you tell him to leave?"

"He came in at 4:58, and my shift ends at 5. There was no time."

"Then why are you still here?" Michael forced the words through his teeth.

"Left my bowling ball." Maureen waggled the leather bag she had slung over her shoulder. "Now outta my way. It's league night, and I'm carrying this team."

Michael and Stephanie shared a look as Maureen tromped down the stairs and out of the building.

"So . . . do you wanna go in first or should I?" Steph asked.

"I really don't want to have to deal with this right now." Michael groaned. "I'm exhausted."

"Alright, buddy. I'll take one for the team." Steph slapped him on the back, but her hand remained as the slap turned into a push and Michael found his feet sliding toward the door.

"What're you doing? I thought you were going to go in and take one for the team!"

"No." Steph scoffed as she started to put her back into it. "I meant I'd just help push you in first since you're so tired."

Michael tumbled through the front door and into the reception area before he could find his words. Luckily, he didn't have to.

"You!" roared the man. He was indeed large and angry as Maureen had advised, but she failed to mention exactly how hairy he was. Nor did Maureen mention that the man and Michael had a pre-existing relationship, although she probably hadn't been aware of that.

"Mr. Doppopopolous?" Michael squeaked. That wasn't his name, of course, but despite having been Michael and Stephanie's overly aggressive landlord for the better part of their adult lives, neither of them had bothered to learn what his name really was.

"You're the Duckett and Dyer Dicks For Hire?" He bellowed, smashing their unfortunate brand trademark into one awkward phrase.

"It's uh . . . P.I.s for Hire," Michael corrected gently.

Mr. Dupopolous's thick black moustache bristled and his eyes burned with the same fury Michael had often encountered in their old apartment. But the way his wide shoulders slumped, and how his thick, clenched fists wavered, there was something else bubbling inside him. Something Michael was more personally acquainted with.

Fear.

"What . . . uh . . . what are you doing here?"

His firm jaw shifted, as did the subject. "Hm. This is your new property, eh?"

"Yeah, it's uh, comfy," Michael said.

"Good, good." Mr. Dualopolis wasted no time bursting through the door of the reception area and into the main office, surveying it with the critical eye of a landlord. His gaze panned across the dark blue walls, and their classical wood paneling which Stephanie had buffed to a soft sheen. He clicked his tongue as if he'd determined there was no way he could hold back any of the security deposit. But he had no power here. "It's a good, decent property. What is the rent?"

"Less than yours." Steph slid out from behind Michael.

"Well, then I'm impressed."

"Thanks!" She added. "It used to be a crack den!"

"Don't tell him that!" Michael frowned for a moment before registering the thought. "Wait. Why didn't you tell *me* that?"

"Never came up."

"We'll talk about this later." Michael turned back to his former landlord, glancing up to his rough, craggy face like some sort of disgruntled cliff. "Seriously, why are you here?"

Duopolos's façade dropped in a snap. No longer was he the tough, angry property owner. His mountain of a body collapsed into a nearby chair and his fiery eyes were now downcast, revealing the tired bags beneath. "I. . . I have come to you because I need your help. A few weeks ago, some. . . men came to my building."

"Men?" Steph asked. "What kind of men?"

"Short men. Glasses. Long coats. They said they wanted to buy my building."

"Why would anyone want to buy your building? No offense, but it's a complete shithole." Michael stopped himself and mulled over his phrasing. "Actually, no, sorry. I definitely meant some offense. Go on."

"When I refused to sell, they said I was standing in the way of science or some nonsense. They said I would sell, or surely pay."

"They threatened you?" Michael arched an eyebrow. "What did you do? Did you call the cops?"

"No, I laughed them off my property. They were puny little nerds. *How dare they threaten me*, I thought." The man growled before his voice went soft. "But then . . ."

Michael and Steph leaned forward.

"They came in the night. These goons in goggles and white coats. Into my bedroom. *My* bedroom! I yelled for Marla—my wife—to run. I fought back, but they managed to inject me with some sort of drug. When I woke . . . Marla was gone."

"They . . . took your wife?" Michael squinted.

He nodded. "And I will not rest until they are tracked down and executed for their crimes!" The landlord leapt to his feet, thrusting his monstrous fist in the air. "So swears Gregor Stavros!"

"Gregor Stavros?" Steph mouthed to Michael, who could only shrug back as their willful ignorance was challenged and shattered.

Mr. Dupopoloose—whose real name was apparently Gregor Stavros—slumped back into his chair having exhausted the last of his rage. "But I cannot do this alone. I cannot. Not without my Marla. My angel. I spent this entire morning crying on the floor of my bedroom. I am useless. That is why I need your help."

"Listen, uh, Mr . . . Stavros." Michael offered a solemn nod, while Steph moved to pat the thicket of back hair exposed by the man's undershirt he wore as an overshirt. "We might not be able to . . . um, execute these people like you said. But we will find your wife. I promise."

"Thank you." Gregor Stavros sniffled and wiped his nose with the back of his enormous hands. "I know I may not have been the most kind to you in the past, but I do appreciate your aid."

"Of course, buddy." Steph winked and clicked her tongue. "We'll be over tomorrow morning first thing."

"Thank you. Anything you need from me is yours." Mr. Stavros bid the two of them goodbye and trudged his way out of their office.

"Weird, wild stuff," Steph said. "Who do you think those guys were?"

"I dunno, but they must've been pretty damn desperate if they wanted to buy our old apartment."

"Property is a cutthroat business, Mike. Should we make a list of real estate agents we think would be capable of a violent kidnapping?"

"Nah." Michael waved her away. "I need some sleep. Marla Stavros'll still be there in the morning."

"Or still won't be there," Steph said as she unfolded the Murphy bed.

"You know what I mean."

* * *

"You awake?"

Michael groaned and turned over. It was Saturday. He wasn't about to let Steph wake him up early.

Steph jabbed him in the shoulder. Her morning voice was a bit gruffer than usual. Like she had a sore throat. "Hey. Are. You. Awake?"

Well, now he was for sure, but Michael refused to open his eyes on principle.

"Just another hour, dammit." he grunted, as turned over on his belly and pulled a pillow over his head.

"Dude. Wake up!"

The pillow flew off of Michael's head and he found himself turned back over and pinned to the bed by his shoulders.

"Steph, what the—Ah! AHHHH!"

It wasn't Steph's goofy face that he awoke to, but the drooling maw of an enormous black wolf. Michael couldn't move under the weight of the beast, so his only recourse was to continue screaming.

"AHHHHHHHH! AHHHHHHH!"

"Hey, man, shut up. People are trying to sleep," the wolf whispered.

This only caused Michael to scream some more.

"Dude, chill out." The springs of the Murphy bed cried out in pain as the wolf leapt off and released Michael. It paced its way back and forth around the bed, eyeing him—hopefully just with interest and not as prey. After a few rounds, it padded its way over to the front of the office and lay down. It was the same size as their huge desk.

"What—what are you?"

"What does it look like? I'm a wolf, dumbass. What the hell are *you*? The world's shittiest detective?"

Michael blinked and sat up. For some reason, the unrestrained amount of sass made him more comfortable with the situation. "You're not . . . Steph, are you?" He had to confirm this wasn't a possibility. He'd had dreams like this before.

"No, idiot. Your partner's downstairs getting breakfast burritos. She left the door open," the wolf chuffed. "What kind of partners are you two, anyway? I thought you were bangin', but judging from the giant anime pillow down the middle of the bed, that ain't happening."

"What? No. Ugh. We're friends. And we, uh, run this detective agency together."

"Yeah." The wolf tilted its head around. "Real high class operation you guys got here. And you sleep in the office?"

"I'm not going to sit here and get bullied by a wolf," Michael snapped. "Why are you here? And what the hell is going *on*?"

"I thought I wanted to hire you. But now I'm not so sure."

"*You*? Hire us? For what?"

"Let's just say, I'm in a little bit of trouble."

"Hey, Mike!" Steph said as she traipsed through the office door in her rubber duck pajamas, hands full of various greasy sundries. "Kashir's doing breakfast burritos now. I didn't know if you wanted me to add M&Ms to yours, too, so I just did it anyw—" Steph froze as she caught sight of the wolf. "Uhhhh . . . what?"

"Oh good," Michael said. "You can see it too."

"Hello," the wolf barked. "Did you get a burrito for me?"

Steph wasn't fazed by much, but this caused the egg, tortilla, and chocolate mixture to fall out of her mouth. Michael couldn't really blame her.

"Yeah, uh, this is . . . um . . ." Michael gestured broadly. "A wolf."

"My name is Gertrude," it insisted.

"Sorry. This is . . . Gertrude," he corrected. "She wants to hire us."

"Oh. My. God." Stephanie's shock was replaced with a childlike amazement and she dropped the bag of burritos, spilling the disgusting contents across the office floor. "This is awesome. Are we getting our own talking dog sidekick?"

"Hey! I'm a wolf, you goddamn racist."

"Sorry! Sorry. I'm just so excited." She sat down crossed legged on the floor. "And I've got questions. Like (a) how can you talk? And (b) do you know White Fang?"

"Stow it, bleached blondie. I'm not here to pal around with you chuckleheads. I need your help."

"Right," Michael said. "You mentioned that. What's the problem?"

The wolf—Gertrude—cleared her throat. "I think I've killed and I think I might kill again."

The silence that fell over the room lasted for a few minutes.

"That . . . um . . . sounds like a personal problem," Stephanie squeaked.

"You're goddamn right it's a personal problem," Gertrude barked. "I don't want to kill!"

"Well . . . you're a wolf," Michael said tentatively. He realized he was mansplaining to a wolf, but couldn't help himself. "That's basically what you do."

"Great. So you're both racists." Gertrude sighed. "Listen, kiddos. I don't want to kill people. It's just that every time there's a full moon, I don't think I can control myself."

"Ooh!" Stephanie smiled as she picked some of her burrito up off the floor and popped it into her mouth. "Go on!"

"Every full moon, I . . ." Gertrude struggled to find the words. "I *change.* Into something uncontrollable. Something evil. I turn into . . . *a man.*"

"Yes!" Stephanie clapped her hands and pointed at Michael. "Reverse Werewolf. I called it!"

"Called it? When did you call it? What—never mind." Michael turned back to Gertrude. "But you're a lady wolf." He wasn't sure of the technical term. "Right? And you turn into a male human?"

"Why do you think I can't stop killing? All that testosterone makes me feel angry, irrational, and violent. Is this how males actually feel all the time?"

"I mean, normally, yeah." Michael shrugged. "But for some reason, in me, all of those feelings just translate to fear."

"It's true," Steph said, munching on some bacon. "I've seen it."

"But what do you want us to do about it?" Michael asked.

"I want you to help me find the bastards that did this to me." Gertrude's growl descended into a whimper. "I . . . I don't want to hurt anyone."

"Someone did this to you?" Steph cocked her head. "I figured it was just some sort of magic spell. Or maybe you got bitten by a wereman."

"Don't be stupid. I was a regular wolf a few months ago, just enjoying regular wolf things. Then a bunch of scientists abducted me and took me to a lab somewhere. I don't remember what they did to me, but I woke up in the suburbs around this city. When the first full moon of the season hit, I started to shape-shift and black out. I tried to piece the events of those nights back together after the fact, and they coincided with some pretty grisly murders."

"You're the Full Moon Killer!" Michael shouted, recalling the newspaper headlines he'd seen, most recently at Gladys' apartment. "They've been chasing that guy for months!"

"Huh." Steph nodded. "So it really was the simplest solution the whole time: a talking, gender-fluid, reverse werewolf."

"Hey! Keep it down, will ya? This reverse werewolf thing isn't supposed to be an open secret."

"Wait, hold up." Steph raised a finger. "Did you say scientists?"

"Yeah," Gertrude huffed. "White lab coats. Goggles. Exactly what you'd expect."

Michael knew where Steph was going with this. It seemed highly unlikely their two cases were connected, but less unlikely than the existence of a talking wolf. "We had a . . . client drop by last night," he said. "Some guys threatened him and kidnapped his wife. He said they looked like nerds."

"You think?" Steph sipped from a soda cup that appeared in her hand. "You think they're gonna turn her into a reverse werewolf, too?"

"Whatever they're up to, it's not good," Gertrude growled. "If we can help save someone else from whatever they've done to me, we have to. Let's go."

"Well . . ." Michael grimaced. "We haven't even brushed our teeth yet, so maybe give us a minute. Right, Steph?"

Steph slurped up more of her soda as she dabbed at a splotch of oil on her pajamas. "Nah, I think I'm good to go."

* * *

After making sure the coast was clear, Michael drove the

Garbagemobile up to the front of their building while Stephanie maneuvered Gertrude—hidden beneath a large down comforter— toward it. The car's metal frame screeched under the stress as Steph shoved the 120-pound wolf into the back seat, before leaping in through the passenger side window.

"This car sucks." Gertrude's muffled growl was all but indistinguishable from the elderly car's grumbling engine. "Did you take out the shocks or did they not come standard?"

"You got a lot of attitude for someone who eats their own poop!" Stephanie shot back. "Mike, are you hearing this?"

"I'm trying not to," he said. Much to his chagrin, the acidic back and forth between his friend and the wolf continued for the rest of the drive.

A strange sense of déjà vu trickled down Michael's spine as he drove up the hill toward their old apartment. He hadn't been there in about half a year, but it felt even longer, given everything that had transpired since then. Up ahead, he saw Mr. Stavros standing off the edge of the curb, saving a parking space for them. Michael yanked the steering wheel and the car chugged its way into the newly vacated space.

"Thank you for coming. Let me take you upstairs." Stavros beckoned.

"Just a minute!" Michael leapt out of the car and rushed to put all his weight against the rear. The parking brake on the Garbagemobile had never functioned, so grabbing a brick from the trunk and wedging it under the rear wheel was Michael's only recourse. He hadn't missed the hassle of parking on a steep incline.

"You good, Mike?" Steph asked as she swung herself out of the car.

"Good lord. What a piece of crap," Gertrude opined as she shoved her snout through the slowly lowering backseat window.

Mr. Stavros's jaw dropped as he pointed at the enormous wolf they'd stuffed in the backseat.

"Aw, crap." Michael sighed.

"Wolf! There is a giant wolf in your car!"

"Ooh. Good eye, Zorba," Gertrude snapped.

"And it can *talk*?"

"Hey, hey, hey." Steph rushed over to him and put a calming arm up and around his wide shoulders. "Mr.—uh—Landlord. Relax. She's with us."

"This . . . thing is *yours*?" Stavros reared back.

"It's not what it looks like," Michael said.

"It looks like you brought a wolf to my property!"

"Okay. Good point. But she's a nice wolf."

"A nice wolf?" Stavros roared.

"Well, she's got a little bit of an attitude," Steph muttered.

"Listen, buddy. I'm the nicest fuckin' wolf you're ever gonna fuckin' meet. So shut your facehole and let's get down to business. Otherwise I ain't gonna find the guys that did this to me and you ain't never gonna find your wife."

Michael winced. Given his experiences with Mr. Stavros, he was expecting a volley of loud obscenities to be lobbed Gertrude's way, with an escalated brouhaha to follow. But instead, no curse words came. Stavros's eyes were narrowed, but held a sort of dark, angry reverence.

"Is what this . . . animal says true?"

Michael blinked. "Well, we think so. According to her, she was drugged and kidnapped in a pretty similar way to your wife. We think the same people may be involved."

Stavros nodded slowly. "Okay, wolf. If you must be involved, so be it."

"Thank you," she said as she leapt out of the car window and shook off her fur. "And I have a name."

"I do not care about your name. Just don't urinate on my

property," Stavros muttered as he clomped toward the steps of the building.

"No promises," Gertrude shot back as she followed him inside.

* * *

Michael and Stephanie had never been inside their landlord's apartment. In fact, Michael had made it a point to avoid contact with Mr. Stavros as much as humanly possible. So it came as quite a surprise to him when the penthouse suite of the building did not share the ramshackle appearance of every other unit. In lieu of the thick flakes of mint green paint fluttering off the walls, a clean, pearlescent white adorned the walls, making the entire apartment look like it was covered in pristine marble. Instead of cramped, windowless bedrooms, there was an enormous master suite with its own bathroom through an open door down the hall.

It made him a little angry.

Stephanie whistled as she walked in behind him. "Ooh. Nice place."

Gertrude's nails clicked across the stained hardwood floor before she turned around three times and settled into the shaggy brown rug nestled between the glass coffee table and the 65-inch TV. "Yup. I could get used to this."

"Get off my rug," Stavros grunted.

"Make me!" Gertrude barked.

"Okay, Mr. Stavros," Michael changed the subject in a bid to maintain order. "You said your wife was taken from your bedroom?"

"Yes. Come. I will show you." Stavros snorted and stomped through a hallway wide enough to contain even his massive frame.

The bedroom was even more impressive than Michael had discerned from the brief glimpse he'd caught earlier. The far wall housed floor-to-ceiling windows allowing in as much daylight as physically possible while giving them a breathtaking view of downtown in the far distance. The streaming sunlight only served to highlight the intense disarray of the rest of the room. Lamps had been knocked over, and there was a hole in the drywall. Scuffmarks littered the floor, and Michael could even see gouges in the paint around the doorjamb, as if someone had desperately clawed at it for purchase. It didn't look good.

"So this is where the magic happens, eh?" Stephanie sauntered into the room, elbowing Stavros in the arm. When she received only a harsh glare in return, she corrected herself. "Sorry. I mean *used* to happen."

"I have kept everything as it was that night. Even after the police came. I couldn't bear to clean it. And I haven't been able to sleep since. My thoughts are only of my dear Marla. I've never felt this powerless before."

"You said these guys drugged you." Michael shifted gears to keep Mr. Stavros from breaking down. "Do you know how?"

Stavros picked up a small silver cylinder from his bedside table and handed it to Michael. "Here."

Michael turned the thing around in his hands and observed the pointy end. "A tranquilizer dart?"

"Man, these are horse tranqs!" Stephanie peered over his shoulder. "They're no joke. They'll knock you clean out for at least eight to ten hours if you don't have food in your stomach. Don't ask me how I know that."

"No identifying marks or anything," Michael said. "These guys mean serious business. You're lucky they didn't kill you."

"No man can take down Gregor Stavros."

"Well, clearly they can—for eight to ten hours." Steph smirked.

"Do you have any clue why these nerds would want your property? And your wife?" Michael asked. "Or what they might want with a wolf?"

"All they said was that this property was highly valuable to them, but did not elaborate."

Steph narrowed her eyes and clicked her tongue in thought. "They wanted your building . . . but they took your wife instead. . ." After nodding to herself a few times, her eyes shot open, bright and inspired.

Before Michael could ask a question, she barreled her way toward Stavros's mid-century modern dresser and tore open the drawers, tossing articles of clothing into the air until she found what she was looking for. "Aha!"

"What the hell are you doing?" Stavros bellowed.

"I have an idea," Steph said, holding up a large black bra that would have been see-through if it hadn't been for the carefully placed patterns around the particularly naughty bits. "Ooh. Hot. Mama like. What's your wife packing? C? D? DD? D+?"

"Steph!" Michael yelled as Stavros seethed. "Put that back!"

"Oh, don't be so embarrassed, Mike. You've seen one of these before . . . I think. Besides, we're gonna need it."

"Why?!"

"Cause we got ourselves a dog." Steph smiled.

* * *

"This is ridiculous." Mr. Stavros stood on the stoop of the apartment, his giant man hands firmly on his hips. "This is supposed to help you find my wife?"

"Not to mention that I find this completely humiliating," Gertrude growled.

Stephanie shoved her nose into the cup of the bra. "Well, if you stop complaining, maybe we'll give you a treat later." Steph smirked.

"You're enjoying this," Michael said.

"This wolf has been giving me lip from minute one." Steph hissed. "Let me have this." She turned back around. "So, girl, do you have something for us?"

"First of all, I'm not your 'girl,' and second—" The wolf stopped, inhaling in short, rapid bursts. Her nostrils were nearly as wide as her eyes. "Goddamnit. I hate you people. But I do have a scent."

"Well, then, follow your nose." Steph gave her a sharp rap on the rear, which Gertrude did not care for. After a quick gnash of her teeth, the wolf sprinted off, clearing the hump of the hill and disappearing from sight within seconds.

"And now," Steph said, "we wait."

* * *

They had been waiting in a coffee shop for the better part of 8 hours. Outside, the pale blue sky had melted into a soothing purple on its way toward an all-encompassing black.

Michael jiggled his coffee cup—which had been empty for hours—against its saucer. "So how is Gertrude supposed to get in touch with us, exactly?"

Stephanie—who was on her eighth muffin of the day—started to speak but could not fit her words past the crumbs. She held up a finger as she worked through the soggy mounds of cornmeal in her cheeks. Eventually, she swallowed enough to say, "She has my number."

"What good is that going to do her?"

"I told her to call me when she's found something."

"How's she going to call you? She's a wolf. She doesn't have a cell phone."

"Uh, she's not stupid. There're still payphones out there she could use."

Michael blinked. "Steph, she doesn't have quarters. Or *fingers*."

"Hm." Stephanie picked the last bits of muffin out of her back teeth with her pinky. If she went any deeper, Michael would have thrown up. "Yeah, I guess that's kind of a stumbling block . . ."

"Are you two just going to sit here and hog the table?" A barista—Janice by the looks of her nametag—squawked at them from behind the counter. "It's for customers only."

"I had a corn muffin!" Stephanie shot back.

"You bought that an hour ago."

"Yeah, but I just ate it now. Shouldn't that reset the clock?"

"What about you, Slim Jim?" Janice waggled her empty milk frothing pitcher in Michael's direction. "You gonna keep nursing those three drops in your cup?"

"I—uh—" Michael froze. She was technically correct. They shouldn't have been there. But where else could they go? If he was on his own, he'd probably have slunk away out of shame, but, luckily, Stephanie was around. He watched her swagger up to the counter, afraid of nothing.

"Janice, if Mike has any more coffee today he's gonna have a panic attack, so mind ya bidness and go practice your latte art. I wouldn't wipe my ass with your piss-poor attempt at leaves. By the way . . ." Steph slid something across the counter. It looked like a picture. "You see this tabby cat at all? Goes by the name Madame Pamplemousse. Don't be fooled, he's a male cat."

Janice merely scowled and shuffled away. Steph shrugged, collected the picture, and sat back down.

"Thanks." Michael gazed down at his cup.

"No worries, but you need to stand up for yourself a little more, Mike."

"Last time I did that, I got fired."

"Eh, they were gonna fire you anyway." Stephanie flipped her hand as her cellphone rang. "Y'know, over the whole monster cult thing."

Michael's eyes darted to the pocket of Steph's oversized green jacket. She let it ring a few more times. "Well?"

"Mike, you can't pick up until at least five rings. Makes you look desperate." It was indeed two more rings before she finally fished her phone out of her pocket. "Yello?"

Michael could only make out a growling mumble. "Put it on

speaker!"

"Oh, right." Steph fumbled with her phone before slamming it onto the coffee table. "Sorry, Gertrude. Could you repeat that?"

"I said," the phone barked, "I followed the woman's scent the best I could, but the trail stops dead. Like it doesn't exist anymore. Which is strange, but not as strange as where it stops."

Michael leaned over the phone. "Where is it?"

"As far as I can tell, it looks like some sort of old industrial laboratory. But it's been abandoned for a while. Should I go in?"

"No!" Michael grabbed the coat off the back of his chair. "Wait for us."

"Where is this place?" Stephanie asked.

"It's by the old LXR Chemical plant," Gertrude said. "Industrial district. You know it?"

Michael unfortunately had a passing familiarity. "We'll be there."

"Great. See you soon."

"Wait, Gertrude," Steph interjected. "Quick question. Where are you calling from?"

"Payphone," she grunted before the line went dead.

"Damn. Didn't get to ask about the fingers."

"C'mon." Michael grabbed Steph's phone and tossed it at her chest as they ran out the coffee shop door.

"Hey!" Janice shouted after them, probably sore that they hadn't left a tip.

* * *

Dusk had long fallen by the time Michael finished coaxing the Garbagemobile down the narrow streets winding through the dark, empty buildings of Industry Way. He had been here months ago under similar circumstances which he didn't really want to relive. Slamming on the brakes a full 300 feet before the abandoned laboratory, the

Garbagemobile eventually ground to a halt an inch from the curb. Even from a distance, it was apparent the lab had seen better days. Its crumbling façade resembled more of a decrepit warehouse than anything. But it was enormous. So it had square footage going for it, at least.

"This place is huge," Steph whistled as she crawled headfirst out of the window. "What do you think it was for?"

"Shitty, terrible science. What else is any laboratory for?" came a guttural growl. Michael jumped back as the rainbow sheen of two wide eyes glinted in the deep shadows. "Where the hell have you two been?" Gertrude snarled. "It's been an hour."

"Well, my car isn't as fast as I'd like it to be . . ." Michael said. He removed a heavy black flashlight from the trunk.

"Stow the excuses, string bean. The scent of that hairy oaf's wife disappears right here. So whatever we're looking for, it's in there."

"Why would they take her to an abandoned industrial laboratory?" Michael asked.

"And if they had this much space, why were those nerds hassling Mr. Duopopolous for his real estate?" Steph added.

Gertrude looked up at them. "Who're you asking? Me? Because I don't have a goddamn clue. Let's just get inside and snoop around and maybe you get some answers to your dumb questions. Alright, pea-brains?" The wolf used her powerful bulk to smash through a thick set of metal double doors and jumped inside.

Michael looked at Steph before walking through the newly-made entrance. "She does have an attitude."

"I know, right?"

Michael clicked the flashlight on, illuminating a banner of harsh red lettering beyond the door.

"Innovative, Groundbreaking Science, Heuristics, and Infinite Technologies," he read aloud. "What does that even mean?"

The name 'Pembroke' had been hastily stenciled atop the logo in a clashing but more modern font, as if the place had been acquired by a different firm. But as Michael swung his flashlight beam down the entryway, the state of the place—largely empty, aside from a few scattered wooden crates caked in dust—implied it hadn't been cleaned since the acquisition. Behind him, Steph snorted, biting her lip before her face burst into a peal of laughter.

"What?" Michael asked.

She pointed back at the first letters of the sign. "PIGSHIT."

Michael looked at it and frowned, before snorting himself in a vain attempt to stifle his chuckling. "Was it an accident or did they do that on purpose?"

"I really don't know what would be funnier."

"Are you two morons done giggling at nothing?" Gertrude's raspy wolf-voice echoed off the corroded aluminum siding that passed for walls.

"Sorry," Michael whispered, "we're coming."

Michael and Steph's dull footfalls were quiet but had nothing on Gertrude's silent padding. Nose pointed down, she slunk through the wooden crates with disconcerting flexibility and swiftness.

"This place," she growled to the floor. "It's familiar. I think I was taken here before."

"For what?" Steph asked.

"I don't know. Probably to make me the way I am."

"But there's nothing here but some sort of empty warehouse." Michael waved his flashlight around the bare walls and floors. "If these weirdos are kidnapping women and turning wolves into . . . talking wolves. I would've expected to see some mad scientist accoutrements all over the place. Big machines, giant tubes full of liquid, those tall towers with balls on the top that shoot electricity to other tall towers with balls on the top."

"I know exactly what you're talking about." Steph pointed at him.

"Right?" Michael shrugged.

"Wait," Gertrude snapped. "Do that again."

"What?" Michael repeated the shrug. "This?"

"Look," the wolf raised her paw and pointed her nose toward the center of the room. "Shine your light there."

Michael did as he was told and angled the flashlight as he did when he shrugged, allowing the beam to cut a wide swath through the dust and darkness in the center of the rough concrete floor.

It was there just for a second, but he saw a glint.

"You see it, right? Something's wrong with the floor over there." Gertrude padded over and sniffed at it.

"Hm," Steph followed, and as she passed the wolf, the timbre of her footsteps changed, a bit more hollow than two steps prior. To hammer the point home, she started jumping up and down, resulting in a dull clanging sound. "Yup. Something's different, alright!"

"Steph, stop that!" Michael scolded.

To her credit, Steph did as she was told, but it was too late. A loud groaning vibrated through the structure of the building. Spouts of vapor hissed into the air, blasting up dust that had filled and effectively hidden several seams in the floor.

"Whoa!" Steph tumbled her way off the moving panels, landing on her butt right beside Gertrude.

The flooring warped and rotated, overlapping and collapsing into itself to reveal an elliptical pit. After some unknown mechanism clanked into place, the whining squeal of invisible gears heralded the appearance of hefty metal consoles and towers, breaking through the pit's inky shadows. Industrial overhead lights thunked themselves on, bathing the proceedings in a harsh glow and turning the empty warehouse into what felt like a car show room. But what exactly it was showing, Michael couldn't understand.

"What the hell is this thing?" He gestured to the machine that had risen out of the pit, a mess of digital and analog interfaces, and bundles of wires lining the edges of an otherwise sleek silver dais in the center. Michael mounted it and ran his hands along the consoles, tracing his fingers around some sort of containment mechanism that held nothing but an empty cylinder with a finish the color of lead.

Meanwhile, Gertrude paced around the edge of it, taking in as much of the scent as she could. "They definitely took your landlady here, but I can also smell me here."

"We can all smell her here," Steph whispered to Michael.

"Shut up."

"You and your weird dog body," Steph whispered again, but louder.

"Listen to me, you wiseass. The science guys took me here. Maybe that machine is the reason I am the way I am. And I'll bet you dollars to doughnuts that they used it on your landlord's wife."

"You think they turned Mrs. Stavros into a genderfluid reverse werewolf, too?" Michael arched an eyebrow.

Steph sidled over to Gertrude and slowly extended a finger, poking her in the ribs. "*You're* not the landlord's wife, are you?"

"No." Gertrude grumbled. "I think I'd remember that. But wherever she is, we need to find her before it's too la—" She stopped midsentence, wrinkling her black nose. The creases disappeared as her ears pricked up and she emitted a low rumble from the back of her throat. "Someone's coming."

"Crap!" Michael leapt off the metal platform and darted behind the nearest pile of crates, with Stephanie following suit. "Gertrude, c'mon!" He hissed.

"Why do I have to hide? I'm a giant wolf."

"Because we—" Michael froze as the door directly behind them, a door he—and, indeed, everyone, had failed to account for—swung open, slamming into the opposing wall. The elongated shadow of a trenchcoated man cast over them.

"Who the hell are you?" he asked, gruffly. "What are you doing here?"

Michael felt his jaw move, but was at a loss for words. Steph, as usual, was not.

"Duckett & Dyer: Dicks For Hire at your service." She popped up, grinning. "Well, not at *your* service. But you might be more familiar with our client?"

Steph clicked her tongue twice and pointed at the man. Gertrude leapt out at him with a snarl like a chainsaw, aiming straight for the man's neck. The man let out the sort of high-pitched squeal Michael never would have expected to hear from a shadowy figure, before dashing back out from whence he came, a large wolf hot on his tail.

Michael was all ready to follow but was distracted as something metallic clanked to the ground by the door. It rolled over to Steph, who scooped it up.

"What is that?"

"Some sort of . . . uh, thing," Steph said, scrambling to her feet.

"Could you be more specific?"

"No time! Let's follow the bouncing dog!" Steph shoved the mysterious thing into her jacket and took off, with Michael trailing behind, as was customary.

* * *

The man had raced through the industrial district with a speed fueled by sheer terror. A giant, angry wolf was certainly a great motivator. Michael and Stephanie decided to give chase in the Garbagemobile, which was, as expected, a great deal slower than a giant, angry wolf. Truth be told, it would've been slower than a giant angry sloth, but that, while a funnier image, wasn't as relevant a comparison. But with their luck, in a couple of months, it could be extremely relevant. Since the giant interdimensional monster showed up, things had been getting increasingly weird around here. But not so weird that a giant wolf attack was old hat. So, though they were miles behind and in the dark of night, all Michael and Steph had to do was follow a trail of light destruction and extremely shocked faces to close the gap. The path led them out of the industrial district and up through the greenspaces of downtown where chunks had been torn out of manicured lawns, and there was more than one upturned fruit cart.

"This is . . . not good," Michael huffed.

"I'll say!" Stephanie yelled back as she stuck her head out the window to get a better look. "I've always wanted a dog, but this is making me reconsider. Maybe something not so furry. Like a shark."

"You're not bringing a shark into the office."

"We'll discuss in further detail later." Steph pointed toward a riverside park as a small group of people bolted the hell out of it. "I think we've found 'er. Over there, past that upturned fruit cart."

Michael peeled into a parking spot and leapt out of the car.

"Hey! Wait for me!" Steph cried out as he dashed into the park, lit only by the glow of the streetlamps lining the perimeter.

Michael saw the hulking shadow of Gertrude atop a small hill. Her hackles raised, she was pinning down her quarry with her powerful front paws. As he ran up to her, he could start to make out the face of the man trapped beneath her, even in the dimmed light. He wasn't a man, more of a man-child, really, as he couldn't have been older than 20.

"I'msorryI'msorryI'msorry!" He squealed in quick succession. "Don't eat me!"

"Don't make it look so appealing." Strands of drool dripped from Gertrude's mouth. Michael wasn't sure if those were a show of intimidation or if she actually planned to eat the kid. "Now what do you science creeps want with me? Why did you do this to me?"

"I don't know, I swear! I'm just the intern!"

"Intern?" Michael repeated to himself. "Gertrude. Let him go."

Gertrude gnashed her teeth against the kid's neck, to prove she was serious, before she backed off and started pacing back and forth on the grass. Even as Michael helped him up, her golden eyes never strayed from the intern's throat.

"Hey, ho!" Steph ran up beside Michael. "What'd I miss?"

"Where have you been?"

"Picked up an apple. These night fruit carts are a lifesaver." Steph waved a granny smith in Michael's face before ripping a bit out of it. "oo's dis guy?"

"He says he's an intern." Michael looked back at the kid. "Spill it. What's going on?"

"Listen, seriously. I don't know. I accepted this gig at these Pembroke Labs because I needed something science-related for credit. I have no idea what they're doing, man. I suck at science."

"oo're naw a very goo' shudent, are ya?" Steph said, her mouth still chewing.

"They said it'd be an easy three credits if I just found and delivered the fuel cannisters to their lab and made sure nobody saw."

"Fuel cannisters?" Michael asked. "What fuel cannisters?"

"'ike dis?" Finally swallowing her bit of apple, Stephanie extricated a rough metal tube, the color of lead, from her jacket. "You dropped this."

"Yeah, that." The kid nodded.

"What's in it?"

"They told me it's pl—" The rest of the intern's sentence was drowned out by a loud retching, and the sickening crack of bones. As the sounds of pained grunting filled the air, the intern, looking past Michael and Stephanie, began to scream. "Uh, ah! Ahhh! What the hell is going on? What is this?"

Michael wheeled around to see Gertrude writhing in the throes of agony. She howled—loud, staccato wails punctuated by wet gasps for air.

"Gertrude? Gertrude! What's wrong?" Michael wanted to take a step forward, but found himself retreating backwards down the hill instead. "What's happening?"

"Uh, Mike?" Steph waggled her apple at the sky. Thin, wispy clouds drifted across the night's full moon, cutting scars across its sickly yellow glow.

"Aw, crap."

Gertrude continued to howl as she twisted and contorted into impossible positions on the grass. Her legs snapped like twigs, allowing them to bulge and deform. Bubbles of pale oily goop—which Michael eventually recognized as skin— sucked in Gertrude's thick, dark fur, replacing it with red peach fuzz that just barely caught the ambient light. With each passing second, the wolf's canine musculature was replaced with the taut, rippling features of a particularly buff primate. Eventually, the only part of Gertrude's that remained were the wildness of her eyes, shrouded by a mop of fiery red hair and contained within a pale, nude human male who could do nothing but growl and seethe.

"Well, that's some shit," Stephanie said, doing her best to avoid looking at the man's genitals.

Michael spun around to face the intern. "You need to run. Now."

And run he did, though the man formerly known as Gertrude was after him in a flash, after bowling Michael and Stephanie to the ground, causing her to drop the dull grey cannister, and something much more important to her.

"Hey! My apple!" Stephanie mourned over the fruit as it rolled away.

"I'll get you another one." Michael was already up and dragged her to her feet. "We can't let our only lead get murdered!"

Michael and Stephanie gave chase, leaving the park behind and tearing down the sidewalk after the man formerly known as Gertrude. If people on the street hadn't been terrified of the giant talking wolf from earlier, they certainly were now as a nude man foaming at the mouth streaked through the night while bellowing a torrent of unintelligible gibberish.

"This is ridiculous," Michael said. "Even for us."

"I'm having fun," Steph replied, her worn out sneakers slapping the pavement. "Are you not having fun?"

Michael could see the intern racing through the streets up ahead, making great strides in putting an adequate distance between himself and the shrieking nude man with only murder on his mind. This kid was fast and was clearly wasting his talents in science when he should have been running track.

It wasn't long until Michael was doubled over in pain from a searing stitch in his side. Stephanie, trailing with what appeared to be a similar ailment, caught up to him, leaning on his back.

"Oh god," Michael said between gasps. "How the hell are we supposed to catch up with—" His labored breathing caught in his throat as up ahead, a black and white police cruiser, sirens blaring, screeched off a side street. The car accelerated suddenly and rammed into Gertrude mid-chase, sending his body flying into the brick wall across the way, then tumbling to the pavement like a limp rag doll. "Oh. Well, that's one way."

"You think he's alright?" Steph said from behind him. "Aside from the whole murderous rage thing."

Before Michael could answer, the cop behind the wheel of the cruiser emerged, gun drawn. Even from this distance her crisp white shirt practically glowed in the night, especially against her dark olive skin.

"Alright, on the ground! Hands behind your head!" she yelled at Gertrude's nude, unconscious body.

"He's already on the ground, douchecanoe!" Stephanie rushed up closer to the scene, as a small crowd of locals began to form.

Michael pushed his way past the gawkers to catch up to her. As he did, he got a closer look at the man formerly known as Gertrude, whose body was a tangled mess of twisted limbs. But he saw no blood. "Oh, my god. You killed him!"

"I saw a threat and I neutralized it. You see a crazy person running around and accosting people, you stop it hard. And hell, a night like tonight? This bastard might just be that Full Moon Killer everyone's talking about. Now wouldn't that be something." The cop didn't meet their gaze. "In any case, you can get off my back. He's still breathing."

Upon closer inspection, Michael had to admit he saw the man's bare ribcage rising and falling. Maybe reverse werewolves were impervious to damage like regular werewolves. But if they were a truly *reverse* werewolf, wouldn't that mean they would be super susceptible to damage? Michael didn't have a firm grasp of the mechanics. Nobody probably did.

The cop finally took her eyes off their mangled friend. They were a light, but piercing hazel that, when coupled with her tightly bound bun of hair, screamed that she knew every law and regulation in the book and was desperate to prove it. Michael didn't recognize her, but he couldn't shake the nagging feeling that he should.

"You know this guy?" she barked.

"Well, we thought we did," Michael offered.

"And who exactly are you?" the cop nodded to Michael and Stephanie, respectively.

"Duckett & Dyer: Dicks For Hire." Stephanie gave a salute. "At your service."

Michael sighed and rolled his eyes.

"Oh, god. It's you two." The cop narrowed her eyes to a squint. Something about that squint struck Michael as all-too familiar, but he still couldn't place the face.

"So you've heard of us!" Steph waggled her eyebrows and clucked her tongue. "Nothing good, I hope."

"Sorry, who're you?" Michael interjected before Steph could parley her way into a bit. "Do we know each other?"

"Detective Kiara Hobson." She holstered her gun and readied her cuffs at once through some sleight of hand. "Now, if you'll just get out of my way, this crazy bastard has a date with a jail cell."

"Kiara . . . Hobson?" Michael felt the name leave his mouth, and only then did he realize where he knew her from.

Steph got it too, and smacked him in the shoulder. "It's that old lady from the mountain!"

"Excuse me?" Hobson turned back slightly.

"Sorry. No. We know you. Kind of." Michael winced. They had met once before, well, not directly. Months ago, during their disjointed and admittedly nonsensical travel through the various dimensions that comprised the multi-verse, Michael and Stephanie had found themselves atop the snowy mountains of a dead earth. The only one there to greet them was an old crone who somehow knew who they were, and how they could traverse universes. Her name was Kiara Hobson, and she was a far cry from the woman who was standing before them.

"What are you talking about?" she said with a curt coldness as she squatted down to cuff the ex-Gertrude, whose limbs had relaxed into somewhat normal positions. "Are you high? You want to spend the night in holding, too?"

"Nah, lady, we actually know you. Not *you* you," Steph said, watching Hobson shove Gertrude into the back of the squad car. "But lemme just say, you, uh . . . age poorly."

"Who the hell do you think you are?" Hobson spun around and her eyes narrowed.

Michael noticed a flash of pure anger behind them. Steph must have seen it, too, and stiffened. This was a whole new ballgame they were playing.

"You wanna keep running your mouth?" said Hobson. "See what

happens."

"Uh. No. No, ma'am." Steph looked down at her feet.

Michael glanced across at her. Steph rarely cowed to an authority figure. He didn't like it. And he really didn't like this version of Hobson.

"Good. And don't let me catch you following me to the precinct." Hobson pointed her finger squarely at them. "I don't have a soft spot for people who pretend to wield the authority I had to earn. And trust me: I'll show it."

Hobson squawked her sirens to part the crowd, and drove slowly away, her cold gaze never leaving Stephanie and Michael until she was well out of sight.

"What happened?" Michael asked. "Hobson stopped you in your tracks. You're usually thrilled to talk back."

"Yeah. Usually. When I can sense some sort of warmth in 'em. But Hobson. She, uh . . ." Steph's eyes were still firmly planted on her sneakers. "She kinda . . . her vibes remind me of my uncle."

"Oh." Now it was Michael's turn to clam up as he remembered how Steph felt about the uncle and aunt who had taken her in after her parents died in a car accident. She'd mentioned they'd never been the most affectionate of relatives, but never elaborated. Michael bit his lip, recalling that he had recently received a package of information on them—and the rest of Steph's family—if he so wished to use it. But he was still waffling on whether or not that would constitute a betrayal. Best to table that debate for another day. Right now, she needed him to be present.

"So what do we do now?" Stephanie finally met Michael's gaze. "Ex-Gertrude is locked up, and that intern is probably halfway out of the city by now."

"Kiara Hobson really mellowed in her old age. This one's got a stick up the ass of the stick that's up her ass."

"She's aggressively by the book."

Michael cocked his head and smirked.

"You have an idea?"

"Oh, yeah." Michael offered her up a smile. "I think we should do things by the book, too."

Steph chuckled weakly. "Yeah. You *would* say that."

* * *

"Name?" the sour faced desk sergeant asked from beneath his baggy eyes. His hang dog expression hung dog all the way over the edge of his raised desk toward Michael and Stephanie.

"Michael Duckett."

"Stephanie Dyer." Steph smiled, having perked back up to her usual self after a night of cramped-yet-restful sleep in their shared Murphy bed. "We're Duckett & Dyer: Dic—"

"No." The desk sergeant sighed. "The name of the person you're here to see."

"Um . . . Anonymous?" Michael frowned.

"What?"

"Try John Doe," Steph added.

"Kids, I'm sorry." the cop set his pencil down. "Do you actually know who you're looking for? Because I can't help you find some rando."

"We don't know his name, but he was picked up by Detective Hobson last night around 10pm. Does that help?"

"Hobson, eh?" The cop turned and begun clacking away at his computer. "Man, that lady is a real hardass."

"Tell me about it," Steph muttered.

"Gets results, though." The cop stopped clacking. "Ah, here he is. Nude guy? Raving derelict?"

"Sounds about right."

The desk sergeant inhaled through his teeth. "Looks like we put him in his own cell. Didn't seem stable enough for the drunk tank."

"That's probably wise." Michael nodded. "Can we . . . uh, go see him?"

"I, mean, if you really wanna. Says here guy's a maniac. Booked under . . . attempted murder? Oh, damn. You guys are friends with the Full Moon Killer?"

"Allegedly," Steph said.

"Your funeral. Lemme get someone to escort you." The cop picked the phone up off his desk and punched in a number. "Hobson, some kids want to see the Full Moon Killer. Say they're friends."

Detective Kiara Hobson emerged out of the back hallway like a wraith. It had been nearly 12 hours, but her eyes had not lost the cold, strict rage they had the night before. If anything, her batteries had been recharged, and she was more alert than ever.

"You again." Hobson sipped her coffee through clenched teeth.

Michael felt Stephanie seize up, so he stepped forward. "Yes, uh, we'd like to see our friend please?"

"He's your 'friend' now, is he?"

"Yeah. We're here to bail him out." Michael reached into his wallet and blindly slapped whatever money he had in front of the desk sergeant.

"This is five bucks and a gum wrapper," the sergeant said.

Michael didn't remember having any gum.

"Alright, you little shits," Hobson growled. "I'll take you to him, but I'm gonna make sure the Chief knows about it. And, boy, will he rain hellfire down on you."

"Is that right?" Michael followed Hobson's hyper-focused death march through the station's back hallways and into the holding cells. Steph trailed a safe distance behind.

"You're messing with me," Hobson muttered. "I don't like people who mess with me."

"Detective, I assure you we're not messing with you." Michael cleared his throat. "We just want to get our friend and leave."

"Well, if you can't pony up the bail, all you can do is visit."

"That's fine, too."

"And it's gonna be a long visit." Hobson turned around to showcase a caustic smile. "Cause I'm chucking you morons in with him."

"What?" Stephanie cried. "You can't do that!"

Michael raised a hand out to calm her down, although he was a little freaked out, as he hadn't counted on this as part of the plan.

"Listen, Hobson. We know you. We're actually kind of friends," Michael offered.

"I wouldn't go that far," Steph murmured.

"True, but still. We don't have the kind of relationship where you'd want to lock us up."

"You keep saying that you know me." Hobson grimaced. "The me that you know. Would she be annoyed with you at all?"

"Well, uh, yes," Michael admitted. "A bit."

"Great. So then we *do* have the relationship where I'd want to lock you up." Hobson kept an eye on them as they approached the final cell in the block. She removed her keys from her belt and grabbed the bars on the door, swinging it open. "Now get in here with your lil—agh! What the hell?"

Hobson jumped back, shocked at the giant wolf she found sleeping behind the bars, just as Michael hoped she would. He wasn't familiar with the mechanics of reverse werewolves, but they couldn't have been too far off from regular werewolves.

Hobson slammed the door shut just as the wolf formerly known as the man formerly known as Gertrude awoke and caught wind of what was going on. She lunged at the bars, roaring and gnashing her teeth, letting her spittle fly. For a wolf, she was a hell of a good actor.

"Where's our friend, Hobson?" Michael bit his lip, suppressing a smile. He glanced over to Stephanie who suddenly looked a great deal more relieved. "What the hell did you do to him?"

"This is ridiculous!" Hobson backed up against the hallway wall, all the fire gone from her eyes. "Is this some sort of prank?"

"I was just thinking the same thing," a gruff voice echoed from behind Michael and Stephanie. The voice was so familiar that Michael could practically hear the exasperated crossing of arms inherent in the delivery. Rex Calhoun stared daggers past them and into Hobson's soul. Steph's resulting smile brightened Michael's whole day.

"Oh, uh, Chief!" Hobson's face blanched. "Hello."

"Just the man we needed to see." Michael jumped to the offensive, eager not to lose the momentum he'd gained. "How's it going, Rex?"

"Shut up. It's fine," Rex snapped before looking at the incarcerated Gertrude—who had reverted to doing quiet dog-like things—and back to Hobson against the wall. "What the hell is this? I thought you collared the Full Moon Killer."

"I, uh . . . uh . . ." Hobson stammered.

"Great point, Rex," Michael said. "But, since you're the new Chief, I've got two questions for you: (a) What kind of dog and pony show are you running over here? And (b) where's the pony?"

"What in god's name are you doing, Hobson? You were one of the better cops I knew before they shoved me behind a desk and now you're turning my holding cells into a friggin' pound?"

"No, Chief! I swear, I arrested a maniac who could've been the Full Moon Killer! He's in the books with a mugshot and everything."

"Then explain this," Calhoun gestured broadly at Gertrude who was now thoroughly licking herself.

Hobson's mouth hung open, at a loss for words.

"And what the hell do you two have to do with this?" Calhoun wheeled on them.

"That's our dog," Steph said, with some of her pep back. "She arrested our dog."

"Hobson, not only did you arrest a dog, you dragged these two weirdos back into my day? I oughta bust you down to prison escort duty."

"Yes, sir—I mean—no, sir. Sorry, sir." Now it was Hobson's turn to be cowed.

"Duckett, Dyer." Calhoun pointed to each of them in surprisingly correct succession. "Take your damn dog and get out of here."

Calhoun had Hobson unlock the cell and—to her credit—Gertrude exited with the calm of a well-trained retriever that was the size of a Shetland pony. With a smile and a nod, Michael led the group out of the cell block.

* * *

After doing their best to ignore the bewildered stares they received from cops and criminals alike in the lobby of the precinct, Michael, Stephanie, and Gertrude piled into the Garbagemobile.

"How're you feeling today, Gerts?" Steph asked the monster in the backseat.

"Like I got run over by a car," she grunted. "Also, if you guys ever call me a dog again, I'll eviscerate you."

Michael shot her a quick glare from over his shoulder, and she hung her head.

"But . . . thanks. Thanks for coming back for me. I'm sorry for being . . . moody. I need to be a better wolf."

"Apology accepted." Steph nodded.

"I . . . I didn't kill anyone last night, did I?"

"No," Michael said, "but you sure as hell tried to run down that intern kid. For all her faults, Hobson managed to stop you. Even if it was with a car to the body. But now the trail's gone cold. And we lost that cannister to boot."

"Yeah, if the intern was telling the truth, we could've used it to power up that metal platform machine," Steph said. "Now we're back to square one."

Michael's phone vibrated in his pocket. It was an unknown number. Against his better judgement, he picked it up and put it on speaker. To his surprise, it was not an urgent call about his vehicle warranty.

"Uh, hello?" A tinny, shy voice emerged from the phone. "Hey, uh, is this Duckett & Dyer: Dicks For Hire?"

"No," Michael sighed. "We're not—"

"Yes, that's us!" Stephanie chimed in. "No case too tough, no case too crazy. Who may I ask are we speaking to?"

"Dylan Reynolds. We've met before. I'm the . . . intern. From last night."

"Oh, uh, hi Dylan." Michael's eyes widened. He grabbed a notebook from the dashboard and tossed it at Steph, urging her to start writing. "Nice to uh, speak to you again?"

"Yeah. I just wanted to thank you guys from saving me from that monster."

Gertrude emitted a low, rumble from the back of her throat.

"Well, no harm no foul, Dylan," Stephanie said. "But we actually want to ask you a few quezzies."

There was a pause. Steph stopped her scribbling.

"That's short for *questions*," she clarified. "We need you to flip the deets on your lab. That's short for *details*, and *laboratory*, respectively."

"Yeah, I got it. No problem. Those guys suck. Ever since they got acquired by the Pembroke Group, they've been going kinda nuts with their company. I just needed some science credits, but these guys are off the wall."

"What exactly do you mean by off the wall, Dylan?" Michael

asked.

"Well, I can't really go into details, because I signed an NDA, but that giant wolf . . . man . . . thing was totally their fault. You think that thing was the Full Moon Killer that's been mutilating people?"

"We're . . . looking into it." Michael shrugged.

"Well, they were working on a lot more stuff than that."

"Can you tell us where they were working on these . . . things?"

"No. I can't. That NDA I signed is scarier than you know. If I tell you anything specific, they're gonna turn me into some sort of science experiment. All I can tell you is they hired me to find and deliver those cannisters."

"Right, the cannisters," Michael said. "Where are you getting those from?"

Dylan paused. It sounded as if the line went dead.

"Dylan?" Steph asked.

Suddenly, Dylan was back on the line rattling off a string of numbers. Michael hoped Steph was writing them down.

"What was that?" Michael asked.

"I can't tell you any more. I'm sorry. With their tech, they could be listening right now."

With that, Dylan's line went truly dead.

"What the hell was that?" Gertrude raised whatever her equivalent of an eyebrow was.

"I bet it's coordinates," Steph said.

"Why?"

"Whenever anyone gets a series of numbers on TV, they always say 'Those aren't numbers. They're coordinates.' And they're always right."

Michael shrugged and inputted Dylan's numbers into his phone's search bar. And, well, they weren't just numbers. They were coordinates. But that wasn't the most surprising thing about them.

"Goddamnit," Michael sighed.

* * *

"What do you mean the trail led you back here?" Mr. Stavros bellowed through the crack in the door, a single brass chain cutting across his scowl.

"You said these scientists wanted to buy your property," Michael said. "Maybe this wasn't about your building at all. Maybe there's something here that they want access to."

Stavros slammed the door in his face, but Michael could hear the drawing of the chain. Soon, he was staring back up into his burning eyes once more.

"So how's about it, Hagrid?" Stephanie said from over Michael's shoulder. "You got anything here worth hiding?"

"Nothing! This is a pre-war apartment building with all the original fixtures."

"Believe me, I know," Michael said. "But has there been anything different going on lately? Since these goons started showing up?"

"I was planning on building an extra unit on the ground floor. Over the backyard."

"Squeeze some more blood out of this stone, eh?" Stephanie waggled her eyebrows.

"Wait." Michael grimaced. "We had a backyard?"

"*You* had nothing," Stavros clarified with a raised finger. "*I* had a backyard. But the builders I hired refused to dig it up. I have had a hard time sourcing new ones."

Michael blinked. "Well, what made them stop?"

* * *

Calling the eight-foot by ten-foot patch of dried grass and dirt a "backyard" was generous at best and wildly inaccurate at worst. But if Stavros managed to slap a barebones studio apartment on it, he could've rented it out to desperate millennials for over a thousand dollars a month, easy. Heat and hot water wouldn't be included. And, of course, no pets.

Contrary to that last condition, Gertrude was sniffing her way around the perimeter with exaggerated snorts, pausing only to paw at the ground for a moment before moving on.

"You find anything yet?" Michael asked.

"Hold on." Gertrude stopped in her tracks, and nearly inhaled a loose pile of dirt. Michael, Stephanie, and Mr. Stavros looked on curiously as the giant wolf turned around and urinated all over the spot. "Nope. Nothing here."

"Great. Thanks. Good work there, Scoob." Stephanie rolled her eyes.

Michael turned to Stavros. "Where'd your workmen start digging?"

"They didn't. After taking a soil sample, they told me to find other builders." Stavros crossed his thick arms and harrumphed. "Didn't even return my deposit. The scum."

"Speaking of which." Michael raised an eyebrow. "Where's our deposit? We moved out of here months ago."

"You were evicted. There's a difference. You get no deposit."

"Okay, fine, whatever," Steph jumped in. "Where'd they take the soil sample from?"

"Back toward the building. Near the water spout and hose, I believe."

Steph crossed back over to the rear wall of the apartment building, kneeling down beside what looked to be an aged garden hose trickling water into what appeared to be a rough patch of recently dug up land. "I thought you said your builders didn't dig."

"They didn't." Stavros narrowed his eyes.

"Gertie. Mind digging this area up . . . again?" Michael asked.

"Screw you. Do it yourself," Gertrude spat. Her glare softened as she actively worked to check her attitude problem. "Okay. Sorry. Fine. I'll do it."

And so the wolf set to work against the constant protestations of Mr. Stavros, who threatened to sue if they damaged his valuable land. Michael and Stephanie waited as the dirt piled up, and before long, Gertrude announced she'd found something. A gray cylinder, roughly the size of Michael's forearm, shot out of the hole and landed at his feet.

"Oh, sweet! Another canister." Stephanie picked up the object and turned it around in her hands. It did seem identical to the cylinder Dylan had been carrying last night—dull coloring and all.

"It's what they use to power their machine," Michael said.

Stephanie cracked a smile, pointing to a label on the canister, "Hahah. Pee-Yew. Maybe their machine is powered by farts!"

"Gimme that!" Michael yanked it out of her grasp and read the label—one that hadn't been on the other cannister. "It's Pu, Stephanie. This is Plutonium." Michael shrieked as he realized what he was handling and dropped it to the ground immediately, scrambling away. "There was Plutonium underneath our apartment?"

"Eh." Stavros shrugged. "A few industrialists paid me some cash to store their waste decades ago. How do you think I renovated my penthouse?"

"But this is radioactive material!"

"They said it was safe. Contained in tubes."

Gertrude, who had since clawed her way out of the hole, took a cursory sniff at the cylinder. "This thing is made of lead. And there's a whole bunch more sitting down in that hole next to your water pipes,"

Michael glared at Stavros, who couldn't seem to care less. "You really are the worst."

"Well, what are we waiting for? Let's go back and plug this thing into the machine," Steph said. "Then maybe we can find out what happened to his wife."

"Alright, fine, let's go." Michael started back toward the building.

"Good luck," Stavros said, before he was met with a low growl.

"You think you're hanging around here?" Gertrude snarled. "Your wife. Your plutonium. So your cheap ass is coming with us."

Stavros refused to move, but a few snaps of Gertrude's jaws changed his mind real quick. Soon, the now four-strong team had shoved themselves into every crevice of the Garbagemobile's limited interior space for what was certain to be a very uncomfortable ride, especially given the bag of plutonium resting in the trunk.

* * *

The abandoned lab building was much less oppressively creepy in the daylight, but the overhead lighting, still on since last night's escapades, emitted an unsettling buzzing noise.

"So this is where you say they took my wife?" Stavros surveyed the warehouse-like structure with his keen sense for property.

"Yeah," Gertrude grunted. "Even now, I can smell her perfume. But it stops right around the machine."

"This machine?" Stavros narrowed his eyes at the round metal dais and the various consoles and doodads that rested atop it, forming an odd sort of miniature city skyline, except with inscrutable machinery. "What is this?"

"Great question." Steph said as she grabbed a plutonium cylinder out of the duffel bag she was carrying, letting the rest clank to the floor. "Don't know. But there's only one way to find out."

"Apparently, the same people who kidnapped your wife and mutated Gertrude here have been using plutonium as a power source," Michael said. He stepped up onto the platform and moved to what appeared to be a control system beside Stephanie. He gestured to the cylindrical shaped containment unit, and—thankful they all stopped to buy gloves on the way here—reached in to pull out the empty cylinder before tossing it far, far away. It landed with a dull clatter. "If we shove one of the new canisters in there, it should activate."

"And do what, exactly?" Stavros arched a brow.

"You're really killing it with the questions today, buddy." Steph shot him a gun finger.

"You still don't remember my real name, do you?" Stavros grunted.

"Uh . . . well, I . . . uh . . ." Steph wheeled around and shoved the canister into the machine.

"Steph, what the—" Michael couldn't finish as his entire body felt like it was being carbonated.

The entire building disappeared in a flash.

* * *

When Michael Duckett fizzed back into existence, he threw up. Then, a second later, he threw up again. The experience was not dissimilar to the feeling he got when he and Stephanie had been traversing the multi-verse a few months ago. Another ordeal he'd done his best to forget. He didn't like it then, and he certainly didn't like it now.

"Whoo! What a rush!" Stephanie, as usual, felt the exact opposite.

"What the hell did you do?" Michael said, in between gasps of air.

"Things were getting awkward, so I shoved the thingy into the other thingy. It's not rocket science."

"Steph, we could have been killed!"

"But we weren't, so stop your whining."

Michael was about to shoot Stephanie a dirty look, but opted to use the time constructively to evaluate their surroundings. He took off his gloves. "Where the hell are we? Did we . . . teleport here?"

The walls around them were a white so bright that Michael couldn't exactly determine the dimensions of the room. The only thing he could use for scale were his two puddles of vomit and the round metal floor they rested on. It was precisely identical to the platform in the lab they had come from.

"I have no idea," said Stephanie. "But maybe this is where they took Gertrude."

"And where they took Mr. Stavros's wife."

"Ah!" Steph snapped her fingers in the air. "Stavros! That's it."

Michael frowned, as he felt around the room for a means of egress. As his fingers brushed across a slight seam, the wall whooshed open, revealing an equally white hallway beyond. "C'mon, let's go."

Michael speedwalked down the hall, looking for any signage or labels that could help them identify where exactly they were, but to no avail. All he saw were open doors to what appeared to be black voids. After a quick peek into one, his eyes adjusted to the stark contrast from the bright hallways, and Michael could see these rooms for what they really were.

"Holding cells," he whispered. "These guys were keeping people in a bunch of sensory deprivation rooms . . . or something. Man, what is this place?"

Steph let out an amused breath over his shoulder. "Seems like you're taking a real shine to this detective stuff."

"I guess, yeah." Michael nodded, returning back to the main hallway. He had to admit, it was growing on him. "I guess it's just problem solving and I like that kinda stuff. Plus, we're helping people, which is nice."

"Yeah." Steph sighed. "So, I know I never say this, but thanks for doing this with me. I know it's not your first choice or whatever. But I really appreciate us working together. Even if it's for a rude reverse werewolf."

"I've been meaning to talk to you about that," Michael said as they turned the corner. "Is it just me, or have things gotten weirder in the past year? The whole vampire thing. And the Santa Claus? I felt like I was going insane." Michael leaned his head into another darkened room. He could see something glint off the fall wall, like a window. But as his train of thought shifted, he unintentionally ignored it. "I think there might be something else behind this. Something big. Do you know anything about something called the Black Ki—"

Before Michael could get the next words out, a sharp pain shot through his neck. Then, two between his ribs and one more in the back of his thigh. The black void around him swam and bubbled before his increasingly heavy eyes. He could feel himself losing his balance and tumbling into the holding cell, blacking out before he could feel the impact.

* * *

A bright glow pierced through the slight crack in Michael's eyelids like a thin white blade, coupled with a strange bold hiss, like a vacuum seal. He blinked, trying to rub the blurriness out of his vision, but found he could not. His wrists were shackled at his sides by cold metal bracers. His ankles, too, though his pants kept them mercifully warm. The intense panic that flooded his chest broke him out of his grogginess at lightning speed, and he could finally take in what was before him.

To his surprise, it was not another pitch black jail cell, but instead something resembling an enormous laboratory. A myriad of messy desks, blinking consoles, whirring computers, and strange mechanisms littered the floor, including a pair of those towers with balls on them that shot electricity between one another. That brought him a strange sense of calm familiarity—an island oasis in a sea of unease. It also gave him the presence of mind to notice that Steph was shackled beside him. Man, he was really tired of being shackled to things.

"Steph!" His voice sounded echoey and hollow.

"Heyo." she offered a slight wave from within her shackles. Her voice was strangely muffled.

The bright sheen of the lab reflected in Michael's vision.

Tubes.

They were both being held in their own separate, human-sized glass tubes. Two in an array of four, with the other two occupied by beings suspended in a strange liquid the color of mint mouthwash. One was an older woman in white pajamas Michael could only assume was Mrs. Stavros, and the other was a common tabby housecat.

"It's Madame Pamplemousse," Stephanie said.

"Steph, what happened?" Michael yelled, hoping for his voice to carry through the two thick sheets of glass.

A crackle of radio static drowned out her response.

"Ah, it seems our two uninvited guests are awake." A haughty yet stern voice drew Michael's attention five feet down to the lab floor. There, a relatively young man draped in a white lab coat met his gaze, a vicious sneer plastered beneath his safety goggles. Behind him had gathered a cadre of similarly dressed scientists, some still scurrying from behind their desks. "Now I'll ask you this only once. Who are you?"

"No," Steph said. Michael heard her voice clearly now. The static had activated some sort of speaker system. "I asked you first. Who're you?"

"You couldn't have asked me first!" The scientist shot back. "You just woke up!"

"Yeah? Well, we're asking now." Michael backed her up.

"My name is not important!"

"So, what?" Steph huffed. "Are we just supposed to call you *scientist*?"

"Stop derailing the conversation!" the scientist said with an overly aggressive gesticulation. "Now who the hell are you? And how did you get here?"

"Duckett & Dyer: Dicks For Hire," Stephanie said, attempting a salute. "We found your little teleportation device and the stash of plutonium fuel you were trying to muscle our old landlord out of. All thanks to your intern."

"I'll have that little cretin's head!" the scientist snapped. "Who hired you? Is this some kind of corporate espionage? Mr. Pembroke won't take lightly to someone trying to sabotage Project Skinwalker."

"What the hell is Project Skinwalker?" Michael reared back at the name. "We're just here for Marla Stavros. And, as a happy coincidence, the cat."

The scientist squinted behind his safety glasses, lowering his gun. "You really don't know about Project Skinwalker?"

"Well, no," Steph shrugged. "But we do now."

"What do you mean?"

"Mike here got like an 1800 on his SATs so I'd say he's pretty good at putting together context clues." She nodded in his direction. "Mike?"

Michael blinked, he had absolutely no clue what could possibly have been going on here, but then, Gertrude's snarling faces—both human and wolf—flashed across the front of his brain as he stared over at Mrs. Stavros floating half-alive next to the cat, and it hit him. "Oh goddamnit. That's what these tubes are for. You guys are crossing humans with animals, aren't you?"

"Ugh. Gross." Steph said. "Didn't any of you read *The Island of Dr. Moreau*? I mean, *I* didn't, but there's like a hundred of you nerds here. I figured someone must have."

"What the hell are you doing that for?" Michael snapped.

"We're merely trying to release the untapped potential of the organic genome." The scientist paced toward them. "Soon, we'll have combined a human with a jellyfish, and we shall harness their regeneration capabilities to become effectively immortal."

"So then why'd you steal a cat?" Michael waggled his chin in the direction of the comatose floating kitty.

"You're not very bright, are you?" the scientist sneered. Michael would've felt insulted, but this guy was just such a jerk. "We can't go straight to jellyfish. That's not how science works. You got to work your way up to it. We started with a wolf, then a frog, a koala, an ibex and will proceed in that order until we reach the jellyfish."

"That's insane! You're so preoccupied with whether or not you could, you didn't stop to think if you should!" Steph nodded to Michael. "Jurassic Park," she whispered.

"Yeah, I *know*." Michael turned his attention back to the scientist. "And now you're reached the cat phase, apparently. So what happened to all those other animals?"

The scientist turned and started pacing away from them. "That's none of your business."

Stephanie smirked. "You guys screwed up, didn't you?"

"No. No!" He toed the line between righteous indignation and a temper tantrum. "We did not screw up! Missteps are all part of the scientific process."

"Missteps?"

"Some were . . . unstable. Others just plain exploded. So we . . . disposed of them in public areas. About once a month, around the full moons. Public hysterics effectively covered our tracks."

"So you nerds are the real Full Moon Killers?" Stephanie shouted. "What ever happened to your Hippocratic Oath?"

"That's for doctors, you moron."

"You guys don't have PhDs?

"Actually," the scientist clarified, "we're mostly graduate students."

"Well, that explains a lot." Michael exhaled, recalling Matteo Carrera, the grad student who'd accidentally flung them halfway across the multi-verse so many months ago. "The big ideas. The high-and-mightiness. The mistakes."

"They were not mistakes!"

"What it doesn't explain is where you got the money for all this." Stephanie chimed in. "Aren't real graduate students supposed to be laughably poor?"

"Well, when Mr. Pembroke purchased our lab, he provided us with a bunch of dimension-breaching equipment from his older scientific ventures. We were able to reverse engineer it into more useful teleportation technologies. That, and he gave us a stupid amount of money to pursue our experiments."

"Great. What do you weirdos need with portal equipment anyway? Just for funsies?" Steph sighed. "Ugh. There's nothing worse than a grad student with a sugar daddy."

"You two are just not intelligent enough to comprehend the gravity of what we do here."

"Oh yeah?" Steph said. "Well, if you're so smart, how come your acronym spells PIGSHIT?"

The scientist moved toward a control panel between Michael and Stephanie's tubes, placing a hand on a dial. "Enough with your disrespect. Now you know far too much."

"What're you gonna do? Turn us into orangutans? Or bees?" Steph laughed. "Wait, actually, if I get a choice, can I be like a shark or something? A street shark?"

"Again with the shark stuff?" Michael scolded.

"Would you two shut up? We're not going to turn you into anything. We don't have any other animal subjects on hand. Instead, we're just going to drown you. To death."

"That's usually what 'drowning' means." Steph rolled her eyes. "Your grad degree isn't in English, is it?"

"You can't murder us," Michael scoffed. "Even if you don't care about ethics, I'm pretty sure the law will. And we have a few friends in high places."

"Oh, yes. The 'law.'" The scientist mocked Michael with air quotes. "Did you ever ask yourself why we can perform our outrageous experiments here with no oversight? It's because when I say Mr. Pembroke gave us a stupid amount of money. I mean he *gave us an absolutely stupid amount of money.*"

The scientist gestured to one of his white coated minions, who scuttled off to the far edge of the lab, where an impressive array of mechanical controls fed into the very structure of the building. After a bit of a struggle, she flipped a heavy switch, and the ceiling of the lab whirred and creaked, sliding down into the lower wall of the room, revealing a clear pressurized bubble. Beyond the glass lay the pin-pricked black of outer space. And there, along a grey, lifeless horizon, he saw Earth hanging in the sky.

The scientist laughed, "And technically, there's no law against murder *on the moon.*"

"Murder is illegal everywhere, you dork!" Steph shot back. "Even on the moon."

"What're you, a moon lawyer? Shut the fuck up." The scientist sneered. "Now, if you'll excuse me, we need to cross a lady with a cat, and you two are wasting my valuable time." He turned the dial on his console, and a loud gurgling commenced, followed by the rapid gush of flowing fluid as Michael and Steph's tubes began to fill with the strange mouthwash-looking liquid occupying the other two tanks.

"Oh, man, Mike," Steph shared a worried glance. "We're boned."

As the liquid began rising past their ankles, a loud, hollow banging began echoing through the vast lab, drawing the attention of the ethically-challenged grad students to the large metal double doors on the far side. The sound even carried through the glass of the tubes. Since the scientist had mercifully left Michael's glasses on, he could make out some slight deformations in the metal that deepened with every pound.

"Marla! Marla!" Stavros's voice slipped through a newly made crack in the door.

"Who the hell is that?" the scientist yelled.

"That," Steph said, "is one large, angry man."

One final bash and Mr. Stavros stormed into the room, growling and seething like a man possessed. Immediately his eyes fell on his beloved wife, floating unconscious in her tube. "Marla!"

"Oh, now you're gonna get it." Stephanie smiled as Stavros roared and charged through the herd of grad students like an enraged linebacker, before leaping toward the console beneath the array of tubes. Heaving his breaths through his teeth, he adopted a fighting stance and stared down the scientist.

"Give me back my wife, or I will not be responsible for what I do to you," he snarled.

"Oh, I think you'd better reconsider," the scientist drew a pistol from beneath his lab coat. Stavros looked to shrink a bit in the face of the gun, but Michael could still see the rage roiling through his eyes.

"Aw, crap," Steph muttered, as the rising liquid reached her waist. "I should've figured you would've had guns."

"Hah!" The scientist forced a laugh, waggling his gun. "There's nothing you can do to stop us. We have the money, we have the power, and we have the intelligence to bend the laws of the universe to our will. What could you possibly have that could rival us?" The crescendo of the scientist's melodramatic monologue was met only with a repetitive clicking. The clicking of the nails of a large animal trotting down the floors of a metal hallway.

"Hey guys," Gertrude said, as she squeezed her way through the hole in the door. "What's going o—" Her words caught in her throat as she stared wide-eyed at the room's open window, looking out at the floating Earth hanging silently above the surface . . . of the moon.

"We have a genderfluid reverse werewolf." Michael smiled.

Gertrude crumpled to the floor and begun to convulse, her bones cracking and her flesh and sinew tearing. In a matter of seconds, Gertrude had completed her grotesque transformation from a broken mess of fur and deconstructed entrails and was now a six-foot tall, nude red-haired man with nothing behind his eyes except uncontrollable rage.

"Whoo," Stephanie breathed. "Okay, *now* you're gonna get it."

Gertrude leapt across the room with his superhuman legs, clearing the mess of people that Stavros had bowled over and zeroed in on the scientist, who, suddenly terrified, fired three quick shots from his pistol. Gertrude took them in stride as they impacted his shoulder, torso, and bounced off his forehead. Ripping the gun from his hands, Gertrude grabbed the scientist by his collar and lifted him clean off the floor, before proceeding to give him the beating of a lifetime. As some of the lab coated minions approached to help, Gertrude screamed unintelligible nonsense at them, and they backed off right quick.

Even Stavros had to step aside and avert his eyes from the brutality. Michael and Stephanie did the same and just looked at each other as the mint-colored liquid that smelled more like anti-septic than mouthwash reached their shoulders.

"So Gertrude turned just by *seeing* the moon?" Steph asked. "That's not how werewolves work, is it?"

"Well, maybe that's how reverse werewolves work?"

"I guess." Steph's eyes darted downwards as a splash of blood hit the outside of her tube. She turned back to Michael. "So this is kind of dark, isn't it?"

"I guess, but that guy was nuts. Nobody should have the money or power to do any of this."

"Hey, did you hear that?"

"What?" Michael asked.

"Nothing." Stephanie was right. The cries of the scientist and the thuds of Gertrude's beatdown were now silenced, replaced only by a faint squelching.

Michael looked down and saw Gertrude, who was no longer nude, but rather, clothed entirely in blood. There was something else different about him as well, which kept Michael from averting his gaze in terror. His eyes. They were no longer those of a savage beast, but a moderately well-adjusted human. Behind him the chest of the grievously wounded scientist rose and fell in labored, shaky breaths.

"Wow . . . uh . . . wow." Gertrude held his head as he spoke the first coherent words of his human life. "I think that was . . . uh just what I needed."

"You're . . . okay?" Steph asked.

"Yeah, I think so." Gertrude said calmly. "I think I got all that rage out of my system. I've leveled off and I think I'm more comfortable now."

"That's good to know," Michael said.

"I feel kind of bad, though," Gertrude hung his head, gesturing weakly at the scientist struggling to breathe behind him. "I messed him up."

"Ah, don't worry about it. He was an asshole, anyway." Steph said. "And on the bright side, it looks like you were never an uncontrollable, insane murderer, after all. Just a normal person who needed some good old-fashioned human vengeance."

"Besides," Michael smirked. "We've been told there's no laws on the moo—blub glub!" While he was attempting his witty rejoinder, the liquid, still pouring in, surged up and filled the remainder of his tube. He and Steph shared a wide-eyed glance and fought against their shackles.

"Mmm! Mmm!" Michael said through clenched lips, looking down at Mr. Stavros and the console he was standing beside. He tried to indicate the tube control dial with his eyes.

"I think he wants you to reverse the liquid in his tube with that dial," Gertrude said.

"Mmhm! Mmhm!" came Steph's cries.

Stavros ambled over to the control panel and placed his hand on the dial. He looked up and met Michael's frantic gaze—for far too long than was necessary. Finally, he sighed and turned the dial down, letting the liquid drain out.

"You bastard!" Michael coughed.

"Do not make me regret this." Stavros frowned. "Now let us bring my wife home."

* * *

It had been two days since Michael and Stephanie's return from the rogue grad students' moon base, and it still felt odd to say that. After they had released Marla Stavros and Madame Pamplemousse, they rounded up the nerds, including the one Gertrude had beaten half to death, and teleported their way back down to Earth, dumping the whole mess of them in front of the local precinct. There they were met by Detective Hobson, who summarily was saddled with all the relevant paperwork.

And now they were here, at an apartment building they'd hoped never to see again.

Stephanie rapped on Mr. Stavros's door.

It creaked open fully, unheeded by a chain, and he greeted them with open arms. "My friends! Please, come in."

Unaccustomed to his overzealous display of affection, Michael and Stephanie crept in, wary of any traps waiting to be sprung. No, the only trap was Marla Stavros bussing in a tray of homemade cookies and milk Michael hoped was not homemade. She placed the tray on the coffee table and rushed over to envelop Michael and Stephanie in a big hug, with a flurry of kisses. Michael would have been lying if he said his heart wasn't warmed a little.

"Thank you, thank you, thank you! Thank you so much for saving me from that awful, awful place."

"No worries, Mrs. Stavros. Happy to help!" Stephanie beamed before pushing her way underneath the hug. "Now, if you'll excuse me, there are some baked goods that require my attention."

"If you ever need anything, please let me know." Marla Stavros planted one last kiss on Michael's forehead before picking up her purse. "Gregor, I need to pick up some more milk from the store. Make sure you treat these children like kings!"

"Of course, my sweet. I will see you soon." Stavros escorted his wife to the door and blew her a kiss as she left. "She is the greatest woman in the world."

"Yeah, she's real sweet," Steph said from behind a glob of chewed up cookies. "So Stavros, we, uh—"

Steph's muffled sentence was interrupted by a knock at the door. Stavros opened it to find the man formerly known as Gertrude, his hair slicked back, decked out in a crisp gray suit that looked rather fetching on him. In his arms was the plump little potato body of Madame Pamplemousse, snoring away.

"Oh, hey! You clean up good." Steph clucked her tongue.

"Thanks," he said as he walked in.

"I'm sorry we couldn't find a way to split you back into both man and wolf," Michael said.

"It's okay!" the man smiled. "I actually kind of like who I am now. And I've gotten pretty good at controlling my shifts."

"That's awesome," Steph said.

"Yeah. And it's been a lot easier since Mr. Stavros and his wife let me rent a place here."

"Really?" Michael raised an eyebrow.

"I can come and go as I please, and I have a flex-time job down at a financial consulting firm. I go by the name John Wolfe now."

Steph sucked air in through her teeth. "Isn't that a little on the nose?"

"It's spelled with an 'e' at the end."

"Yeah, that changes everything." Steph rolled her eyes.

"Anyway," he continued, thrusting Madame Pamplemousse into Michael's arms. "This is yours. Probably not a good idea to have him hanging around me."

"Thanks." Michael winced as the cat awoke and dug his claws into his arm. "We'll make sure he gets back to his owner."

"Cool. I'll see you later, then," John Wolfe said. He paused on his way out the door. "And thanks. A lot."

"What a nice fella," Steph said in between glugs of milk. "Almost makes you forget he's also a wolf."

"He is a good tenant." Stavros nodded as he turned his massive frame toward the coffee table to clean up the mess Stephanie had left behind. "Always pays his rent on time. Why should I care if he is also a wolf?"

"Good point. And speaking of which," Michael segued, "we were wondering if you had any view on when you'd be able to pay for our services."

Stavros put the tray back on the coffee table and stiffened. "Pay for your services?"

"Yeah, we run a detective agency," Steph said. "Not a charity. Going rate is $500 a day plus expenses. Cough it up."

Stavros turned around, "I believe the cost of digging up my backyard more than covers your bill."

"Oh, you can't be serious." Michael groaned. "There was plutonium down there! If anything, you should be paying us for getting rid of it for you."

"We saved your wife, buddy! How come John Wolfe gets a pass and we don't?"

Stavros's eyes darkened as his face assumed his familiar angry scowl. "I was quite clear that he pays his rent on time. Unlike you two hooligans."

"Wait, so we can't even move into a new apartment here? Even if we pay the rent on time from now on?" Michael whined.

"Yeah, that Murphy bed is really cramping my style." Steph rubbed her back.

"No." Stavros put his foot down. "Now take your damned cat and get out."

The door slammed shut behind them, and Michael and Stephanie could do little more than to slink away with Madame Pamplemousse in their hands. After all they had been through, Michael hoped at least Gladys would give them a fair shake and finally pay her tab for the numerous cat retrieval services they'd provided.

She did not.

In the criminal justice system, the people are represented by two separate, yet equally important groups: The police, who investigate crime, and the district attorneys, who prosecute the offenders.

This story isn't about any of that.

It's much more irritating.

Duckett & Dyer
Dicks For Hire

Executive Producer

Dick Wolf

IN CITY CIVIL CLAIMS COURT

MICHAEL DUCKETT; STEPHANIE
ALOYSIUS DYER, co-owners of
DUCKETT & DYER: P.I.s FOR HIRE, LLC

       Plaintiffs,

vs.

FRANCO CONSETTI; ABRAHAM
RESTREPO, co-owners of
2 DICKS 4 HIRE, LLC

       Defendants

Case No. 4:10-cx-00234-DMZ

City Court House
June 18th, 2014

       Before the Honorable Wallace Toshida

Transcript of Proceedings

Trial Day 1

Proceedings reported and transcript prepared by:

Tracy James, RDR, CRR City Official Court Reporter

Proceedings reported by stenographic shorthand; transcript prepared with reporting software.

On Behalf of the Defendants:

Conway Grimsby Esq.

Grimsby Law Associates, LLC

213 West 18th Street

Against all advice, the Plaintiffs have opted to represent themselves.

PROCEEDINGS

(Proceedings commenced at 9:06 a.m. as follows:)

JUDGE TOSHIDA: Good morning. Be seated.

MR. DUCKETT (whispering aside): Steph, where's our lawyer?

MS. DYER: Uh, right here, baybeeee!

MR. DUCKETT (whispering aside): What? Are you [expletive deleted] kidding me? You didn't tell me you were going to represent us!

MS. DYER: Because I knew you'd throw a fit about it. Relax. This is an open and shut case.

JUDGE TOSHIDA: Ms. Dyer, is there a problem?

MS. DYER: Not at all, your highness. My client here is just being a [expletive deleted].

MR. DUCKETT: Your *client*? You're the one who wanted to sue these guys! And I'm not a [expletive deleted]! You're a [expletive deleted]!

MS. DYER: Don't be immature, Mike.

JUDGE TOSHIDA: Ms. Dyer, if you can't control yourself and your client, I will have to ask the bailiff to restrain the two of you.

MS. DYER: As hot as that sounds, sir, it won't be necessary. We'll cooperate.

JUDGE TOSHIDA: Good. Now, as I understand it, you two are the owners and proprietors of Duckett & Dyer: P.I.s For Hire, LLC.

MS. DYER: Actually, it's Dicks For Hire, your grace.

MR. DUCKETT: Objection! No, it isn't.

JUDGE TOSHIDA: Objection overruled. So why have you brought Mr. Consetti and Mr. Restrepo — to court today?

MS. DYER: Ladies and gentlemen of the jury, I aim to prove —

JUDGE TOSHIDA: Ms. Dyer, this is a small claims court. There is no jury.

MS. DYER: Oh. Well, uh, then I aim to prove, beyond a shadow of a doubt, that the plaintiffs have —

JUDGE TOSHIDA: Defendants.

MS. DYER: What?

JUDGE TOSHIDA: They're the defendants. *You're* the plaintiffs.

MS. DYER: Are you sure? That doesn't sound right.

MR. DUCKETT (to himself): I hate everything about this.

MS. DYER: Okay, then the *defendants* have purposefully named their competing corporation 2 Dicks 4 Hire to cause intentional confusion with our — frankly, more successful —

copyrighted brand.

MR. DUCKETT (whispering aside): Did you actually copyright that?

MS. DYER: Yeah. It only cost like $750.

MR. DUCKETT: Wait, that's why you wanted to borrow $750?

JUDGE TOSHIDA: Now what evidence do you have that the defendants have willfully aped your copyright to cause confusion?

MS. DYER: Well, it's pretty obvious, your majesty. Since the Future Group incident, Duckett & Dyer: Dicks For Hire has become a household name in this city. Calling their business 2 Dicks 4 Hire? That's just asking for a copyright strike. And, second of all, it's pretty lame, which devalues our business.

JUDGE TOSHIDA: And so you're suing them for . . .?

MS. DYER: 300 million dollars.

JUDGE TOSHIDA: Again, Ms. Dyer. This is small claims court.

MS. DYER: Go big or go home.

MR. DUCKETT (standing up): For the record, I did not agree to any of this.

JUDGE TOSHIDA: Mr. Duckett, please be seated.

MS. DYER: Fine, then. Let's dial that back down to $750. The cost of the copyright. Does that fall within your limits, my liege?

JUDGE TOSHIDA: That is acceptable.

MS. DYER (to herself): Just because you can't run with the big boys, we all have to suffer.

JUDGE TOSHIDA: What was that?

MS. DYER: Nothing! We can proceed.

JUDGE TOSHIDA: Very well. Now, Mr. Conway Grimsby will present his opening arguments for the defendants.

MS. DYER: Hah! Conway Grimsby? Was he born in a Coen Brothers movie?

MR. GRIMSBY: Ahem, your honor. I aim to prove that not only is the case that these two . . . layabouts have brought before you invalid, but in fact it is *they* who owe *my clients* $750, or more!

MR. DUCKETT (whispering aside): Steph, could that be true?

MS. DYER: No way. We're not layabouts! I consider myself more of a ragamuffin.

MR. DUCKETT: That's not what I'm talking about.

JUDGE TOSHIDA: Mr. Grimsby, could you please elaborate?

MR. GRIMSBY: I'll let my clients' testimony speak for itself. Mr. Consetti?

MR. CONSETTI: Yes, um, hello, your honor. My name is

Franco Consetti and myself, along with Mr. Restrepo here are the owners of 2 Dicks 4 Hire LLC.

MR. GRIMSBY: Your company, Mr. Consetti. Is it, as the plaintiff argues, infringing on their brand as independent Private Investigators?

MR. CONSETTI: No, your honor. Our services are entirely different.

MR. GRIMSBY: And what are your services?

MR. CONSETTI: Well, Mr. Restrepo and I can be hired as . . . well, intimidation personnel.

MR. GRIMSBY: Could you clarify the meaning of that? Or provide an example?

MR. CONSETTI: Uh, so say you've got someone you don't like and you want them, I dunno, bullied. Or harassed. Nothing too physical or violent, of course. Nothing illegal. Just like followed around and insulted all day. Maybe we accidentally bump into them and make them drop their coffee. Or maybe we don't hold the door for them and laugh. Just basically treating someone like a jerk or like . . .

MR. GRIMSBY: . . . like dicks, to use the colloquial term.

MS. DYER: Objection! That's not a real job.

MR. GRIMSBY: Neither is private investigator.

JUDGE TOSHIDA: Objection overruled. Mr. Grimsby, you

may continue your arguments.

MR. GRIMSBY: Let's turn to you now, Mr. Restrepo. Could you stand up please? Let the record show that Mr. Restrepo's arm is in a sling and he has slight bruising around his eye. Mr. Restrepo, as you handle the legal and financial matters of your company. Could you please tell the court when you filed the copyright for your name?

MR. RESTREPO: November 16th, 2013, your honor.

MR. GRIMSBY: The day after the fall of the Future Group. Is that correct?

MR. RESTREPO: That is correct.

MS. DYER: Hah! Nice try, [expletive deleted]. We started our company in September.

MR. GRIMSBY: Yes, your company, Duckett & Dyer: P.I.s for Hire LLC. And what exactly is the date on the copyright for the alternate wording? The Dicks For Hire?

MS. DYER: Um . . .

MR. GRIMSBY: Ms. Dyer, is there *any* official documentation regarding the copyright for Dicks For Hire?

MS. DYER: Uh, objection?

MR. DUCKETT (aside): Steph, what the hell? Now we're going to be on the hook for this!

MS. DYER (aside): Relax, Mike. I've got a strategy they

haven't thought of. If we just strike all their arguments from the record, they won't have a case.

MR. DUCKETT: What? Where are you getting these ideas from?

MR. GRIMSBY: While I believe I've proven my case, your honor, I have one other point to raise, if you don't mind.

JUDGE TOSHIDA: Proceed.

MR. GRIMSBY: Mr. Restrepo, your injured arm and bruised face. Could you explain to the judge exactly what happened there?

MR. RESTREPO: Well, we were in our office, minding our own business, when that crazy lady over there bursts in and starts beating the [expletive deleted] out of us!

MR. GRIMSBY: Let the record show that Mr. Restrepo pointed to Ms. Dyer when he used the phrase "that crazy lady over there."

MR. DUCKETT: Steph, did you actually go beat these guys up?

MS. DYER: N-no!

MR. RESTREPO: So I'm heading out for coffee, and I'm standing by the door at the time, and this psycho just kicks the damn thing in and sends me flying. And she yells "Alright, which one of you [expletive deleted] [expletive deleted] stole our name?" Then she comes flying at me like some sort of rabid monkey. It took three of our guys to peel her off me!

MR. GRIMSBY: And so you're seeking damages of $1500 for door repair and minor injuries?

MR. RESTREPO: That is correct.

MS. DYER: Objection! That guy's face is stupid.

MR. GRIMSBY: Objection! Irrelevant.

MS. DYER: Counter-objection! PHHHHBBBBTTTT! Please let the record show that I blew a raspberry. And it was *moist*!

JUDGE TOSHIDA: Ms. Dyer, if you do not settle down I will have you held in contempt! Now is what Mr. Restrepo alleges true?

MS. DYER: . . .yes, sire.

JUDGE TOSHIDA: Well, then that makes the ruling pretty simple. Mr. Duckett, Ms. Dyer, you are ordered to pay the defendants a sum of $1500 for door repair and minor injuries.

MS. DYER: Objection! Strike that from the record! Strike *everything* from the record. Ha-haaa! What're you gonna do now, Grimsby?! According to the record, you don't even *exist*.

JUDGE TOSHIDA: You can't do that. This Court is adjourned.

MR. DUCKETT: This has been the worst day of my entire life.

MS.DYER: Hey, Mike. Could I borrow $1500?

THE PASSION OF THE HEIST

Stephanie's last memory of the City Museum's stone façade and polished marble pillars was indelibly coupled with the warmth of her mother's hand—and the absurd faces her brother pulled to imitate the wax figures of cavemen. Not since the accident that took her parents' lives and resulted in her brother's disappearance had she returned here. It had been fifteen years since, however, and the wounds had long scabbed over. So, as Steph shoved another slice of dark chocolate cake into her mouth, she regretted not returning here sooner.

"Oh, man," she said, swallowing the moist morsels. "Why didn't anybody tell me about this? This is the best cake I've literally *ever* had."

The rest of the patrons at the museum coffee nook did their best to ignore her gluttony, but Steph needed them to know exactly how outstanding this experience was.

"Amaaazing cake, get in my mouth," she sang, to the tune of a public domain hymn. "I am so hung-a-reeee!"

"Those things are like five dollars each." Mike set their coffees on the table and sat down. "And you've gone through three of them."

"So?" She shrugged, speaking through her last mouthful of cake. "Juff wrife it off as uh bidness meal."

"Steph," Mike pinched the bridge of his nose and winced, an expression she had long become accustomed to. "Our business is touch-and-go as it is without committing light tax fraud."

"Then write it off our personal taxes."

"*Our* personal taxes?" Mike leaned in, raising his eyebrows.

"You, uh"—Steph absently sucked the chocolate off her fingers, avoiding eye-contact—"don't file us jointly?"

"What? No!"

"Oh." she drew a sharp, nervous breath and tugged at her collar. "Then I might need help with something when we get home."

"You're on your own with that one. Now are you done? The museum is going to close in fifteen minutes. I'd like to at least see the damn jewel."

"You're just jealous you didn't get your own slice of cake."

"C'mon." Coffee in one hand and Steph's elbow in the other, Mike yanked her off her chair and far away from her beloved desserts. She would have shed a tear if she wasn't so busy chewing.

The "damn jewel" Mike was so adamant to see was a teardrop-shaped black rock Steph honestly didn't find that appealing. But she might have been alone in that opinion, as the museum had set up a lavish exhibit dedicated specifically to showcase the thing. They'd even gone the extra mile and hired a graphic designer to produce a logo introducing it as "The Holy Bloodstone."

The whole affair was set down an expanse of royal purple hallways emblazoned with the logo, amidst bits of history about the stone that Steph willfully ignored, though a picture of the Pope holding it aloft caught her eye. She wasn't sure which Pope it was. As far as she knew, however, it could've just been a random old man in a hospital gown. Still, it was a nice picture.

In fairness, Mike was also ignoring all the poignant historical context in an effort to see the jewel proper. After passing a few more dry paragraphs of history, the false purple walls gave way to a large rotunda with multiple exits. Presumably, the Holy Bloodstone was in the center, but Steph couldn't see it over the mass of people crowding the area.

"Great," Mike sighed. "I've been waiting for the Bloodstone to debut in public for years, and now we can't even see it."

Now it was Steph's turn to grab Mike's arm as she shoved and elbowed her way through the crowd. She made sure to spit rapid-fire nonsense so no one could get a word in edgewise. "'Scuse me. Pardon me. Dying child here. He really wanted to see the rock, but we couldn't afford Dwayne Johnson, so he's gonna have to settle for this stone. Close enough, am I right? I *am* right."

After a bevy of dirty glares and muttered curse words from the crowd, Steph successfully navigated them to the front. There, in a glass case with some seriously excessive underlighting, sat the Holy Bloodstone, its deep black surface sucking in every photon that dared stray near. Steph's eyes widened. She hadn't expected it to be as big as her fist. Maybe there was something to it, after all.

". . . is why the City Museum is so honored to have hosted the Bloodstone before its return to the Vatican." The small, mustachioed curator standing by the case nodded as he finished his spiel.

"Oh, great. We missed it," Mike muttered.

"Any questions?" asked the man from behind his oversized glasses.

"Yeah!" Steph raised her hand. "Could you run through absolutely all of that again? 'Cause we totally missed it."

She could see the tiny curator's soul begin to break, as his tweed-draped shoulders slumped and he rubbed his temples. "Okay, yes.

Fine. If nobody else has any more relevant questions, I will stay behind and repeat the narrative before we close for the day."

"There you go, bro," Steph whispered.

"Gee, thanks," Mike grumbled.

The majority of the extant crowd dispersed with a low murmur, aside from Steph, Mike, and a few other stragglers. One person in particular—a man in a jean jacket, sunglasses, baseball cap and a hoodie—caught Stephanie's eye. Not because of his unorthodox, overly warm dress, but because of the perfectly waxed grey curlicues on his epic handlebar mustache. Frankly, it put the curator's dry, bristly one to shame. There was also something oddly familiar about him. Something Steph just couldn't place.

"Well, let's start from the top, shall we?" The curator cleared his throat and drew Steph's attention back to the dark jewel. "The appeal of the Holy Bloodstone is a unique anomaly, because there's nothing particularly valuable about it. It *is* old, with the earliest recorded description of it going back over two millennia. But ultimately, it is just a piece of common onyx, albeit impressively cut for its age.

"But it's the *story* of the Bloodstone that makes it so prized. The earliest legends state the stone crystallized around a drop of Christ's blood from the crucifixion—hence the name. And similar to the myth of the Holy Grail, the Bloodstone was said to grant whomever possesses it true immortality."

Steph ooh'ed. "Is that true?"

"Of course not," the curator scoffed. "I told you. It's just a stupid rock. There's no blood inside. But, ironically, a lot of blood has been spilled over it. For centuries, through deadly means, it was passed from king to king, emperor to emperor, and, eventually, museum to museum—all while being the target of several attempted thefts—before ultimately ending up in the private collection of multi-billionaire Armitage Pembroke.

"Luckily for all students of history, Mr. Pembroke recently

relinquished his claim of the item and removed it from his private vault with the intent of getting it back to its permanent home in Europe. Which is why the City Museum is so honored to have hosted the Bloodstone before its return to the Vatican."

Steph squinted as a mustachioed, jean jacket-wearing thought snuck across the front of her brain, "Uh, did you say 'thefts?'"

"William DeFaux," Mike said under his breath, like he usually did when he didn't want to look like a know-it-all but wanted to confirm to himself that he did—in fact—know it all. Steph figured it was a self-esteem thing.

"Yes. Exactly!" the curator confirmed. "In the late 80s and early 90s before it went into Mr. Pembroke's private collection, the Bloodstone was targeted on seventeen different occasions by the infamous gentleman cat burglar known only as William DeFaux."

Steph blinked. "Willem Dafoe? The *actor?*"

"No, Steph," Mike chided. "William DeFaux."

"Willem Dafoe," she repeated sternly.

"WILL-EE-AM DE-FAUX." He enunciated, as if she were a child.

"Willem Dafoe!" she snapped. "I'm saying what you're saying! Y'know what? Forget it." Steph turned her attention back to the curator who had his head in his hands. "See? He's fed up, too. So, this guy, is he behind bars now or what?"

"Well, no. William DeFaux hasn't been seen since his last public burglary attempt back in 1999. And law enforcement hasn't been able to track him because nobody really knows what he looks like."

"Nobody knows what he looks like?" Steph frowned. "He was the bad guy in Spider-Man One!"

"The point is"—the curator cleared his throat in an attempt to reassert his tenuous authority—"whether or not William DeFaux is still active, the City Museum has employed a state-of-the-art security solution to keep the Bloodstone secure even during its transport to the

Vatican."

"So you think he's gonna try again, don'tcha?" Steph waggled her eyebrows. "That'd be pretty cool. Wouldn't it?"

"Steph, don't egg him on," Mike said, but as he turned to the curator, his expression changed. "But it would be pretty cool, right? I've been obsessed with the Bloodstone for years and I just find the whole robbery angle kind of fascinating. DeFaux never actually got ahold of it, but his methods and tricks to even get in the same space were amazingly clever. Oh, man. The Venice Escape of 1986. The Highway Robbery in Ibiza in 1999. The Heist of the Traveling Exhibit at the Taj Mahal!"

Steph was surprised that Mike didn't audibly squee.

"Well rest assured, if DeFaux does attempt to steal the stone again, we'll be waiting." The curator took an exaggerated glance at his watch, belaboring the hint he was trying to make. "Alright! Looks like that's all the time we have today, folks. The museum is closing. Please find your way to the exits and have a good day."

"Do you guys have like a giant steel cage that falls from the ceiling?" Steph asked, looking up. "Or what about one of those laser grids from the movies?"

"*Please* find your way to the *exits*, and *have a nice day*." the curator grunted as he shambled off through the back way of the exhibit.

"Hmph." Mike crossed his arms.

Steph looked around. She and Mike were the only people left in the rotunda.

"Hey, Mike," she jerked a thumb over her shoulder. "Where'd he go?"

"Where'd who go?"

"There was a guy here! Don't tell me you didn't see him."

"I have no idea who you're talking about."

"The guy in the jean jacket and the hoodie with the gnarly moustache."

"A jean jacket *and* a hoodie? I think I would've noticed someone like that."

"You were too busy nerding out over the stone. But he was definitely here. He must have snuck out." Steph bit her lip. "There was something weirdly familiar about him."

"Wait." Mike froze in his tracks, grabbing Steph's shoulder. "You don't think . . ."

Steph felt a jolt of excitement flit down her spine. "Oh, crap. You might be right."

"Are you serious right now?" Mike shook his hands out like a toddler who'd just eaten something spicy. "Are you telling me we could actually be part of the historical saga of the Holy Bloodstone? That we could be the ones to catch *William DeFaux*?"

"That must've been him doing one last case of the joint before springing his plan," Steph said. "I never knew you were so into this stuff, Mike."

"I have hobbies, too, y'know," Mike said. "Now come on. He might still be in the building!"

Steph followed Mike as he tore back down the halls of the Bloodstone exhibit and into the main atrium of the museum. The lights were dim, and the last few stragglers were quietly making their exit out the array of doors beyond the marble pillars. Across the way, a skeleton of a diplodocus and her child looked on soulfully.

"Hm." Mike whipped his head around, scouring the premises. "Where do you think he could've gone?"

"Uh . . . maybe over there . . ." Steph said, inching slowly toward her own agenda. "By the closed and unguarded cake place."

"Steph," Mike droned, his voice echoing across the floor a bit. "Stop with the cakes."

"Fine, fine. But the museum's closing. If the guards start doing their rounds soon, they'll find us before we find DeFaux and kick us out."

"Alright," Mike rubbed his chin in thought. "Well I guess we'll have to find a place to hide."

"Like where?"

"I dunno! I've never had to hide myself away in a museum before. Have you?"

"No," Steph nodded. "But common sense says there's always one place you go when you don't wanna be found."

"Where's that?"

* * *

"Rgh. Why did we have to hide in the bathroom?" Mike asked as he shifted his body weight in an attempt to get comfortable in the supremely uncomfortable position of squatting on a toilet seat.

"I didn't hear you coming up with any other ideas." Steph wasn't too comfortable either, as they were sharing the same toilet seat, struggling to keep their feet from being visible through the gap between the floor and the stall door.

"Well, couldn't we have at least used the handicapped stall so we could, y'know, have more room?"

"What if someone in a wheelchair came in, Mike? I bet you'd feel like crap then."

"The museum has been closed for three hours," Mike hissed at her. "Nobody in a wheelchair is coming into the bathroom!"

"It's been three hours already? Wow. Time sure flies when you're hiding in a stank-ass bathroom."

"Shh! Shh!" Mike said. "Somebody's coming!"

"How do you kn—" Steph was silenced as Mike slid his hand over her mouth.

"Hello?" a deep voice called out. "Anyone in here?"

The clicking of hard-soled shoes echoed across the tile between the sink and stalls, with the glow of a flashlight softly bobbing with each step.

"Thought I heard something." A flashlight beam cut through the darkness and illuminated a spot just two inches above Mike's head, before arching away. "Clarence, you goddamn fool," the voice mumbled. "You need to lay off the bourbon before work. If Mr. Armond tests you again, that's it for you. Then Adriana's gonna kick you to the curb."

The footsteps clicked away, followed by the rhythmic creaking of a swinging door.

Mike let his breath out once the door was still. "Goddamn. That was close."

"I'll say." Steph cocked her head. "Time to go? That guard's probably not gonna do another round for three more hours."

"I guess this time's as good as we're gonna get." Mike hopped off the toilet before turning back up to her and hissing. "Just be careful and *pay attention.*"

"Mike," Steph scoffed. "Name *one* time I haven't paid attention."

Mike shot her a wordless glare as he unlocked the stall door and the two crept out of the bathroom into the now, much darker museum hallway. Steph did as she was told and made sure to pay extra close attention to every single tiptoe. She matched Mike's tentative pace exactly, as they darted from behind one exhibit to another, ensuring they couldn't be seen. As a result, it took them the better part of fifteen minutes to make it back to the pillared edges of the main atrium, within striking distance of the Bloodstone exhibit.

Mike held up his hand, demanding they stay hidden behind this particular pillar. Steph could only roll her eyes at the ridiculous authority he had assumed. And so there they sat, waiting.

It was another twenty or so minutes before Steph saw something stir. She slapped Mike in the shoulder and repeatedly pointed at the skeleton of the diplodocus. From beneath the jagged shadows of its gently arcing ribs slipped the lithe body of a man clad all in black. He silently glided toward the Bloodstone exhibit.

"Shit!" Mike whispered. "It's him! Let's go."

Finally able to release all her pent-up energy, Steph dashed after the thief with her usual reckless abandon. She could hear Mike trailing behind her and whining something, but opted to ignore it. Now was the time for action!

Steph rushed into the exhibit, tearing down the hallways before skidding to a stop before the main display. There, the thief was in the process of opening the Bloodstone's glass case with his gloved hands. He was working both quickly and carefully to prevent tripping any alarms that may have been hidden within. Hearing the screech of Steph's sneakers on the marble floor, he snapped his neck around, allowing her to take in his soft, sparkling blue eyes, well-moisturized skin, and a mischievous smile neatly tucked away beneath his tightly waxed grey moustache.

Steph cocked her head, squinting at him. "You're not Willem Dafoe!"

Not-Dafoe tipped the brim of his black beret-style hat up with his thumb, revealing a head of thick salt-and-pepper hair. "Quite right, young lady." He said with a charming transatlantic accent. "And who might you be?"

"I'll be asking the questions here, buddy."

"Oh." The thief crossed his arms. "Very well, then. Go on."

Steph blinked. "Okay, you got me. I don't actually have any questions. But there ain't no way you're getting that jewel."

"I beg to differ. I've been planning and re-planning this heist for decades. I'm not about to lose the Bloodstone again. And I don't believe you'll be able to stop me."

"Well, believe it!" Steph lunged at the thief who simply side-stepped away and let her crash to the floor.

"Well, that was anti-climactic." He huffed.

"I wasn't going for you." Steph smiled as she rose and knocked her knuckles on the glass display case. Almost instantaneously, an array of lasers materialized, crisscrossing their way around the atrium, creating a seemingly impenetrable grid. Now, both she and the thief were caught in a tight web of red laser light, preventing them from even flinching. "One false move and the cops'll be here in seconds." It had been a gamble that there even *was* a laser grid. But now that the plan had paid off, Mike just needed—when he eventually got here—to go get the guards and take the credit.

"Oh, you think you have it all figured out, do you?" The thief contorted his body in skillfully lithe gyrations, narrowly avoiding the lasers until he got into a more comfortable position. "Well, good luck." Detaching a gun from his belt, the thief shot a rope into the air, its metallic end clinking into an open vent above. "Ta!" He waved as the rope went taut and the vent practically sucked him up.

"Aw, crap." Steph blinked again and took stock of her situation. "I keep forgetting to bring my grappling hook."

It was at this time that Mike skidded into view at the edge of the atrium, just short of the laser alarm grid. "Goddamnit, Steph. What did you do? Where's DeFaux?"

She pointed excitedly up at the ceiling. "I tried to catch him with the laser grid, but he wriggled out of it and escaped through an air vent."

"That's . . ." Mike's conflicted emotions were clear on his scrunched-up face. ". . . extremely cool."

"Yeah." She nodded. "It was!"

"Just like his escape from the Smithsonian in 1992!" Mike's amusement shifted to his more usual disappointment. "Goddamnit. I told you not to run ahead and that we'd take him together!"

"Well, in my defense, I was too busy running ahead to hear that," Steph said.

"Great. Now if you even move a muscle, you'll trip this grid, it'll set off the alarm and then we're gonna be in some serious trouble."

"Don't worry, Mike. I think I got a way out of this." Steph slid her hand into her pocket and removed her phone, careful not to stumble. "If he can do it . . ."

"Oh, no. Steph, please don't tell me you're gonna do what I think you're going to do."

Gingerly plugging in her earbuds, Steph nodded with a wide smile. This was something she had wanted to try since forever. Mike's protests were instantly muted by the bold, brassy voice of Tina Turner who reassured Stephanie that she was, well, simply the best.

Closing her eyes and getting in touch with her inner Zeta-Jones, Steph extended her arms upward in a long stretch before sliding down onto her knees and angling her back low to the ground, shimmying herself forward. After rotating on her back, she kicked up into a standing position before arcing back forward and nearly touching her toes. She flipped onto the ground with a hard impact to her butt, then leaned back and slid herself beneath another laser.

As the chorus kicked in, Steph spread her legs in a wide V then slowly rotated around and hopped back to her feet. She found her nose inches away from a laser and nearly toppled into it, but found a way to shift and regain her balance. Mike, slack-jawed and shocked, was only a few feet away, behind a few more arrays of the grid. Steph smiled to herself and took a deep breath. She shut her eyes again and pivoted, angling her shoulders and snaking her way through the next section, before dropping to the floor and downward dogging herself through the last set of lasers and into the hallway beyond.

Steph popped to her feet as Mike simply stood there in front of her, brows knit and mouth agape.

"Hahah. That was awesome. Didn't think I could do that, did you, Mike?" Steph smiled back, but as she removed her earbuds, the continuing affirmations of Tina Turner were replaced by the sustained blare of sirens and alarm bells. "Wait. What's that?"

"You. Hit." Mike forced the words through his teeth. "Every. Single. Laser."

"Oh," Steph winced. "Uh, whoops?"

* * *

"Why in God's name did you close your eyes while you were doing it?" Michael grimaced as the cold metal of the police cruiser's trunk met his cheek.

"I thought it would look cool," Stephanie shot back, as if that justified everything, despite the fact they were both being handcuffed.

"Well, now we're going to have to get Rex to pull our asses out of jail again, and I'm sure he's not going to like that."

"He doesn't like *anything.*"

"Is this them?" A reedy, vaguely familiar voice cleared its throat behind them as the uniformed cops spun Michael and Stephanie up and around to meet its source face-to-face. Well, face and top of balding head, as it were. The tiny exhibit curator who had given them his spiel about the Holy Bloodstone stared daggers up at them from behind the thick frames of his glasses. "So you two thought you could get away with it, huh?"

"Hey, we were trying to help you, little man!" Stephanie said. The curator's moustache bristled.

"Steph, don't call him a little man." Michael admonished her. "He has a name. Although I don't know what that is."

"How could you possibly be helping us by stealing the Bloodstone?" The curator shouted.

"Well, first of all, we weren't stealing it," Steph explained. "We were trying to keep it from being stolen. By Willem Dafoe."

The curator reared back. "William DeFaux?!"

"That's what I said." Steph nodded.

"He was here? Impossible!"

"It's not impossible," Michael said. "We saw him. Well, Steph did."

"Did you see his face?" The curator leaned in, squinting. "What did he look like?"

"He looked like . . . uh, I don't know." Stephanie shrugged. "An old guy. Blue eyes. Grey hair. Kinda hot, actually. I might have a thing for him now."

"That's incredibly vague. How do I know you aren't just making this up?"

"Well, he had a better moustache than yours." Steph smirked.

The curator frowned, before looking over to the cops. "Take them away, and I will be pressing charges tomorrow morning."

"That will not be necessary." A voice with a sharp English accent and a strong undercurrent of authority sliced through the crowd of curious onlookers who had gathered to witness the proceedings. The gawkers parted, and a tall blonde nun strode through them like they were the Red Sea and she was two million Hebrews, though that metaphor wasn't exactly accurate on religious lines.

"Sister Malone!" The curator gasped with such reverential surprise, Michael thought he was about to take a knee.

"Mr. Armond." the nun addressed the curator but didn't deign to look at him, instead keeping her steely gaze fixed on Michael and Stephanie. "It seems you've had an incident regarding the Holy Bloodstone."

"Uh, yes, but it's been confirmed safe and has been moved into the Museum's storage vault for security purposes."

"Regardless," the nun flipped her hand, "his holiness will not be pleased that the property of the Catholic Church was put in certain peril. And, needless to say, that would put my head on the chopping block, as well. As a result, I've made the decision to expedite the transition of the Bloodstone to the Vatican early as tomorrow."

"But—but the exhibit is scheduled to go on for at least another week!" Armond stammered.

"I'm sure you'll find some bones or fabrics or something similar that can fill the space. But we will be taking our holy relic back into more secure custody. And since these two"—she gestured broadly in the direction of Stephanie and Michael—"seem to be the only ones taking this attempted theft seriously, they will be in charge of its security from now on. That is, if they are amenable to it."

"Oh, hell yeah," Steph said before Michael had a chance to answer. But, to be fair, he would have been just as excited. "Duckett & Dyer: Dicks For Hire is at your service, m'lady."

"Don't call us that." Michael buried his face in his palm. "And don't call her m'lady."

"Hm." the nun raised an eyebrow. "Yes, I've heard stories about you two. If your reputation matches the rumors, I will be quite impressed. I trust your rates are reasonable?"

"Yes," Michael interjected. "We're competitively priced. We'll submit an invoi—"

Steph double-interjected, "We'll do it for some of that cake!"

"Steph!"

"Excuse me?" asked Sister Malone.

"The chocolate cake in the museum. Give us a dump truck full of that. It's *literally* the best cake I've ever had."

"Steph," Michael forced the words out of the corner of his mouth. "Are you insane? We need money."

"This cake tastes better than money, Mike," she said, before dropping her voice down to a whisper. "Trust me. If we keep our rates this cheap, they might even give us a closer look at the Holy Bloodstone. And then we'd be immortal."

"What're you talking about?" Michael could do nothing except sigh. "Steph, weren't you listening? It doesn't work that way."

"I meant figuratively."

"It doesn't work that way, either!"

"Are you two quite done?" tutted Sister Malone. "Now, we agree to your terms. I plan to have our security convoy depart the museum tomorrow at 0600. And I want you on it." She pointed at Michael. "Do *not* be late."

"Sir, yes, sir!" Steph saluted the nun.

Sister Malone offered only a curt nod before performing an about face and melting away into the crowd.

Mr. Armond followed slowly without taking his eyes off Stephanie and Michael. "I still don't trust you as far as I can throw you. So you buffoons better watch yourselves. Because I'll be watching *you.*"

"Great! See ya later!" Stephanie waved, before turning back to Michael. "This is going to be fun."

Michael grimaced. "You're still hopped up on the sugar from all that cake, aren't you?"

"Maybe."

* * *

Michael struggled to fall asleep. He was incredibly excited to be such an integral part of the history of the Bloodstone. When Steph had forced this detective agency on him, he never once thought it would put him face to face with the awesome stuff he obsessed over as a kid. And to work directly for the Vatican? Who knew their accidental, half-assed LLC would have provided so many opportunities?

The other reason Michael couldn't sleep was Steph running around like her head was on fire, unable to calm down. She kept pacing back and forth across the office's creaky hardwood floors, muttering to herself aloud.

"*How* do I know him? How do I know *him*? How *do* I know him?"

Michael tried to block it out with a pillow, but with limited success. It was only once Steph's sugar mania sent her tunneling down an internet rabbit hole about William DeFaux that he finally managed to get some rest. The rapid, rhythmic pitter patter of her fingers across the laptop keyboard provided the white noise Michael needed to drift to sleep.

When he opened his eyes at 5am the next morning, Steph's bloodshot, baggy eyes were peering over the anime body pillow between them.

"Geeze!" Michael nearly rolled back off the edge of the bed.

"Hey, man. You awake yet?" Her teeth chattered in her skull, as her fingers idly traced the old bullet holes in the body pillow.

"Yes, damn it!"

"I think I'm onto something," she whispered.

Michael rubbed grains of sleep from his eyes as he swung his legs off the bed. "Does it involve cake?"

"No." Steph held up a lumpy, grease-stained paper bag. "This stuff goes stale fast. I'd chip a tooth if I bit into it."

"Great. Now what are you talking about?"

"I can't tell you." Steph dropped her voice to an even lower register. "It's a *secret*."

"Why is it a secret?"

"Because I'm not sure I'm right, and I don't want to look like an idiot in front of that nun if I'm not. Those ladies hit you with rulers, y'know? And not in the fun way, like you want."

"Alright, whatever." Michael didn't think any of her sugar-crazed conspiracy theories would hold any water. "We don't have time for this—whatever this is—anyway. The convoy leaves the museum in an hour. And I'll be damned if I miss working on the first case I'm actually interested in."

"Well, hurry up then. I'm all ready to go!" Steph jumped up to reveal yesterday's wrinkled clothes, which she still wore like a badge of honor. "I'll make the coffee!"

* * *

The Garbagemobile creaked and groaned as it skidded to a stop in front of the City Museum. Michael had always enjoyed the place, but its white marble columns were even more strikingly beautiful in the first light of the morning. Less striking were the two black armored trucks and their pair of guardian Humvees. They looked like squatting shadows in the street, although the shiny limousine at the rear of the convoy was quite nice.

They exited the Garbagemobile as professionally as possible—but between the welded shut passenger door and the driver's side door jamming at the most inopportune occasions, it was difficult. Once they navigated the car's intricacies, they walked over to meet Sister Malone and Mr. Armond, who were casually waiting by the doors to the limo— as casual as people could be when flanked by heavily armed guards.

"Good morning," Sister Malone lilted, in a surprisingly better mood than she had been last night. Mr. Armond just glared.

Michael's gaze shot down at the metal briefcase handcuffed to the nun's left hand. She quietly crossed her wrists to block his eyeline.

Steph whistled, pointing at the armed—and armored—men. "You guys are packing some serious firepower. Remind me why you need us again?"

"We don't." Mr. Armond sneered until Sister Malone elbowed him in the shoulder. Michael hadn't fully realized how tall Sister Malone was. She nearly towered over all of them. Or perhaps that was just the illusion of authority.

"I am not leaving anything to chance, Mr. Armond." She tutted. "If there's even a 1% chance that these two have seen William DeFaux in action, their assistance will be quite valuable to us."

"Yeah, Mr. Armond. If that is your real name!" Steph jabbed.

"My real name?" He furrowed his brow. "Of course it's my real name! What the hell are you talking about?"

"Also, and I've been thinking about this." Steph shifted gears like a rally driver. "Why don't you guys just *mail* the stone to the Vatican? That'd be safer and cheaper, right? 'Cause messing with the mail is a federal offense."

"Please don't listen to her, she's been up all night, *and* she just had coffee," Michael offered. "But we're happy to help in whatever way we can. Just tell us where you need us to be."

"Very well," Sister Malone said. "We shall be riding in this limousine, while the rest of our security detail remains in the armored cars and military vehicles."

"And what about the Bloodstone?" Michael asked.

"There are three fireproof, reinforced cases spread out between us and the armored cars," Sister Malone held up the metal attaché cuffed to her hand. "Only one contains the true Holy Bloodstone."

"Cool. So which one is it?" Steph asked.

"Steph, she's not going to tell us." Michael chided.

"Yes, I'm afraid I'm going to have to keep that information to myself and on a strict need-to-know basis. Once the convoy safely reaches a private airstrip outside the city limits—with your assistance—I will re-take possession of the correct case for my secure flight to the Vatican."

"Okay, well, that seems simple enough," Michael said.

"I'm sure it won't be," Armond muttered.

"I'm tiring of your pessimism quite rapidly, Mr. Armond." Sister Malone admonished. "Please try to be a little more chipper. Now, then, if you'd all make your way into the limousine." She flourished her left hand, while her right kept a tight grip on the handle of the case. "We can begin the day."

* * *

Having gotten used to the jostling and bouncing of the worn-out shocks on the Garbagemobile, Michael found riding in the limo akin to drifting on a particularly luxurious cloud and allowed himself to relax a bit. Conversely, Steph was beside him twiddling her thumbs and staring intently at the metal box on Sister Malone's lap. Michael thought she would have had a sugar crash by now, but she was still very much on edge. He shrugged to himself. Perhaps this was the kind of frantic behavior Steph had to deal with when *he* became nervously obsessive about things.

With the two Humvees covering the front and rear of the two armored trucks, and the limo following carefully behind, the convoy thundered its way out of the city. Traffic was light, and within twenty minutes, they merged off the highway and onto a stretch of wide four lane road winding south through the badlands—a vast expanse of arid, rocky dirt no one had bothered to develop. Though they were now out in the open, the remarkable flatness of the area made it easy to see if any threats were incoming. So far, as Michael looked out the tinted windows, he saw none.

. . . aside from Steph staring absolute daggers at Mr. Armond, which would certainly threaten their pay scale.

"Stop looking at me like that!" he finally snapped, pushing up his thick glasses.

"Make me."

"Steph, stop."

"Why, Mike? There's something shady about him."

"What? My name is Elmore Armond. I'm 57. I have a Master's degree in anthropology and have been employed at the City Museum for over 30 years. I pay my taxes on time. I own three cats! What's so shady about me?"

Steph's eyes narrowed. "Why not *four* cats?"

"Alright, you two," Sister Malone—who up until this point looked like she was actually enjoying the back and forth—hushed them. "Stop these shenani—" The sister was interrupted as the limousine lurched sharply to the right, nearly careening off the road. Luckily, the driver managed to regain control just in time to avoid a large, dense brush.

While they regained their bearings, a dark blur whizzed by Michael's window on the left side. "What the hell was that?"

"Bikes!" Steph disengaged her seatbelt and leapt over to Michael's side. Leaning over him, she shoved her nose against the glass as a second blur—a light, speedy dirt bike with a black leather-suited figure balanced atop it—passed them.

"Bikes, plural?" Michael raised an eyebrow. In all his past heists, William DeFaux tended to work alone.

"He must be getting desperate," Sister Malone chimed. "This is his last chance to seize the stone before its locked away in the Vatican vaults forever." She rapped twice on the closed divider behind Mr. Armond's head. "Keep driving!"

"This is *so* cool," Stephanie rolled down Michael's side window and stuck her entire torso out. The roar of air rushing into the limo was quickly shattered by a distinctive *brrap-brrap.* "They got guns!"

"Are you crazy?" Michael shouted, clawing at Steph's coat in a bid to drag her to safety. "Get back in here!"

"No!" Sister Malone shouted over the din. "Can you identify the assailants? Are either of them DeFaux?"

Against his better judgment—which had been rapidly eroding as of late—Michael shoved his face in between Steph's ribs and the side of the window. His glasses shielding his eyes from the crackling desert winds, Michael tried to identify the riders, but their sleek black helmets made that almost impossible. Not to mention the flashes of their gunfire being quite distracting.

"I can't tell!" Michael shouted back. "Steph, do either of these guys fit his body type?"

"Sorry, Mike! I'm not sure either."

"What're they doing?" Mr. Armond's tweedy voice shouted from inside the limo. "Why're they shooting at an armored car?"

The dirt bikes wove in and out of the convoy in a gracefully coordinated highway ballet. They were targeting the first armored truck in line. The bikes were alternating, one strafing the truck with gunfire, while the other got up close and hung onto the side. The frontmost Humvee had a man in the gun turret, but the bikes were darting back and forth so quickly, he couldn't get a bead.

"Michael!" Mr. Armond squealed, knocking him out of his concentration. "What's happening!"

"I don't really kn—" Michael saw the armored truck's driver leaning out his side window. He couldn't make out the look on the man's face, but, judging by the fact that he leapt out the door seconds later, Michael guessed he was *terrified*. He blinked, and then his eyes went involuntarily wide as he figured out what was going on. Without thinking, he wrapped his arms around Steph's waist and dragged her back into the limo before the first truck exploded. The two of them, along with Sister Malone and Mr. Armond, tumbled around the back seats as their limo driver once again swerved artfully to avoid the sudden maelstrom of fiery, distressed metal flying through the air and bouncing across the pavement.

The explosion caused the convoy to splinter around the remains of the destroyed vehicle. To the credit of the drivers behind the wheels of the Humvees and the remaining armored truck, they coalesced back into formation once they cleared the debris.

"That was nuts!" Steph screamed. "I mean, *holy shit*!"

Sister Malone shot Stephanie a disapproving eye, which was promptly ignored.

"This was similar to how he attempted to heist the stone during its transit from the British Museum in 1984," Armond said. "Although it was just him then, and the damage was much less . . . severe."

"I remember seeing footage of that!" Michael said. "I don't know how he managed to get away."

"Well, let's make sure he doesn't escape this time."

Michael peeked his head out the window and looked back, spotting the bikers roll-up, dismount, and begin to paw through the wreckage. "They're searching for the stone."

"Well, they're certainly not going to get it." Sister Malone turned up her nose at the mere suggestion.

"Ah-ha!" Steph pointed. "So it wasn't in that truck! I knew it."

"No, you didn't." Michael frowned.

"If he's this determined," Armond said, turning to the nun. "With his intellect brought to bear, *and* hired muscle, we could be in very real danger, Sister."

A dour resignation swept Sister Malone's once stoic face, and she nodded. "Driver." The nun rapped on the divider between them and the front seat. "Radio the others and tell them to divert to alternate route 21-C. They'll know what it means. Follow them closely."

Moving as one, the remainder of the convoy swerved off the main road of the freeway at the next exit. This new route took them down a narrower, two-lane road that stretched off into the distance before being swallowed up by the rocky teeth of a range of red-orange buttes.

"I've been advised that this route is out of our way," the nun clarified. "So we will need to double back to the airstrip. But it is relatively isolated."

As the rocky outcroppings loomed larger and cast their shadows over the convoy, Michael could make out the arc of a small tunnel carved within the foot of the butte before them.

"Heh. Hey, Mike." Steph pointed as they passed a green highway sign. "Butt Tunnel."

Michael stifled a chortle.

"Hmph." Armond crossed his arms. "And here I thought you were the sensible one."

The concrete and metal maw of Butte Tunnel swallowed the convoy whole, ushering it out of the hot desert badlands and into its cool, sterile innards with the sun's rays replaced by the glow and hum of the tunnel's fluorescent lighting. The convoy slowed down, and Michael felt the limousine shift to give the Humvee in front of it a wide berth.

"Why're we slowing down?" He asked.

"The guys in the Humvee up front radioed everyone to give each other space," said the driver—whom Michael hadn't heard speak until now—over the intercom. "In case of any sudden stops. And so they can get a clear view of each car."

Michael leaned back in his seat, and the rest of the passengers in the limo did the same. Something felt off, though. Real off. And Michael's anxious, repetitive jiggling of his leg didn't help quell his nervousness. A quick glance told him Steph's leg was doing the same, but probably for hyperactive reasons.

The ride through the tunnel was smooth but long. Michael didn't realize the butte was so wide. That thought gave him the urge to chortle again, but he stamped it down as much as he could. Fortunately, nobody heard him, as they were distracted by the growl of an engine.

As the limousine drove past a maintenance passage perpendicular to the tunnel proper, two headlights blazed into existence, and a dark, heavy form screeched across the asphalt into formation behind them.

Steph was the first to snap around and peer through the limo's rear window. "It's another armored truck."

"Are we supposed to have a backup?" Michael asked.

"I—I don't believe so," Sister Malone stammered.

They were treated to three more screeches of burning rubber coming from in front of them. Another armored truck, identical to the first, peeled into line in the space between them and the next Humvee. Michael could only imagine there were more that had cut in line ahead.

To his surprise, the new armored trucks made no moves to attack them, like the dirt bikes had. Instead, they kept the procession moving in an orderly fashion—even if they were a bit too close for comfort. The convoy continued to trundle along the tunnel in a state of mutually assured confusion.

After a few more hundred feet, the tunnel ended and the convoy was back on the open two-lane road again, with the butte shrinking behind them. As soon as the first sliver of blue sky was visible from the limo's back seat, the armored car inches from their bumper roared to life and charged ahead, disappearing from view.

"Where the hell are they going in such a hurry?" Steph asked.

In response, the armored truck in front of them changed lanes and sped up. Two others slotted out of formation into the opposite lane, shifting back to take up positions at the rear of the convoy.

"Good lord. He's trying to confuse us!" Sister Malone said.

"It's a shell game!" Michael and Armond said in unison. They looked at each other. "Like the Ibiza heist in 1988!"

"Now this is more his speed," Michael continued. "Nice and clever."

"Well, if you two know what it is," Sister Malone scolded. "Tell us what we can do about it!"

"Just the obvious," Michael said, beaming. "We need to keep our eyes on the right armored truck."

Sister Malone nodded and rapped on the driver's partition. "Get into the oncoming lane and speed up. We need to identify each truck in the convoy."

The limo driver did as he was told and swerved around the rearmost truck, speeding up so that they were now running parallel to the entire convoy.

Steph, all too eager, jumped up on her seat and hit the sunroof button with the toe of her sneaker, allowing her torso to poke out of the top of the limo. Michael followed suit.

"So which one is it?" He called back down. "The one that has the stone. Give us a license plate or something."

"I . . . uh . . . can't! I told you. The information must be kept on a need-to-know basis."

"Well, if you don't think we need to know"—Michael ducked back down into the limo—"then you'd better stick your head up here yourself!"

"Mike!" Steph called from up top, with an uncharacteristic fear in her voice. "We've got a problem!"

Michael scrabbled back up to see Steph pointing, her eyes wide. The once clear oncoming lane was now blocked by the unfriendly face of a bright red eighteen-wheeler barreling out of the horizon straight toward them.

Michael slapped the roof of the car, "Driver! We have to fall back. Can't you see the truck?"

"I see it," the driver squawked across the intercom, "But I need the Sister's go ahead."

"No, keep driving!" Sister Malone shot back. "We can't lose them!"

"What?" Michael ducked back down as the truck's horn blared. "We'll die if we don't!"

"We need to stay the course! The safety of the Bloodstone depends on it!"

"Are you insane?" Armond shouted. "I'm not dying for this!"

"Mike!" Steph tugged anxiously at his sleeve. The truck sounded its horn repeatedly. "We've got like thirty seconds. We need to move!"

"Sister, give the order!" Michael barked.

"No! We can't lose them!" She repeated.

"Ten seconds!" Steph called.

"It's my responsibility!" the nun shouted.

"Five seconds!" The truck's horn was now a sustained scream.

"Okay, okay!" Sister Malone cried. "Do it! Driver, fall back!"

"Too late!" Steph tumbled down through the sunroof as the limo cut a sharp turn and juked and jostled, sending them crashing against every seat and wall in the car.

When Michael finally decided to open his eyes, the truck horn was receding angrily into the distance. He found himself bent in awkward angles against the limo's minibar, but otherwise generally unharmed.

"What happened?" he said, his vision swimming as the minibar door opened and a handful of tiny vodka bottles fell out onto his face.

"Hey, I didn't know we had alcohol!" Steph grumbled from the opposite side of the limo.

Sister Malone and Mr. Armond, both upright and safely in their seats, unclicked their seatbelts. While Sister Malone clutched her case for dear life, Mr. Armond peered out the window.

"We veered off the road just in time," he explained. "But it looks like the rest of the convoy are already too far for us to catch up to."

Sister Malone averted her gaze and said nothing, inadvertently speaking volumes.

As Michael pushed himself back upright, he glanced at Steph, just in time to see her eyes dart down to the case still chained to Sister Malone's arm. The constant tossing and tumbling had left bright red sores around her wrist. When Mr. Armond turned back around, everyone in the limo finally knew what everyone else was thinking.

"So you're holding onto the real stone, eh?" Steph, as usual, was the one to put it into words. "I should have figured. I always pegged you as kind of a control freak."

The nun's nervous, worried, mask fell back into her usual stoicism. "Of course I'm holding the real stone. This holy gem belongs to the Vatican, and I was under strict orders not to let it out of my sight."

"And why were you willing to let us die?" Mr. Armond screamed. If he hadn't, Michael surely was thinking about doing some yelling himself. "That truck would've taken you and the stone along with it."

"I made a vow, Mr. Armond. And this holy stone"—Sister Malone patted the case—"is worth more than any of our lives combined. I was ordered to keep the true location of the stone on a need-to-know basis. So, in the interest of committing to the ruse, I feigned ignorance to make sure none of you really knew where the true stone lay. I was only authorized to break my act if our lives were truly, unavoidably in danger." She cleared her throat. "Even then it was a massive risk. You can never be too careful. There are eyes everywhere these days."

"You're crazy, lady. But I kinda admire that," Steph said. "At least we're sure the stone is safe now."

"Well, actually, I wouldn't go that far." The opaque screen that divided the driver from the rear seats slid down with a slow mechanical whir. A mellifluous voice with a manufactured transatlantic accent floated through the open partition over the barrel of a silenced pistol.

"Hey!" Steph pointed at the man behind the gun. "I know you!"

"William DeFaux," Michael said, savoring every syllable. He'd finally gotten his first look at the larger-than-life cat burglar he'd romanticized in his youth. He was as Steph had described him, a stern-jawed older man with a prodigious grey moustache. A thick head of salt-and-pepper hair hid under a chauffeur's cap. It was then that Michael realized that he should never meet his heroes. Especially if his heroes were actually villains who wanted to shoot and rob him.

"Now, sirs and madams." DeFaux waggled the pistol. "If you could please hand over the Bloodstone?"

"Over my dead body," spat Sister Malone.

"Yes, well, that's certainly an option." DeFaux smirked.

"You don't kill people," Michael said, his hands in the air. "That's not how you operate."

"And who exactly are you to tell me how I operate?" DeFaux raised a silver eyebrow.

"You're not violent," Michael insisted. "Just sneaky and clever."

"Am I now? Well, how's this for sneaky and clever?" DeFaux fired off two silenced shots into the floor of the limo, causing everyone to jump back. By the time Michael regained composure, Sister Malone's metal case was firmly in DeFaux's grasp, with the handcuffs dangling limp and free from the handle. The thief flicked a small lockpick at them while admiring his prize. "Now, I do appreciate the challenge you've given me. So a sincere thanks to all of you. This really has been a pleasure. Ta!" With a tip of his chauffeur's cap, DeFaux bolted out of the car, stage left.

"I—I can't believe it. How did he—" Sister Malone stammered in shock. "How did he get past our security?"

"Amazing," Mr. Armond growled. "Absolutely amazing. This has been a complete disaster. At least if we'd left it in the museum nobody would've gotten hurt."

"What the—" The staccato thunder of helicopter blades shook the roof of the limo as Michael spun around, realizing Stephanie was nowhere to be found.

* * *

It didn't take long for Steph to catch up to William DeFaux on the deserted shoulder of the highway.

"Hey! Stealy Dan!" She shouted. "Where do I know you from?"

DeFaux squinted. "I'm sure I don't know, madam. But, if you'll excuse me, my ride is here."

Steph felt the kick up of dust from the hovering helicopter before she registered the deafening noise of the rotors and the shadow passing overhead—so deep had she dug into her mind to figure out where exactly she had recognized DeFaux's charming face.

And then it clicked.

"Yes!" Steph clapped. "I got it!"

"WHAT?" DeFaux shouted over the noise of the chopper as a small rope ladder unfurled down in front of him.

"I KNOW WHO YOU ARE," she shouted back.

"I DON'T HAVE TIME FOR THIS, MADAM." DeFaux merely shook his head before mounting the ladder. "GOODBYE."

"OH NO YOU DON'T." Steph took a running start and grabbed the last rung of the ladder as the helicopter rose. Pulling herself up, she worked her way toward DeFaux, who drew his gun with his free hand—the other tenuously holding onto both the ladder and the handle of the case containing the Holy Bloodstone.

"ONE MORE RUNG AND I'LL SHOOT," he said.

"I'M BETTING YOU WON'T." Steph smiled and grabbed the handcuffs dangling off the handle of the Bloodstone's case. She clicked them firmly around her wrist.

And then everything went black.

. . .

. . .

"HEY, WHOA!" DeFaux's violent exclamation brought her back to reality. His cold metal pistol tumbled past her head on its way to the desert floor hundreds of feet below.

"SORRY!" Steph yelled, shaking her head. "FINALLY HAD THAT SUGAR CRASH!"

Steph found her sudden narcolepsy had caused her to let go of the rung, and the only thing keeping her hanging was DeFaux's rapidly straining grip—one hand on the ladder, the other on the opposite handle of the case she was chained to. With a faint clack, the box's clasps gave way under the pressure, and the case flung open! Falling several feet, Stephanie's heart caught in her throat. Fortunately, DeFaux was stronger than he looked, and kept her dangling, albeit more perilously. Amidst everything, Steph noticed the Bloodstone squeak its way out of the case's foam holder. Snapping out with her free hand, she caught the cold black gem before it plummeted to certain doom.

Using her experience maneuvering herself out of the Garbagemobile's passenger-side window, Steph levered her bodyweight forward and grabbed back onto the ladder.

"WHOA! OKAY!" She said. "WHOO. THAT WAS A BIG MISTAKE." Steph climbed up a few more rungs until she was just below DeFaux's moustache, staring up at him from the opposite side of the ladder, waggling the stone in his face. "Now tell flyboy up there to touch down and let me off. Or I'll tell everyone who you really are.

"Also." Steph glared at him. "I like your little hat. Give me your little hat."

* * *

"Hey, so I got the Bloodstone back."

Michael's jaw couldn't help but drop as Steph sauntered up to the limousine with the case shackled to her left hand.

Sister Malone looked even more dumbfounded as she took possession of the case, removing it from Stephanie's wrist using a key she'd secreted away. She clicked it open to find the dark black rock staring at her in the face, before shutting it immediately. "Thank you! But—but how?"

"Listen, Sister. You hired Mike and me to do a job, and we delivered. Don't ask questions. Now I suggest we get to that plane of yours in case DeFaux changes his mind and turns around."

Sister Malone nodded and ducked back into the limo. Mr. Armond followed suit but turned around at the door. "I have to say, I'm quite impressed. I'm sorry for doubting you two before. I won't make that mistake again."

"Thanks, pal." Stephanie flashed a finger gun. "I appreciate that."

Michael turned to her. "Steph, I don't understand. What the hell did you do?"

"Don't worry about that for now. First we need to get Sister Malone on that plane. And we need a new driver, so . . ." Steph yanked DeFaux's chauffeur's cap from the inside pocket of her jacket and slapped it onto Michael's head. "Let's roll."

* * *

With Michael behind the wheel, the damaged limousine limped along the remainder of the desert highway, eventually turning into a small private airfield. Flanked by several hangars in a state of disrepair, a surprisingly smooth length of runway extended off into the distance. A medium sized personal jet idled at the top, its engines emitting a low whine.

"Well, that was more excitement than I've had in a while," Sister Malone admitted as she approached the plane's boarding stairs. With the Bloodstone case once again safely cuffed to her left hand, she extended the other in gratitude. "Thank you, Michael. And thank you, Stephanie. Without you, this holy relic would be in the hands of a common thief. I'm certain His Holiness will be very pleased with your efforts."

"Tell him we're happy to help," Steph said. "And we'll be even happier when the check clears."

"Mr. Armond." The nun turned to the irritable curator. "I trust you will escort these two young people safely back to the city?"

"Yes, Sister. I can do that much."

"Lovely. Now, then, I really must be off." Sister Malone walked halfway up the stairs, before turning around and giving them her steely blue stare one more time. "Please don't take this the wrong way, but I hope we never see each other again."

"It's fine," Michael said. "We get that a lot."

The boarding ramp folded into the plane's fuselage and the aircraft thundered to life, rocketing down the runway and pivoting into the sky. Once it shrunk into a tiny black dot and disappeared into the wispy clouds, Michael let out a long breath. "Wow. That really was . . . something."

"I'll say." Steph smirked, before turning to Mr. Armond. "Hey, Chuckles. Quick question. Do you know if there's a specific address to Vatican City? Or do you just write 'Vatican City' on the envelope? Like, 'care of the Pope?'"

"What?" Armond squinted behind his glasses. "Why?"

"'Cause you might want to mail this there." Steph removed the Holy Bloodstone from the pocket of her green jacket and tossed it underhand at the curator, who understandably panicked and fumbled, managing to catch it just before it hit the ground.

"What the hell?" He shouted.

"Yeah, Steph! What the hell?" Michael echoed.

"Oh. Awesome. I've been waiting for this," she said, smiling.

"Waiting for what?" Michael snapped.

"We're finally at the part of the heist where I get to explain everything!" Steph cracked her knuckles. "Alright, I'd say you're going to have to sit down for this, but I don't see any chairs, so here goes: turns out I was right about DeFaux from the beginning."

"He's NOT Willem Dafoe," Armond croaked, cradling the Bloodstone in his palms as if it was a hatching egg.

"Right, but you guys said the real DeFaux never showed his face to anyone. This guy was putting his face out there like it was his job! Because it was. He was an actor! No way he's refusing some good facetime. And that's when I recognized him. He was in that traveling production of Rent I'd seen back in 2011. I promised not to tell anyone who he was if he just let me go with the stone."

"You're kidding me," Michael said.

"Yeah, but he was objectively terrible in Rent, so when we get back to the city, remind me to tell Rex to put out an APB on Randall Albertson."

"So there's no real William DeFaux?" Armond cocked his head.

"Well, there was," Steph said. "When I was hopped up on caffeine and sugar last night, I did like five hours of googling, and pieced something together from like 15 different websites. The reason DeFaux stopped trying to steal the Bloodstone was because he got caught when it passed into the Pembroke Collection, and he was put in prison under the fake name Hiram Jones. If you look it up, his final mugshot kinda looks like the make-up job Randall had going on. Handlebar moustache and everything. Unfortunately, Hiram Jones died in prison in 2009.

"But," she smiled. "He had a daughter. And that—coupled with the fact that a Vatican Nun probably shouldn't have an English accent—is why I'm really hoping one of you two got the tail number of that plane before it took off."

Michael and Armond shared a blank look.

"Well, crap." Steph frowned. "Whatever. Fine. It's fine. At least we have the stone, right?"

Michael had to admit, he was floored by Steph's handling of the situation. She had been leagues ahead of the dubious anti-hero he'd admired during his youth. But there was one thing Michael still couldn't wrap his head around. "Wait, there was a Bloodstone in Sister Malone's case. How could you possibly manage to switch it out?"

"Oh, please." Steph scoffed, waving away the question. "That was a piece of cake!"

* * *

Anne Poole a.k.a. Tammy Bowers a.k.a. Irina Haverstone a.k.a. "Big" Melinda Babbage a.k.a. Billiam 'Billie' DeFaux released her flowing blond locks from suffocation beneath the confines of her nun's habit and breathed a sigh of relief. It'd been a long, convoluted road to this point, but her father had taught her that the best victories were the ones most cleverly designed. Billie had planned for every contingency, even factoring those two bumbling idiots into the equation. And if she hadn't gotten ahold of the Bloodstone now, at least her hired actor would have been able to pass it off to her at a later date when the heat died down.

Staring out the circular window of her jet, Billie played idly with her hair. After decades of planning, she could finally rest easy knowing she had secured her father's legacy. Armitage Pembroke was a vengeful, spite-filled man, sending her father away to die in prison like a nameless, common thief—robbed of the notoriety he'd spent years cultivating. But now the DeFauxs would have the last laugh—even though that wasn't their real surname.

The only question now would be what she was going to do with the Bloodstone. Her father only found value in the chase. If he had still been alive, he would have insisted the actual trinket itself was worthless, and would have tossed it out the door with a hearty chuckle. But Billie, at least, had more economic sense. The stone was way too hot at the moment, but if she held on to it for a while, she could probably fence it and reap enough cash to retire to her own private island. It was stupid how much people idolized this simple rock.

Reaching out to the sleek metal case on the table before her, Billie clicked open its clasps to gaze upon her spoils. There, within, the dark stone sat in its protective foam cushioning. She drew in a long breath and, along with it, an overpowering, yet intoxicating smell of coffee and dark chocolate. Billie reared back before opting for a closer sniff. The scent was indeed coming from the Bloodstone. As she picked it up, she realized the stone was far more pockmarked than she'd realized, and, though it was as hard as a rock, tasted far better.

And, in the end, all Billie DeFaux could do was laugh.

HANDLE LIKE EGGS

The cobbled street was dark and cold, and the rain did nothing to help except pitter patter on the roof of his car in an uneven staccato. It was so late that it was actually early, and Rex Calhoun was on his sixth cup of coffee, attempting to keep his dry, bleary eyes focused on the warehouse across the way.

By all accounts, he shouldn't have been here. He was the chief of the goddamn police now. Chiefs didn't sit in on sting operations until the wee hours of the morning. They sat behind desks for the most part, dealing with administrative bullshit, pushing around papers, and yelling at people. And although Calhoun enjoyed that last part, the rest of it just wasn't visceral enough for him. It wasn't real. He belonged out here—in the thick of it.

And so he had convinced—rather, told—the Narcotics Bureau that he'd personally be sitting in on their operation down at the docks. There had been word of thousands of pounds of cocaine entering the city en masse via a coordinated operation between a local gang and a small subset of the stevedores on the docks looking to make a little extra scratch on the side. What's worse, the rumors said this cocaine was tainted. Bodies of addicts described only as "burned out" were piling up in the underworld. At least, that's what he'd been told. Calhoun had never seen any of these bodies—but he sure had done the paperwork for them.

By the time Calhoun had brought himself on board, they'd already managed to get a man on the inside posing as a new dockworker. It'd been months until he was able gain enough trust to be let in on the next handoff—the handoff that was supposedly happening in the warehouse across the way right now. And, despite no visible activity, Calhoun couldn't take his eyes off it.

Truth be told, he could if he wanted to. He'd set up enough officers on the surrounding rooftops to cover the area. But Calhoun so desperately wanted to be a part of some normal, by-the-books police work again, even though he'd never really been much of a "by-the-books" guy in the first place.

After the absolute nonsense task of weeding agents of a giant monster death cult out of the force over the past few months, a drug bust felt—for the lack of a better word—right to him. Things were finally getting back to norm—

Calhoun's head jerked to the side as the passenger side door of his car opened. An unwanted guest slid in, her green jacket sopping wet. "Hello, Reginald!" Her hair hung over most of her face and wide smile, dripping its damp onto his upholstery before she shook herself like a dog and sent it everywhere else.

Calhoun shielded his face and—more importantly—his coffee with his arms. "Jesus Christ!"

"Sorry about that! Hell of a storm we're having," Stephanie Dyer said.

"What the hell are you doing here?" Calhoun growled. "Can't you see I'm in the middle of something?"

"Middle?" Dyer reached into his back seat, picked up the giant box of coffee he'd purchased and gave it a little shake. "I'd say you're about three-fourths done. Man, don't you have to pee?"

"Not the coffee, you idiot! A Sting!"

"What, like 'Roxanne?'"

"No." Calhoun rubbed his eyes with the heels of his palms. "Not like 'Roxanne.'"

"Oh! Right. Like crime." Dyer was silent for a moment, rubbing her chin. "Wait, is that why he's called Sting? Because he's part of The Police?"

"I don't know! Just get the hell out of here."

"Reginald, is that any way to talk to one of your oldest friends?"

"*Oldest* friends?" Calhoun glared at her.

"Yeah! What're you, like 60?" Dyer bit her lip. "55?"

"I thought we had a truce. I let you two goombas do your own thing with the monsters and the aliens or whatever and you leave me well enough alone to do serious, actual police work. For real people."

"Please." Dyer waved off his anger. "There were never any aliens."

"Good!" Calhoun almost threw his hands in the air before remembering his coffee. "I don't care. The less I hear about all your sci-fi nonsense, the better. Now will you get out of my car? We're trying to stop some bad guys from flooding the streets with drugs."

"Oh, come now, Reginald," she started.

"You use that name again and I'll have you arrested. What are you even doing here?"

"I need to ask you a favor." Of course she did.

"If I do it, will it get you out of my car?"

"It might," she smiled, faux sweetly.

"Fine, fine! What do you want?"

"That young lady you always pal around with. The forensics girl. Carrie McDermott. I'm gonna need her phone number."

"Jesus. Really? Again with this?" Calhoun rested his weary forehand on the steering wheel. "I told you. I'm not giving you her phone number."

"Well, that's quite a shame." Dyer ran her finger slowly across the dashboard of Calhoun's car, picking up the odd mote of dust and bits of sticky unknown residue. "This is a nice car you've got here, Rex. It'd be a shame if something . . . happened to it." she punched the glove box, which levered open and sent a bunch of papers flying into her lap, as she cradled her hurt fist. "Ow!"

Calhoun was too tired to do anything but stare. "I'm not giving you her phone number because I don't know it."

"How do you not know her number? You work with her!"

"I've never had to call her! I heard your stupid favor, now get out of my car." Calhoun swiftly pointed to the door, because he couldn't be sure if this goofball knew where it was.

"Geeze." Dyer huffed. "Fine. I'm going, I'm going!" Dyer hit the button on the armrest to lower the window, letting in both the quiet roar of the rain and much of the rain itself. She grabbed the handle above the door, lifting her butt as if she was going to climb out through the window.

Calhoun dragged his palm across his face. "What the hell are you doing?"

"Oh," She said, catching herself and sitting back down before opening the door. "Old habits, you know?"

"No. I do not know," Calhoun said, indicating the way out again.

Dyer exited the vehicle like a normal human being but, to Calhoun's chagrin, refused to vacate the premises. Instead, she leaned the top half of her body through the window, letting the rain in.

"Why aren't you going?" Calhoun pinched his eyes shut. "We had a deal."

"Rexy, I know you must have had a rough childhood, or marriage, or divorce, or something—maybe all three—and can't express many emotions other than anger, but I just wanted to let you know that we love you. And we know you love us, too."

Calhoun took a deep breath and composed himself, but before he could respond, a muffled, digitized novelty Halloween song forced its way out of one of Dyer's pockets. After rooting around in her cloak-like green jacket, she extracted the phone and took a look at the screen.

"Oh, sorry," she said, holding up a finger. "I've gotta take this."

Calhoun flipped his hand and rolled his eyes. "Go ahead."

She stepped away from the car into the rain. "Hey, Mike. What's the sitch? You're where? Oh yeah? Nice. Hmm. Hold on. Let me ask him." Stephanie disengaged from her phone and leaned back in. "Hey, Rexy. Would you say I was a huge distraction or just a minor one?"

Calhoun stared at her, wishing he could burn a hole in her head.

She put the phone back up to her ear. He could hear a garbled, faraway yelling on the other end. "Yeah, I'm gonna say huge distraction. Cool. Yeah, no, that's great. I'll see you soon." She shoved the phone back into her pocket.

Calhoun sighed, knowing he had better things to do than pry. "What was that about?"

"Man, Rex, I'd tell you, but . . ." Dyer sucked her teeth. "You said you didn't want to hear about all our sci-fi rigmarole."

Up ahead, through the dark, Calhoun could just barely make out a group of shadowy figures fleeing the warehouse into the rain, heading down toward the docks.

"Aw, shit! They're getting away!" Calhoun cranked his engine on and reached for his radio. "Team 312, this is—"

Dyer, suddenly back in the passenger's seat, slapped the radio out of his hand and turned the engine off."

"What are you doing?"

"I would keep a low profile right now if I were you." Dyer whispered before pointing to the sky as the waning moon was covered by a mass of clouds. But they were too fast to be clouds, as the moon returned mere seconds later.

"What . . . the hell?" was all Calhoun could get out before a massive lizard touched down on the street in front of him, sending a shockwave through the ground that spilled the remnants of his cold coffee directly onto his lap. He struggled to take in the entirety of the beast, managing to focus only on the bright yellow eyes and the off-white claws slipping into the grooves between the street's cobblestones. Its scales rippled, offering bright blue glints of color as they reflected the moonlight. Only when it folded them did he clock the leathery wings that flanked a lone figure hanging perilously off the creature's back.

"Goddamnit," he whispered to himself, as the thing arched its serpentine neck and let out a mighty roar. The deafening sound was eventually muffled by the torrent of sulphureous flame erupting from its throat, setting the fleeing criminals alight.

Immediately, Calhoun's radio was awash with rapid chatter that devolved into white noise with only one resolvable word.

"It's a dragon!" Dyer smiled as the lizard thundered slowly away down the streets. "Isn't that badass?"

Calhoun had no words.

"STEPHANIEEEEEEEE!" an anguished cry pierced the air. It could only be Michael Duckett.

"Sorry to cut and run. But the drugs these guys were selling had crushed up dragon eggs in 'em. Dragons! Isn't that wild? Turns out they were living in the sewers! And we couldn't let you get directly involved, because the big ol' mamas can smell the egg residue on anyone who touches them. And they kinda incinerate everyone who does. Also, Mike drew the long straw so he got to ride the dragon, even though he really didn't want to." Dyer was ejecting words with such a rapid-fire stream of consciousness that everything sounded like one word. "It was a whole thing. I'm actually kind of jealous." She slammed the door shut and ran toward where the dragon was turning a corner. "We'll talk more later. Tell Carrie I said hey!"

Stephanie leapt onto the tip of the creature's tail as it performed one last swish before it disappeared around the next building.

As the shockwaves, screams, and trailing glow of fire receded into the distance, Calhoun released the death grip he'd maintained on the steering wheel and slumped down in the driver's seat. After letting a lungful of air out, he picked up his radio. "Attention all units in the vicinity of the docks. This is Calhoun. Fall back."

He sighed.

"It's being handled."

THE HUNT III

The Black King never thought it would be easy to harness the power of the corpse of an interdimensional monster. But he didn't expect it to be as hard as it was.

It was nearly two thousand years hence before the floating, purple brains of the Infinite French Shadow Empire achieved the technology the King needed to process the energies of the undecaying monster body. But those millennia passed in the blink of an eye. Someone as ageless as the Black King had no need for time.

The parts of the monster necessary to probe the unknowable spaces between and across universes were finally extracted and processed to add their power to the King's throne. Donning the black and red visor once more, the Black King found it easy to traverse the bounds of the multi-verse with his mind alone. He could speak to beings through the vibration of the subatomic particles in their universes and will them to do his bidding.

But thousands and thousands of universes later, he had still not found the one he was looking for. That is, until he heard the screams.

Screams of anguish and torment from a poor old man, who had been ripped from his native universe into another and experimented on by unscrupulous scientists. Something the King could partially empathize with. What was more, the man was dressed not unlike a figure from his youth. A figure he'd never thought he'd think of again.

This gave the Black King pause, but he proceeded with his probe of this universe. The one where this. . . Santa Claus was currently trapped. Using the powerful capabilities of his throne, the King explored this dimension and this time. He saw much that looked familiar, but bits also seemed new, though that could be accounted for in a time differential.

Most importantly, he saw Michael Duckett and Stephanie Dyer.

The two he had looked for, found, and exterminated in other universes. Those he destroyed were clearly not of his home universe. The ones—particularly Stephanie—he wanted to see again. No, these versions were cowboys or spacemen or synthetically intelligent automobiles. These two, though, looked correct enough to indicate that this universe was where he was supposed to be. But he had been wrong before.

Reaching out to the aging jolly fat man, the Black King attempted to twist his mind with promises of help and revenge, as long as he guaranteed that he would bring Michael Duckett and Stephanie Dyer to him. It had nearly worked, too, until Michael and Stephanie actually showed up and brought the entire operation crashing down on his head.

Stymied, the Black King nearly tore his helmet off in rage, but not before he heard another voice. One desperately searching for absolute control in a random, meaningless universe. No one was as easily manipulated as those seeking what they could not have.

The Black King smiled, for his hunt was now over.

It was the psychic.

She was the one responsible for all of this.

Armitage Pembroke glared out the window of his study. The roiling black clouds hurled dagger-like rain drops against the reinforced glass. As the view continued to darken, Pembroke found his aged, gaunt features increasingly reflected like some sort of cruel taunt.

Wrinkling his nose in displeasure, he shuffled away to rest his creaking bones on the wingback chair beneath his looming bookshelves.

In an effort to ignore his aches and pains, he grumbled to himself as he sat down. It had been 30 years since his third wife Mathilda—now long his ex—had dragged him into that den of grift on his 63rd birthday.

"It'll be fun," he remembered her saying. "Just for a lark!"

Hah! Pembroke scoffed to himself. *Fun.*

Mathilda had always been like that. Carefree. Concerned more with enjoying herself than material goods or ambitions of status. Because, of course, she was young—much younger than him—and therefore free of the sort of baggage he'd accumulated over his long life. It was what Pembroke had originally loved about her. It had made him feel young by association. It was also, unfortunately, what made Mathilda such a goddamned idiot.

But that was his opinion now, older and wiser. Armitage Pembroke, three decades prior, had allowed his love for this woman to make him equally as foolish. Though he was at the top of his game when they met, she had softened him, and he was on the verge of giving up his robber-baron lifestyle for an ordinary one with her.

But it was not to be.

And, technically, he had the psychic to thank for that.

Once they were within the psychic's inner sanctum—little more than a disused storefront disguised as a mystical hovel—a young woman clad in gypsy clothes parted sets of tattered purple and gold cloth and glided into view.

Taking a seat before them, she assured them—through an outrageous accent—her predictions were one-hundred percent accurate. Client testimonials allegedly proved she had never been wrong before, and she never would be. And that she would stake her reputation on it.

Pembroke had rolled his eyes, for which Mathilda elbowed him in the ribs, so he merely nodded at the so-called psychic to proceed.

"Armitage Pembroke." The woman's smooth yet spindly hands hovered over the glass ball in the center of the table and danced arhythmically across the surface. "You are a very wealthy man. You believe that through your hard work and gumption you have built one of the largest corporate empires in the world. And it enabled you to expand your reach and eat well. But it garnered you many rivals . . . and enemies."

Pembroke had shrugged, with a condescending smirk. All of that had been true, indeed. But nothing one couldn't garner from a careful reading of the trades—or, for commoners, the Wall Street Journal. But that was the old him. The greedy, acrimonious life he'd led would soon be fading in the rearview. It would just be him and Mathilda. He squeezed her hand softly.

The psychic continued, "Your competitors wish you dead so they can usurp your throne. The laborers you've exploited to earn your riches wish you dead so they may be free of your penny-pinching wages. Even members of your family wish you dead so they can reap the rewards of your horded wealth." The psychic paused and met his grey eyes with her green gaze. "And they will be granted this boon in time."

Pembroke's eyes narrowed, and darted quickly to Mathilda at his side, who was drumming her fingers on her knees, nervous. This was no longer a lark. This was out of line.

"Wait a minute," he started. He felt the weight of the "psychic's" words pushing down on his shoulders. And more worrisome, the truth of them.

"Eventually," the woman continued, unabated, "you will be all but robbed of your riches, and you will die at the hand of the one person who wishes it the most. Be aware of your transgressions, Armitage Pembroke, for no matter how you proceed, they will come due, and your debt will be paid in gold and blood."

"Alright, that's enough!" Pembroke shouted, leaping from his seat. He grabbed Mathilda's wrist and dragged her through the purple drapes and out of the building. "That was idiotic and sadistic."

"It—it was just a bit of fun, Armie," she said. "I'm sure she didn't mean anything by it. It's all fake, anyway."

"You're damn right it's fake. None of that garbage is going to happen! And I can make sure it doesn't!" He yelled out of anger or, now with the benefit of hindsight, fear. Fear that cut into his mind. Fear of losing his life. And, if he was honest—really honest—with himself, his riches. And within him, a sense of low, churning unease that he had quietly suppressed for years was finally bubbling over, with Mathilda in the firing line. She was trying to get him to give up the only thing that had brought him peace of mind in this world. He was Armitage Pembroke, for God's sake! He had amassed his fortune through wit and bravery, and now all he felt was powerless. He hated that feeling and promised himself he would do everything he could to prevent this psychic's prediction from coming to pass.

And now he had.

Over the last three decades, Pembroke had invested heavily in the means to stave off the finality of death, at the expense of his company, his relationship with Mathilda and others, and any other minor annoyance standing in his way. And what he found was beyond his wildest expectations.

It was something brilliant.

Something powerful.

Something nigh unstoppable.

Now here he was today, smiling to himself as he sized up the rainstorm outside and found it beneath him. Although it had taken a third of his life, Pembroke had finally discovered a way to conquer nature and become more than any man had ever dreamed.

His smile grew wider as he thought about the host of people he had summoned to his manse tonight, milling about in the drawing parlor below. They were his greatest rivals, his fair-weather associates, and his greedy family . . . and two asinine private detectives. He had lured them here, allowing them to blissfully sharpen their knives, certain they would get his coveted wealth when he passed.

Only one thing was certain, however. After tonight, Armitage Pembroke would

Never.

Ever.

Die.

THE MYSTERY OF THE MURDERED GUY

Michael Duckett warbled a sigh through his lips as he absently flipped through the mail Stephanie Dyer had once again neglected to collect. He'd been visiting his mother in Boca Raton for the past week, and their narrow mailbox was now stuffed to bursting with furniture catalogues, credit card pre-approvals, and good old reliable bills.

With one arm busy dealing with his overnight bag, Michael tucked the roll of junk mail into his armpit and made his way up the three flights of creaky wooden stairs to the detective office doubling as their apartment. He sighed again when greeted with the red graffiti that turned the name of their operation from that of a semi-reputable business to a mere crude joke. With both arms full, Michael executed a coordinated yet awkward dance to extricate the keys from the pocket of his khakis. If anyone were around to notice, he would've been embarrassed. But, then again, he usually felt that way about just walking down the street.

Keys finally in hand, he clicked open the door and let it swing open before dropping his bag and kicking it into the narrow space they called "the waiting room" —a small portion of the entryway overrun by a slapdash IKEA desk for their erstwhile secretary and former professional assassin Maureen Whelan. If you squeezed your way left past the desk, another small doorway led to a five-foot-by-three-foot nook generously called a kitchen. It housed a minifridge, a hotplate, a trashcan, and, at this moment, it also housed a horrendous smell.

"Steph!" Michael scrunched up his nose beneath the bridge of his glasses. "I'm home! What the hell is that stench?"

Michael didn't know where Stephanie was in the office, but was hardly surprised when her head peeked out of the "kitchen."

"Oh, hey, Mike. What's up? How was your trip? Did you tell your mom I said hey?"

"No, no, no. What did you do? Why does it smell like a yak exploded in here?"

"Well, that's a very specific metaphor."

Michael merely tapped his foot in response.

"Fine." Stephanie sighed. "If you must know, I got a little . . . tipsy last night. Y'know, as one does at the club."

Michael frowned and shimmied his way over to the kitchen doorway.

"And when I got home," Steph continued, "I decided to make a drunk omelette."

"Clearly," Michael retorted. "That's why the eggs are all over the floor!" He took in the full scope of the curdling liquid disaster spread liberally across the tile. "Geeze. How many eggs did you use?"

"You know what they say, Mike. If you want to make a drunk omelette, you've gotta break all the eggs you own and puke in the trash can."

"Goddamnit, Steph." Michael pinched the bridge of his nose.

"Listen." Steph crossed her arms. "You can either stand there finding fault or you can help me clean this up. Because we totally ran out of paper towels."

Michael rolled his eyes and passed Steph some of the more useless pieces of mail he was still carrying. "Here. Just use this, I guess."

"Oh, sweet," Steph grabbed a particularly thick catalogue and frowned at the cover. "CB2? Who thought Crate & Barrel needed a sequel?"

A small lavender rectangle slid out of its hiding place between the pages of the catalogue and hit the tile with a quiet plink, narrowly avoiding the puddles of rotten egg juice. Michael raised an eyebrow and picked it up. Turning it around in his hands, he found a particularly luxurious card envelope with a golden wax seal securing the contents inside. There was no return address, but swirling golden script indicated its recipient.

"Who's B.L. Ayer?" Michael asked, not expecting an answer.

"Oh, snap!" Steph snatched the card out of his hands. "It worked!"

"What worked?" As the words tumbled out of his mouth, he instantly regretted them.

"You know Armitage Pembroke?"

The name sounded familiar. It felt like something he ought to have recognized, but he just shrugged.

"Well, he's this really old rich guy—I'm talking like a gazillion dollars here—and he's throwing some kinda party for his birthday. So I tried to get us invited."

Michael furrowed his brow. "But why?"

"Pembroke's old wrinkly finger has been involved in everything we've been working on lately. The Dracula at the hospital's Pembroke wing. The mall that we burned down *and* the Bloodstone. Not to mention the freakin' *moon base.* This guy has some serious capital, and he's been spending a lot of it messing with us in particular, and I intend to find out why."

The film reel of Michael's memories unfurled on a projector before getting caught and ripped to shreds. "Wow. How could I forget that?"

"Eh, little details. But I realized this can't be some sort of weird coincidence. This Pembroke guy—whoever he is—must really be out to get us for some reason. So I figured we take the fight to him. And so I started planting some seeds and well . . ." Steph tore open the envelope and pulled out the invitation within. The thick purple cardstock carried more of the same swirling golden writing, which, as Steph said, offered an invitation to Armitage Pembroke's 93rd Birthday Party for Friends, Family, and Well Wishers, to be held at Pembroke Manor this Saturday at 6:30pm sharp. But it wasn't Michael and Stephanie who were invited. Instead . . .

"But who's B.L. Ayer?" Michael repeated, tapping the name on the card.

"Oh, right. Well, I wanted to keep Pembroke off our trail, so I created a fictional rich guy identity for you. You're very wealthy."

"Me?" Michael reared back. "*I'm* B.L. Ayer?"

"Uh-huh!" Stephanie nodded excitedly. "The L stands for Leon."

"B. Leon Ayer." Michael spat out each dumb syllable with the disdain it deserved.

She waggled her eyebrows, entirely too proud. "The B stands for Bill!"

"Yeah, no, I got it!" he snapped. "You really think this wealthy industrialist is stupid enough to fall for something like this?"

"Please, he probably hires people to do all of this stuff for him. I think *they're* stupid enough to fall for something like this. Besides, your costume is really gonna tie together the entire act."

"Hold on. What do you mean 'my costume?'"

Steph merely smiled, and Michael felt the bile rise in his gullet.

* * *

Four days hence, Michael and Stephanie sat in silence as he forced the Garbagemobile to struggle its way up the winding hillside roads toward Pembroke Manor. It wasn't a particularly difficult gradient, but Michael's 1982 Mercury Zephyr had only half of a horsepower under the hood. And it wasn't even the good half of the horse.

It was the top half.

Even if they could hear each other over the grinding crunch of the car's gears, Michael would still have not said a word to Steph. No, he was too busy stewing in his "costume:" a purple crushed velvet suit over a puffy, lacy shirt, all complemented by a pencil thin mustache she'd drawn over his lip in eyeliner.

"This isn't what billionaires wear!" he had shouted. "I look like Austin Powers and Prince got horribly mangled together in an accident!"

Steph had simply smiled in her typical idiom and went to don her own costume: a worn, somewhat familiar tuxedo t-shirt she dug out from the dregs of their closet. Evidently, she'd put less thought into her get-up than his. Michael swore she had done it on purpose.

Of course, he could have just walked away and refused to go. But, deep down, Michael really didn't want to be left home alone on a dreary Saturday night.

Pembroke Manor was part of a sprawling estate set atop the lush hills beyond the northern edge of the city. Even from below, Michael could spy the spindly tips of the house's spires looming above the thick pine forest that straddled the single paved road leading up to it.

They were about halfway up the hill when the Garbagemobile sputtered to a halt and refused to go any further. Michael pressed the accelerator to the floor, but all it produced was pained groaning from the engine and copious amounts of thick, grey exhaust. Taking his foot off the accelerator, however, caused them to roll backwards down the hill.

"Goddamnit. This piece of crap." Michael grumbled as he eased the car back down to a flatter part of the road and coaxed it onto the shoulder beneath a pair of trees.

After getting out and securing the back tires with his trusty brick for good measure, Michael met Stephanie, who was sitting on the edge of the pavement.

"Well," he said. "What now?"

His question was answered first by a distant rumble of thunder, and then by Steph's meager offer: "I guess we better get to steppin'."

And so they ended up trudging the last mile of uphill road. It was hell, given Michael's tiny Italian leather boots.

"This is awful," Steph said between heaving breaths. "Really awful."

"It was your idea!" Michael hissed.

"Maybe you should buy a new car."

"Maybe you shouldn't be spending all our money on crushed velvet suits because you think that's what rich people wear!"

"Mike, that's what I would wear if I was rich! You think rich people have better taste than—"

The trees rustled as a swift wind blew through them. Somewhere out in the woods, a large tree groaned and snapped, followed by a mournful wailing sound.

"What the hell was that?" he hissed as the sound faded away.

Steph grimaced. "Uh, I dunno. A moose or something?"

"A moose? Are you sure? All the way up here?"

"What are you, the wildlife inspector? It could be a moose. Or a monster."

"It's not a monster."

"Hey!" Steph cupped her hands around her mouth and yelled.

"Are you a moose or a monster or some kinda third thing?"

"Steph, stop!" Michael grabbed her shoulder but froze when the wailing returned. It deepened and rose in pitch before being drowned out by the sound of cracking branches and dull thuds barreling off in the opposite direction.

"Monster Moose," Steph said. "Probably more scared of us than we were of it."

"That's ridiculous."

"Or the Mothman." She waggled her eyebrows. "It could be the Mothman."

"Steph, It's not the Mothman," Michael said as they trudged on. "It's never going to be the Mothman."

"Oh, we'll see about that."

* * *

Adorned with the most fanciful gold filigree Michael had ever seen, a set of wrought-iron gates marked the entrance to Pembroke Manor. As if by magic, they swung open silently, and Michael and Steph trudged their way up the last stretch of driveway, flanked by wide tracts of well-manicured lawn and hedges on either side. The manor itself towered like a castle, its rough-hewn stone walls insisting they were the only defense from the amassing rain clouds.

"Aw, man." Steph eyed the manor's spires extending into the sky, intent to poke out the eyes of God. "If I was a ghost, I'd totally want to haunt this place."

With the large wooden double doors before them, Steph stabbed her finger at the manor's pearlescent doorbell. It pealed with such a timbre, it might have been rung by a hunchback.

After a pause that seemed interminable, the doors silently swung opened to reveal a tall, lanky man in a black suit so well pressed, it made the wrinkles in his dour face look that much deeper. Light but sharp, beady eyes stared down over his beak-like nose, penetrating the depths of Michael and Steph's souls and finding them desperately wanting.

"Yesssss?" He droned, with the skeptical ennui one would expect from a butler.

"Um, yes, uh, hi. Ahem. I'm, uh . . . B.L. Ayer," Michael struggled. He motioned to Steph, whose wide smile was almost blinding. "And this is my manservant . . ." He paused to sigh. ". . . Manuel Cervante."

"But you can call me Manny." Steph extended an overzealous hand to the butler, who hadn't blinked once since he opened the door. She shoved her hand back in her jeans and attempted to lean past the old man to take a peek at the manor beyond. "We're here for the party? Y'know? The . . . birthday party?"

The butler's already tight lips formed an even tighter line as he took a short, exasperated breath. "Yes," he said, to Michael's surprise. "Master Pembroke has been expecting you. We'll be beginning formal celebrations in the parlor in a short while. But until we ready the space, I urge you to proceed to the cocktail reception in the rear gardens." The butler gestured to the left with a sweep of his long arm and a snap of his white gloved hand. "Please make your way around the house and you should see the other guests."

"Oh, uh, well, thank you?" Michael stammered.

"Do enjoy." The man's flat tone implied he didn't really know what the word "enjoy" meant. But Michael would have to take it, as he shut the door almost instantly, and the two oddly dressed friends followed the stone pathway to the back of the house.

"I refuse to believe that worked," Michael grumbled.

The grounds opened up even further to a wide expanse of flat grass, dotted by the occasional decorative hedge, and groups of mingling social gadflies all with a drink in one hand, hors d'oeuvres in the other, and smiles of dubious authenticity on their lips.

"Oh, this is gonna be tight," Steph said as she raced over to one of the many servers carrying a platter full of devilled eggs. After her third, she glanced back at Michael. "What're you doing? Go, mingle! Figure out what everyone's deal is."

"Me? What're *you* gonna do?"

"I'm gonna follow this egg guy around until I have a heart attack." Steph shoved more into her mouth. "An' gef me uh drink eff yew can!"

Michael exhaled and slouched toward the other partygoers, mumbling to himself. "She really needs to cut down on the snacks."

As he made his way across the lawn, a large shadow jumped out at him from behind a hedge, nearly knocking him backwards.

"Hullo! Ja! I am ze maid!" A portly woman shouted over a tray of salted meats and cheeses. If what she said was true, she certainly looked the part, with the platonic ideal of a maid outfit draped over a body that was the same basic shape as the teapot from *Beauty and the Beast.*

"Uh, yes, hi." Michael reached for the charcuterie and tentatively placed a slice in his mouth. "Th—thank you?"

"Ja! I am ze maid!" the maid repeated, with flushed cheeks red as apples. She waggled her stumpy little legs toward the next guest she needed to accost.

"Don't mind her," groaned a jaded voice with the consistency of sandpaper. "Armitage never hired anyone that spoke English."

Michael glanced over his shoulder to find a woman roughly the age of dust glaring down at him. Her dark eyes were rimmed with bags caked in heavy blue eyeliner, clashing harshly with her red sequined dress. Switching her cigarette holder to her non-dominant hand, she managed to lift him to his feet with little trouble.

"Gee, thanks." Michael dusted off his crushed velvet suit. "But I talked to the butler earlier, and he seemed to speak English pretty fine."

"Bartleby?" The woman scoffed. "Well, yes. I meant the women. None of them speak English. Makes them easier to take advantage of, I'm sure. Delia." She extended her limp hand. "Delia Dahlia."

As he took it in a quick shake, Michael suddenly felt less bad about his alias. "Uh . . . B.L. Ayer."

"Well, Mr. Ayer," Delia gave him a quick glance up and down. "How has my ex-husband wronged you?"

"Wronged me?" Michael cocked an eyebrow.

"The man doesn't have any friends, Mr. Ayer. So it stands to reason he'd only have enemies left to invite to his birthday."

"I mean I guess that makes sense? What'd he do to y—"

"We were lovers for a time." Delia spun around. As she put the back of her skeletal hand to her forehead, Michael realized he had better settle in for a monologue. "The early days, you see? Years before his riches built him up into the harsh and unyielding edifice you know today. I was there for him as a young man. When we adventured across the globe, searching for the next big score, making love under different sets of stars every night . . ."

"Could you . . . uh . . . move it along?"

Delia glared at Michael, shutting him up, "But it was a mistake. Once his money got the best of him, I was tossed aside like a used washrag. I was nothing compared to the next pretty little thing that came along. And once I caught him . . . in congress with 'the help'. . . I was forced to go my own way, eking out a survivalist's existence as a mere socialite and art critic. And until now, I thought he had forgotten about me. About the times we spent making love under different sets of stars every night—"

"Yeah, you, uh, covered that already," Michael said, not so subtly backing away.

"And this is to say nothing of the effect it had on our son!" she rasped.

"Your son?"

"Mother means me." A broad-shouldered man with locks of golden hair asserted his presence beside Michael. He was maybe twenty years Michael's senior, but he wore a light beige suit that made his tanned skin pop, knocking a few decades off his age. "Ethan Allen Pembroke." He swirled and introduced a glass of whiskey to his all-too-white teeth.

"Nice to meet you? B.L. Ayer?" Michael, overwhelmed by the idea of introducing himself to yet another weird rich person, made every statement a question.

"And this is my son, Ethan Allen Pembroke Junior." He gestured with a flick of his chin to a smaller, scrawnier version of him that hovered behind his father's back, nose buried in his smartphone. A teenager.

"Enh," the kid said, not looking up.

"You might be wondering why such a chiseled, well-put-together man-about-town such as myself might be attending his absentee father's birthday party," Ethan Allen Senior said through his smile.

"No, I'm really no—"

"When Father left mother and I to go off on his lecherous dalliances, I became the man of the house and had to use my scrappy wits to scrabble my way to the top of the cologne business my father had divested from years earlier."

"I mean, it sounds like both of you did alrigh—"

"After years of slaving away managing the company's finances, I met the love of my life, Kathryn Spirit, heir to the Spirit Halloween fortune. Mother disapproved, of course, but that could not stop our whirlwind romance."

Michael glanced over Ethan Allen's shoulder, to discern any negative reaction from Delia, but instead she was wrapped in her son's story, dabbing at the corner of her eyes, proud of her son's inherited penchant for drama.

"Soon after, we conceived Ethan Allen Jr. while on our honeymoon—a sailing trip around the world. Our lovemaking was fierce, passionate, and repeated, which I am sure Ethan Jr. draws his own internal fire from."

"Buh," Ethan Jr. grunted, stabbing at his screen.

"But then tragedy struck and I lost her at sea in a terrible storm." Ethan Sr. dashed his empty whiskey glass to the ground in a dramatic gesture undercut by its impotent bouncing across the sod. "It was weeks later when we finally found her pale, lifeless body smashed against the pylons of an oil rig. A Pembroke Industries oil rig. Once again, my father was the fly in the ointment of my life."

"Wait, uh, hold on. Could you back up for a second? She died on the sailing trip just *after* you guys uh . . . conceived?" Michael furrowed his brow, pointing between the young and old Ethan Allens. "But, then, how did she . . . like . . . the kid is *here*."

"Certainly my memory has been blurred by time. I am only human." He chuckled quietly. "Well, aren't we all? But tonight I intend to finally confront my father about the ills he's bestowed on his only begotten son."

As he delivered his intent, Michael noticed the dark clouds rolling toward them across the sky, the slight rumble of thunder from earlier growing into a dull roar.

"Alright, well." Michael backed away again, his hands up and palms out as if to indicate he wasn't a threat. "It's been really lovely chatting with . . . this family. Now if you'll excuse me, I've got to hit the bathroom."

After receiving slight nods of acknowledgement from everyone except Ethan Allen Jr., Michael gathered himself and dashed toward the rear wall of the manor, where more finger foods were being served on an array of long tables draped in white linen. There he found Steph, still stalking the server with the deviled eggs.

"What do you mean you're all out? Mama like! Mama wants to eat!"

Michael grabbed her by the shoulder and spun her around. "Where the hell have you been?"

"Mmm. Yum. Yes, this'll do in a pinch." Steph picked a salmon canape off the table and slid it into her mouth before turning to him.

"Why? What'd I miss?"

"I spent the last 15 minutes getting talked at by the strangest family on Earth!"

"Who? Those guys?" Steph pointed back toward the tree, but Michael slapped her hand down.

"Don't point! They'll know I'm talking about them and they'll come over for another rambling speech about how they hate this Pembroke guy and are painfully oblivious to how goddamn fortunate they really are."

"Aw, I'm proud of you, Mike." Steph slapped him on the back. "Putting yourself out there and meeting new people."

"Steph, this shit is bizarre. Why would Pembroke invite all these people who harbor such a personal hate for him? And us—or me—or B.L. Ayer or whoever I am? Something really strange is going on."

"Well," she said. "Then it's a good thing we're here."

"No, it's not. I don't want to deal with these weirdos."

Steph raised her eyebrows and smiled as she grabbed a chocolate covered strawberry and took a bite. "Don't look now, but here comes more of them."

"Oh, goddamnit." Michael spun around to the olive visage of a smiling man sporting a thin moustache quite similar to Michael's fake one. In fact, the man's purple suit—though not crushed velvet—also bore a striking resemblance to Michael's current outfit. The man, however, held a martini glass aloft in one hand, while his other arm curled around the waist of a grey-haired woman in a powder blue sundress. "Okay, I'll bite." Michael sighed. "Who are you supposed to be?"

"Ah, Bill Ayer, we meet for the first time," the man said in a thick Castilian accent. "I have admired your prowess ever since I happened upon your interview in GQ."

"I may have submitted a short piece to GQ," Stephanie hissed in his ear.

"Of course. Great." Michael pinched his brow beneath his glasses.

"You truly are one of the titans of business and industry."

"Yes. Look at me," Michael deadpanned. "With my business. And my industry."

If this man had been paying any attention to what he was saying, Michael would have been quickly found to be a fraud. But, just like all the other ridiculous people at this garden cocktail party, he was so preoccupied with his own opinions on whatever he was thinking about, Michael could've spewed absolute gibberish and gotten away with it.

"It is a pleasure to meet you!" The man spun with an exaggerated flourish, nearly dropping his martini and his woman. Setting the drink down, he extended his hand. "Enzo Credenza. I'm certain my reputation precedes me."

"Enzo . . . Credenza?"

"Of *Credenza and Associates*. The shining jewel of Italy's Corporate Sector."

"Italy? Then why do you sound Spanish?"

"Do not concern yourself with that." Credenza stepped away from his woman—who seemed perfectly content—and covered the distance between him and Michael. Tossing an overly friendly arm around Michael's shoulder, he leaned in and whispered, "What you should concern yourself with is the offer I am about to propose."

"Uh . . ." Michael glanced at Stephanie, who was enjoying this all a little too much from the sidelines. "What?"

"An alliance! Between my resources and your acumen, the two of us shall topple Pembroke and be the premier industrial powerhouse of the twenty-first century."

"I'm not even sure exactly what it is you do."

"It was only a scant decade ago when I made my dramatic entrance into the dangerous world of high stakes industrial technologies. They say you have to be willing to get blood on your hands to succeed in this business—"

"See what I'm talking about?" Michael whispered back to Steph. "Everyone here is doing some sort of goddamn soliloquy."

"—and certainly, I made my fair share of mistakes. But if it wasn't for Pembroke—that swine—dogging my progress at every turn, I would not have had to make some of my more regrettable choices. But I had the last laugh, though, when I stole his wife." Enzo returned to the side of the woman he was with and gave her waist a tight squeeze.

"Second wife," the woman clarified. "Armitage had once seemed a stable partner who could provide for me. I had heard the tales of how he had treated his first, but I thought certainly our relationship would be different. Especially given the ferocity of our love-making—"

"Christ. Here we go again." Michael took a page out of Steph's book and turned his attention back to the fingerfoods. To be fair, they really were quite delightful.

"—but that was the last straw. I absconded in the night with a sizable chunk of Armitage's assets and went straight into Enzo's arms and I have not regretted a moment of it."

"Yes, thank you, Carol." Enzo turned back to Michael. "And he has never forgiven me."

"Okay, that's fine. Good to know. Thanks for your time." Michael turned to Steph. "I've heard enough. Steph, let's go."

Before Michael could grab her wrist and make an earnest attempt to leave, the rainclouds were upon them, and water fell from the sky. Drops quickly turned to sheets, and soon everybody was running for cover, yelping and shouting. While Steph was trying to save more canapes from getting soaked by placing them in the safety of her mouth, the servers directed everyone inside to the rear dining room, a grand space whose bright white lights and clean wood floors stood in stark contrast to the dark hell brewing outside.

"Whoo, boy!" Steph burst in after them. Her shout echoed across the room as she shook herself like a dog, spraying a fine mist into the air. "That turned bad fast."

The rest of the guests, equally drenched, were not as amused. Neither was Michael, who found the inky remnants of his pencil moustache on his cuffs after he wiped off his face. He flagged down one of the servers. "Yeah, hi. Is there anywhere we could maybe get changed or dry out our clothes at least?"

"Yes," said Ethan Allen Sr. "I simply must slip out of these wet clothes and into a dry mar—"

"Shut up, Ethan," snapped a voice Michael didn't recognize. Whoever she was, she didn't have the wistful, entitled twang of the other guests.

"Rest assured, sirs and madams." The butler who had met Michael and Stephanie at the door—Bartleby, if Pembroke's first wife was to be believed—had slipped quietly into the room, causing Michael to jump a bit. "Master Pembroke has prepared for this eventuality. There are several vacant bedrooms upstairs for each of you, with appropriately sized attire."

"Ah, yes," "Fantastic," and "Finally that old skeleton is good for something," were just some of the murmurs rising from the crowd.

"But first, he would like you to assemble in the drawing parlor so that he may welcome all of you personally."

"But we're all drenched to the bone!" cried Delia Dahlia.

"Do not worry, madam." Bartleby the butler wheezed. "All the furniture has been covered in plastic."

"My father did this on purpose!" Ethan Sr. shouted. "He wants us to wait in these chilly wet clothes. He gets off on having total control!"

"Well, I'm certain I know nothing about that," Bartleby said. "Now, if you will just follow myself and the maid—"

"Ja! I am ze maid!" The portly maid at his side piped up but had little more to offer.

Everyone blinked.

"Yes," the butler continued, unfazed. "Well, please do follow us."

Michael shrugged at Stephanie as they joined the loquacious group of Pembroke's various invitees slopped their way after the help in their soaked suits and dresses. Even though he was sopping wet as well, Michael harbored a small smile at seeing the rest of them forced to be uncomfortable.

Stephanie, on the other hand, might as well not have been wet at all. She was trotting happily behind the butler and next to an older, raven-haired woman in a simple purple sweater and jeans chewing on the end of a cigarette. Michael had never seen her before. She was far too normal looking to be in the same league as the rest of these yahoos. Despite the slipperiness of his leather dress boots, Michael caught up to them after only two false starts.

"So, Mr . . . Butlerino?" Steph had already started her hyperactive schtick. "How big is this place? And where is Mr. Pembroke? Or is that supposed to be a secret? You can tell me. One manservant to another!"

"Master Pembroke is in his chambers. He assures me that any and all questions you may have will be answered in due course."

"Oh, that's great, because I have a lot."

"Me too," Michael, wiping fog off his glasses, muttered to Steph, before turning to the woman who hadn't yet said a word. She avoided his gaze, preferring instead to concentrate on the glow at the end of her cigarette. "Hey, uh, sorry, is everything okay?"

The woman nearly jumped in surprise as if she hadn't expected anyone to address her. "Oh, uh, yeah. Sorry. It's fine. I'm fine. Your moustache is . . . uh, running, by the way."

"Oh!" Michael wiped the rest away with the back of his hands. "Right, never really . . . got the hang of it."

"Got the hang of a moustache?" The woman cocked her head in a way that confused and intrigued Michael.

"Yes, well, uh . . . anyway, I'm, uh . . ." He considered dropping his fake identity for a second, but for some reason went against his own internal voice. "B.L. Ayer."

"Mathilda Valance."

Michael cringed, expecting the worst.

"What?" Mathilda asked.

"Sorry, force of habit. Judging from my time out in the garden, everyone here wants to wax poetic about their lives like they're in goddamn drama class. The only person who wasn't insufferable was the creepy silent kid."

Mathilda stifled a chuckle. "Yeah, I never really fit in with that crowd."

"I didn't see you outside," Michael said.

The group entered a long, narrow hallway in the main house, with oak paneled walls and dark green wallpaper broken only by the occasional painted portrait or landscape. There was limited light, and what was present was the meek orangey glow of dated Edison bulbs. It was odd, but the place felt a little cramped, as if the house somehow had less space inside than the monstrous castle-like edifice should contain.

"I stayed on the edge of the canape delivery routes. Closer to the house," Mathilda said, puffing on her cigarette. Michael wasn't fond of smoking, but he had to admit, it did make her look cool. "I learned it's the smart move if you want to avoid getting talked at. These people have always been full of themselves."

"So you know them?" Michael cocked his head.

"We've met. Hard not to when you're married to Armitage Pembroke."

"You're his wife?" Michael almost stopped in his tracks.

"Ex," she clarified. "Third."

"But you look so . . ."

"Normal?" she said. "Yeah. That was the point." They passed the wooden double doors of the manor's main entrance and entered the foyer. "He wanted someone down to Earth. He was looking to give up his fortune and turn over a new leaf. I was really young, and I thought I could help him through that. And it went pretty well until he became, well . . . obsessed."

"Obsessed?"

"It was weird." Mathilda shook her head. "And I'd rather not get into it. How about you, though? How do you know Armie?"

"Me?" Michael was knocked out of the strange glow he had started feeling for this mysterious woman. "Well, uh, I'm another independently wealthy billionaire. And I . . . uh . . . am new in town?" He regretted never coming up with a fully fleshed out background with Steph, who was now too far ahead—babbling the butler's ear off—to add her admittedly ingenious lunacy to this story.

"Yeah, uh-huh." Mathilda wasn't buying it. "And what did you say your name was again?"

"B.L. Ayer," Michael said through his teeth, and glanced away.

Mathilda squinted. "And the B.L. stands for . . ."

"Uh . . ."

But Michael was saved from revealing his double life by the butler.

"Ladies and gentlemen," he said, indicating an archway with a wave of his gloved hand. "We have arrived. Please make yourselves comfortable and Master Pembroke will be with you shortly."

The drawing parlor looked exactly how Michael expected a room called a 'drawing parlor' in the house of an aged multi-billionaire to look like, except darker. The green walls felt almost black, helped in no way by the storm clouds gathering outside nor the few weak bulbs situated around the room. Towering bookcases filled with intimidating leather-bound tomes loomed over a triad of long crimson sofas—lovingly covered in plastic—which, in turn, surrounded a cold, unlit fireplace. Two sets of cherrywood staircases flanking the fireplace led to an uninviting second floor landing. It looked more like a balcony from which to deliver a fascist address to the assembled hordes. Michael's attention, however, was drawn to the giant taxidermy bear standing upright in the corner.

"Dude's got one of them 'rich guy' bears." Steph sidled up to him with a whisper. "That's how you know he means business."

Two by two, the group shuffled their way into the room. There was plenty of space on the couches for the eight of them, but after extinguishing her cigarette in a nearby ashtray, Mathilda opted to lean against the wall by the archway instead. Michael decided to do the same, while the rest waddled to the couches and squeaked their wet butts down.

"Bleh," said Ethan Allen Jr, his phone the only source of modern-quality light in the entire room.

"You said it, kid," coughed Delia.

"This is an outrage," Enzo pouted, his arms crossed like a child. "I demand that Pembroke not keep us waiting a second longer!"

"Easy, dear." His wife Carol wiped some of the moistness off his forehead. "You know what your doctor said about stress."

Enzo's cries went unheard, as the butler and the maid had silently departed their posts to parts of the house unknown. And so the group sat, eyes darting from one to another, saying nary a word. Steph, however, was staring directly at Michael. She narrowed her eyes and smirked, pointing at him, then nodding ever so slightly toward Mathilda, and performing an obscene gesture. Luckily, no one noticed except Michael, who wrinkled his nose and shook his head in disapproval. Steph, relentless, continued to nod lecherously at him.

"What's taking him so long?" Michael asked, hoping to break the silent conversation.

"Well, he is 93 years old." Delia Dahlia flipped her hand, depositing ash from her cigarette holder onto the rug.

"Oh, that makes sense. He's probably busy replying to an email from Methusel–" Steph's witty rejoinder was cut short by the bright flash of lightning through the windows followed by a faint rumble, which unnerved everyone.

"Keeping us waiting could be another power move," Michael said.

"Almost certainly," Ethan Allen Sr. said.

"Or maybe he's . . ." Mathilda trailed off, muttering.

"What'd you say?" Steph asked.

"Maybe he's . . . uh . . . waiting for someone," she mumbled a little louder.

"For who?" Michael scrunched up his forehead. "Aren't we all here?"

Another lightning flash illuminated the faces of everyone in the room, their eyes haloed in shadow for a brief second before the deafening thunder caught up and vibrated the very ground beneath the house, causing even the books on the shelves to shudder.

The crowd in the drawing room had barely a second to regain their bearings when a sudden slam reverberated down the hallway outside. Even the weird Ethan Allen kid jumped at that one.

It was the two giant doors in the entryway foyer. They had blown open. A howling gust of cold wind, buffeted by the white noise of the torrential rain outside rushed through the mansion, and the lights in the drawing room and hallways flickered off as the crowd gasped collectively.

"Oh, relax," the confident voice of Ethan Allan Sr. carried through the dark. "This old house does this kind of thing all the time."

"Does it do the ghost noises too?" Steph asked. The eerie, rhythmic clanking and clattering of chains moved toward the parlor across the hallway floor. The main doors slammed shut, sealing the storm out—and the source of the noise in.

"Oh good lord," Delia Dahlia's creaky voice cried out. "We're all going to die!"

"Meh," grunted Ethan Allen Jr., his phone a floating beacon cutting through the inky black.

"Gimme that!" Michael seized the opportunity and the shitty kid's phone. Using the screen as a quick makeshift flashlight, he illuminated the immediate hallway beyond the arch. Much to his chagrin, there was indeed a shambling figure in chains there. But it was worse than any ghost.

"You cretins thought you could start without me, didn't you?" Helena Pembroke growled. Michael had somehow blocked out all memory of her and her high-speed rail horror show. When the lights finally flickered back on and revealed her bright orange prison jumpsuit, he realized why.

"Oh, no," Michael whined quietly.

Surprisingly, Helena's steely gaze flashed first to Mathilda. "Hello, mother. I trust you're well."

Michael's jaw went slack, and out of the corner of his eye, he saw Steph nodding with psychotic glee. She was about halfway through mouthing the word "nice" when she caught view of a second woman passing through the archway behind Helena.

"Ahem." The dark-skinned, leather-jacketed form of Detective Kiara Hobson brought with it a tension that Michael could feel, with Steph immediately clamming up.

"Sorry," Helena said. "This is my police escort, Officer—"

Hobson's eyes darted from Helena up to Steph and then across to Michael who could only offer a meek wave. "Oh, Jesus Christ. You've gotta be shitting me. What're you two doing here?"

"Wait." Enzo Credenza rose from his seat. "How do you know B.L. Ayer and his manservant?"

"Manuel Cervante," Steph whispered under her breath.

"B.L. Ayer?" Helena tilted her head at Michael, who gritted his teeth, preparing for the poorly built house of cards to finally come falling down.

"What the hell are you talking about?" Hobson snorted. "Did they tell you they were billionaires? And you really bought that shit?"

"Then who is B.L. Ayer?" Ethan Allen demanded.

"There is no B.L. Ayer, you bunch of idiots," Hobson continued. "They must've made it up. They do things like this to sneak into places they don't belong."

"Preposterous!" Enzo Credenza stamped his Italian booted foot. "We are not such fools to be hoodwinked by such a puerile ruse."

"Hmph. Well, then." Hobson, knowing where to strike, wheeled in on Stephanie, who stiffened and sent her gaze down to the tips of her shoes. "Tell me what the L in B.L. Ayer stands for."

"Uh . . ."

"Now."

"Leon . . ." Steph mumbled.

"Uh-huh. And the B?"

"Bill."

"Bill Leon Ayer?" Mathilda sounded it out, and Michael winced.

"Yeah," Hobson declared. "That's what I thought."

"Oh, now I get it," said Carol Credenza.

"Wait." Mathilda—the last person here Michael wanted to disappoint—turned slowly toward him. "Then who are you, really?"

"Duckett & Dyer: P.I.s for Hire," rasped a voice from the upper landing, as a heavyset man draped in a royal purple silk robe waddled his geriatric body into the light. Everyone craned their necks up to meet his grey gaze. From beneath a crooked nose, he smiled an equally crooked smile at all of them. "Isn't that right? I'm very glad you could make it."

"Oh, Armie," Mathilda whispered quietly. "What have you done with your life?"

"Father . . ." Ethan Allen grumbled. "We meet again."

"Whoa. *That's* Pembroke?" Steph, taking the opportunity to put distance between her and Hobson, leaned over to Michael. "He looks like he's going to order us to kill all the jedi."

"Hello, everyone," Pembroke's words slipped through the gaps in his yellowing teeth. "Welcome to my 93rd birthday. I trust you are all sitting comfortably."

"We've been soaked to the bone and forced to sit in this miserable room, you old goat." Enzo Credenza shot to his feet and shook his fist at Pembroke. Carol Credenza placed a hand on his arm as if to protect him from his own rage.

"Ah, Enzo. Ever the firebrand." Pembroke paced slowly across the landing above the fireplace, turning and walking back as he got to the stairs. he clearly never intended to descend to their level. "I apologize for the wait, but I was hoping Carol could have kept you warm. That is what she's there for, isn't it?"

Michael was shocked by the level of trash talk this nonagenarian was dishing out, and expected Carol to respond in kind, but she merely narrowed her eyes and shot back a glare. He admired the restraint.

"Why have you brought us all here, Armitage?" Delia Dahlia droned. "And why all the theatrics? We all have better places to be."

"Oh, yes," Pembroke said. "I'm sure there's a bottom of a bottle waiting for you." He turned down toward Helena. "And what time do they need you back in solitary?"

"Go to hell, Skeletor," she told him off. "You're loving this, aren't you?"

"No one steals from me without consequences, girl. Not even my youngest daughter. You should have remembered that."

"And what of me, Father?" Ethan Allen Sr. boomed. "What did I ever do to deserve your ire?"

"I can barely remember," Pembroke said. "And that's the most infuriating thing of all. That you have the family name, but never did anything even remotely notable with it. Good thing that Kathryn woman got out while she still could."

"She died!"

"I am aware."

"And what about these two idiot private eyes?" Hobson piped up.

"Well, they're quite . . . essential to the process." Michael didn't quite like the gleam he saw in Pembroke's milky eyes as he said that.

"Enough of this!" Mathilda shouted. "Armie, stop your games. Why are we here?"

"Oh, Mathilda." Pembroke paused to gaze down at her. Something in his manner softened, but only for a second, before he cleared his throat and stood up as straight as he could. "If you must know, I have brought you here to finalize the execution of my will." He raised an arthritic finger and waggled it at the shadows behind him. A thin, tightlipped man in a neat pressed gray suit and the wide, eighties-style glasses of a stereotypical accountant stepped into the light just before the railing. "This is my lawyer."

"Oh, you goddamn son of a bitch, Stephanie stabbed her finger in the air toward the stern face of Conway Grimsby, Esq., of Grimsby Law Associates. "You owe me like 1500 dollars!"

"Is there no one here you haven't personally jerked around?" Hobson sneered.

"Ma'am, I can assure you that is not how the law works," Grimsby intoned. "I am merely here to officiate Mr. Pembroke's last will and testament proceedings."

"Wait," Ethan Allen said. "Does this mean we're all beneficiaries?"

"Oh, my!" Delia squealed. "Oh, my lord! Thank you! Thank you, Armitage. I may have misjudged you."

Enzo's eyes grew twice in size. "I cannot believe it! I apologize for all the slanderous things I've said about you and your family!"

"Yes, yes," Pembroke said, tenting his hands. "I would hold on to those words if I were you, Enzo. Mr. Grimsby?"

Grimsby popped open a briefcase he swung up onto the railing and removed a single sheet of paper which he began to read from. "As per the last will and testament of Mr. Armitage Pembroke, he leaves to all those in this room . . ."

The air in the drawing room felt as it had been sucked out during the lawyer's seemingly infinite pause.

". . .absolutely nothing. And you should all go"—Grimsby cleared his throat—"expletive deleted yourselves."

"What?" Enzo shouted. "How *dare* you!"

Michael and Steph exchanged glances and a little bit of a stifled chuckle. He was glad they never really had a dog in this fight.

"I'm not in the business of giving away my wealth, Mr. Credenza." Pembroke scowled, his sarcastic warmth now replaced with a shark-like tenacity. "I'm a businessman, and intend to be a businessman long after you're all deep in the cold, cold ground."

"Hahahah." Ethan Allen's booming laugh echoed through the drawing parlor. "I'd say we'd be giving you a eulogy in the next three weeks at best, old man, but you know none of us is coming to your funeral."

"In that, my detestable son, you would be correct. But not in the way you intended. And as you will soon see, this 'will,' or lack thereof, is nothing but a formality." Pembroke grinned. "Now, there's quite the storm outside, so you might want to spend the night. I've had Bartleby and my maid set up quarters for you, so please follow them so that you can get changed in time for dinner."

"Dinner?" Helena growled. "If you think we're having dinner with you, you miserable old—"

"Tut-tut, my dear daughter. It is non-negotiable. But trust me, you will want to stick around."

"Sir?" Conway Grimsby coughed.

"Oh, yes. Grimsby. Your duties here have been fulfilled. You're free to stay if you like. You're off the clock."

"Thank you, sir." Grimsby nodded and descended the stairs to join the ranks of the rest of the group. Steph frowned angrily at him.

"I'll be seeing you all shortly." Pembroke sneered as he hobbled away into the dark and out of sight.

After a long, hushed silence, punctuated only by the incessant tapping of rain drops on the windowpanes and the occasional, distant lightning flash, Michael finally decided to say something. "Well, that was a horrible experience."

And that was when the tension burst and the room devolved into a cacophonous argument with no rhyme or reason. Before anyone knew it, Delia Dahlia had her hands wrapped around Carol Credenza's throat while Enzo fought to tear them apart. Ethan Allen's arms were entangled in Helena's manacles and Hobson was threatening him with jail time. Ethan Allen Jr. slunk his way around the brouhaha just to yank his phone back out of Michael's hands.

"Wait, wait, wait!" Mathilda, the only relatively sane one of the bunch, rushed into the center of the room and threw out her hands. "Every one of you stop! This is ridiculous! This is exactly what Armie wants. All of us fighting with each other while he sits back and laughs."

"Yes! He's trying to sow dissent and confusion!" Ethan Allen said as he untangled his way from Helena's chains, shaking off his berserker rage. "It helps him keep his claws in all of us."

"What a weirdo," Steph said.

"Uh-uh. Don't you try and deflect." Hobson glared at her. "You think you can get away with whatever it is you're doing, don'tcha?"

"Uh . . ." Steph stammered. "Uh . . . no ma'am."

"Hobson!" Michael said, dashing over and placing himself between the cop and his friend. "Back off. Steph and I didn't do anything."

"Wait . . ." Mathilda walked back over to them. "Duckett . . . and Dyer? You're them! The Future Group private eyes. The dicks for hire!"

"Well, technically I never agreed to that branding . . ." Michael sucked in air through his gritted teeth.

"Now why would a pair of private eyes make their way into my ex-husband's 93rd Birthday Party?" Delia Dahlia raised a sharp, penciled-on eyebrow.

"Father said they were essential." Ethan Allan rubbed his chin.

"Listen, guys," Michael said. "We really don't know what he was talking about. We've never even met the guy before tonight. This whole thing has gotta be some sort of coincidence."

"Ahem," Bartleby the butler cleared his throat from the archway. "Ladies and gentlemen. If you would once more please follow me and the maid . . ."

"Ja!" The maid's round face popped out from behind Bartleby's gaunt figure. How she managed to hide the rest of her body behind him was nothing short of miraculous. "I am ze maid!"

"Yes, well, if you would like to follow us, we will direct you to your quarters."

Michael noticed Steph letting out a surreptitious breath of relief, only to suck it back in as Helena, still in chains, passed before them, with Hobson following—her fiery glare staring straight into Steph's soul.

I'll be watching you, she mouthed as they disappeared around the corner after the maid.

* * *

"Thank you, Bartleby," Mike said as he closed the door to their room. He slumped against it, slid nearly halfway to the floor, and let out a deep breath.

Steph had already rushed in and collapsed on the king-size bed, her heart still in her throat from having to see Kiara Hobson again. The way that woman carried herself just sent shivers down her spine. It was just so overbearing and mean without even a sliver of humor. She thought she had left that kind of treatment behind once she'd moved out of her uncle's house. It was something she still could not deal with.

"You okay?" Mike said. She hadn't noticed him sitting on the edge of the bed until now.

"Oh, uh, yeah," she lied, shifting her eyes down to the bedspread and changing the subject. "But you ever see a bed this big? We don't even *need* Oshinko tonight."

"Right," Mike nodded, mercifully steering away from her trauma. It wasn't his problem to deal with, but deep down, if she wasn't lying to herself, sometimes she wished he'd ask. But would she tell him anything? He knew about her parents, a bit about her uncle, and nothing about her missing brother. Not to mention the fact that she hadn't told him that an alternate universe version of herself had foretold his death. That was a whole other story. And certainly not one for right now.

"Anyway." Steph swallowed her feelings and bounced upright on the mattress. "So how's about you and that MILF? Looked like something was going on until we found out she's train girl's mom."

"First of all, Steph, there's nothing there. Second, they have names."

"Yeah, but you know I don't pay attention to that." She shrugged and began to jump up and down on the bed. "Ooh. Springy."

"Steph, get down from there! Or at least take off your wet shoes."

She brought her legs up at the apex of her bounce and came down at an angle on her butt, propelling her directly onto her feet into a walk toward the wide in-built wooden closets. "Hey, didn't they say they had clothes for us here? My wet jeans are starting to get a little itchy."

"Oh, yeah, good idea," Mike said, stripping off his crushed velvet jacket. "If I have to wear this for another minute I'll go insane. You see anything useful in there?"

Steph drew open the closet doors and scanned the array of outfits. "Nothing as stylish as what I picked out for you, but I'm sure there's something here we can put to use."

It took them about ten minutes to get ready, taking turns behind the old-school changing screen in the corner of the room. Steph wasn't super happy about having to ditch her tuxedo t-shirt, but when she came across an actual tuxedo, she couldn't put it on fast enough. The tux was a little too big for her, with more sleeve length than necessary, but it fit exactly like her brother's old green jacket that she cherished. It felt like home.

She looked at Mike, who went his usual conservative route, donning a powder blue button down and khaki pants, pretty much identical to his usual wardrobe. She frowned. Where was the creativity? As long as he was comfortable, she supposed.

Then, the lights in the room, a little brighter than those in the drawing parlor, flickered off for a second, then back on again.

"Hm," Steph said. "The wiring in this place must really blow."

"So what do we do now?" Mike asked. "Just sit here and wait for the butler to ring the dinner bell?"

"I guess." Steph shrugged but then felt a telltale tingle. "But I really need to go pee."

"Yeah, you should probably go take care of that." Mike bit his lip, as if suppressing some of his own historical trauma. "Do you know where the bathroom is?"

"No." She already had half her body out the door. "But I'm sure it'll be easy to find."

Whistling to herself, Steph exited their room and stalked the hallways of the upper wings of the house, trying each door she could find that looked, well, bathroomy. After about the eighth door, she realized she had no idea where she was and where she was going. Rather than go find the butler—because that would be admitting defeat—she continued to open as many doors as she could. It was a smattering of bedrooms, closets, libraries, and one room which had a pool table. Steph made a note to come back to that one later. Eventually, she happened upon a wide, lustrous teak door.

"Huh," she said to herself. "Could be this one."

If it was a bathroom, it was probably Pembroke's personal privy and all the signs pointed to it being real luxe. Besides, when else was Steph gonna be able to pee in a billionaire's bathroom?

She tried the knob, but it stubbornly refused to turn.

"Why I oughta . . ." Steph reared back and slammed her shoulder into the door. Remarkably, she felt it give a bit, so she backed up and tried again. Then a third time, and a fourth, and a fifth until the door burst open. Skidding to a stop, Steph found herself not in a beautiful bathroom with porcelain fixtures but in a cavernous study lined with well-stocked wooden bookshelves, a titan of a writing desk, and windows that spanned the entire length of the far wall, allowing an up close and personal view of the torrential storm raging outside.

But what really tied the whole room together was the dead body.

* * *

Michael was flipping through a magazine he'd found on the bedside table when Stephanie creeped back in the room.

"Nobody's called us down for dinner yet," he said from behind the pages as he heard the door click. "You find the bathroom?" When he didn't get a response, Michael lowered the magazine to find Stephanie standing at the foot of the bed a little more pale and stoic than usual. "What? What's wrong?"

"Uh, Pembroke," she said.

"What about him?"

"Remember how the last time we saw him he was all walking around, and talking?"

"Yeah . . ."

"Well, he's not doing much of that anymore. Dude's dead."

"What?" Michael jumped to his feet. "You could've opened with 'he's dead,' y'know!"

"Yeah, well, I was in shock."

"You? You're never in shock."

"There's a first time for everything, buddy."

"Alright, alright," Michael put up his hands. "What happened? Start from the beginning."

"Well, I kept looking for the bathroom, and I thought it was behind this really large door. But it was locked, so I had to break it down."

"You managed to break down a door?"

"I'm as surprised as you. But it was Pembroke's study, and he was just lying there, stone cold dead on the ground."

Michael let out a pained breath. "Steph, why'd you have to break the door down?"

"I needed to use the bathroom!" she whined.

"Believe me, I understand that more than you'll ever know, but you know we're going to get blamed for this."

"But we didn't do it!" She paused in thought for a second. "Unless . . . maybe we *did* do it?"

"Steph, we didn't do it! But you know what we have to do now."

She frowned with terrible realization. "No, no we don't have to do that."

"Yes, we do," Michael said. "We have to tell Hobson."

* * *

Pembroke's ancient, bloated body, loosely wrapped in his purple robe, lay sprawled on the floor of his study by the corner of his desk. His ankle and, more importantly, his neck were bent at odd, uncomfortable angles, making him look a bit like a rotund bird that had flown headfirst into a window. Particularly disturbing were Pembroke's eyes—frozen open, with his jaw hanging open in a permanent expression of shock.

Detective Hobson squatted down on her haunches by the man's torso, "Yup. He's dead."

To her credit, she had been all business when Steph and Mike had showed up to her room after finding the butler and the maid. Wasting nary a second, Hobson followed them to the study, but unfortunately had to bring the still manacled Helena with her.

"I'd like to say I'm sad," the young Pembroke said, "but I really hated his guts. Good riddance to bad rubbish."

"Careful what you say, Helena," Mike chided. "Hobson could and would use it against you in a court of law."

"I'm already in prison, you moron." She waggled her cuffs at him. "Because of *you*. Besides, Hobson's had her eye on me all night. I didn't do it."

"Would you two be quiet?" Hobson snapped, before turning her attention back to Pembroke's body. "Definitely broken neck and ankle. Must've fell. No blood or visible wounds. No blunt force trauma. Could've just been a heart attack."

"Well, that's pretty coincidental, isn't it?" Mike asked.

"I'm sorry, did I ask for your opinion?" she glared at him.

"No, but I think Pembroke ending up dead when he gathered together a bunch of people who hate him the most just to insult them, case in point"—he gestured broadly at Helena, who simply shrugged— "is more than a little suspicious."

"Listen, kid. This isn't some dumb Scooby-Doo mystery like you're used to solving. This is real life. It's entirely possible that a 93-year-old man died of a heart attack."

"And I'm saying it's also entirely possible it's not."

"You." Hobson pointed at Steph, who up until now had been trying to watch quietly from the door, then pointed down. "C'mere."

Steph nodded and did as she was told.

"You found him, right?"

Steph nodded again.

"And you said the door was locked?"

She offered another curt nod.

"Do you see any other way someone might have gotten in here?"

Steph looked around and shook her head no.

"There." Hobson turned back to Mike. "Even your partner says you're overthinking it." She hopped to her feet and strode to the door where the butler and maid were waiting. "I'll call the coroner as soon the storm lets up. Until then, I suppose I have to go break the news to his surviving family."

"Excuse me." The soft voice of Mike's MILF—Mathilda was it?--floated over the butler's shoulders as he stepped aside to let her through. "I'm sorry, I was heading to the bathroom and saw the light and—" Her eyes fell upon the broken body of her ancient ex-husband. She could only whisper "Oh, no" as she rushed over to his side.

"I'm sorry for your loss," Hobson murmured. She gestured to Helena to follow her.

"Serves him right, mother," Helena pointed to Mathilda with her manacled hands.

"C'mon." Hobson yanked at her chains.

Helena offered her mother one last glare and shuffled after the cop, the butler and the maid following behind.

Now that Hobson had left the premises, Stephanie felt like she could breathe again and did so with gusto. "Whoo, boy."

The MILF, however, was, surprisingly, on the edge of tears. "How did this happen?"

Mike put a hand on her shoulder. Steph felt a smirk forming. Of course he did.

"Hobson thinks it was a heart attack," he said. "We're not so sure."

"Seems more likely . . ." Steph thrust her way forward, harnessing her renewed vigor. "He was *murdered.*"

"It's just like the psychic said . . ." Mathilda whispered.

"I'm sorry." Mike's hand retreated from her shoulder. "What was that? Did you say psychic?"

"Yeah, no," Steph started. "I heard that, too. There's a psychic in the mix. Now we're cooking with gas."

"It was 30 years ago," Mathilda said. "We were finalizing plans to donate Armie's wealth to charity and start a new, more socially conscious life together. We really did love each other, y'know?"

Mike nodded, and Steph felt she had to, too.

"I took him to a crappy little city psychic after his birthday dinner. It was just supposed to be a little fun. But then she predicted something about his death. And he . . . well, he lost it."

Steph whistled. "Pretty damn good psychic, I'd say."

"Steph!" Mike elbowed her in the ribs.

"That's what started his downward spiral. He was scared and became so invested—obsessed—with proving her wrong. Armie started pouring all of his time and effort into finding artificial ways to prolong his life. It eventually tore us apart."

"So thirty years to the day?" Steph asked. "This is definitely more than a coincidence."

"Did anyone else know about the psychic's prediction?" Mike paced his way around Pembroke's giant desk. "Yow!" he yanked his hand back as it caressed a silver teapot on a platter. "Hot."

"No one knew about the psychic, I don't think," the MILF explained. "But everyone in his circles heard rumors about what Armie was trying to do. You can't try to live forever without making a few waves."

Steph was about to say something she thought was genius, but a grinding and scraping noise interrupted her as it rumbled throughout the walls of the house.

"What the hel—" Mike, still clutching his singed hand, was also interrupted by the echoic baleful lowing that followed—a haunting mournful sound that was instantly recognizable.

As the animalistic call faded into the walls, Steph whispered, "Monster Moose."

"It's not a Monster Moose!" Mike shouted.

"If you have a better idea than Monster Moose, I'd like to hear it," Steph snapped back.

"*Anything!* Anything is a better idea than Monster Moose!"

"Monster Moose?" The MILF cocked her head. "What are you talking about?"

"It's a long story." Mike rubbed the bridge of his nose beneath his glasses. "Our car got stuck and we had to walk up through the woods and we heard this sound . . ."

"When you were married to uh . . . this guy." Steph pointed at the corpse. "You ever see any Monster Meese around here?"

"No . . . nothing like that." The MILF scrunched up her face. "This house was in Armie's family for generations. It's probably some stuff settling. I used to hear a lot of creaks and groans and scrapes. Made it hard to sleep. Sometimes it even sounded a little like people screaming."

A shrill shriek pierced the air through the doorway, echoing up from the lower levels.

"Something like that?" Steph asked.

"No." The MILF blanched. "That was a real scream."

The three of them wasted no time rushing out of the room and down the closest stairwell. A second scream, less shrill and more labored, guided them from the landing and down two adjacent hallways until they ended up in the kitchen. Mike skidded to a stop and threw out his hands to prevent Steph and the MILF from running any further.

"Oh, man," Steph said as she peered over Mike's shoulder to see what he was shielding them from.

There, across the black-and-white tiled floor, lay the body of the butler, twisted and contorted, with blood leaking from every visible—

and probably non-visible—orifice. The crimson pool below him continued to enlarge, seeping into every crack and cranny in the tiles beneath him. Beside the butler, the maid, her apron and dress similarly stained with blood, lay motionless. If they were taking bets, Steph could have guessed her last words with certainty.

"Alright." Steph sighed. "Well, I guess this time the butler didn't do it."

"Steph, shut up," Mike whispered.

Steph's eyes traveled upwards, where she found the crusty old woman in the bright red sequined dress from earlier holding a knife and an apple.

"Delia?" Mike's MILF asked. "What are you doing here?"

"I . . . I . . ." she stammered. "I just got so hungry waiting for dinner that I came down to ask Bartleby to prepare me an apple. But when I couldn't find him I decided I could not wait. When I came to the kitchen . . . I found them. Like this. Dead." Delia's eyes darted to her raised knife, which she immediately dropped. "Oh, no." It skittered across the floor and into the puddle of expanding blood. "It wasn't me. I certainly did not do this."

"Relax, Dilly Dally," Steph said. "I believe you. The same thing happened to me."

"It did?"

"Yeah. I remember it like it was yesterday."

"It happened like 30 minutes ago!" Mike hissed.

"Oh, right. I'm sorry to have to tell you this, but Pembroke is dead, too."

"Good lord!" Delia cried out and dropped her apple, which also bounced into the blood pool. "Armitage? What happened?"

"We thought a heart attack, but we're definitely thinking there's a little more at play here now," Mike said, glancing down at the butler and the maid.

Ethan Allen Pembroke Sr. and his weird son—nose still in his phone, and altogether uninterested—skidded into the kitchen behind Delia, followed shortly by Detective Hobson. Steph's eyes went wide, and she stepped back.

"Good lord!" He echoed his mother's earlier sentiments. "Mother, I just heard the terrible news about father. What happened here?"

"Don't worry," Steph offered meekly. "She didn't do it."

Hobson either didn't hear or purposefully ignored Steph's statement as her gun was already drawn. She began advancing on Delia. "On the ground. Hands above your head!"

"Hobson, stop! She's innocent," Mathilda cried.

"I mean, you'll probably find her prints on the knife, but . . ." Mike added, out of anxiety.

"Shut up!" Hobson said as Delia lowered herself to the ground. "This is officially a crime scene."

"I . . . I think you're being a bit too harsh," Steph started.

"Shut it!" Hobson growled. "It's because of you two that I'm on escort duty and this is just the sort of collar I need to get back in Calhoun's good graces."

"You're not gonna get on Rex's good side with shitty police work, Hobson," Mike said. "No matter how much you hate us."

Steph was stunned by his curt response. She'd never actually heard Mike talk to other people like that before. Truth be told, it was a little inspiring.

"Listen, you little shit—"

The house made its sounds again. A grinding, sliding noise, like stone rubbing up against stone, gears turning, and the *ka-thunk* of something large slotting into place. This time, it sounded as if it was coming from the floor above.

"What the hell was that?" Hobson looked up.

Hobson's question was answered only by a slow, rhythmic thud, followed by the braying of the terrifying Monster Moose clearly haunting the mansion. Another loud set of thuds and crashes made the walls tremble, followed by another sustained scraping and creaking. Then, everything went silent.

Steph looked around at the shocked faces in the kitchen, before focusing on Mike, who was doing the same.

"Hobson," he said. "Where's Helena?"

"She was supposed to be—oh, goddamnit!" Hobson jumped up, grabbing Delia by the arm and rushed back out, with both Ethan Allens bringing up the rear. "C'mon." She grunted before calling back. "And don't touch anything!"

Mike and Steph shared a shrug.

"If Helena might be in danger, I should . . . I should probably follow them." Mathilda pointed at the door and promptly scurried off.

"Hey, Mike," Steph whispered when they were alone. "Thanks again for having my back with Hobson. I . . . can't tell you how much I appreciate it."

"Of course. I've always got your back, Steph. We're a team, remember? Duckett & Dyer!"

Steph grinned. "Dicks—"

"Don't push it." Mike waved his finger at her.

"Should we, uh?" Steph indicated the exit on the other end of the kitchen.

"Yeah." Mike glanced down at the twisted bodies of the butler and maid. "They're not going anywhere."

* * *

Michael and Stephanie caught up to the group clustered around the door of Hobson and Helena's shared room three floors up. Hobson was cuffing Delia Dahlia's hands behind her back while Helena was sitting calmly, dangling her legs off the side of her bed like a child.

"Oh, mother," Helena smiled at Mathilda. "What did I miss?"

"The butler and the maid are dead," Mathilda said. "Delia found them, and Detective Hobson thinks she did it."

"Well, as long as I'm not to blame."

Steph tapped Michael on the shoulder. "She knows something," she whispered.

Michael nodded, spotting the twinkle in Helena's eyes that wasn't there earlier. "Okay, Helena, cut the shit. What's going on?"

"I'm just having fun watching you guys run around like chickens with your heads cut off."

"Helena," Mathilda scolded. "Do you know what's going on here? Do you know where these weird noises are coming from?"

"I might have an inkling." She shrugged. "More of an educated guess, to be honest."

Everyone turned to face her, Hobson and Delia included. The only person who wasn't actively looking at her was Ethan Allen Jr., his nose still buried in his phone screen.

"Like what?" Michael asked.

"There are secret passages all over this house, Michael." Helena rolled her eyes. "Any basic engineer could've told you that. Sliding panels. Moving walls. What did you think was making those noises?"

"Well, what about the monster?" Steph piped up. "What's making *those* noises? Is it killing people? Is Delia Dahlia innocent?"

"I am!" Delia shouted, before Hobson directed her to sit on her bed—which she did wordlessly.

"I can't opine on that," Helena continued, staring directly at Mathilda. "But I spent a lot of time here as a kid—not of my own free will, of course—but my father never paid attention to me, so I really got to know what was going on, literally behind the scenes."

"I grew up in this house, too, and I don't remember any secret passages," Ethan Allen declared, turning up his nose.

"They were all built long after your time," Helena clarified, "when the old bastard went all crazy and paranoid."

"So you're the only one who can guide us through the house?" Michael cocked his head.

"What can I say?" Helena smiled. "But I'd be happy to do it . . . for a pardon."

"Oh, how convenient." Hobson crossed her arms. "Absolutely not."

"Well, then, I'm afraid my hands are tied." Helena waggled her bound wrists with a smirk.

"Hobson," Michael said. "C'mon. We have to figure out what's going on."

"I am not entering into some 'Silence of the Lambs' pact with this woman," Hobson grumbled.

Helena rolled her eyes. "Fine. I know you don't have any reason to trust me . . ."

"If you wanted us to trust you, you'd tell us everything right now," Hobson said.

"Well, then there's nothing in it for me. Quid pro quo."

"Cogito ergo sum," Steph whispered.

"That's not . . ." Helena sighed. "Never mind. Okay. I'll give you the first one for free. That scraping and creaking you heard earlier? That came from just down the hall on this floor."

"Our room?" Ethan Allen asked.

"I don't know where your room is," Helena stated.

"He's past the den on this floor," Hobson said. "I was there informing him about Mr. Pembroke's passing when we heard Delia scream."

"That's not far enough," Helena said. "This particular noise came from the walls of the bedroom at the very end of the hall."

"That's where I was headed next." Hobson blanched. "To see

Enzo and Carol Credenza."

"Oh," Helena said coyly. "Well, then I suppose someone should check up on them."

"Don't move a muscle." Hobson shot a glare at Delia before rushing out the door. Mathilda, Ethan Allen, and his kid followed. Helena rose to her feet and strode out past Michael and Stephanie, who were left gawking.

"Well?" Helena said, looking back at them. "Are the two famous detectives going to come or not?"

"Why are you like this?" Michael groaned as he and Steph jogged to catch up with her. "Who hurt you?"

"Who *hasn't?* Haven't you been paying attention to anything around here?" Helena frowned. "God, you're the worst."

"Goddamnit!" Hobson's yell indicated that they were already too late, but Michael, Stephanie, and Helena picked up their pace.

Once again, they were treated to an absolutely gruesome spectacle. The entire bedroom had been turned upside down, with the standing armoires, dressers, and side tables smashed to pieces against the wall and strewn everywhere. Decorative plinths and their associated marble busts were lying in pieces across the hardwood floor. What was more, the two queen size beds that had taken up most of the floor space were somehow stacked on top of one another.

"Oh my god." Mathilda covered her mouth with the tips of her fingers. "Where are they? Are they . . . dead?"

"We're here!" came the muffled, accented cry of Enzo Credenza from somewhere within the room.

"We're under the bed!" followed Carol's more kindly voice.

Michael walked in and bent over, peering under the wood footboard of the bed. The floor beneath was empty. "I uh . . . I don't see you."

"Not that bed!" Enzo's voice was coming from higher up, and

Michael realized that the Credenza couple was sandwiched in the tight space between the two-bed stack. At least they were laying comfortably on a mattress.

"C'mon!" Michael said to everyone. "Help me get this off."

Steph moved to one side, followed by Ethan Allen, while Hobson and Mathilda took the other. Helena remained off to the side, enjoying that her handcuffs gave her an excuse not to participate. With a coordinated heave, the group lifted the first bed up off the second, allowing Enzo and Carol to slide out between the frames and onto the floor.

"Credenza!" Hobson immediately launched into the third-degree. "What happened?"

"I have no idea!" he shouted.

"We were waiting to be summoned for dinner when the wall suddenly opened up," Carol said, shaking, "and this . . . this . . . thing just barged its way into our room and went on a rampage."

"What was it?" Michael asked.

"Was it a moose?" Steph followed up, which earned her an eye roll.

"We didn't get a clear look at it. It was too busy trying to kill us!" Enzo yelled. "I thought we were going to die when it picked up that bed and slammed it down on us."

"So . . . it had hands," Steph said.

"No! No longer." Enzo fumed, indicating his surroundings with a series of violent hand gestures. "Enough of this. Fake billionaires, an insulting will reading, and now some sort of maniacal monster? I will not risk suffering another insult to the Credenza name. Come on, Carol. We are leaving."

"But, Enzo, it's still pouring outside," Carol protested as he grabbed her arm and dragged her out of the room.

"I do not care if it's hailing fire and brimstone!" His anger echoed down the hallway. "I will not spend another minute in this madhouse!"

After he heard them tromp down the stairs, Michael looked around at the faces that remained. "Well, at least now we know they didn't do it."

"No, we don't," Hobson countered.

"This clearly isn't the work of a person." Michael put his hand on Steph's shoulder. "We've got to admit it. Steph was right from the beginning. There's some kind of . . . thing here."

"Oh, a monster?" Hobso's dark eyes flared. "You must be out of your damn mind. There's no such thing."

"Remember when we clowned you for accidentally arresting a dog?" Steph stated. "Werewolf."

"Reverse werewolf," Michael corrected with a grin.

"Goddamnit. I've had it up to here with this nonsense!" Hobson yelled. "People have *died*. And you're telling me it's because of a *monster*. You two are infuriatingly useless."

"Detective." Steph stepped forward with a sense of purpose about her, which surprised Michael a bit. It also made him a little proud. "Mike and I have seen our share of strange stuff. And we're talking some really out there shit, so, believe me when I say, this kind of thing is absolutely our wheelhouse. And so far you've just been yelling real loud and making a scene. So you'd better step the fuck back and let us do our thing. We might not know what we're doing, but *we know what we're doing*. Right, Mike?"

Michael nodded, smiling.

"Beh." Ethan Allen Jr. grunted at his phone.

Michael jumped, startled by the teen who was hovering near his elbow. "Goddamn! I keep forgetting this kid even exists."

"Alright. Fine." Hobson scowled. "You think you're hot shit? Well, go ahead." She flourished her hand over the room. "Do your thing."

"You heard the lady, Mike," Steph said with a soft grin. "Do your thing."

"Uh . . . uh . . ." Michael had no clue what this specific thing was, but he'd be damned if he was gonna leave Steph high and dry right now. It was time to fake it till he made it. "Sure! Okay, so what do we know?"

"Well, the monster has hands, and it's strong enough to lift up a bed," Steph said. "So the moose theory is out. But it's also crawling up the walls of this place."

"It came *through* the wall," Ethan Allen Pembroke clarified. "Enzo said it emerged from a false wall. Probably from one of the secret passageways Helena keeps talking about."

"Everyone start feeling up the walls of this room!" Steph said.

"Or . . ." Michael strode over to the door and flicked the room's lights off and on again, pausing for a second in between each switch.

"There!" Mathilda pointed to the wall behind the smashed marble column. "I saw something. Like a little orange seam."

Michael rapped on the wall Mathilda identified with his knuckle, producing an echoing hollow sound. In fact, the false wall had not been entirely shut, creaking open with little resistance. It revealed a darkened tunnel through the structure of the house.

"If I could clap, I would." Helena smiled, revealing canines that could cut glass. "Took you long enough."

"I guess we should . . . uh, go down the tunnel?" Mathilda said, the paragon of certainty.

"Well, if we want any goddamn answers, we better," said Steph.

"So that's it? Clearly, we all value answers over our lives?" Hobson asked.

Everyone nodded.

She sighed and drew her gun. "Fine. You two win this round. I'll bring up the rear."

Michael snatched Ethan Allen Jr.'s cellphone out of his tiny, clawed hands once again. He turned on the proper flashlight and led the way through the open wall. The kid grunted angrily and followed suit, with the rest of them close behind. Hobson, true to her word, covered their rear flank.

As the wall slid shut behind them, shrouding them in darkness, Michael had only one thought: *Oh, god. We're following a monster down a scary tunnel. Have we all gone insane?* But he stowed it for the greater good and pushed forth.

The tunnel was about one and a half shoulder-widths wide and made of cold, crumbling brick. Michael couldn't see much of it beyond a foot in front of the cellphone flashlight, but he could feel the delicate, pockmarked edifice as his other hand brushed against the wall.

"So where does this take us?" Mathilda asked from somewhere behind him.

"Oh, I'm quite familiar with this one," Helena said, amusing only herself.

Up ahead, a faint orange light flickered, and after a few more feet of tunnel, the passage opened up into a small, dimly lit workshop filled with parts, tools, and, up on the wall, a skeletal half-corpse that hung from chains.

"Gah!" Hobson shouted, nearly jumping back.

"Relax, officer." Helena approached the torso and knocked on it with her knuckles to the tune of a soft clang. "It's just metal."

"Your robots?" Michael grumbled.

"My father's prototypes, anyway. He never perfected the consciousness upload, as far as I could tell, so he never made a real, working robot body to put his undying mind in. But he didn't much care for my upcycling of his efforts, as I'm sure you know."

Steph wiggled some of the wires dangling from the thing's spine. Its metal head toppled off and into her hands. She rolled it around a bit before sticking her hand up its neck. "Yeah! It does kinda look like him. Hey, Mr. Pembroke! I heard you just got back from the doctor. How'd it go?"

"Not good," Steph's terrible ventriloquism said as she waggled her tux's bowtie with her other hand. "He says I've got termites."

"Steph, stop it. That joke doesn't make sense if it's a robot." Michael squinted. He had to admit, with the faint lighting, the shadows cast on the robot skull did make it look a little like the dead man in the study.

"Let's keep moving," Ethan Allen Sr. said.

Michael raised the cellphone up and proceeded down the tunnel on the other end of the workshop, which narrowed again. If a huge monster had been crawling around, it must have been real careful to squeeze down here.

It took about three more minutes for them to reach a dead end.

"What now?" Hobson grunted.

"Relax," Steph said pushing her way through the group and sidling between Michael and the wall. "There's always a switch or a button or a—oh, there it is." She hit a loose brick and the wall creaked and groaned as hidden gears rotated to allow it to slide away.

Michael took a large step forward. And then a huge thing fell on him, its teeth bared, and its powerful arms outstretched, ending in sharp claws black as night.

"Agh!" He screamed and instinctively put up his hands. "Monster!"

Steph came to his rescue and, together, they shoved the bulky, hairy mass back. With a final, brusque push, they managed to topple it to the floor with a loud thud, where it remained motionless.

"Huh," Michael looked at it, and then the room beyond in recognition. They were back in the drawing parlor, and the 'monster' was merely Pembroke's taxidermied trophy bear.

"Well, that's embarrassing, Mike." Steph smiled as she strode past him and into the parlor. Michael could only roll his eyes and ignore the judgement as the rest of the group made their way past him. Mathilda gave him a merciful pat on the shoulder, while the Ethan Allen kid did nothing but snort and grab his precious phone back.

The rain outside persisted, hitting the windowpanes in wet spatters, as the seven strong group filed back into where they started. As they arrayed themselves around the crimson couches, they were surprised to find an eighth person in the room, staring at the cold black emptiness of the unlit fireplace, his spindly hands clasped behind his back.

"Oh, hello. I see you've finally made it back here." Conway Grimsby slowly turned around. A flash of well-placed lightning glinted off his piercing gray eyes and the wide frames of his glasses. "I wondered how long you'd take."

"Lawyer!" Steph thrust her finger toward him, despite the fact that it was covered in her oversized tuxedo sleeves. "I knew it was you the whole time."

"No, you didn't," Michael chided. "We still don't."

"Well, I knew he was up to no good! And I was right!" Steph declared, before dropping her voice. "What were you up to, by the way? Was it good or not?"

"My plans have been in motion for years." The lawyer smiled. "And now they've finally come to fruition."

"Did you know anything about this?" Mathilda glanced at her daughter.

"Uh, no." Helena looked genuinely surprised. "This is a new one for me."

"You fiend!" Ethan Allen leveled a dramatic finger across the room at Grimsby. "You've spent your time at my father's side plotting his death, haven't you? Not to mention the deaths of his closest servants."

"Your father?" Grimsby's eyes filled with a fire that belied his buttoned-up appearance. "*Your* father? He was *my* father before you were a twinkle in his eye!"

Ethan Allen Sr. took a step back, looking genuinely shocked. Ethan Allen Jr., however, could not be less interested.

"Your maid," Grimsby continued. "When you were growing up. What was her name?"

"What?"

"Say her name!" Grimsby yelled.

"C-c-claudia. Ms. Claudia."

"Ms. Claudia . . . Grimsby," the lawyer finished. "My mother. She and Pembroke lay together years before he met Delia Dahlia, and I was birthed and hidden from the family. Raised by my mother in secret. Pembroke never even knew I existed."

"Okay, this is all getting to be really too much—" Michael started.

"So for years," Grimsby ignored him. Everyone else had; Michael didn't know why he thought this moment would be any different. "I sat, and I studied and I vowed to wreak my vengeance against my father no matter how long it took."

Hobson pulled up her gun. "Hands up, Grimsby. I'm placing you under arrest."

"Oh, please." Grimsby waved at Hobson's firearm in a posh dismissal. "I killed no one. My machinations"—he grabbed the briefcase that had been leaning against the side of the fireplace and patted it—"have been entirely legal.

"As you all know, Armitage Pembroke hired me to draft up a will out of spite. One that gave every one of his most hated associates nothing. What he didn't know is that I altered the wording on the digital copies he e-signed."

"Because he's old," Steph said, finished the thought.

"Yes, and now that he's dead, everything belongs to his eldest heir— me! This house? His business? His fortune? All mine!"

"So you did kill him!" Mathilda said.

"It turns out the *real* monster was the lawyer the whole time." Steph narrowed her eyes. "I can't say I'm surprised."

"No, I didn't kill him." Grimsby shook his head. "He was inviting you all here to rub your failure in your faces. I figured one of you was going to kill him."

"Yeah, well we didn't!" Steph said. "At least, I don't think so."

"Then who—" Grimsby's thought was interrupted by the sliding clank of a metal door. An enormous, soot-covered hand, roughly the size of the lawyer's torso, burst out of the darkness of the unlit fireplace and grabbed him by his ankles. The man's frantic screams were drowned out by a deep primitive bellowing. Grimsby clawed at the hardwood floor with his free hand, the rest of his body dragged back through the hole in the fireplace. Michael, Steph, and the rest of the assembled crowd could only stare on in terrified awe.

"No! Please help! Help meeeeee!" He screamed as his body disappeared into the blackness. His fingers slipped from the handle of his briefcase, sending it sliding across the parlor floor. A soft squelching and crunching trickled out of the shadows and was soon replaced by silence.

"So it turns out the *real* monster," Steph whispered, when she was sure it was over, "was a real monster the whole time."

Michael jumped, and everyone shrieked as the giant blackened arm thrust itself out of the fireplace again with a sustained, angry growl. Its enormous hand flailed about, grabbing at the air, as the group retreated to the back of the room, safely out of its grasp. This only made it angrier, and when it couldn't find anything to grab on to, it retreated somewhat, then surged forward. Whatever monstrous body was behind the fireplace impacted with a savage fury, sending dust and debris falling. Cracks snaked through the pale bricks.

"Ah!" Ethan Allen Sr. screamed as the arm retreated and slammed into the fireplace again. "It's going to break through!"

Once more, the arm pulled back and readied itself for another full-body tackle, so that it could make its entrance through the wall, like some sort of horrifying Kool-Aid Man. But before the final impact could come, the fireplace erupted in flame, incinerating the wood scraps and Grimbsy's briefcase. With a pained screech, the giant arm retreated from the flame, its owner thudding away through the back walls of the house.

"Okay, what the hell just happened?" asked Hobson. She had backed up the furthest against the wall.

"Do you believe there's a monster now?" Steph said.

"What . . . what is that thing?" Mathilda's voice shook and rightly so.

"I'm certain I don't know, Mistress." said the butler from the archway.

"Augh!" Everyone shouted in unison. Had they not already been against the wall, they would have leapt back even further.

"Zombie!" Steph pointed.

"Madam, I assure you. I am not a zombie."

"Well, you better not be a vampire." Steph pointed between herself and Michael. "Because we already did the whole vampire thing, and I'll be *damned* if we're gonna repeat ourselves."

The butler looked mildly annoyed. Then again, everyone usually did when dealing with Steph. "I am not a vampire, nor a ghost, nor a revenant, nor a lich, nor any other supernatural boogedy boo. I'm quite corporeal."

"No, no, no, no, no!" Hobson ran up to him. "We saw you bleeding out in the kitchen down the hall."

"And believe me, it was a *lot* of blood," Michael added.

"Madam and sir, I must protest." The butler sighed. "And my presence here would dictate otherwise. If that did indeed transpire, I remember absolutely none of it."

"I . . . I don't get it, Bartleby," Ethan Allen said. "We saw you. You were dead."

"If I was dead, sir"—Bartleby frowned—"I wouldn't have been able to save you using the remote start for the gas fireplace, now would I?"

"Oh, yeah, that was a smooth move," Steph said. "Nicely done."

"Bartleby." Ethan Allen Sr.'s voice quavered. "What Grimsby said . . . was it true?"

"Perhaps," Bartleby said. "But given the circumstances, it hardly matters now."

Ethan hugged the butler. "I'm so glad you're alive. You were always good to us."

Bartleby slowly patted the man on his back. "Thank you, sir."

"Smeh." Ethan Allen Jr. shrugged, avoiding any eye contact as usual.

"Okay." Hobson put her gun away and waved her hands around to get everyone's attention. "This is all great, but can we get back on track here? Whatever that thing was—and I'm *not* saying it was a monster"—she glared at Steph, who amazingly glared right back—"is still loose in the bowels of this place, and we don't know what it will do next."

Following a sudden rumble, the thing's harsh keening echoed through the house, ending in a splintering smash. Outside the nearest window, a hail of jagged glass pieces tinkled down, only just distinguishable from raindrops by their size.

They were followed by a frail body in a sparkling red dress.

"Mother!" Ethan Allen Pembroke let himself gape for half a second before tearing out of the drawing parlor and down the hallway toward the main foyer, the butler steps behind him.

Hearing the main entrance doors slam caused Ethan Allen's shitty teen to finally crane his pencil neck up from his screen. His eyes wide at his sudden abandonment, he chased after his father.

"Wait!" Mathilda called out, before following suit. "Ethan!"

"This isn't a good idea!" Hobson pulled her leather jacket up over her head and rushed out after them, despite her advice against it.

"So . . . uh," Michael said to Steph, "should we go?"

"I feel like we should." Steph looked down at the borrowed tuxedo she was sporting. "But I really don't wanna ruin this tux. I think I'm really rocking it."

"Likewise," Helena said, her butt plopped safely on one of the long couches. "I don't wanna get my hair wet, so I'm gonna be waiting right here."

"Good for you." Michael rolled his eyes. "Let's go, Steph."

After Steph carefully hung her tuxedo jacket on the arm of the closest couch, they were off. Opening the wooden double doors in the foyer, Michael and Steph stepped into the downpour. The rain was coming down harder and faster, and before they reached the corner of the house, they were already drenched to the bone. Michael's hair was instantly matted, and rivulets of water streamed through it, guided by thick strands hanging over his glasses. He could barely make out where he was going, but he grabbed Steph's arm and guided them toward the crowd gathered before the first-floor window—visible only during the occasional lightning flash.

The wet ground sucked at his shoes as they approached the group. Ethan Allen Sr. kneeled in the muddy garden bed beside the broken body of Delia Dahlia, her back arched and her arms askew like bare wings. Bartleby the butler gently put his hands on Ethan's shoulders.

"Oh, man," Steph said quietly, her words mostly drowned out by the rain.

Michael looked at the broken window from which she had fallen, three floors up, but due to the high ceilings of all the rooms in the manor, it was more like six. A hulking shadow hovered behind the broken pane, but it disappeared after the next lightning flash.

"We've gotta get out of here," Michael said.

"Oh, no, you think?" Hobson raised her voice to fight against the rain; she just barely won. "We need to come back here tomorrow with a team of real officers."

"We're not leaving her!" Ethan Sr. cried. His son—now 90 pounds soaking wet—stood off to the side, closer to the garden wall, struggling with how to handle genuine emotion. "We're not!" he repeated, standing up and moving toward Michael.

Steph stepped forward and put a hand on the man's shoulder. "Listen, guy, I'm sorry. I know how hard it is to lose . . . family. But Mike's right, we need to leave. This is getting out of hand." Michael was taken aback by Steph's sudden turn of responsibility. Maybe now *he* was rubbing off on *her.* "If we stay, more people could die. It's not worth the risk—"

"No!" Ethan Allen Sr. swatted her hand away and ran back to his dead mother's side. "You definitely don't understand! She's my mother, I won't leave her! If I have to, I'll wait here until I die!"

Had he remained alive for another second, Ethan Allen Pembroke Sr. would've immediately regretted those words. Fortunately for him, his body—and his mother's by proximity—was instantly turned into a puddle of human goo with bone bits. Everyone else, however, was tossed back to the ground by the shockwave as the monster, who had leapt out of the third-floor window, made landfall atop Ethan and Delia's bodies. Michael had the wind knocked out of him as he splashed backwards into a small puddle of silty water.

"Holy shit!" Steph yelled as she rolled ass over head into a nearby bush.

As he struggled to his feet, Michael tried to wipe the mud off his glasses to get a better view of what was going on. There, in an indent of its own making, was a hunched, hulking, vaguely human shape riddled with unnatural bulges of muscle towering over everything. It was covered in black and white tattered clothing, its loose fabric flapping aggressively in the storm. A sopping wet black hood shielded its face from view, but one large purple eye peered through a well-placed hole in the cloth.

"Crap." Michael whimpered as the thing threw its arms back and practically dislocated its jaws to release a guttural roar. The sound knocked him back with as much force as the monster's impact. "Run!" he shouted and flailed around, grabbing Mathilda's hand. Together, they fought their way across the muddy ground and back toward the mansion's doors. "Steph!" he called back.

"I'm fine! Let's go, let's go!" Through the rain, he could see Steph grabbing the shoulders of Ethan Allen Jr.—still shocked at seeing his father turned into a liquefied pulp—and forcing him forward.

"Hobson!" Past Steph, Michael spotted the detective, who was standing her ground and looking up at the deformed monstrosity. Staring directly at its single, bulging eye, she drew her sidearm and began to unload her clip into its body.

Each shot drove it slightly back, causing it to screech and shield its face with an arm as big as a human torso. When Hobson's gun finally transitioned from bullets to empty clicks, the thing dropped its arm. Just before it let out another earth-shaking roar, Michael could have sworn he saw it flash a broken smile. Flailing around randomly with its other arm, the monster managed to snag Bartleby, who had the misfortune of being sandwiched between the thing and the mansion walls. Its massive hand enclosed around the man's balding head and crushed his beak-like nose with a soft squish. With a loud crack, it broke the skull, and the butler's blood and brain matter oozed from between its fingers.

"Not again!" Michael whispered to himself.

Using the now lifeless body as a makeshift cudgel, the monster sent Hobson flying into the mansion walls. She thudded to the muddy ground, unmoving, but hopefully only unconscious.

Michael and Mathilda were both frozen by the corner of the house. Fortunately for them, Steph was still in control of her faculties and pushed them forward, along with Ethan Allen Jr.

"C'mon! C'mon!" Steph's cries fought for purchase against the ringing in Michael's ears as they ran back to the wooden double doors of the entrance. Even as they slammed them shut, they could hear the terrible thudding of the approaching monster.

Helena down the hallway toward them. "What? What happened? Where's Hobson!"

"Helena, we need to barricade this door, now!" Mathilda shouted.

"Okay, okay!" Helena directed them to several chairs and tables lining the hallway. The group moved each one into a quickly engineered pile in front of the doors.

The first thud against the doors caused the barricade to shift slightly, but it held. Outside, the monster gurgled with rage and tried again. This time the shift was bigger.

"This isn't gonna last," Helena said.

"Thanks for the heads up," Steph snapped.

"We've gotta get out of here!" Mathilda cried.

"Where can we go that this thing can't follow?"

"Uh . . ." Ethan Allen Jr. said, attempting his first real word since he set foot in this house. He pointed back down the foyer and hallway toward the drawing parlor. "Fireplace?"

Michael's eyes widened in realization.

"He's right," he said. "That thing can't fit through the hole in the fireplace."

"Well, what're we waiting for?" Helena shouted. "Let's go!"

The group, now only five strong, had made it around the archway and into the drawing parlor when the front doors exploded. Several chairs and tables crashed into their surroundings, destroyed instantly. Their splintering mixed with the dull roar of the rain outside, and the angry, piercing shriek of the monster bent on vengeance.

Michael got on his hands and knees first and crawled his way through the black soot and pale gray ash of the fireplace. The rear was now open, the black metal sliding door wedged ajar by the damage the monster had done earlier. Slipping through the opening, Michael found himself in another secret passage, similar in structure to the other, but much wider and longer, and with more consistent, blue lighting. Maybe it was the thick drops of rain fogging his glasses, but he didn't think he could see the end.

Michael helped Ethan Allen Jr. through, then Mathilda, who

helped Helena, her bright orange jumpsuit now utterly soiled by dirty black patches. The clomping thuds of the monster inched closer outside.

"Steph!" Michael called out. "Where are you?"

"Hold on!" came her voice through the fireplace hole.

The heavy footfalls of the monster caused the walls of the tunnel to rumble, sending debris falling from the ceiling.

"Steph, what're you doing? Hurry up!"

The monster's steps quickened, now closer than ever before. Seconds later, Steph's body slid through the hole headfirst. She hit the ground running and dashed past them, her tuxedo jacket flapping behind her like a victory flag. "Can't forget this!"

"Goddamnit, Steph!" Michael shouted as the monster's arm shot through into the tunnel, limited once again by the size of the hole. Luckily, no one was in grabbing range this time, and they were all already far down the tunnel and moving at a decent clip. Feeling nothing, the monster's arm eventually disappeared, and Michael heard it faintly clomping away in disappointment.

"One of these days, your love of dumb little things is going to get us killed," he grumbled to Steph.

"I just hope I'm alive to see it." Steph smiled as they turned the corner, leaving the monster and the fireplace in the dust. They descended into the bowels of the manor's hidden underbelly.

* * *

Steph felt a weird feeling of déjà vu escalate as they proceeded further and further down the tunnel. They had long left the mansion behind and were spiraling deep into the very hill Pembroke Manor sat upon. The air developed a chill, which was certainly less than optimal since they were all soaking wet.

But thanks to the blue glowing wall sconces, at least they weren't stuck in the dark.

"So . . ." She broke the silence that had fallen upon the group. "Does anyone know where we we're going?"

Mike turned back toward Helena who was following her MILFy mom and the now orphaned weirdo teen. "Helena, you're the expert here. Where does this tunnel go?"

To Mike's surprise, but not necessarily to Steph's, Helena simply shrugged. "Beats me."

"Beats you?" Mike cried. "What do you mean 'beats you?'"

"I thought you said you knew these tunnels like the back of your hand!" Mathilda said.

"These tunnels weren't around when you abandoned me here, mom," Helena said angrily. "They're all new."

"First of all." Mathilda looked to be on the verge of cracking. "I didn't *abandon* you here. I brought you here every summer so you could get to know your father and maybe have some fun. So I'd appreciate it if you'd stop blaming me for how you've squandered your life!"

"Oh . . . kay," Steph rolled her eyes and stepped back. "Looks like we're bringing up some stuff."

"And secondly," Mathilda continued. "How new are we talking?"

"I dunno," Helena shrugged again. "Ten, fifteen years?"

Steph rubbed the stone walls, slick with cold moisture that shone in the light of a series of blue wall sconces. The tunnel certainly looked and felt a lot newer than the creepy passageway through the walls they had walked through earlier.

"You think it just goes . . . down?" Mike asked.

Again, Helena shrugged.

"Down where?" Mathilda asked.

"Really only one way to find out, isn't there?" Helena said.

"Gweh," mumbled Ethan Allen Jr.

As they descended further, the thin layer of water on the stone walls slowly transitioned to a thin layer of ice. It was only when the tunnel opened into a rotunda with multiple branching exits did Steph clock exactly where she had seen this before.

"Extreme Clausing!" she shouted.

"What?" Helena screwed up her face, and rightly so. "What is that?"

Steph turned to Mike. "These are the same kind of tunnels I found when I rescued you from that evil Santa Claus!"

"I'm sorry . . ." Helena glanced between them, befuddled. "This is a thing that actually happened?"

"We live . . . colorful lives." Mike bit his lip, but at Mathilda, not Helena. "Steph, if you've seen this before, which tunnel did you go down?"

"Uh . . ." Steph glanced away. "I kinda . . . picked one at random."

"Oh, good," Helena said. "This is going be a disaster."

Steph stood up straight and smiled, holding out her finger toward the leftmost tunnel.

"Eeny.

Meeny.

Miney.

That one."

Her finger landed on the middle tunnel.

"We should go down there," she said.

"Are you sure?" Helena asked.

"She's quite right, madam," an unfortunately familiar, droning voice intoned. "That is a good choice."

The group wheeled around in unison to find Bartleby the butler in the dim cold tunnel behind them.

"Gah!" Mike jumped. "Goddamnit! How many times?"

"Bartleby, what the hell?" Mathilda furrowed her brow. "We thought you were dead. Again."

"I don't presume to know what you're talking about, Madam. I've been here the entire time."

"You damn well know you haven't!" Mike shouted.

"Yeah, we saw your *skull being crushed* by a giant monster," Steph said. "You're dead, dude."

"Yeah! The monster! Big thing? Weighs a ton?" Mike stopped his line of questioning when he realized the butler was absorbing none of it. "It killed you . . . for a second time."

"I have no idea of what you speak. And my presence here would dictate otherwise. If that did indeed transpire, I remember absolutely none of it."

"That's what you said the last time," Mathilda narrowed her eyes. "Bartleby, is there something . . . wrong with you?"

"No, madam, I don't believe so," the butler said. But it was not the butler they were all looking at. From behind them, a second, identical butler emerged from the shadows of the closest tunnel on the left.

Then another from the adjacent tunnel.

"Hello, madam."

And another from the next.

"Hello, madam."

And yet another from the next.

"Hello, madam."

Only the last, leftmost tunnel remained butler free.

"Oh, God." Mike's eyes widened. "Is everyone else seeing this?"

"Yeah, uh, quick question," Steph raised a finger. "How many of you are there?"

The butlers slowly turned their heads left and right and were surprised to find themselves staring back. "Well, that is indeed disturbing," they droned in unison.

"You're telling us!" Mathilda said. "What did Armie do to you?"

"You know, Madam. I'm not quite sure," came the echo.

"Guh," Ethan Allen Jr. said.

Mike wheeled and turned to Helena. "You knew about *this*, right? This is what you were hinting at earlier."

"I had an inkling." She cocked her head. "Cloning's one of the first things you try when you're trying for immortality. I saw my father's basic research years ago—stolen from a shadowy group trying to resurrect Hitler—but I didn't know the extent of it until today."

"I guess the butler didn't do a lot of dying while you were growing up?" Stephanie shot back.

"If he did, I didn't know about it."

"I wish you wouldn't speak about me as if I weren't here, madams," said five voices simultaneously, turning their monotones into a dull chorus.

"I'm really happy this is as weird for everyone as it is for me," Mathilda said.

"If his cloning was this successful"—Mike indicated the existential horrorshow before them—"why did Pembroke keep looking into everything else? The vampire. The Bloodstone. Project Skinwa—"

Mike's list of recent, important events was cut short as the cloned butlers bodies began to shudder unnaturally. Steph watched tears of blood trickle from each of their eyes. Their limbs turned into jelly, and they collapsed, one after the other, to the cold stone floor. Warm red geysers erupted from their gaping maws and spilled over their chests, resulting in a rapidly growing pool of blood that pushed the group closer together to avoid getting any of it on their shoes. It was a full few minutes before the butlers stopped vibrating and settled into a state of peaceful, yet disgusting rigor mortis.

Ethan Allen Jr. audibly suppressed a gag.

"Did their bodies just *do* that?" Steph asked when she was sure there wouldn't be any further lingering spasms. "Is that what happened to the butler upstairs?"

"I guess dad really didn't hit the nail on the head with the cloning," Helena admitted. "They're completely unstable."

"So, um." Steph looked around at the blood-stained, corpse ridden floor. "Does anyone else want to move on from this, or is it just me?"

"Yeah," "Yes," "Okay, let's go," were the various mumbled assents as the group proceeded down the only branching tunnel that didn't have a dead butler in front of it—as per unspoken consensus.

"Okay, this is *not* what I call moving on from this," Mike said a few minutes later. The tunnel had terminated in a room taken up by a pile of dead butler bodies so high they nearly scraped the ceiling with their beaky noses. Fortunately, the frigidness of the catacombs had kept the bodies from decaying too much.

Fortunately.

Ethan Allen Jr. suppressed another gag.

"Wow." Steph scrunched up her nose. "He sure went through a lot of butlers."

"Goddamnit," Mike muttered. "Where do we go from here?"

The other notable problem with this room—aside from the obvious mountain of corpses—was the complete lack of any additional exit, making it both a figurative and literal dead end.

"Maybe we should go back," Mathilda said softly.

"You think the other tunnels that the cloned Bartlebys crawled out of will yield better results, mom?" Helena sneered.

"It's an option!" She yelled back.

"Wait," Steph held up her hand. The butler pyramid had—presumably over time—shifted to keep its stability by slumping its collected mass against the rear wall. And while the limbs of all the rest of the butlers hung languid and loose as their muscles atrophied away, the corpse at the tippy top—a relatively recent clone, Steph figured—had its left arm outstretched, with its hand grasping onto something with dear life, or dear death, as it were.

It was a big metal staple driven into the stone wall. She blinked with realization. It had to be part of a series, with the rest hidden beneath the bodies of the butlers, which led up out of the room through a sewer pipe-like exit.

"There," she pointed at the staple. "It's a ladder."

"I'm sorry." Mike squinted up at where she was pointing and did a double take. "Are you telling me we have to climb up over all these dead bodies?"

She turned her head slowly, to meet Mike's gaze with a dark sincerity, before breaking into a wide grin. "Race you!"

Steph, harnessing her ability to black out the most traumatic of things by sheer willful ignorance and an admittedly insane desire to commit to a bit, clambered her way up corpse mountain, using the bodies' arms, legs, and noses as macabre handholds. It took her surprisingly little time to reach the top.

"C'mon," she shouted down at the rest of the crew who she could see were retching. "I think I can see my house from here!"

"If you can believe it," Steph heard Mike say to his MILF, "this is the second mound of corpses and corpse parts I've had to climb up in so many months. But the first was a lot smaller."

It took the others much longer to reach the summit, but when they did, they moved much faster up the wall staples. Steph noted the motivational power of wanting to increase the distance between oneself and a metric ton of dead bodies. With Helena bringing up the rear due to her obvious impairment of handcuffs, Steph led the group up the rungs and through the vertical tunnel above.

There were no sconces here, and her eyes needed a bit to adjust. Fortunately, the ladder was long, giving her ample time. Unfortunately, the ladder was also *infuriatingly* long. The darkness of the ladder's tunnel faded to a slightly bluer darkness up ahead, but Steph could not tell how long that transition would take. Even once the muscles in her arms started seizing up and screaming at her, they still had about thirty or so rungs to go before the tunnel ended in a large metal grating, haloed by violet-blue light.

"How much further?" Helena's voice echoed from below.

Steph stopped, allowing herself a rest, and looked back down. Mike was right behind her, followed by Mathilda, and the silent but repeatedly traumatized Ethan Allen kid.

There, so far below that she was barely visible, her black stained jumpsuit partially melting into the dark, was Helena. "Um, hello?"

"Nearly there!" Steph shouted back. "Try to keep up!"

Fighting against her aching muscles, Steph pressed forth, rung by rung. When she finally reached the top, her head butted up against the grating. It felt like cold cast iron against her scalp. Through the holes, she could see carved out rock formations bathed in deep violet lighting, but when Steph tried to push it open, she found her muscles so well-saturated with lactic acid that they could barely make it budge.

"You doin' okay there, Steph?" Mike asked from behind her. She could hear the strain in his voice.

"Yeah, just dandy!" Steph forced through gritted teeth.

"Hey, can you move to the left? I think I can help."

Despite the lack of room to maneuver, Steph repositioned herself, allowing Mike to clamber up beside her.

"I'll get this side, you get the other? Alright?"

"Alright," she nodded.

Mike angled into position, with his head down, pressing his back against the left side of the grate. Steph aped him on the right side, staring down into the wide eyes of the MILF, the kid—and somewhere down below, Helena.

"One," Mike said.

"Two," Steph nodded.

"Three," they grunted together and jammed their legs upwards, their feet pressing against the rungs. The cast iron grating dug into their backs, but they strained harder. A second later, she felt the grate slip a bit, but they had to stop before they broke something.

After another pained count of three, Mike and Steph tried again. This time the grate slipped up further out of its inset slots in the floor above. Steph was able to slide her hand in the narrow crack and push it a fair bit aside. Mike, elated, did his part and moved it further, and eventually, both of them, Mathilda, and the kid collapsed on the cold stone floor of wherever they had ended up.

After a few minutes on his back, Mike managed to push himself to his feet. Removing his glasses and rubbing the sweat-fog off them, he looked around with a slow spin. "Steph," he said. "Where the hell are we?"

Steph, still breathing hard, raised a silent finger from the floor, urging him to pause. After about five more minutes, during which Mike transitioned to glaring at her and tapping his foot, she found the strength to rise and take in the surroundings.

It was a wide cavern, meticulously chiseled out of the rock in the hills beneath Pembroke Manor. Steps had been carved into each wall flanking the center of the round cave. One stairway to the left was carved at a great height and had a separate set of wrought-iron spiral steps leading up to it.

The other walls were also carved into smaller, individual steps, working as makeshift pedestals to hold a vast array of computer towers, actively blinking a staccato set of blue lights with no discernible pattern. Behind them was yet another dark tunnel that led off into God-knows-where, but before them was an enormous display that loomed over everything with a blank, black face that displayed only their reflections. Ostensibly, it was connected to this hardworking array of computers, which led Steph to the only obvious conclusion.

"Waitaminute. Is Pembroke . . . Batman?"

"Steph, not everyone is Batman." Mike frowned.

"Most assuredly, madam, Master Pembroke is not a Batman." A new butler emerged from the shadows.

"Fuck me!" Mike grabbed his heart.

"*A* Batman? There's only one Batman, chief." Steph sneered before abruptly realizing her mistake. "Except I guess if you count all those other ones."

"Bartleby, how many of you are still alive?" Mathilda asked, just slightly exasperated.

"I'm not certain what you mean, madam."

"What a surprise. Of course you goddamn don't." Mike growled. "Could you maybe be useful for once instead and tell us what this place is?"

"This is the final resting place of Master Pembroke."

Mathilda narrowed her eyes. "What do you mean 'the final resting place'? He *just* died, and we haven't dug his grave?"

"No, not at all Mistress Mathilda. He is very much alive."

Steph bit her lip. "More clones?"

"No, nothing like that, madam. The cloning process we experimented with was very much temperamental and resulted in some unexpected side effects."

"Right. Like the spontaneous bleeding and that pile of corpses?" Mike said brusquely.

"I'm sure I don't know what you mean."

"That's news to me."

"Master Pembroke went through copious amounts of research and development in his attempts to remain alive, although most of them were failures. The Holy Bloodstone. Project Skinwalker." Bartleby sighed. "The medically-licensed vampire was a particular disappointment."

"I'll say." Mike smirked.

"But in recent months, he achieved limited success on one front. He returned to his initial aspirations of robotics and artificial intelligences with more up-to-date technologies. He was on the verge of a breakthrough, but this past Christmas, he shifted his focus to other endeavors he believed to be more fruitful." The butler cast his hand over the cave. "So now, the computers housed in this cave merely store an imperfect imprint of his consciousness, backed up during his non-waking hours."

"His mind is . . . inside the computer?" Steph whistled. "That's badass."

"So, we can speak to Armie again?" Mathilda balled her fists. "Though this thing?"

"Yes, madam."

"But how do we turn it on?"

"I'm afraid it's keyed to his biometrics, madam. Even I cannot—"

Ethan Allen Pembroke Jr., in his first truly proactive move, was already silently striding toward the input devices beneath the giant screen. He toggled around with them for a bit, and the screen blinked on. Miraculously, the array of computers started humming and the whole thing booted up, bathing the entirety of the cave in an even brighter blue ambience. The shitty teen, his genetically-fortuitous hand on a touchpad, simply turned around and shrugged.

Slowly, but surely, dots appeared on the screen, followed by connecting lines that warped, twisted, and rotated, eventually forming a rough wireframe model of Armitage Pembroke's balding old head. Each polygonal frame was filled in with a flat pale skin tone with gained an off-putting metallic sheen when rotated. It was quite rudimentary. These were barely PS2 level graphics. Hell, they weren't even good enough for a Sega Saturn.

"What the hell is going on here?" It was Pembroke's angry, raspy voice alright, just slightly digitized and distorted with a subtle echo.

"Hello, sir," the Bartleby clone said. "It's good to see you again."

"Bartleby, what latest happened?" Pembroke's digital head bounced around the display like the blob in a Windows 95 screensaver. "Who the hell are you peo—Mathilda?"

"Armie!" She stepped forward with blue-lit tears in her eyes. "Is—is that really you?"

"Mathilda. It's been so long."

"It really has, Armie. What . . . what did you do to yourself?"

"I backed myself up. Portions of my consciousness exist on this computer. I can live forever like this. Just as I intended."

"But why?" Mathilda pleaded. "Why did you spend so much of your life doing this?"

"Because I couldn't let them win."

"Who?"

"Everyone! The vultures out there just circling, waiting for me to die so that they could scoop up my hard-earned wealth. And least of all that insufferable psychic." If the cyber-Pembroke had arms, this was where he would have been flailing them in anger. "No one—and I mean no one—tells Armitage Pembroke how his life is going to go, except Armitage Pembroke."

"Well, sorry to burst your bubble there, buddy." Steph stepped forward, sensing her opening. "But you are very much dead."

"What?"

"She's right, Pembroke." Mike said. "You—the real physical you—are dead. Murdered."

"That's impossible. This computer back-up was a minor fail safe, but I was on the verge of something big. Something permanent that would allow me to live forever. And I was murdered before I could put it into action? How?"

"Heart attack, you old bastard," Helena's smiling face finally popped up beside the dislodged grate. She turned to Steph and Mike. "Thanks for waiting for me, you jerks."

"I mean, we thought it kinda could've been a murder," Steph said, turning back to Pembroke.

"Murder?" The simulation blinked. "Who would have been able to get to me?"

"We were hoping you'd be able to tell us," Mike said.

"I'm a months-old computer back-up of my mind, you fool. I can't give you any new information."

"Damn it," Mike grumbled. "Should've thought of that."

"What about the monster?" Steph asked.

"Monster?" Pembroke seemed confused.

"Armie, there's a giant deformed monster that's been chasing us through the halls of the manor." Mathilda paused and looked down. "It . . . it killed Delia and Ethan Allen."

"Oh," Pembroke's digitized voice wavered. "Oh, no. I suppose if I was indeed murdered before I could achieve true immortality, then my security system might have been triggered. It would not have harmed me, just anyone who threatened me." He cleared his artificial throat. "My son . . . is dead you say?"

"Wait, hold on." Mike raised a hand as if he were in school. "Security system?"

"Yes, well, I certainly wasn't going to let my death be an excuse to disburse my funds. So, I uh . . . had one of my earlier failed experiments programmed to destroy anyone who might have tried to kill me for my money."

"That explains why he tried to kill your lawyer," Helena stepped forward. "That guy was planning to bilk you out of all your cash."

"Grimsby was on the take?"

"He said he was your secret son," Steph said. "And he deserved all of it. You really shouldn't have had all these shitty kids."

"Grimsby? My son?" Pembroke's digital eyes widened cartoonishly. "That's . . . entirely possible."

"And then you hired him to write a will to taunt everybody out of spite," Mike said, recapping the beginning of this escapade, "So he pulled a fast one on you and got you to sign a document that left your estate to him."

"Hm." Even through that one syllable, Pembroke's juddering voice acquired something Steph hadn't expected to ever hear from someone like him—a twinge of remorse.

"Well, don't worry about now." She sighed. "The monster killed him too, and I'm never gonna get the $1500 he owes me."

"Steph, you were never gonna get that $1500 back anyway," Mike said. "Let it go."

"That whole business . . . was regrettable on my part. I can certainly see why someone would have tried to kill me. Mathilda." Pembroke's head turned to his third ex-wife. "I truly was a monster, wasn't I?"

"No, Armie," she said. "You were just . . . scared. I'm sorry I couldn't help."

"No, I am sorry." Pembroke's chin indicated the caverns around them. "Time passes slowly in these . . . computers, and I've used it to gain a bit of perspective. I should have realized that I was misguided and hurting myself and my family. For that I apologize."

"Sir, if I may interject." The Bartleby clone cleared its throat. "As you are more . . . program than man, your estate will still need to be transferred to those specified in your will." The clone picked up a small tablet from beside one of the computer towers and scrolled through it. "According to the lawyer's electronic documents, it is to go to the eldest child."

"That's me." Helena's eyes widened in the blue light as she started bouncing around the cave. "That's me! I have everything! I can buy my way out of prison and back into the public limelight. And I'll build the most complex, intricately-plotted interactive entertainment experience the world has ever—"

"I'm sorry." Bartleby cleared his throat again. "Eldest male child."

After everyone processed this new information with the most pregnant of pauses, all eyes in the cavern turned toward the spindly frame of Ethan Allen Pembroke Jr., who was once again tapping away at his phone.

He looked up at everyone staring at him.

"Guh?" he said.

"FUUUUUUCCCCCCCCKKKKKKKK!!" Helena screamed to the heavens, although she was in hell.

"That's a real relief." Mike leaned over and whispered in Steph's ear. "If I had to go through another one of those escape rooms. . ."

But Helena's deafening cry had done more than just vent her anger. From the darkness of the carved tunnel behind them came a slow rhythmic tremor.

"Oh, no," Mathilda whispered.

The tremor resolved into dull thuds, causing the ground to quake as they sped up. With a horrible bellow, the hulking behemoth that had been chasing them through the halls of Pembroke Manor loped on all fours into the light, its grotesque, bulbous muscles shifting below its taut skin. The ambient glow of Pembroke's screen allowed the group to get a clear glimpse of the creature for the first time, and it was, unfortunately, irritatingly familiar.

In the better light, Steph could make out the tattered black and white rags hanging over the thing's body were actually the remains of a formal black and white suit, and its face—no longer covered by the stray fabric of a makeshift hood—was wrinkled, and saggy, with its most prominent features being an oversized beak-like nose, a balding head of gray hair, and one bored, beady eye—the other being a deformed purple bulb.

"Goddammit. How many damn butler clones do you need?" Steph

yelled. The monster grabbed its smaller, normal butler counterpart and bit a chunk out of his torso. Bartleby screamed in pain before being dashed into blood and chunks against the cavern wall. The monster then gathered up the remains of Bartleby's lower half to use as a club, aping its strategy from earlier.

"This was one of my first attempts at the cloning process!" Pembroke's computer shouted. "And I opted to reuse rather than destroy it! You think I got rich by just wasting things?"

"Okay, now is not the time to get defensive!" Mike screamed as he dodged another swing of the monster butler's smaller butler weapon. "Pembroke, can you stop him?"

"Bartleby! Cease this nonsense at once!" Pembroke's voice came garbled from speakers mounted in the rock. But the monster continued his rampage, swinging the dead body into several of the computer towers, sending them crashing to the floor. The graphic of Pembroke on the screen began to fritz in and out, with occasional blocky artifacts clouding its eyes and head. His voice switched between a high-pitched squeal and a deep baritone, never remaining consistent. "Stop it! I order you now!"

"It's not working!" Steph tackled Mike to the ground, moments before his head would have been crushed by a flailing monster arm. She dodged the next giant fist by rolling aside, tumbling over by a set of rocky stairs.

"He's programmed to respond to my voice!" Pembroke said in a nasal whine. "But he's damaged too much of the system."

"Well, that's just great." Helena shouted. "Can any of you do a good impression of my dad?"

"I think I can do that, yes," Steph said in her best approximation of a Pembroke accent.

"Steph," Mike called across to her. "That's Orson Welles!"

"Isn't that close enough?"

"It's way off!" he yelled back. "But it's a pretty good Orson Welles!"

"Thanks!" Steph said as she ducked to avoid another wild blow from the monster. The attack ripped a gouge out of the computers directly behind her, sending sparks flying.

Pembroke's digital floating head was getting all sorts of messed up, with his form undergoing such severe squashes and stretches that he looked like edgy animation from the early-90s. "Stop, stop, stop!"

"We're trying, but I think we're out of options!" Mike shouted over the din of the screaming, charging monster butler. He dove out of the way just in time for the creature to slam headfirst into the cave wall, knocking itself out of commission for the time being, but the faint twitches in its hands made clear it would not be down for long.

"Armie, there must be something you can do!" Mathilda yelled.

Pembroke let out a digitized garbled sigh. "Okay."

"It'd be nice if you let us in on your plan, Pembroke!" Mike said.

"You must take the spiral staircase to the left beside the computer console. It will lead you back up to the main house, and it's too narrow for this . . . version of Bartleby to follow. There is a self-destruct sequence included in my program. I will activate it, which will collapse this cave, trapping and killing Bartleby."

"But . . ." Mathilda stuttered. "You'll be destroyed. All your work will be for nothing."

"If what you've all told me is true, I am already dead. Perhaps my last action can be one of kindness rather than greed. I can at least save you, too, Mathilda. I loved you very much, and I am sorry for turning myself back into the monster you wanted to help me overcome."

Steph stifled her laughter. It would have been a sweet, touching sentiment from the computerized Pembroke, had his modulated voice not been so far distorted to sound like he'd inhaled an absolutely poisonous amount of helium. Mike shook his head at her and she bit her lip into silence.

"Thank you, Armie." Mathilda whispered, though the pained echoes of her voice bounced off the cave walls.

"Alright, c'mon people. Let's go! Let's go!" Helena, in all her self-serving glory, was already halfway up the set of metal spiral stairs. Steph grabbed Mike's wrist and dragged him forward, with Mathilda and the now incredibly wealthy, but still kinda shitty teen orphan catching up behind.

A strained screech resounded off the cavern walls as the Butler Monster struggled to its feet. It looked even more horrific, its nose crushed, broken, and bleeding from its impact on the ground.

"Go! Go!" Pembroke garbled as his screen switched from a bright blue to an ominous blood red, with a clear minute long countdown.

Mike, Steph, Mathilda, and Ethan Allen Jr. leapt up and swung around the stairs as the monster lunged forward, bending the wrought iron bannisters in its enormous fists. Their screams were lost in the depths of its angry roaring, but they still proceeded up, spiraling twice as they ascended the helix. Eventually, they reached the transition to a second set of rocky carved stairs leading to a darkened outcropping jutting off the cave wall.

"So long, you dumb, ugly bitch!" Steph stuck her tongue out at the creature, who was struggling and failing to fit into the metal staircase. Unfortunately, it could somewhat understand English and did not take kindly to the insult, roaring again before digging its rough-hewn fingers into the rock wall itself and heaving itself up, closing the distance between it and the group in seconds.

"Goddamnit!" Helena shouted back. "You idiots!"

"Steph, how many times have I told you to stop antagonizing monsters!" Mike screamed. The group ran down a narrow passageway, following Helena's scream.

"Yeah! You'd think I'd learn!" Steph looked back to find the creature forcing its way through the narrowing rock walls and inching toward them. It had been slowed, but not by much since it was fueled by pure rage. It did its level best to squeeze its gargantuan, muscular body through the cracking and crumbling passage, but not without immense pain.

But the monster's roars were suddenly overshadowed by a set of repeating blasts and a low angry rumble.

"The self-destruct sequence started!" Mike called. "Keep moving!"

The group did as advised, barreling forward until they came to a sudden stop in front of a wall which held nothing but another small computer console on a small carved shelf.

ENTER PASSWORD, the screen said, upsettingly.

"Goddamnit!" Helena swore. "We're screwed."

"Password?" Mike asked, before turning to his MILF. "Mathilda, do you have any idea what the password would be?"

Mathilda pushed forward and entered a string of numbers. The screen flashed red and returned to the blinking password cursor. "It's not my birthday." She tried again twice, to the same results. "And it's not his. Nor Helena's birthday."

"Jesus, mom." Helena rolled her eyes. "It's not going to be anyone's birthdays. Especially not mine."

Steph turned back as the monster's pained groans were inching closer, crumbling rocks and rising flames visible over its bulbous shoulder.

"Ethan," Mathilda asked. "What about you?"

The kid merely shrugged.

"C'mon! C'mon!" Mike tried to hurry them along, but refused to be of any actual help. The monster's gnarled fingers had barely reached them, mere feet from the starched white collar of Ethan Allen Jr. "We gotta go!"

"Alright! Fine!" Steph surged forward, taking control of the console and jabbed at the keyboard. The screen pinged green and the rock wall slid open. "Yes!"

"Go go go!" Helena rushed past, with Mathilda and the kid following as quickly as possible.

Steph leapt forward as the tunnel behind her disintegrated, setting the monster free from the crushing walls just in time for it tumble into the abyss below and shatter its mutated clone bones on a pile of rocks.

"Phew!" she wiped the sweat off her brow. "That was a close—"

"Dammit, Stephanie!" Mike was currently hanging for dear life on the edge at her feet, while screaming his head off. His legs flailed wildly over the flaming pit of jagged stone and debris below. "Help me!"

"Oh, c'mon!" Steph reached down and dragged her best friend over the ledge with a giant heave, sending them tumbling backwards through the secret cave door.

* * *

Michael sniffed idly at a faint, bitter smell. Whatever it was, it worked as good as any smelling salts. It stung at his nostrils and when his eyes jolted open Michael came face to face with a corpse—its eyes frozen open and its blue lips contorted into a silent scream. Squealing like a little girl, he scrambled backwards like a frightened crab until he hit a wall.

"Ugh! Ow. OW!" he grunted as a few old books tumbled onto his head. Blinking twice, Michael finally managed to get his bearings. It was Pembroke's corpse he'd reintroduced himself to, and he was now up against one of the bookcases in the study. Steph, Helena, Mathilda, and Ethan Allen Jr. were on the far side of the dead man's enormous desk. "What the hell? How the hell did we get here?"

"Secret door." Steph jerked her thumb over her shoulder. "Behind the bookshelf. Hobson was wrong. This was some real Scooby-Doo shit."

"Huh." Michael frowned.

"I don't get it," Mathilda rubbed her arm and turned to Steph. "How did you know Armie's password?"

Steph shrugged. "Dude was like a million years old. It had to be 1234." she paused. "Or password."

"Or admin," Michael offered as he got to his feet.

"Yeah!"

"That's probably how the murderer got in," Mathilda said. "Through the caverns. They must've figured out the password like you."

"It still could've been the monster." Helena countered.

"No, Pembroke said it wouldn't harm him." Michael waved the theory away. "The thing is dead now, anyway. And besides, how would we have brought murder charges against a monst—"

Michael was thrown back by the explosion of splintered wood and flying books as the cloned monster butler—not nearly dead enough after all—tore its way through the rock wall and the hidden door behind the bookcase, screeching like a banshee.

"Goddamnit!" he cried as he slammed against the study's giant windows with a dull, vibrating thud.

"This guy's harder to kill than Steven Seagal!" Stephanie yelled from the opposite side of the room. The monster shoved its grotesquely muscled body further into the study. Upon receiving no response, she doubled down, as usual. "C'mon, guys. *Hard to Kill?* It was his best movie."

"No, it wasn't!" Helena shot back. "None of his movies were good!"

"Uh, *Executive Decision?*" Steph yelled as she ducked beneath a flying plank of wood—a former shelf—the monster had wrenched from the wall.

"He was in that for like five minutes!"

"That's what made it good!" Steph shouted back.

"Would you two shut up? We've got a problem here!" Mathilda yelled, backing toward the door to the main hallway, with her body between the monster and Ethan Allen Jr. to shield him from harm.

The monster bellowed into the air, the loose skin in its neck shuddering. It pivoted on its gargantuan heels to face Mathilda and the kid. With a terrifying broken grin, it advanced, flexing its enormous hands in terrible anticipation.

"Oh, no you don't!" Steph clambered onto Pembroke's writing desk, soiling the papers with her shoes. She leapt off the edge, jostling the silver teapot sitting atop the desk, before landing on the monster's back, in an attempt to engage it in a sleeper hold. Of course, this was a less than effective strategy. "Nighty night, monsty!"

"Steph, he's not going to pass out! He's a monster!" Michael's eyes shot toward the desk and the teapot. The smell from earlier triggered a faint memory of the silver metal burning his fingers. He glanced down at Pembroke's corpse and squatted, putting his ear to the ground. There, beneath the desk, lay a shattered teacup and a cold pool of tea. "Yes!" Michael shouted as he shot up and grabbed the teapot by the handle. "Steph!" He yelled to draw her attention as he flung it through the air. "Poison! The tea is poisoned!"

Steph nodded, grinning, and caught the pot. "Bottom's up, Butlerino! Teatime!" The monster opened its mouth to roar again, and Steph dumped the entire contents of the teapot down its gullet, then the teapot for good measure. It's already bulging eyes widened as it staggered backward, clutching at its throat. Steph leapt off the thing's shoulders, tucking and rolling when she hit the ground. The monster finally succumbed and fell, crashing through the floor and down several more floors to the ground level of the building.

"Whoo!" Steph cheered as she leaned over the massive hole. Ethan Allen Jr. and Mathilda joined her. "That was *awesome*. Good thinking, Mike."

"Yeah," Helena said. "How did you know there was poison in the tea?"

"When I was on the floor, I caught a pretty sharp bitter smell from under the desk. It was Pembroke's spilled tea. I figured unless the milk was *really* off, it had to have been poison."

"Oh, Armie." Mathilda sighed, shaking her head.

"I'm sorry, Mathilda," Michael said, slowly putting pieces together.

"I suppose he drank the tea, and when he started feeling the effects of the poison, staggered and broke his neck against the desk on the way down."

"But if that's true, who poisoned him?" Helena asked.

"The better question to ask would be: where'd homeboy get the tea?" Steph narrowed her eyes.

* * *

Magdalena Norris had fled down the hilly terrain by foot, with her hidden bag of clothes smacking her repeatedly in the back. It hadn't been easy in the unyielding downpour, but after slipping out of Pembroke Manor, she did not have much of a choice. Taking any of the guests' fancy cars would draw unnecessary attention and would have allowed them to track her easily. Even the two stupid "detectives" would've been able to find her.

So instead, she stumbled her way through thick deciduous forestry, losing one of her heels in the process. Not to mention faceplanting into gross accretions of mud not once, not twice, but thrice. Her entire disguise was ruined, caked in brown and black slop that, despite the never-ending sheets of rain—refused to slough off. At least it covered the blood soaking through her dress. She had lain motionless in the pool of that butler's blood for what seemed like hours. How the man died, she had no idea, but she didn't shy away from the opportunity.

It had been more than worth it.

After a few near stumbles, Magdalena reached a road midway down the hill, and, to her surprise, found a car hiding amongst the trees. The rusting hunk of metal wasn't in the best condition—one of its doors had been replaced by the door from a completely different car, in fact—but it was such a jalopy nobody would look at it twice.

Magdalena threw open the trunk and shed her disgusting, blood- and mud-soaked disguise. After taking a moment to bathe her bare body in the rain with only the trees as witnesses, she donned her back-up clothes and jumped in the driver's seat before cranking the key. It took a few tries, but the old thing chugged to life. She set off, leaving that ugly rotting corpse in the dust.

After the car struggled its way out of the mud, she cut down through the remainder of Pembroke land before merging back onto the main highway. The junker's yellow headlights cut through the darkness and sheets of rain, clearing her view of the empty roads in front of her.

Finally.

She was free.

Free from the insatiable hunger for payback that had clouded her mind for the past thirty years. That man, that monster, had come into her psychic booth—dragged by his wife, mind you—for a simple reading. But when Magdalena offered what she had intended to be a playful prophecy of his death, the glassy, rage-filled stare of Armitage Pembroke burned its way into her soul.

She had initially thought nothing of it, but when she returned the next day, Magdalena found the entire building housing her business razed to the ground—eventually replaced by what was to become another unnecessary monument to capitalism—a garish, neon-tinged shopping mall.

That sat with her for decades until she came up with a way for her to truly reap her revenge. The old fool barely left his house anyway, and even then, he had been so obsessed with his batshit 'immortality' projects that he'd never noticed her—the parasite slowly worming its way into his inner circle, waiting to strike.

But all of that was behind her. Now where would she go? What would she do—no longer having to endure the indignities imposed on her by Pembroke. Eugh. Even the name left an acrid taste in her mouth. Spotting an all-night diner two exits off, Magdalena decided to pull off and grab a coffee to wash off her tongue.

The waitress was a kindly woman—around her own age—who offered her a clean towel to help dry her hair. Sliding her way into a booth by the window, Magdalena picked up a giant laminated menu and gazed at the specials. Maybe she'd get a pie. She deserved it. But which kind? Banana cream? Blueberry? Apple was always a classic. Oh, or cherry.

She was so distracted by the sheer selection available, she didn't notice the nondescript blue Chevy pulling up outside her window. It wasn't until a woman in an absolutely drenched tuxedo and her glasses-sporting compatriot sidled their way into the vinyl seat across from her did Magdalena realize she was out of time.

It was them. The *detectives.*

"Hey, lady." The man wiped the rain off his glasses with the edge of Magdalena's hair-drying towel. "Give me back my shitty car."

"Yeah!" The woman shook her loose hair, splattering her partner's glasses with water once again. "And also, you're under arrest."

Magdalena looked past them to the door, where the angry police detective in a leather jacket stood guard. The dark-skinned woman had one arm in a sling and the other nursing an icepack against her forehead, but she was still staring daggers at her.

"Oh, I'm sorry," the man mocked, turning to his friend. "Maybe we weren't clear enough for the *psychic lady.*"

"How about we put it in terms you can understand? I dunno, maybe something like," the woman paused, before launching into an exaggerated accent. "Ja! I am ze maid!"

Magdalena cursed to herself. She should have foreseen this.

The rain continued its assault against the windowpane as Armitage Pembroke glared out of it. The elements were out of his control, but maybe once he was unshackled by the burdens of time, they could be.

A sharp rapping at his study door drew his attention. The thick, reinforced wood made the sound weak and tinny, as if a bird were pecking at it.

"Come!" he bellowed.

The door creaked open and the maid peered in. While she struggled against the weight of the wood with her right hand, she kept a sterling silver teapot and cup balanced carefully on the platter in her left hand.

"Ja?" she asked in her cartoonish accent. "I am . . . ze maid?"

"Tea?" Pembroke cocked an eyebrow, pretending to understand her intent. "Certainly."

The maid waddled in and stood stupidly before him. Her hand no longer burdened by the door, she lifted the teacup on a saucer, already filled, and proffered it toward him.

"No," he said. "Leave it on the desk."

"Ja," she started. "I am ze—"

"I said the desk!" He pointed.

Shaking, she placed the silver platter on his writing desk and hurried her way out.

"And be sure to lock the door when you leave," Pembroke called after her. "I do not need any more botherations."

"Ja," The maid said as she shut the door behind her. Pembroke fixed his stare on the brass knob until he heard the locking mechanism click firmly into place.

His gaze shifted to the tea on his desk. What kind of fool did the woman take him for? Clearly a rather big one, as she had not expected him to recognize the very psychic that had set the course of his life for the last thirty years. Especially when she applied to be a part of his housing staff with an absolutely insane manner of speaking.

And now, on the eve of his immortality, there was certainly no way he was going to drink any tea offered by that woman. He knew the machinations of revenge all too well. Once he had sealed his deal, the "maid" would learn them, as well.

Pembroke moved past his desk and toward the bookshelf closest to the window. Pulling down on a red leather-bound volume of Dorian Grey, the shelves split apart, revealing a metal arch made jagged and uneven by the plethora of wires and mechanical bits running off it. Just another one of the many secrets he'd installed in the manor, but the only one that would grant him what he desired, if the man on the other side was to be believed.

Flipping a switch on a nearby console and typing in his password—keeping it so simple was a personal triple bluff—Pembroke booted up the arch. With a sputter and a jerk, the empty space within the metal archway filled with the crackling glow of violet energy. The lights in the room flickered and dimmed for a minute, adjusting to the sudden draw of power, before returning to their original brightness.

Pembroke heard a faint whisper in his ears.

It was time. He was coming.

The whispers steadily increased, reaching a grand crescendo.

"Armitage Pembroke," the voice said.

It was him. He was nearly here.

Nearly three decades of consistent failure had led Pembroke to this point, but each one of those failures was a necessary steppingstone toward his goal. He set his original sights upon supernatural means—believing the occult to have the power to grant him eternal life. But when the Holy Bloodstone proved to be nothing but a bauble, and his research into vampirism revealed it came at too high a personal cost, Pembroke re-shifted his focused on some of his more conventional, scientific approaches.

Hiring a team of young physicists and biologists and providing them with carte blanche sped up development considerably. They set up shop first beneath the mall Pembroke had built intentionally atop the ruins of that psychic's hovel. But when they stumbled upon a method of interdimensional portal technology—the specifics of which were beyond him—the research was deemed too dangerous to continue. Instead, his engineers dumbed down the technology and used it to transport materials large distances, allowing them to establish a laboratory on the moon where they could carry out some of their more morally questionable experiments.

That was where Project Skinwalker came in—it was their name, not Pembroke's—an earnest attempt to extend a human lifespan with the regenerative abilities of animals. But that, too failed with the scientists captured and tried for violations of "moon law." And even his most recent breakthroughs in the robotic AI technology he had started out with— and which his disappointment of a daughter Helena had stolen— was all too lackluster.

In the end, ironically, Pembroke had to move backward to move forward. Upon finding his old mall destroyed, Pembroke went out to survey the area to ensure no one would be able to recover the dangerous research his team had buried down there long ago. Instead, what he found was a voice. One that called out to him through the ether, vibrating the fabric of the universe rather than his eardrums.

The voice called itself 'The Black King'—a pretentious title to be sure, but who was Pembroke to argue with a being that could reach across universes? The Black King could even read his mind to sense what he was seeking. He said that in his myriad travels across universes he, too, sought immortality, and was willing to share the secret he found, as long as Pembroke would provide him a few simple things.

First, the Black King instructed him on how to build a new gate to allow him access to the plane of this universe—something he was having a great deal of trouble breaching. Second, upon his arrival, he required the presence of two very specific people.

Michael Duckett and Stephanie Dyer.

These two, he said, were essential.

Pembroke fancied himself as shrewd a businessman as there ever was, and immediately noticed the King was bargaining not from a position of power, but of desperation. Pembroke was desperate, too, so he agreed to the terms, but made sure to keep the upper hand for himself.

Over the next months, Pembroke—with the faint whispers of the King lingering in his ears—toiled with his remaining engineering team to build a doorway within the confines of his study behind the disguise of a non-descript bookshelf.

Once the device was finalized, he reached out to his bloodsucking relatives to invite them to the unveiling on his 93rd birthday. What was immortality if you couldn't rub it into the faces of the people you hated most? He had relished the thought of seeing the anger seethe out of their slack jaws when they realized they would never receive any of the inheritance they felt entitled to.

All that remained was to find this Duckett and Dyer. Pembroke had heard their names in passing. They had been involved with the recent Future Group fiasco in some capacity. But he knew little more than that. Fortunately, they were trying to contact *him* for some reason, albeit through an obvious fictional alias. They were all too easy to rope in. And now, here, today, all the pieces were in place, and the Black King was coming to give Pembroke his due reward.

The purple glow of the portal rippled and crackled, giving way for the body passing through it. The thing that stepped through wasn't exactly how Pembroke had pictured a Black King. No, this man was encased in a thick suit of dark armor, with tubes of foul yellow liquid running from each limb. They extended backwards before disappearing into a cloak blacker than any shadow Pembroke had ever seen. The man's face was obscured by a visored helmet, with two decorative, yellowing horns curving flamboyantly up into the air before him.

"Ah." The Black King sighed with relief, his voice filtered and modulated through the suit—sounding nothing like his interdimensional whispers or the terrible dreams that sprung from them. "This feels . . . right."

The helmet hissed as seams appeared in its façade, separating out and revealing the pale, scarred face of a surprisingly young man beneath. Pembroke felt like he had seen this person somewhere recently, but he could not place the face. No matter, at least he now had confirmation that the Black King was a human. Or at least looked like one.

The King's dark eyes wandered around the room as he rubbed his stubbly beard with his gauntlet, eventually focusing his fierce gaze on Pembroke himself. "Armitage Pembroke. It's good to put a face to the name. How *are* you?"

"I—I am . . . well?" Pembroke stammered, having not expected to answer such a nonchalant question.

"Good! Good. That's always nice to hear." The King, his midnight black cloak trailing behind him, paced the perimeter of the room, exploring the space like a predator in a cage. "Beautiful place you have here." He rapped sharply on the thick wooden door. "Oh, lovely. Is that teak? I love me some teak. Very sturdy."

Pembroke tilted his head ever so slightly. Even the Black King's cadence was familiar, but he still could not identify where he recognized it from.

"Sorry." The King's face transitioned from playful wonder to a disappointed frown. "It's been a while since I've spoken to a human face to face. My manners must be appalling."

"No, it's quite . . . alright," Pembroke said. "But I was wondering if we could, well, get to our deal?"

"What?" The Black King lifted his head, distracted away from running his armored finger across Pembroke's bookshelves. "Oh, yes. The deal." A toothy smile spread across the King's face and he strode directly to Pembroke's desk, taking up residence in the large chair behind it. The King grabbed a set of coasters from the corner of the desk and placed them down, before clanking the heels of his metal boots onto them and leaning back in the chair. "Then let's get down to brass tacks. Have you procured the two people I requested?"

"Well, yes," Pembroke said. "They're in a bedroom a few hallways over."

"Excellent. Excellent." The king's smiled faded, replaced by a face all too grim. "Bring them to me."

Pembroke narrowed his eyes. "First, the secret of immortality."

"Oh, Armitage." the smile returned as the King moved his feet back to the floor. But it wasn't the same smile. There was no humor behind it. Just an unsettling darkness. "Don't worry. That will come in time, as you continue to serve me."

And there was the rub.

"No." Pembroke frowned. "I don't believe that was part of the deal."

"I don't think you quite understand." The Black King rose from behind the desk. "There really is no deal. Now that you've led me to this universe, things are finally under my control. Now bring Duckett and Dyer to me."

Pembroke cleared his throat with purpose and slipped his hands into the pockets of his robe—hopefully surreptitiously enough to evade detection. "I will do no such thing. Not until you have completed your end of the bargain."

In two short strides, the Black King covered the distance between them, and gingerly grasped the sides of Pembroke's head. The combination of his sweat and the cold metal of the King's gloves caused Pembroke to shudder. He stared deeply into the King's bottomless black eyes as he felt a jolt run down his back. And suddenly, as if a movie were broadcasting directly into his brain, he saw everything the King intended to happen.

Pembroke saw the world aflame, a multitude of indescribable horrors running rampant as existence broke down and the very atoms of creation sublimated into nothing. And there, at the top of an infinitely tall pile of debris, sat the Black King in his terrible throne, with a figure ensconced in shadow at his side and him—Armitage Pembroke—his body flayed and bloody on a chain leash, his mouth blabbering away incoherently.

"You see, Pembroke. This is what is to come," the King said calmly. "At least in broad strokes. I don't necessarily *need* you anymore, but I do want to be true to my word—at least in theory. You will live forever." He donned his helmet once more, his voice deepened and distorted. "But it will be on my terms. And that slight tingle you just felt, running down your spine? The process is beginning. Soon you will be immortal and in service to my ends."

Pembroke was shivering, shaking now, but soon found the wherewithal to force a word out of his trembling lips: "No."

"What?" The Black King reared back.

"No!" Pembroke extricated the remote he had been tightly gripping in the pocket of his robe and pressed a button. Immediately, the color of the portal from which the Black King had entered snapped from a roiling purple to a bright, flaming yellow.

"You fool!" The King shouted, as his body dragged backwards toward the portal. "What have you done?"

"I had my men program in a contingency." Pembroke offered the King a harsh smile. "Reversed the functionality of the dimensional doorway. I don't much understand it myself, but I'm sending you back to where you came from."

The King roared in anger, trying to pull against the portal's forces with all his might. Pembroke was afraid he might make progress, but it appeared that even he could not fight the tidal forces of the universe.

"And now I have the immortality you offered with none of the strings attached. I'm not a fool, King," Pembroke said. "If you make a deal with the devil, you must plan to be burned."

Even as he was being dragged back into what was ostensibly oblivion, the King simply threw back his head and laughed. A maniacal, disconcerting laugh that was made all the more terrible by the vocalizer in his helmet. "Oh, this isn't over, Pembroke. Not by a long shot. All those things I showed you are still to happen. I've destroyed entire other universes, and I won't stop until I rewrite existence to *my design*. I promise you will suffer forever when I return. And now that I know the location of this universe in the tapestry of the multi-verse, I *will* be able to return." The Black King's body receded into the bright yellow glow of the reversed portal. "I will see you, Pembroke. I will see you very soon."

With a hiss and a snap, the Black King disappeared from view and the portal blinked out of existence, with the bookshelf sliding into place as if nothing had ever happened. As if everything was okay.

But Pembroke knew it wasn't. He could not stop playing those terrible images back in his head over and over. The symphony of destruction and systematic dismantling and reforging of everything that was and is and ever would be. It was enough to drive a man mad, and according to the visions—that was exactly what was going to happen to Pembroke.

This terrified him. Even with immortality he would lose his grip and control—things he valued the most—over himself and his identity. What good was immortality if you weren't around to use it? But the process had started and soon all of it would come to pass. The Black King was right. He had already won.

Or maybe, he hadn't. Pembroke's wavering eyes caught the glint of the sterling silver tea set and the teacup that rested, still steaming, atop the platter.

Pembroke rushed over to the obviously poisoned tea. If this immortality was a process, maybe he could interrupt it. The teacup shook as he brought it to his lips and hungrily slurped down the poison. Hopefully this would stop it dead in its tracks, and he could expire on his own terms.

A burning sensation coursed down his throat and through his veins. Yes! His death would be under no one's purview but his own.

Pembroke's knees buckled, and he took a violent tumble forward, slamming his neck against the corner of his desk and twisting his ankle on the way down. He could feel his spine break, the bone shards of his vertebrae splintering and embedding themselves in the surrounding flesh and muscle.

Pembroke crumpled to the floor, his eyes wide and his mouth contorted into a ghastly open frown. His body stiffened as his breathing halted.

And yet, he could still comprehend everything.

It took him months to realize this but, at that point, the Black King's promised immortality had not yet spread to his corporeal body, but it had already infected his mind.

He remained entirely present as his family and the two detectives investigated his study, and eventually tore it asunder while fighting his horrific cloned butler.

He was present as the coroner dragged his corpse from its resting place and out of his beloved manor.

He was present as his remaining family sealed him up in a pine box, said their—very limited—respects, and buried him six feet beneath the ground.

And from then on he could do nothing but watch the darkness silently for the remainder of time, as the universe passed him by and eventually ended. Though when existence collapsed into itself, what little of Pembroke's mind remained had already been shattered beyond all reckoning.

A NIGHT OFF

To his complete and utter surprise, Michael Duckett had recently found himself becoming more accustomed to the day-to-day tasks of private detective work—even when each day brought on its own crop of unusual anomalies. But meeting contacts in disgusting alleyways under the cover of darkness wasn't something he ever saw himself getting used to. He absently ran his finger across the chipped green paint of a rusting dumpster before yanking it away when he realized what he was doing. Grimacing, Michael turned his attention to the half-eaten pizza floating crust up in a puddle of dingy water. A rat sniffed its way out from behind the fence at the rear of the alley and made a beeline to the edge of the puddle. But before Michael could get more invested in this macabre saga, a voice drew his attention.

"Michael," it said with a husky, alluring tone. "Hello."

Michael whirled his body around with such ferocity that he almost spun himself into the side of the dumpster. Regaining his bearings, he straightened up and smoothed down his shirt before meeting the sharp blue eyes of the raven-haired, trench-coated stranger in front of him. Well, she wasn't exactly a stranger. If you were to count the experiences they'd shared, they were kind of close.

"I hope I didn't keep you waiting long." Her bright white smile radiated enough energy to melt his heart in his chest like microwaves over a candy bar. He would've flirted back with her if he wasn't so cripplingly anxious around women. And if he actually knew her real name.

"Yeah, uh, just a bit. But it's fine." He scratched the side of his head and looked away. "Uh, lady."

The Woman, as she had come to be known between Steph and himself, was a member of a super-secret organization known only as STEEL. Michael didn't know what that stood for either, if indeed it stood for anything. She had helped the two of them take down The Future Group and the marauding, interdimensional horror known only as Korthuu. She was also incredibly attractive. But that went without saying.

The Woman crossed her arms over the front of her trench coat, popping her hip out to the side. "So, what did you call me for? And how did you even get my contact number? It was Maureen, wasn't it?"

Straight to business. Michael took in a breath and shifted focus. He removed the large manila folder he had been carrying in the messenger bag dangling from his shoulder and extended it toward the woman. "Take it back."

The Woman leaned back. "Did you read any of it?"

"No," Michael said. "I don't need it."

Contained within the folder was a deep dive into the family history of Stephanie Dyer. Every single little detail about her and her parents— who had died in a tragic accident before he and Stephanie had ever met—reported, collated, and triple-checked as only a super-secret organization such as STEEL could. Michael once thought that he needed this to be a better friend. To learn about all the things he had never asked Stephanie about due either to anxiety, stubbornness, fear, or all three. But if the last few months had taught him anything, it was that he'd be an even better friend if he just sat down and talked to her. Things were better between them now, and he honestly believed he could. The only thing stopping him was the temptation of an easier but inherently dishonest way. And Steph didn't deserve that from him.

"Take it back," Michael repeated, waggling the folder. "Classify it. Shred it. Burn it. Whatever it is you people do in your shadowy spy world."

"Okay." The Woman nodded. "Are you sure?"

"It's not right. I think I can—I know I can be better than this."

"That's incredibly sweet of you."

"Yeah." He smirked. "I'm kind of an amazing guy." Then, as the rat from earlier scurried halfway up his pant leg, Michael let out a glass-shattering shriek and swatted at it. "Get it off! Get it off! Get it off!"

With one quick hit, the rat flew off and splashed back into the gross puddle, before righting itself and scurrying away. But the damage had been done. In the commotion, Michael had dropped the folder, allowing much of its contents to flutter across the dirty concrete below their feet.

Both Michael and the Woman bent down almost instinctively to scramble for the papers. Michael was careful to shut his eyes so he didn't accidentally get a peek. But in the urgency, the side of his hand brushed against hers. Michael opened his eyes a crack to find her smiling. Not overtly, of course. She was too much of a spy for that. But the corner of her eyes gave her away a bit. Peering over her glasses, she brushed a strand of hair behind her ear. It would have been romantic if they weren't both squatting by a dumpster in the middle of a filthy alley.

When they'd finally grabbed all the loose sheets and shoved them safely back into the containing folder, they both stood up. Michael pushed the folder gently back into her hands and patted it awkwardly just for emphasis. "There you go!"

"Thank you." She patted the folder and tucked it under her arm. "By the way, I have the other thing you asked me for." The Woman handed him a small sticky note with a series of numbers scrawled across it.

"Oh, great!" Michael snatched it up and shoved it in his pocket.

"Definitely a much better use of STEEL's exhaustive database."

Michael nodded. "So, uh . . ." He scratched the back of his head, deciding whether this new leaf he was turning over was worth branching out to other opportunities. "I'm, uh, supposed to meet Stephanie in a bit for a drink. Did you maybe, uh, want to . . ."

The Woman smiled, but it was a weak one with an averted glance that sent Michael's heart sinking without a word. "Ha, yeah. I'd like to, but—"

Michael let out a breath.

"It's not that I don't want to!" She scrambled to say. "It's just . . . I can't. Because—"

"Yeah, no, of course. You've got your whole . . . thing going on. I'm sure there's more world-ending threats you've got to take care of."

"Sure." She nodded and swiveled around on her heels, with the tails of the trench coat swirling about her ankles. She glanced back over her shoulder and smiled with her eyes. "But maybe I'll see you around? And since you have my number, you could call me sometime."

"Maybe." Michael kicked a few pebbles at his feet as the Woman started to stride out of his life again. "Wait!"

She stopped and offered him a half turn.

"Are you ever going to tell me your name?"

"You can call me Ace." Her eyes smiled again and when Michael blinked, she was gone. He sighed and looked at his feet for a while before making the executive decision to leave the alley.

"Ace," he said to himself, feeling the syllable out as he strode around the corner and down the next two blocks. "Ace, Ace, Ace. Ace what?"

Michael knew he was likely never going to get an answer to that question and instead decided to pull out his phone. With the sticky note in the other hand, he fumbled at the screen with his thumbs, eventually managing to hit all the numbers.

"Hey . . ." Michael said tentatively when the person on the other line answered. "It's Michael Duckett. You know, of Duckett & Dyer—yeah. Of course you remember. Listen, this is gonna be a bit weird, but I'm heading to Jasper's Karaoke Bar over on East and Fifth. And I thought—Yes. With Steph. That's kinda the—Oh. Great. I'll see you in a bit, then."

Michael blinked and shoved his phone back into his pocket. That was easier than expected. How was that so simple, but he had so much trouble getting a single normal word out with Ace? That was something he knew he needed to work on.

But maybe some other time. Tonight, if Steph was to be believed, was going to be all about fun. They'd had a pretty insane few months—to say the least—and even Michael could admit they needed to take a night off.

But in the back of his mind, something rankled him. Something disturbing. It had been months, but he still had no idea who, or what, the Black King was. When he had first heard about it around Christmas, Michael had filed it away as something to bring up to Stephanie later, but he never had. Given the absolute batshit things they'd done over the past year or so, their cavorting across the multi-verse felt far in the rearview—but certainly this Black King was too—no. He was not going to let his anxiety drive his train of thought. Not tonight. No cases, no weirdness, just relaxing. Right now.

Drizzle spattered from the sky as Michael approached the bright buzzing neon logo of Jasper's, a speakeasy-style karaoke bar pseudo-hidden behind the false front of a mom-and-pop hardware store.

Michael had never been much for karaoke—he once had accidentally tried to buy a hammer here—but after a couple of drinks, who knew? At least maybe that would distract him from—

"Yo!" Stephanie tapped him on the shoulder. Michael jumped, but as she slid around him into his field of vision, he was glad to see her. "You ready to get schwasted?"

"I would put it a bit more delicately," Michael said. "But yes. I don't wanna be hung over, though. I landed us another case tomorrow, so I think—"

"Bup bup bup!" Steph put a finger to his lips. "Ix-nay on the ase-cay."

"Yeah, okay. You're right. Let's just get in here." Michael grabbed the door handle and swung it open, letting Steph go first.

"There we go!" She punched him in the arm as she passed. "That's what mama like! Race you to the tequila!"

They proceeded past the fake counter and shelves full of tools Michael had found were most decidedly *not* for sale. They passed through a second, heavier back door that opened into a wider, darker bar space lit only by strings of Christmas lights and a single spotlight on the main stage—which currently held a very drunk man singing KISS. Steph ran up to the bar almost immediately, and Michael followed.

"Two tequila shots, por favor." Steph held up her fingers, and the guy behind the bar poured them so fast, it was as if they had materialized out of thin air.

"Alright, ready?" Steph said, grabbing a saltshaker and the thin slice of lime the bartender slid over.

"Yeah, no. I always forget is it shot, salt, and then lime?"

"Wow. What are you, new? You couldn't be more wrong." Steph demonstrated the proper order to Michael, then slammed the shot glass on the bar demanding the bartender reload. "Did you catch that?"

Admittedly, Michael hadn't. He was too busy staring over Steph's shoulder at the woman who had just walked into the bar, clutching a purse over her shoulder.

"Hey, actually, before we take any more shots, I know the whole thing you had about working with Hobson was tough on you . . . for whatever reason," Michael said dancing around things and feelings he didn't want to touch. He wasn't avoiding it. No, this was just not the time. Maybe later. "So." He cleared his throat, issuing a curt wave over Steph's head. "I thought I'd, uh, do something for you."

"Oh?"

"Well." He nodded past Steph at the smiling woman with the bouncing red hair who was excitedly approaching.

Steph spun around. "Carrie!"

"Hey!" The young CSI beamed, setting her bag down on the nearest barstool. "How's it going guys?"

"Whoa! What're you doing here?"

"Michael gave me a call and told me you guys were doing karaoke. And I wouldn't miss that for the world." Carrie's infectious smile persisted. "Something tells me it's going to be an absolute train wreck."

"Yeah." Michael looked away as he absently took a sip of his tequila shot and made a face. "It probably is."

With a thud that drew their attention, the drunk man collapsed halfway through "Strutter" and had to be dragged off. The rest of the small crowd around the stage looked at each other, not wanting to follow that act.

"Wanna do one together?" Carrie asked Steph. "I always start off with 'You're the Best.'"

"Around?" Steph finished. "The Karate Kid? Hell yeah."

"Awesome! I'll go set it up." Carrie bounded away toward the stage, before stopping and turning back. "It's really good to see you guys outside of, y'know, work."

"Mike, man, you're amazing." Steph placed a hand on his shoulder as Carrie made her way onto the stage to submit their request. "Thank you. Seriously. How did you even get her number? I've been trying for ages."

"As it turns out"—Michael took another sip of his shot, and made an even worse face—"I'm a pretty good detective."

"Aw, bro!" Steph enveloped him in an oversized bear hug. "You're the best! Drinks are on me!" She added, "Figuratively, though. You've still got this, right?"

Michael raised his shot glass in a silent mock toast.

"You gonna come up and sing with us?" Steph asked.

"I'll need a few more drinks before I hit that point, so you get started."

Steph nodded her appreciation before moving toward the stage.

Michael sighed. He had to admit, things were going pretty well. Even though his day-to-day life now more closely resembled the fever dreams of a lunatic rather than, well, a day-to-day life, he was finally getting into the groove of it. And he found himself more confident and less anxious than ever. More importantly, things with Steph were good. The best they'd probably ever been. And maybe, just maybe, Michael would be able to be that deeper, emotionally supportive friend he desperately wanted to be.

And that she deserved.

"Hey!" Steph ran back over to him and placed both hands on his shoulders. "Listen, I'm sorry. I'm really sorry, but there's something important I absolutely have to tell you. And it can't wait."

"Huh? What?" Michael was knocked out of his introspection, nearly spilling his still pretty full shot. What was this? What could she possibly want to say?

Steph's pause felt interminable as her eyes darted down and then back up to meet his. "You've got some crap stuck to your shoe."

"Huh?" Michael looked down to find a small scrap of paper

flapping around the toe of his sneaker. When he looked back up, Steph had dashed away and was already leaping up the stage stairs toward Carrie as their music began to play.

Michael reached down and pulled the paper off, squinting at it under the limited glow of the bar's Christmas lights. Before he could process exactly what it was, it was already too late. It was a corner piece of a meticulously typed and formatted report about one Stephanie Dyer. It was just a fragment, mostly inscrutable outside of the larger context, but it did contain one word that Michael would regret having read.

"… brother?" he said out loud as the music drowned his voice out.

Will Return In

The Curse of Hitler's Tomb

ACKNOWLEDGEMENTS

And here we are again at the end of yet another Duckett & Dyer book. So, first of all, thank you for sticking it out with my weirdness and the truly bizarre places this book went. I thought putting together a collection of shorter novellas would go quicker than a full novel, but it turned out I was wrong. As usual. But once again, it's painfully obvious I couldn't have done it without a ton of support.

Emily Spear, my supportive and loving girlfriend. Thank you for giving me the space and time to write this absolute nonsense even though there were a lot more important real life things that I could have been focusing on. Thank you for taking most—read: all—of that off my plate.

Tareque Powaday. Once again, your amazing covers are what get the eyes on the page and the asses in the seats. Thank you for bearing with my aggressive deadlines (due to my own procrastination) and tiny nitpicks. If anyone else ever does covers for Duckett & Dyer, they'd surely pale in comparison to yours.

Thank you to Roman Levant, my best friend, who's been reading this thing in print, even though he mostly just does audio books. That's a hell of a lift. And I promise I'll get to my dreams of a full-cast audio drama at some point.

Thank you to C.D. Tavenor, who continues to like my work and work with me even though I throw ridiculous books his way. Your work continues to be great and I hope you're ready for the rest of the nonsense.

Thanks to very much to Hugh Howey and Duncan Swan for creating the Self-Published Science Fiction Competition. As of this writing the original Duckett & Dyer is a semi-finalist, which is due entirely to the brilliantly weird Team Space Lasagna. Without all of you, my rinky dink sci-fi/mystery/comedy would've gotten the early boot it deserves.

Of course, thanks to my mother and father. While they don't read my books, they often ask about them, and save their quiet judgment on the twenty or so dollars I make a month.

And a final thank you to my grandfather, who always supported my writing and creativity whenever I brought something new to show him.

And thank you for buying the third (?!?) book in this bizarre series. I know your time is short and valuable, so thanks for spending a few hours of your life with Duckett & Dyer. These characters mean a lot to me, and it warms my heart that you love them, too.

ABOUT THE AUTHOR

G.M. Nair is a crazy person who should never be taken seriously. Despite possessing both a Bachelor's and Master's Degree in Aerospace Engineering, he has written comedy for the stage and screen, and is the author of the highly unlucrative Duckett & Dyer series.

The Mystery of the Murdered Guy is his third book, but he's not yet out of material.

G.M. Nair lives in New York City while his volcano lair is remodeled.

You can find him trolling the internet at:

 NairForceOne@gmail.com

 @GaneshNair

www.ds-df.com